Lost In T

Kiki Archer

Title: Lost In The Starlight
ID: 19241226
ISBN: 978-1-326-76719-8

K.A Books *Publishers*

www.kikiarcher.com

Published by K.A Books 2016

Editors: Jayne Fereday and Diana Simmonds

Cover: Fereday Design

Image: 123rf.com/profile_pitju

Author photograph: **Henry Abel Jimenez Villanueva**

ISBN: 978-1-326-76719-8

M.C.C & P.P
Forever in my heart.

CHAPTER ONE

Honey Diamond sensed the shifting gazes and hidden whispers as she took her seat in the exclusive London eatery, the staring eyes a testament to her stardom. The members' only section of the already-impossible-to-get-into restaurant was lavish with chandeliers, Champagne and celebrities complimenting the minuscule portions of haute cuisine presented on slate chalkboards and other novel vessels, standard plates never to be seen in the up-market establishment.

The Muse, as it was called, had a waiting time that ran into months and a much coveted membership to a private balcony room, reserved for the brightest and richest of stars. Yet here they were, A-listers in their own right, staring in awe at Honey Diamond, lost at the sight of her beauty. Her glow, radiating from the table in the centre of the room, dazzling through the glitz and glam. Honey was a luminary. A light you couldn't help but admire.

Looking towards the sweeping staircase, Honey smiled politely at the watching eyes as she awaited her mother's arrival. It was always the same where Diana Diamond was concerned: a huge entourage planning, preening, preparing and prompting, but none quite able to deliver the package on time. And Diana Diamond was quite the package. If the occupants of The Muse thought dining with Honey was fodder for their fame-hungry friends, they had no clue their anecdotes were about to take a further enthralling turn.

Honey heard the bustle and touched her sweeping fringe in preparation. She could hear diners in the public room below gasping and clapping, the scraping of chairs signalling people were standing in shock, no doubt admiring her mother with over-the-top sycophantic greetings.

All A-list eyes were now on the staircase, wondering who might be causing the stir, ready to tut if it was one of those five-minutes-of-fame reality stars the public seemed so obsessed with, who should never, in their egotistical opinions, gain entry to the prestigious section. But the tuts didn't transpire. Instead, the celebrities held on to their excitement with flared nostrils, raised eyebrows and congratulatory nods as Diana Diamond strode up the staircase, two paces in front of her staff. The woman took a moment at the top, but not to catch her breath. At sixty-two, Diana Diamond prized herself on her fitness, and the pause was instead to confirm the height of her jacket collar and lift of her chin. She entered the balcony room with the regal elegance and no-nonsense assertiveness she was famed for.

Honey got up from her seat, ready for the air kiss.

"Dearest," said Diana, in the middle of the flamboyant greeting. "What, may I ask, are you wearing?"

Honey inhaled the scent of Chanel N°5, a timeless classic that took her back to her childhood, an image of her mother kneeling beside her bed and whispering she was home, bringing warmth then as it did now. "Apparently it's a one-off green velvet gown by Country Couture," she said, smiling into the scent.

Diana stepped backwards and appraised her daughter. "You look like Merida from Brave."

"Jane Fonda wants her white suit back," replied Honey, always willing to give as good as she got.

Diana feigned indignation. "You know old Janey steals my style. I trademarked the high collars and short sassy hair years before she did." She laughed. "Shall we sit? All these eyes are making me itchy."

Honey tried to ignore the staring diners as the hovering maître d' settled them into their seats. She looked towards the staircase instead, at the group of people busying themselves on their handheld devices, her own staff-free, back door arrival quite the opposite of what she'd just witnessed. "Who's he?" she asked, signalling past her mother's PA, her mother's clothes stylist, her mother's hairdresser, her mother's make-up artist and her mother's personal trainer.

"Gorgeous, isn't he? Turned twenty-one last week."

"What does he do?" Honey asked, smiling a thank you as she accepted the delicate gold-leaf trimmed menu.

Diana lifted her hand to stop the offering. "We'll have the Dom Pérignon and the duck. Thank you, George." Her polite snappiness always got the job done.

Honey held on to her menu. "I think I fancy a salad."

"The duck's divine. I had it with Madge last week. Plus the waif look's gone out of fashion."

"I'll have the salmon and dill salad please," said Honey to the nervous waiter, returning the menu to him with a smile.

"And the Dom Pérignon?" he asked gently, not wanting to get on the wrong side of Diana Diamond, The Muse's most loyal of patrons.

"Lovely." Good Champagne was one of the few things the Diamond women actually agreed on. "So," asked Honey again, "what does he do?"

"He's my zhoosher." Diana turned to the staircase and wiggled her fingers, shimmying her shoulders in a ridiculous pre-pubescent flirting move.

"Your what? And stop shaking. You've not got Parkinson's."

"He's my zhoosher. And don't say things like that. The papers still think I'm forty." Diana inhaled deeply, reciting the new boy's talents. "He zhooshes my hair, checks my shoulders for flecks, wipes lipstick from my teeth, squeezes my hand in support."

"Oh, Mother."

"What?"

"You cart your stylist, your make-up artist, your hairdresser and PA around for that."

"He's my finishing touches boy." She grinned wickedly and repeated the shimmy. "Name's José. The energy in those legs. You really ought to get one yourself."

"A twenty-one year old called José? No, Mother. I don't think I shall."

Diana Diamond tilted her head and looked the green velvet dress up and down once more. "Sometimes I question whether you're really my daughter."

Honey smiled, fully aware the restaurant's prying eyes were currently discussing just how alike the Diamond women actually were with their rich auburn hair, high cheek bones and wide smiles. "Is that because my porcelain skin's still intact?" She turned on the smile, knowing which buttons to press.

"Time in the Algarve's essential for my well-being." Diana nodded. "And anyway, the pale look went out with the waif."

Honey laughed. "This pale waif has missed you, Mother."

"I saw you last week."

"I'm surprised you noticed me, squashed into your dressing room, vying for your attention as your hoard of fans fawned all over you with their flowers and their curtseys."

"Honey dearest, the week before that it was I battling the fainting fans in your dressing room."

"They weren't fainting."

Diana nodded. "You're the brighter star in the Diamond dynasty, my darling, and the sooner you embrace that the better."

"I'm not getting zhooshers, and for the umpteenth time we are not a dynasty."

"You need zhooshers, you need a man and yes we jolly well are."

"Jane Fonda, Joan Collins – I struggle to keep up."

"Oh Honey, our Diamond dynasty's far more fabulous than Joan's. Now, where was I?"

Honey paused as the waiter returned with their Champagne, silently pouring the bubbles into cut crystal flutes. She held on to her words, hoping they wouldn't have to revisit again her mother's previous encouragements of her love life. Diana had already used every trick in the book, from double-dating, where Diana's man was often the youngest of the group, to theatre set-ups with adjacent seats always occupied by eligible bachelors, Diana likely claiming both once she finished her performance on stage.

Diana Diamond was known as Britain's Mae West. A child star whose career in the West End and on Broadway spanned almost sixty years, not to mention the move into Hollywood that saw her appear alongside the top players in the business. She was old-school class and her whirlwind romance with Heath Travis had been better than any silver-screen script. Love at first sight with her leading man, the hottest heartthrob in Hollywood. English beauty and American action-hero, idyllic English wedding and a baby girl in the year that followed, only for Heath to die of a drugs overdose before his daughter even turned one. Diana Diamond had embodied the tradition of stiff upper lip and carried on, her career gliding right over the bump in the road. Or so she had said.

Honey Diamond, the little girl left behind, had one abiding memory – an absent mother, always away, always performing, the gentle bedside whisper and warm timeless scent the only things capable of closing her wide eyes under the covers.

Honey remembered things changing when she was nine and was asked to act alongside her mother in what was destined to be a hit West End show. Honey was quickly hailed as a chip-off-the-old-block, Diana Diamond's daughter, more divine than the diva herself, becoming a star in her own right in musical theatre before finding her true passion in concert performance. Singing, song writing, anything and everything involving music. Honey Diamond was leading the pack and at twenty-eight, with numerous platinum albums under her belt, she was a national treasure, made even more glamorous by her Diamond heritage.

"I want to be a grandma," came the announcement from the other side of the table.

Honey sloshed her Champagne back into the flute. "What?"

"Jane Fonda's a grandma."

Honey leaned into the table and lowered her voice. "Go steal her grandkids then. You already steal her style."

"Oh Honey, don't be blasé."

"Me?"

"Yes you, and when I say you need a man I'm not talking about setting up home. You've made it perfectly clear that's not going to happen."

"Mother, people are looking."

"People are always looking." Diana carried on in her loud, frank fashion. "Ask one of your cads to oblige." She nodded. "The world wants you happy, Honey. Not like poor Kylie. Dozens of dates, never the dream." She tapped a bejewelled finger on the table and hushed her words. "And it doesn't matter if the dream is a dame, as long as it's not a dykey looking dame."

"Please Mother, just stop."

"I know you said you'd open up when you had something to open up about, but your PR company can't play the pantomime forever."

"I don't have a PR company and I don't play the pantomime."

"You're a Diamond, darling. We don't get here and stay here without help." She turned to her staff who had been moved to a discreet table in the corner and caught her tech guy's attention. "Benedict," she said, calling him over with a flick of her finger. "Read the latest from SlebSecrets."

Honey rolled her eyes. "SlebSecrets?"

The young man tapped on his tablet, following Diana's instruction without question. "Posted at 10.11 this morning," he said. "Which national gemstone treasures her female PA more than she'd like us to believe? The—"

"May I look?" interrupted Honey, not wanting to make a scene or draw further attention to their table.

The tech guy glanced towards Diana waiting for the nod. He received it and handed over the tablet before stepping away as he'd been taught.

The garish pink and purple website had a flashing SlebSecrets header next to an accompanying shushing finger. "Mother, how on earth are you reading this rubbish?"

"Google alerts. Benedict follows the family."

Honey sighed. Her mother's definition of family included two step-siblings from a later-life failed marriage who neither she nor her mother saw anymore after their abuse of the Diamond name. Then there was a brother who couldn't compete with his sister's fame, now living in a commune on the Shetland Islands. And Diana's two oldest friends, Gerty and Dot, whose missions were to make *Tatler's* society pages each month. And finally, Honey's godmother and now live-in housekeeper, Sofia – her one remaining constant from early childhood.

"It's just trolling, Mother," said Honey, unable to read any more.

"Is there any truth in the trolling?" Diana glanced to her left, instantly getting the maître d's attention. He signalled back with a three minutes gesture, understanding the speed at which Diana liked to be served. "I adore your PA." Her attention was seamlessly back on her daughter. "What's she called? Lesley?"

"It's Liza, as you well know. The same Liza I've had for years." Honey blushed. "Had as my PA." She dropped her eyes to the flashing header. "This probably isn't about me."

"Diamond, gemstone. National treasure. They make a dig about your *Secret Smile* song too."

"There are lots of songs about secret smiles."

"Not as well-known as yours, Honey dearest, and if you search the SlebSecrets archive, there, that tab at the top. That one."

"I'm not touching that tab."

"Touch that tab and search the archives. Search the word gemstone. You'll see yourself mentioned time and time again."

Honey pushed the tablet away. "Ignore it."

"You really ought to get yourself a tech guy like Benedict to keep on top of things and file libel suits where necessary."

"I don't worry about things I can't see."

Diana lifted her collar. "Well I've seen some tweets you should worry about, and I'm not going to mention the Horny Honey Double Dip Instagram hashtag."

"The what? Mother, how do you know of such things?"

"I have people."

"You've successfully reconfirmed why I'll never join social media."

"You'd beat Katy Perry's Twitter record – eighty million followers by dessert if you signed up right now."

"I'm not having dessert."

"Yes, you are. You're wasting away. It's a mother's job to flap."

"How many sixty-two-year-old mothers insist their child join Snapchat?"

"Oh no, not that one, Honey. I've had some near disasters that have cost me a fortune. Who knew you could screenshot?"

"I'm doing perfectly well without social media."

"That's what you said about personal security and look at you now."

Honey rolled her eyes at her mother. Yes, a too-close-for-comfort incident with over-enthusiastic fans a few years back had forced her to give in to her mother's demands for security. But she'd drawn the line at Diana's recommended full-blown professional detail, having instead only two close protection officers working on opposite shifts who Honey insisted were actually never close to her at all. They didn't travel with her, they weren't pictured with her, they were just in the background if ever she needed their help, which since said incident she hadn't. "And that's a waste of their time and your money."

"Do I pay for your men?"

Honey laughed. "Often you've tried, but if we're talking about Alan and Andy then once again I'll reconfirm to you that I don't need them, just like I don't need social media. I live my life in a totally different fashion to you, Mother, and it works. I'm doing okay."

Diana Diamond held on to her words and looked across the table, taking a moment to appraise her daughter. "I'm sorry. You are. I just think with your success you could get a huge following."

"I have a huge following. They follow my music. My shows. They don't need to see what I'm eating for breakfast or what I score on a Facebook *what kind of pizza are you* quiz."

"But you'd have influence."

"I have influence."

"Even more influence."

"Why? I'm the UK's most successful female recording artist. I've signed up for another season judging *Britain Sings* and I've just landed my first big-screen major role."

"You have not!"

"*Excusez-moi*. The duck and the salmon and dill salad," said the maître d', presenting both dishes on interestingly shaped platters.

"Not now, George!" snapped Diana, her tone softening as her nostrils filled with the delicate aromas. "Come back in five."

"Mother, it's fine." The maître d' moved away without query.

"Why am I not involved? You know my influence in Hollywood."

Honey pulled her eyes from the disappearing food back towards her mother. "I wanted to do this on my own." She smiled, her annoyance quickly slipping away. "It's a big screen musical. Think *Moulin Rouge* meets *Sleepless in Seattle*."

"You have the lead?"

Honey nodded.

"Oh darling, that's fabulous." Diana turned towards the diners who had been straining their ears to pick up any valuable titbits they could pass on to their friends. "No need to earwig, I'll shout it loud and clear. She's got the lead. Hollywood. Musical. A singing *When Harry Met Sally* type thing."

"Mother!" Honey reached across the table, trying to pull the fanfare back in.

"What? I'm proud of you. You never let me crow."

"Look," Honey shook her head. "Out come the iPhones, no doubt trying to get an exclusive with someone or other."

"Give an interview then. Beat them all to it."

"You know how I feel about interviews."

The tablet on the table burst to life, tringing with red notifications. Benedict appeared without being summoned. "May I?" he said, reaching for the gadget.

Honey caught sight of her name and beat him to it. "Surely it doesn't happen that quickly?"

"I'd rather you didn't, ma'am."

"Ma'am?"

Diana addressed her daughter's scornful look. "It's what I like staff to call me. Except for José, he calls me..." She stopped. "Give him his tablet back, dearest."

Honey clicked on the notification and the SlebSecrets site flashed up. *Which secret lesbian has landed her first Hollywood role? Is this the end for the pretty PA as the sparkling treasure moves to LA?*

CHAPTER TWO

Honey Diamond's car passed through the manned security gate to enter the exclusive fifteen-plot community known as The Alderley. Each house sat in at least five acres of land, with the estate boasting a golf course, ten tennis courts, four squash courts, a state of the art gym, swimming pool and sauna, a bar and restaurant and its own spa, sold to residents as a unique location designed for high achievers looking for a secure and private home in tranquil surroundings. It had round-the-clock guards and CCTV atop all high perimeters, both obviously discreet, allowing the residents to feel safe yet free.

Of her neighbours, Honey knew there was an oil tycoon, a hedge fund boss, two chief execs, three footballers and a handful of other celebrities. Most kept themselves to themselves due to huge work schedules, constant travel and the desire to just hide away and relax during any spare moments. Residents might host the odd party or fundraiser here and there and pleasantries were exchanged, but no firm friendships were formed, and for Honey sometimes the sheer size of the open spaces made her feel quite alone.

She had looked into buying one of the penthouse suites in the Shard, but the idea of tourists taking pictures every time she came home didn't appeal. At least living at The Alderley her driver, Tammara, could drop her at her door without risk of exposure to prying lenses.

It wasn't being papped that Honey disliked, but the crowd that would quickly appear, making it very difficult to give each and every supporter the time they deserved. She hated saying no to signing autographs or posing for pictures, or just taking her time to talk, but life wasn't like that and schedules had to be kept. Or so said Liza, always rushing them from venue to venue, micro-managing their each and every move.

As the car made its slow approach, Honey looked up at her huge house, glowing under the gentle, yet all-revealing, security lights. It wasn't Liza's fault, she was just doing her job – a job that she'd executed to perfection for the past ten years, always knowing which events to attend, being right about which products to endorse. Honey sighed. Liza worked hard and her perpetually strung-out persona was understandable. Who wouldn't be stressed managing someone like her?

The question came from the front of the car. "Are you okay, Honey?"

"Tammara, sorry, I didn't realise we'd stopped."

"You look deep in thought. Everything alright?"

Honey smiled at the concern. She liked Tammara, always willing to chat no matter the prohibitive protocol Liza tried to enforce among staff. "It must be the day off. I'm not used to free time."

"Anything nice planned for tonight? I'm not booked in again until the morning. Liza's warned me it'll be a long shift."

"Isn't it always?" said Honey, watching her driver in the mirror, noticing the long hair was loose from its usual bun. "Would you like to come in for a drink?" she asked.

Tammara turned in her seat. "Really?"

Honey continued. "We could chat outside of the car for once. It would be novel."

The pitch dropped from excited to peeved. "I'd have loved to. Really I would. And it would be worth Liza's wrath, but it's my dad's sixtieth and we're having a party and I should have been there an hour ago."

"Goodness! That's why your hair's down. Why didn't you say anything? Why on earth are you driving me?" Honey unbuckled her seatbelt and made for the door.

Tammara shrugged. "Have you ever said no to Liza? Plus I wanted to make sure you got to The Muse safely. I'm not sure who scares me more, your mother or your PA."

Honey paused with her hand on the door. "There's always a cab."

"That's what they told me you'd say. But you're far too famous for cabs, and the other drivers are nowhere near as good as me."

"Betty's not bad."

"Don't start choosing Betty Big Boobs over me."

"She's got a nice personality."

"That's what it is."

Honey laughed before pausing as she registered her driver's previous comment. "Why's Mother involved in my movements?"

Tammara shrugged again. "Your mother's involved in everything."

"That woman. I'm sure she thinks she's The Godfather." Removing her hand from the door, Honey lifted her eyes, hoping for one of Tammara's occasional anecdotes offering her a glimpse into a world she'd never known. "How's real life? Normality? Where's the party? Many guests?"

The driver shifted in her seat, discreetly tilting the watch on her wrist. "Well—"

"Stop. I saw that. I'm keeping you." Honey's fingers pressed the door release. "Look at me, trying to fill my free evening. I've no clue what to do with myself. You've got a life to get to." She nodded. "So I'll see you tomorrow, or send Betty if you're too worse for wear."

"Never. Now let me jump out and help you."

"On your day off? No chance." Honey stepped out of the car. "Have fun."

"You're sure you're okay?"

"Stop worrying. I'm fine."

"All part of the job, Miss Diamond."

Honey shut the door and waved the vehicle away, knowing the instruction was to wait until she had entered the building. "Go!" she said with more vigour. "I'm fine!" She stood still and watched, wondering just how much of their friendship was indeed part of the job, willing the car and its driver away to the real world with real lives and real people who were desperately awaiting their arrival. She turned to the house and wondered what it would be like to have one person, just one person, standing in her doorway desperately awaiting her arrival.

****

"How sure are you?" Jo eyed her flatmate with suspicion.

"I was there! The dotty old Diamond woman announced it. I grabbed my phone and uploaded. Yes, maybe I should have thought about it for more than one millisecond, but it was a scoop."

"Come on, Meg. This isn't like you." The head moved from side to side in thought. "The old you, maybe, but I thought you were past posting the small fry."

"She's got the lead in a Hollywood musical!"

"You know what I mean. It's just gossip. You said your site was about righting the wrongs in the world." Pulling out a chair, the buxom blonde sat at the small kitchen table, nodding towards the open laptop and flashing pink website. "And that bit about the PA?"

Meg shrugged. "What?"

"You're obsessed."

"She's a lesbian."

"You think everyone's a lesbian."

"The PA is, and they're close. Honey's only ever pictured with beards. If she were sleeping around with lots of different women someone would have sold their story by now, but they haven't, so she must be getting it somewhere." Meg nodded. "Her PA's the most logical explanation."

The scoff was loud. "She must be getting it somewhere? Like you, you mean?" Jo lifted her finger and tapped the side of her flatmate's black-rimmed glasses. "Maybe if you got more sex you wouldn't be so obsessed with what everyone else is getting up to in bed."

"I've not met the right person and I'm not obsessed."

"Start dating then!"

"I've tried." The brunette shrugged. "People don't get me."

"I don't get you. You say your site's about untold truths, news that needs to be known, but this is just gossipy speculation."

"Oh Jo, stop acting so saint-like. You're far worse than me."

"Only when I've had a few."

Meg paused. "Three days now?"

"Three days." The smile was one of relief and appreciation. "I owe you, Meg. Once again I owe you. But just to confirm, I'm not giving it up, I'm just taking it steady. Social drinking yes, solo drinking no."

"Sounds like a start. I just want you happy."

"And I want the same for you too." The blonde smiled. "You're twenty-eight. This is your time. It your time for sex, or dating, or affairs – just anything other than sitting in front of your screen and speculating about strangers."

"Honey's twenty-eight."

"And I bet she's not shy of bagging some booty."

The eyebrows rose above the frame of the glasses. "See."

Jo paused. "Oh, you clever geek. Why do you always do this? Using your words to lure me into your traps? Maybe she's not then. Maybe she's just busy."

"Like me."

"You're a top journalist, Meg, and founding SlebSecrets sleuth, but you're not creating worldwide hit album after hit album, or judging the nation's most popular talent show."

"And I don't have one of the richest mothers in the land covering up my indiscretions either." Meg turned in her chair until she was knee to knee with her flatmate. She reached out and held on to the slender thighs, smiling up at the blonde hair and blue eyes. "You're a beautiful straight girl, Jo. You don't know what it's like to be a geeky gay girl desperately clinging on to the idea that lesbian role models might one day be the norm."

"You've got Ellen, and you're not that geeky. You're like Alex Vause and everyone fancies her."

"*Orange is the New Black*? I am not," she smiled, "but I do like you like this. You're giving compliments. You've said I'm not *that* geeky, and you've compared me to Alex Vause. I can't remember the last time you said anything so nice."

"You're right. I'm a better person without the slosh, but you're also a better person when you dump that weight-of-the-world expression and let me do your hair and make-up."

"Never."

"Lead beautician on the set of *Reality Rules*! Who wouldn't jump at the offer?"

"Anyone who wants to look normal."

"That's what's wrong. You're too happy being normal and plain." Jo lifted her hands to the chaotic mess in their tiny London flat. "This is lived in. This is life. Compare this with your stark and lonely bedroom. Well?"

Meg pushed a finger onto her flatmate's lips. "Shush, you were doing so well and Pia's coming later so we need to tidy."

"Oh god, don't!" Jo flicked the finger back towards the laptop. "I'd rather you carry on with your tittle-tattle than have us clean for the cleaner."

"I haven't posted tittle-tattle in months. My new job's changed me. I'm like Perez. I've turned over a new leaf. Each entry has to have purpose. I only post indiscretions that need to be outed. Hiding your sexuality's not okay. Having an affair's not okay. Taking drugs whilst being a spokesman for an anti-drugs charity is just not okay. The world needs to know the truth about these people."

Jo moved from her chair, begrudgingly picking up some empty bottles and discarded pizza boxes. "I can't believe that one's not public."

"The papers won't touch some people. Like Honey. That's how SlebSecrets started. That's why I'm needed. You know this."

Dumping the rubbish on the kitchen counter, Jo turned to her friend. "So you haven't changed? You're still going to be pimping me out? Even with this new hoity-toity job of yours?"

"You love it, sober or sloshed. But now you can be my plus one to the *really* posh dos. No more flirting with crap reality hunks to see if they stray. This time you'll be breaking the big news."

"Meg, that's your day job."

"Yes, but it's the stuff I can't print that drives me the most. The papers are so scared of libel, and then there are the PR companies paying us off. HotBuzz were quite daring, they'd let me loose as much as they could, but look what I had to put on my site. They just wouldn't risk it." She sighed. "It's so frustrating, knowing the truth, the lies and the spin, but no one having the guts to call it."

"So stop with the Honey trash now you're a," Jo put on her poshest voice and flicked her hand with affectation, "proper journalist."

"I've always been a," Meg tried to mimic the voice, "proper journalist." She shrugged. "My new rag's just a bit more up-market."

"And then some," said Jo, using the pizza boxes to try and shove the mound of rubbish further into the overflowing bin. "God, this is gross."

"And it's not trash." Meg moved her glasses further up her nose and refocused on her laptop. "SlebSecrets prides itself on unspoken truths."

"Unless it's Honey Diamond. With her, personal speculation's just fine." The box and pile of rubbish pinged back up, littering the floor even more. "We need a new cleaner."

"No, I like Pia. She speak-a no on-glay."

"She do-a no cleaning either."

Meg laughed. "And I feel a connection with Honey. We're both twenty-eight. We're both lesbian." She paused, tapping the SlebSecrets' interface on her laptop. "Pia's perfect. I can't risk anyone catching sight of my site. She's Filipina. She wouldn't know what it was even if I left it exposed."

"One day, Meg. You'll be busted one day."

"Not by our cleaner I won't." She turned to her friend with all seriousness. "It's just you, Jo. Just you."

"I know."

Meg broke the meaningful silence. "So... I've got two all-access press passes for tonight's London Town Football Club charity do. I'll be on official duty, but how about you resume your role as super sleuth?"

"Ha! I knew it wouldn't last long."

"No, it's an indiscretion that needs to be outed." Meg peered over her black rims for full effect. "Louis Laurent."

"Okay."

"New patron of Family First. A rebrand of that coalition for marriage charity."

"Boring."

She shook her head. "That's not the news." She let the pause re-build the moment. "Affair."

"What?"

"With new nanny."

"No!" Jo's eyes were wide with shock.

"Yes."

"No! Jackie's heavily pregnant with their fourth!"

"Exactly. I was interviewing him last week for a piece on his humanitarian work and I noticed—"

"Hang on. You interviewed Louis Laurent, the hottest footballer in the country, and you failed to tell me?!"

"You've been busy with *Reality Rules* and I've been busy working on real stories. It's hard getting back into the swing of writing more than two-hundred-word titbits. It slipped my mind."

"It wouldn't slip your mind if it was Honey bloody Diamond would it. You'd be harping on non-stop, but Louis Laurent—"

"She's a lesbian. I'm a lesbian. We're connected. She matters."

"No she bloody doesn't! She needs to be archived. I'm a straight girl! I'm your bestie! He's Louis Laurent! Louis fucking Laurent."

Meg smiled. "So come super sleuthing tonight."

CHAPTER THREE

Honey walked the fifteen paces from the curved driveway towards the front door, the sight of Sofia snapping her out of her self-induced melancholy. Sofia was standing there smiling, eagerly awaiting her return. How spoilt of me, thought Honey, dismissing her previous thoughts. She had everything. More than any woman could ever dream of. People would always eagerly await her arrival. Fans would camp for hours, days even, screaming and cheering when their moment finally arrived. Their moment to meet her, Honey Diamond, and here was her godmother Sofia, her nanny as a child, her housekeeper now, her friend and live-in confidante, waiting once more with a smile in her eyes.

"Sofia, there's no need to greet me. Go back inside, you'll catch cold."

"I'm not greeting you, dear." The old woman giggled. "I'm off to the hub. Peter's waiting for me at the spa."

"Oh." Honey stepped aside as her godmother bustled past. "Peter the gardener? What happened to Tony the handyman?"

"Caught him playing tennis with that young nanny from the Laurents' place. Your salad's in the fridge. Don't wait up."

"Sofia, your coat. Please, let me grab it."

"And hide this hot little body? No chance."

"Winter's coming."

"Can't hear you, dear! Going to have fun!"

Honey watched as the seventy-something darted down the driveway without a care in the world. "Bye then," she whispered, turning back to the house and the silence awaiting her. Stop it, she told herself, looking across the open hallway towards the imposing staircase. This could be nice. This could be just what she needed. She was rarely home alone with time to spare. Usually it was the early hours when she'd finally get back, tired from filming an episode of *Britain Sings*, or from being stuck in a recording studio for eighteen hours at a stretch, never satisfied unless perfection was achieved. She'd mostly come in, pull herself up the stairs and fall into whichever bed she found first, before waking up to one of Liza's early morning phone calls reminding her of hair, make-up and wardrobe's imminent arrival. She used to try and refuse the fussing, but had long since accepted that Liza knew best and the schedule would only be kept if she did as instructed.

Not tonight though. Tonight she was free. In her own home. Not some anonymous hotel room with minimalist design and the same fruit wherever she was in the world. Her own home. Where she belonged. But Honey stared at the minimalist rooms surrounding her as she walked through. They were as lacking in personality as all the other places she stayed. She rubbed her eyes and kicked off her shoes, making a mental note to find the time to get personal, decorate the house in a fashion that would show guests who she truly was and what she truly liked. She stopped herself. She didn't really have guests and if she was honest she didn't know who she really was or what she really liked. Of course she could recognise nice wallpaper and elegant ornaments, but she had no passions or preferences. Was she drawn to any eras, like art deco? Or any styles, like chintz? The press, according to Liza, hailed her as a style icon, setting trends, leading the pack, but in all honesty it often felt as though people knew her far better than she ever really knew herself.

Looking through the open double doors towards the large lounge, Honey spotted a set of pyjamas folded neatly on the arm of the sofa. She smiled. Sofia did care. She'd often come home to find soft clothes, warm jumpers, bottles of water and pieces of fruit scattered around four or five locations where her godmother had anticipated she might finally lay her head, always insisting she eat, drink and get warm before sleeping. Honey unzipped her dress and padded into the lounge. The curtains were open and the winter night was black beyond, but she didn't question her privacy nor feel the need to seal herself in. The Alderley was secure, and the glow from the lamps on her driveway ran all the way up to the well-lit private road, just a short distance from the estate's hub with spa, bar, restaurant and all the other over-the-top amenities.

Pulling on her pyjamas she settled on the sofa, clicking the projector to see if she could remember how to work the home cinema system. She couldn't, so she lifted the arm of the sofa instead, searching for a remote that might possibly find BBC One. There were seven in total, one dimming the lights, one starting the cleaning system, but none changing the channel, so she opted for the iPad instead, disregarded along with a selection of other gadgets and gizmos, mostly gifts from her mother, and relegated to the compartment in the arm of the sofa, waiting for the day she'd finally become technologically capable.

Honey clicked the home button, pleased to see it had charge. The iPlayer app was easy enough to find, but the list of on-demand programmes just didn't appeal. *EastEnders, Match of the Day, Simply Nigella* and *This Year's Most Awkward Celebrity Moments*. She studied the jpeg on the site. The image was of her. She cringed. They would no doubt be making a big hoo-ha about that damned misheard interview question on that American chat show at the start of the year. Liza had convinced her to take part, claiming people wanted an insight into the "sweetness behind the songs."

Interviews where she had to promote her albums or talent shows were just about bearable, but the idea of talking about herself, who she was and where she came from, never felt right. She avoided them at all possible costs. But this time she'd been persuaded. So she did it, and the questions were coming thick and fast, and she thought they'd said "math". "What are your thoughts on math?" She'd always liked maths. Being home-schooled had been tricky – all the shows and musicals getting in the way. But maths was the one subject she could do on the job. Quick answers.

No need for textbooks or tools. She was good at it. It made sense. So she answered wholeheartedly with enthusiasm and flair. *"I love it. I've always loved it. It makes sense to me. I started when I was about seven and it's something I really enjoy. I'm confident with it."*

Meth. They were asking about meth.

Liza had tried to show her the gifs that followed and an "I Love Meth" Honey Diamond beat-box remix that had done the rounds, all of which apparently made her even more loveable and endearing and were most likely the cause of the huge jump in merchandise and album sales at the start of the year.

Honey stared at the link. What *was* the obsession with celebrity? She was normal. The same as everyone else. Yes, she had a talent, but so did the primary school teacher nurturing a class, or the doctor saving lives. Why weren't these people hailed as heroes? All she could do was sing. Why did people get so obsessed? She thought back to the tringing notifications at The Muse. Gossip spreading like wildfire. Who were these people and why weren't they living lives of their own?

She brought up the Google search box and started to type. She hadn't even got to the second S when the SlebSecrets site was suggested. The pink and purple header quickly filled the screen and the shushing finger flashed like a neon sign luring the punters in. The news of her Hollywood role and the ridiculous presumption about Liza had been relegated to second position. In the top spot it now asked: *Which engaged sleaze is hooking up with online fans? This beefed-up reality star needs to stop pulling the wool over his fiancée's eyes.* Honey thought for a moment. She never had time to sit and watch shows but televisions were always playing in green rooms and she was sure she'd seen a billboard outside the recording studio advertising some sort of farming version of *I'm A Celebrity... Get Me Out Of Here!* What was it called? *Famous Farmers? Fame-Hungry Farmers?* And who was that muscly man holding a sheep on the cover of *Heat* this week? She never bought or read the gossip magazines, but they were always around, always visible. Think, Honey, think. She gasped at herself, suddenly realising the pull of the scandal. Maybe this was the draw: the vicarious excitement of the exploits of others.

Hitting the archives button she entered the search word "gemstone".

- *Which national gemstone treasures her female PA more than she'd like us to believe?*
- *With another bearded beard when will our sparkling gemstone realise the irony of her choices?*
- *Whose eyes were sparkling like a precious gemstone during Shanice and St Lourdes lesbian kiss at the Grammys?*
- *Which gemstone uses beards to appease her mother Lucy in the sky?*

Honey stopped reading. What in god's name was this talk about beards? Yes, she could understand the gossip about Liza, clearly a lesbian and always pictured right by her side, but what was this chat about facial hair? She opened Google and asked the question: What is a bearded beard? Result after result mentioned hipsters, grooming and glitter beards – apparently the must-have accessory this Christmas – but she stopped at the entry from Urban Dictionary. *Beard: Any opposite-sex escort taken to an event in an effort to give a homosexual person the appearance of being on a date with a person of the opposite sex.*

Honey laughed. She'd been escorted to the Bond premiere by Tommy Jacobs. Lead actor, handsome, successful, bearded and gay. Everyone knew he was gay. It was the first thing he'd done years ago when they'd met at a charity do: introduced his then boyfriend. He was gay. Blatantly so.

She nodded, ready to Google the words: Tommy Jacobs gay. But as soon as she'd input his name, her name automatically appeared. *Tommy Jacobs and Honey Diamond.* She clicked on it and scanned down the links. Most were from news sites proclaiming with delight the fact they'd gone public. Romance blossoms. Love is in the air. Year-long secret relationship finally revealed. Honey laughed even louder. How utterly ridiculous. They weren't dating. It wasn't even a date. It was two professional people appearing together at a movie premiere. It was work. It was, as Liza put it, maintaining her profile and supporting events worth supporting. And it was fun. With a friend.

Honey tapped back to the SlebSecrets sites and typed: Tommy Jacobs. Nothing came up. She thought carefully and smiled to herself, searching instead for: Cream Cracker.

- *The cream cracker might have bling on his arm, but we know the story's just cheesy.*
- *His love of cream crackers is out there, so why won't he tell us he's gay?*
- *He's a cream cracker of an actor, so why won't this gay man come out?*

Honey clicked on the most recent entry. She was clearly the bling they were referring to. The story went on to ask if the two of them were ever shaken or stirred by the speculation surrounding their sexuality. Honey smiled to herself. It was actually all rather clever, but the idea of any mainstream sexuality speculation was just nonsense. Never once had she been asked about boyfriends or girlfriends, or dating, or love life, and rightly so. She was there to talk about music, not what went on in her bedroom. No one had the right to ask about that.

She tapped the words into Google: Honey Diamond sexuality speculation. Again, page after page of stories flashed up declaring male celeb after male celeb as the new found love of her life. She scanned through the pictures, finding it rather amusing that most were indeed sporting beards. It didn't have any meaning: it was simply a trend, a fashion. She clicked five pages in: more of the same. People weren't speculating about her sexuality. People were speculating about which hero would claim her heart. It appeared that her mother, for once, might be right: people just wanted her to be happy. Well she was. She was living the dream.

Honey dropped her head against the cushions and sighed. Wasn't she? Wasn't this all she'd ever really wanted? To follow in the family footsteps? To share music? To be known? She thought carefully, unable to remember a time when she hadn't been known. This was her life and she'd learnt how to live it in the best way she could, which included a blanket ban on technology. Liza would inform her of anything essential, any campaigns that had performed particularly well, but there was no need to re-read or re-watch the interviews. She'd been there; she knew how they'd gone. The same with performances: she'd lived them already. Life was short; it was about progress, looking forward, moving on; not obsessing over every past action or critiquing every past thought and word.

She'd decided to turn off the iPad and head to the music room instead to write lyrics, but that's when she saw it, the result at the bottom of the Google page: *The Lesbian ChatBoard. I know Honey's a lesbian. I guessed when I sha**ed her. (16 members 1207 Guests 28 anonymous) Active: SneezyFlavor, LaterBlooms...* Honey hit the link. A message board flashed up entitled *The Lesbian ChatBoard. Hot lezzie gossip and drama.* She had been taken to page 317 of 2872 and the message from *Unregistered* claiming to have sha**ed her. Looking up at the thread title, Honey gasped. *What is Honey Diamond's Sexual Orientation Part 4.* She clicked onto page 2872 and scrolled to the last message, posted exactly one minute ago. Another "Unregistered" user was commenting on a picture she recognised had been taken that afternoon as she was leaving The Muse, her mother insisting they use the front entrance to get into their cars. *Ha, you're right,* it said, *she even dresses like the only lesbian Disney Princess.* A new message flashed up in real time. *Unregistered: She needs to use Merida's bow and go shoot herself some livestock #pale #thin #GetSomeMeatInsideYouGirl*

The reply was instant. *Unregistered: She doesn't like meat ha ha, that's the whole point #HoneyDiamondDoesDykes*

Honey remembered her mother mentioning a hashtag at lunch. What was it? Horny Honey's Double Dipping Dilemma or something equally ridiculous? She scrolled up, reading message after message dissecting everything from her look to her seemingly lively lesbian love life. Where in god's name were these people getting it from? Feeling the heat rising inside she typed quickly, her message appearing as *Unregistered: Who's writing these things?*

The replies came thick and fast ranging from *Go away newbie* to *Hello Honey*. Honey bit the inside of her lip, panicked that she'd somehow left her name, or a link to her iPad, or… she stopped as the bickering continued among the users, fighting about whether celebrities would ever visit the site or not. She typed again. *Unregistered: Isn't her private life private?*

The flurry of replies included:

- *Troll.*
- *Get lost and go read the thread from the start.*
- *Take that pole out your arse, she's a celeb, she sold out, she owes us the truth.*
- *Hello PR slut.*
- *Not now that SlebSecrets site is spilling her story.*

Honey typed quickly. *Unregistered: Who's behind SlebSecrets?*
The reply flashed up. *Now that's the biggest mystery of all.*

Honey put the iPad back down, fuming that she'd been so drawn in. This is why she avoided social media. Reading mean comments in her teens had put her off for life, leading to her self-imposed blanket ban on technology which had for the most part saved her from feeling like this. She paused, shocked at how much worse it had got. Who the hell were these people and where did they get off gossiping about her so aggressively? She reached out and hit the top tab, bringing the SlebSecrets site back onto the screen. Yes, it wasn't as bad as that ridiculous forum, but this site was obviously popular. Who would run such a place? A site about strangers, because that's what she was. People might listen to her songs and watch her on stage, but they didn't know her and they didn't have any right to pretend they did. She pulled herself up and walked towards the old-fashioned house phone, calling the one number she knew off by heart.

"Mother," she said when it was answered, "your tech guy, Benedict. You said he could help?"

The reply came with quiet caution. "That, dearest, depends on what's true."

CHAPTER FOUR

"Ai ai, Meg. No HotBuzz riff raff tonight."

The journalist smiled at the doorman, their paths having crossed on numerous occasions before. "And hello to you too."

Jo tottered up the red carpet, grabbing hold of the lanyard dangling from her flatmate's neck. "Darryl, my man, Meg's moved up in the world. I see you're still working the doors."

"Ow! Your words are as sharp as her glasses." The doorman moved his nod from the black frames towards the buxom blonde's ample assets. "But you, my lady, are as stunning as ever."

Jo slinked towards one of the tall patio heaters and shivered. "It's freezing out here."

Blowing on his leather gloves, the doorman rubbed his hands together before reaching out to warm the goose-bumped arms. "You should have worn a nice sturdy coat like Meg."

Jo smiled at the sarcastic remark, remembering how wicked he had been in other departments. "And hide my beautiful ball gown? I'm sure you wouldn't want that now would you, Darryl?"

"It's been a while," he said, continuing his come-on. "You should have called."

Meg lifted herself onto her tiptoes and waved with two hands, refocusing his flirtation. "Helloooo! My sturdy coat and I would like entry please." She paused, catching sight of the clipboard and guest list resting on top of the stone pillar. "HotBuzz are here, aren't they?"

Darryl stopped the rubbing and turned to Meg. "Nope. It's all that French manager's fault. Coming over here and trying to culture-fy our club." He lifted the list and showed her the names. "It's all the big-wigs, all the proper papers."

Jo smiled sweetly, willing the attention her way. "The club's winning aren't they?" That was as far as her football knowledge went.

"Yes, but we're London Town, and that French fucker's brought all his froggy fuckwits with him. People like Louis Laurent will stop playing. We're a British club, we need British players."

Meg laughed. "Louis Laurent's half French."

"No he ain't. British bloke born and bred."

Jo pouted. "Mmm, Louis Laurent."

"Alright blondie, calm it down. Still here for the ride I see." He turned to Meg. "That press pass better say two."

Jo stepped away from the heater and reached out to wiggle Meg's lanyard once more. "Doesn't matter who she works for, she always gets her wicked way."

"I'd rather have my wicked way with you."

Meg hit the bulging bicep. "Just let us in."

"Always a pleasure." He stepped to the side, allowing them to pass. "Jo, you know where to find me."

With an added wiggle to her walk, the blonde seductress smiled over her shoulder. "We'll see."

"We won't," snapped Meg, marching them forward. "We're working."

"I'm only being friendly," she said, trotting to catch up, only half noticing their impressive surroundings. "Have we been here before?"

"The Children in Need charity dance. Remember? The footballers took part in that spoof Strictly sketch." Meg led them across the plush hospitality arena towards the banquet hall, taking a moment to marvel, as she always did, at the building's ability to encase one of the UK's largest football pitches, not to mention the conference areas, hospitality suites, performance stages and events rooms. She turned to her friend. "Is my coat really that bad?"

"Yes!" said Jo, suddenly remembering.

"Great."

"No, not your coat." She gave it a quick up and down. "Well yes, it's bad, but I was yes-ing about this place." She lowered her voice. "It's where I heard the WAGs in the ladies gossiping about Matty Hardacre's impotence."

"Oh don't, that was one of my early posts."

"What was it? 'Which premier league player's not as hard as his name suggests? The only thing he gets up is the score sheet'."

Meg cringed. "Stop it. It's awful. I'm ashamed of myself. You convinced me on that one, remember?"

"You had a better sense of humour when you were younger."

"It was never funny. It was cruel, and I regret it. My site's so much better than that now." She pointed at the grand placard outside the hall. "Seating plan," she said, trying to change subject.

Jo glanced inside, taking in the quiet buzz of activity. Waiters were in a line receiving instruction and organisers were pushing missing chairs into place. "It's rather empty."

"We're an hour early. They want to brief the press pre-event. Sell us the story before it occurs."

Jo tapped the plan. "Here we are." She scanned the hall finding the position of table three. "There. Look, people are already seated."

"The other papers."

Jo nodded. "So what's the story, and where do you want me?"

"Official story. London Town's new manager is starting an arts charity to increase engagement among young people. French culture comes to football."

"Boring. No wonder HotBuzz aren't here."

"Seems like the club's selected where they want coverage. It's a clever marketing ploy actually. Get press inches in the broadsheets by talking about arts organisations and cultural venues for disadvantaged areas. HotBuzz would only focus on who's wearing what."

"I'd read that."

"Exactly, but the more up-market person wants to read about the new, cultured French manager, no doubt shocked when he found out his youth team had never set foot inside an art gallery, or watched a live theatre performance, or listened to an orchestra."

"London Town's an inner city football club, of course they haven't. Footballers are footballers. That's all they need to know."

Meg shook her head. "They'll feed us the line now, but it'll be about unlocking creativity, raising aspirations, improving communications – all things they'll say a good footballer needs."

Jo pretended to yawn. "This new job's changed you."

"Fine. Unofficial story. Louis Laurent's knobbing his nanny."

Jo grinned. "I'm on it. You sit down and suck up the schmoozing. I'll do my usual."

"Hang around the bar and loiter in the toilets?"

"People talk to me. I've got one of those faces."

"Just don't bid on the auction and don't get too drunk."

"There's an auction?" Jo beamed. "That's the perfect way in!"

****

Honey lay stretched out in her creative position, head back among the cushions on her music room's well-worn sofa. It was the same sofa she'd lain on as a child, the one piece of furniture moved from property to property as she penned her first verses and dreamt her first dreams. She smiled. Because that's what music was. A dream. A place where you could make anything happen. A place where you could evoke emotions with one simple line or one enchanted melody. Music was magic and she'd always had the ability to close her eyes and create. She nodded along to the notes circling around inside her head. This creation was different. This wasn't peaceful or perfected. This was raw. This was angry. She jumped up. This needed new words.

Grabbing the pen and paper from the table next to her feet, Honey moved to the mixing desk and sat at the station, scribbling fast as the heated words poured from inside her.

What does it matter where I lay my head?
Who cares if it's in a boy or girl's bed?
There's so much more to my personality.
What's the importance of my sexuality?
She sang loudly as she wrote the chorus.
Love who you love.
Be true to your feelings.
Who cares who's tugging at your heartstrings?
Love who you love.
Be brave with your choices.
Those who matter will accept our true voices.

She gasped. This was the feeling she'd had with *Secret Smile*. It wasn't that her other songs lacked meaning, they were just rather samey. Like Adele. Like Enya. People knew a Honey song was a hit song, but she wasn't breaking boundaries or making people think. She was producing hit album after hit album of tuneful songs. But what if she changed? What if she became edgy? What if she made a music video that wasn't black and white for once? What if she caused controversy? Honey giggled at the thrill rising inside her. She twisted in her seat and reached back down to the table, finding the discarded iPad and forcefully tapping the SlebSecrets site back to life. She spoke with a smile. "I'm not hiding anything, so put that in your pipe and smoke it, you psychos."

****

Jo hooked her heels onto the barstool rails and lifted herself up, waving her arms towards the stage. "Four thousand, five hundred!"

The elderly auctioneer struggled to take his eyes from the blonde hair and bouncing breasts. "Five thousand anywhere?" he asked, not really moving his attention from her bid.

"Five!" came a shout from the other side of the noisy banquet hall.

"Five," he acknowledged before nodding enthusiastically again towards Jo. "Five, five?"

"Five thousand, five hundred," she shouted, not daring to look towards table three where Meg would no doubt be having kittens. She glanced instead towards the group of footballers further down the bar, hoping someone would take the bait. Gavin Grahams, first team defender, was edging himself her way. *About bloody time*, she thought, praying the other bidder would go higher.

The shout came quickly. "Six thousand!"

The raspy auctioneer peered around at his audience. "Everyone wants this night at the opera with Louis Laurent it seems." He lifted his wire glasses and winked in Jo's direction. "But I'm sure he'd prefer the arm of a beautiful blonde, don't you, ladies and gentleman?"

Jo lifted her hand in shocked apology to the equally pretty, brunette bidder on the other side of the room. "Sorry," she mouthed, genuinely uncomfortable with the elderly man's flirtation.

"That's six five!" he whistled, spotting the raised hand and revelling in his role.

Jo gasped. "No, I…" the jeering was too loud.

"You're making a mistake." Gavin Grahams had positioned himself next to her at the bar. "I'd take you for free."

Jo didn't even turn her body his way. "You're not Louis Laurent," she said, deliberately needling the ego. She signalled towards the brunette. "You go. I'm out."

The voice was annoyed. "Louis Laurent's not even here. Too famous for a fundraiser it seems. Plus he's married."

Jo heard the shout of "Seven thousand" and smiled, relieved to be free. She ignored the inappropriate gesturing the auctioneer directed her way and eased herself back into a seated position, finally looking at the man standing beside her. It was common knowledge that Louis Laurent was disliked by most of his teammates. Mr Golden Shoes. The focus always on him. Yes, he could take free kicks and score the odd goal, but he wasn't a great like Maradona or Zidane. He was good looking, with a famous wife to boot, and if there was something Brand Laurent could sponsor, they sponsored it. The fact most people thought London Town and Louis Laurent were one and the same annoyed the hell out of players like Gavin.

Jo reached for her martini and sipped deliberately slowly, needing to focus on the flirting. "Doesn't stop him playing away though, does it?" she said with a smile.

"I didn't come over to talk about him. I came over to save you some money."

"Because you'll take me for free?" Jo worked all the tricks. The flutter of eyelashes, the crossing of legs. Giving him hope before snatching it all away. "Sorry, like I said, you're not Louis Laurent." She lifted the olive from her drink and started to suck it.

The defender narrowed his eyes. "You know he's a knob so why do you want him?"

"Is he a knob?"

"You said he played away."

"Does he?" It was also common knowledge that Gavin Grahams wasn't the brightest button in the box.

He frowned, confused. "What?"

The fluttering was back. "I thought you knew him." She nonchalantly shrugged her shoulders and smiled. "Fine, let's talk about you. Who would you pick? Me or the nanny?"

"What nanny?"

"Who's better looking, me or his nanny? Louis' nanny. The one he's seeing."

Gavin Grahams paused.

"You paused. It's her isn't it? I thought you were coming over to woo me? To wine and dine me? To take me to the opera?" She dropped her lips at the corners. "But now you're saying you prefer her to me." She straightened on the stool and pretended to strain her ears towards the auction. "I'm going back to the bidding."

The response was quick. "No. I'd pick you. He's a fool."

Jo relaxed her pose and encouraged him with wide eyes. "Because he's married?"

"No. Jackie's always put up with his shit." He lowered his voice. "The nanny's a digger. Us players know them when we see them. Always after the bling." Responding to the lifted eyebrows, he carried on. "And she's a live-in, so she's got access to everything. He'll get unstuck with this one I'm telling you now."

"You wouldn't get unstuck would you? You're bright enough to stay single."

"Too right I am. No bird's pinning me down." He waited for the encouraging eyes, pausing for a second when they didn't come. He coughed. "Unless the right one comes along of course."

Jo nodded. "Of course." She finished her martini in one gulp, thirsty now her job had been done. "If you'd excuse me for a moment I need to check on my friend."

The footballer lifted her empty glass. "Can I get you another?"

Jo eyed the man up and down properly for the first time that evening. "You know what? Why the hell not?"

****

Stepping out of the recording pod, Honey made her way to the control panel and sat down in front of the mixing desk. She'd never made an album at home, but the small soundproofed music room was perfect for times like this when she wanted an instant copy of her creation. Yes, lyrics had been written down and basic notes recorded, but there was nothing quite like a playback of the melody as it came from her mouth. She was forever changing bridges and harmonies and it was helpful to remember where the vision had first started; here with these rough verses and chorus. She pressed play and listened. Just her. Just her voice. There was something powerful about the playback. It wouldn't need much. Some beats and some bass. Stripped back and raw, yet dominant and edgy. She transferred the file onto her iPod: the one piece of technology she did keep in her possession at all times. The iPad next to her suddenly pinged as well and she vaguely remembered setting up the share across devices feature when she'd received it from her mother, thinking she may use the tablet to listen to music. She never did, hence its relegation to the arm of the sofa.

Honey tapped the home button, instantly annoyed as the SlebSecrets site filled the screen. She was about to minimise and check the music app when she noticed the new entry.

"Which twinkle-toed London lad likes to put the boot into his long-suffering wife? Pregnant with her fourth and he's playing away. It's the spoon full of sugar bringing down this brand of medicine."

Honey shook her head. The Laurents were her neighbours. This was clearly about them. They'd received huge stick for their latest endorsement, a family advert for Calpol. Louis claiming it helped when he fell on the pitch. Jackie claiming it helped with her births. The kids claiming it helped them put up with their parents. Honey paused, making the connection. Spoon full of sugar? Not that new nanny? Surely? She wasn't close to Jackie, but they spoke now and then and she'd often see her on the green with the kids.

Honey felt the annoyance rising once more. How dare someone spread such rumours, especially with families involved? It was one thing to speculate about a singleton's sexuality, but to outright accuse a family man of a fling, well. She nodded her head. She'd get it seen to. She'd get this sordid SlebSecrets site down.

CHAPTER FIVE

Honey was seated on the large stool in the centre of her even larger kitchen, living the same morning she lived most days she was home. She watched with a smile. PA Liza was strutting around, PDA in hand, listing the day's itinerary of meetings, rehearsals, appearances and studio sessions. She could feel hair stylist Heidi at her shoulder, coaxing her long auburn layers into a fashion deemed appropriate for whichever outfit clothes stylist Caitlyn had selected for the day. Louisa the make-up artist was in front of her playing her usual role as master fencer, jumping in and out with her blusher brush whenever the curling wand was lowered. Then there was Sofia, adding to the hustle and bustle with non-stop rounds of tea and coffee before presenting all of the pre-packed meals she'd carefully prepared for whoever was involved in the day.

Honey always insisted on no visible entourage when out and about, but most working days involved at least one style change and she'd often find herself back in the company of Heidi, Caitlyn and Louisa as they miraculously appeared at her studio, set or location exactly when needed. Honey knew this was all down to the careful planning and preparation of Liza and her ever-buzzing electronic PDA, but as long as she didn't travel, arrive or hang with a huge crowd of groupies, as her mother was famed for, she could cope with Liza's stranglehold on their each and every move.

"So," confirmed Liza for the third time that morning, "Tammara's coming at eight and we're—"

"Even I've got it today!" yelped Sofia, the high-pitched volume from such a small body shocking everyone in the room. "Sit down, Liza," continued the voice, more calmly this time. The old woman patted the free stool next to her before pointing to the centre of the kitchen where Honey's naturally pale eyes were being transformed into cat-like creations by the expert flicks of Louisa's black pencil. "Watch the show."

"No."

"What is it? You're more on edge than usual. Another love life disaster? Sit down, let it all out."

Liza stayed standing. "I don't have disasters." She turned to Honey. "Is that how you report it?"

Honey smiled to herself. It was wonderful having Sofia around at times like these to keep her grounded, to make her laugh and to say all of the things she was far too polite to say herself. Liza's dramatic love life *was* funny. It was a mishmash of mishaps, reflecting the mixture that was Liza herself. She was short, but not stocky. Slim, but not trim. How one might picture a little dictator: more amusing to her people than feared, her pretty features and pixie haircut paired with her masculine suits and flat shoes bringing all sorts of lady lovers her way.

"I must say you are a tad more jumpy than usual," agreed Honey.

"It's this Hollywood film." Liza lifted her device. "I've had to schedule in hours and hours of rehearsals, sound checks and recording sessions. Plus, we've got *Britain Sings* still in the auditions phase so there are months of that to come. Not to mention the new album."

Honey raised her hand. "About that."

"Which bit?"

"The album bit." She paused, trying really hard not to move her face as she talked. "But why's the film stuff starting already? I thought I'd be in Hollywood for that?"

"On-set filming won't begin until the end of next year, but we're recording the songs and singing bits of dialogue over here as and when time allows."

Sofia laughed. "Oh Liza, I love how you say *we*."

Clothes stylist Caitlyn, who was sitting at the breakfast bar with her role in activities done and dusted, blew on her coffee and looked up and down at Liza's trouser suit, complete with braces and waistcoat. "You're certainly dressed for the part. Going on set at *Bugsy Malone* are we?"

"She's always on set at *Bugsy Malone*," added Sofia. "Have you ever seen her in anything other than a three-piece suit and those bloody brogues?"

Liza huffed at the comments and marched to the spare stool. "Stop it," she said, sitting clumsily. "I'm not in the mood. And brogues are my trademark."

"It's so sweet that you're proud of that," commented Caitlyn.

Liza folded her arms on the breakfast bar. "Decided. You three are signing the new confidentiality contract. You're taking too many liberties."

Hair stylist Heidi moved the curling wand away from a now bouncing auburn ringlet and whispered into Honey's ear. "Definitely a love life disaster."

Honey smiled. Heidi, Caitlyn and Louisa were her longest serving employees, having been with her since things started to get really serious ten years before. Liza had taken up her role as PA and insisted on stylists. Stylists that were exclusively Honey's, on call at all times as the empire was established and expanded. "Quite possibly," said Honey.

"I heard that." Liza checked the clock on the wall, followed by the watch on her wrist and the time on her PDA, obviously feeling the pressure of taking a moment.

Honey raised her hand again. "I'll make you smile. I've written a new song for the album."

Jumping from her seat, Liza's moment was short lived. She started to pace. "Oh good god, we've not got time for that! The album's finalised, it's well into production!"

Honey laughed. "It's good. It's different. It can be a bonus track or something."

"No."

"Special edition version?"

"Absolutely not." The sound of a car horn averted Liza's panic. "Thank goodness. Tammara's here; Alan's already there. Ladies, are we done?"

Louisa and Heidi stepped away from the stool, presenting a perfectly preened Honey Diamond showcasing a silvery chic 1920s look. Caitlyn put down her coffee and joined in the admiration. "It's a one-off Thierry DuBon full-length flapper."

Honey looked at Liza who was double-checking the notes in her PDA.

Liza nodded. "Got it. And the head piece?"

Hair stylist Heidi smiled. "That's my own creation."

Caitlyn continued. "The headpiece isn't DuBon, but it follows the main themes of his winter collection. Silver. Sparkle. Lace. White feathers."

Heidi spoke louder. "Headpiece by hair stylist Heidi Dixon. Get that in your PDA, Liza. Pass that on to the press."

Liza ignored her. "Bobby Brown make-up, Louisa?"

"Yep, and I've flicked the eyes in the Dauragé style."

"Yes, got that."

Honey stood from her stool. "I don't look like a peacock, do I?"

"Does Honey Diamond want a mirror?" Caitlyn laughed. "I think she wants a mirror! Girls, I think we've done it!"

Honey turned to her godmother. "Sofia, do I look like a peacock?"

"No, my dear, you look beautiful. Who's the designer?"

"Thierry DuBon."

Sofia nodded. "Then you're good to go."

It was all Honey needed to know. The name of the designer. Liza would brief the photographers with each and every detail prior to the first picture being taken, and as long as she remembered the name of the designer she could get through the inevitable shouting from the press as she made her way from car to studio, an essential piece of judge showmanship required during the first round of auditions.

Honey trusted her stylists and cringed whenever they brought out the mirrors, parading her with complimentary words that only made her feel uneasy. It was Honey's belief that anyone could look great with a team of stylists and she'd always vowed to never let herself get drawn into the lie that she had some sort of naturally intrinsic beauty or instinctive flawless style. Yes, without make-up she was adequately pretty, but so were most women. She wasn't anything special, yet she understood the role required of her.

"I'm playing you my song, Liza" she said, holding on to her iPod.

Liza shook her head. "No, you're not."

"I am."

"We haven't got time."

"I'll play it in the car then." She turned to her stylists. "Ladies, you'll hear it on the album."

"They will not," gasped Liza, ushering Honey towards the door.

"You will, and thank you for today's 1920s style, ensemble."

Caitlyn laughed. "See Honey, you do care." She paused. "But we'll see you again after auditions. Quick change for your Live Lounge performance."

"Can't I wear this?"

Cries of "don't you dare!" chorused from all three with Liza simply saying: "Stop it."

Honey laughed. "I'm joking. I know the drill. You lot wore me down years ago. Right, Liza, where are we going to first?"

"Haven't you been listening at all?! The London round of the *Britain Sings* auditions, then..." She paused at the look on Honey's face. "Very funny. Tease Liza day, is it? I'm so glad I bring light into all your dark little lives."

"Bye, Liza," said the stylists, waving her out of the room with their giggles.

Sofia kissed Honey on both cheeks. "Play her your song, dear. She'll like it."

Liza marched towards the front door, shouting back towards the kitchen over her shoulder. "Not on the new album I won't."

****

"Looking lovely today, Honey," said Tammara, opening the car door as she appraised her employer. "Like a ginger-haired Greta Garbo."

Liza rushed forward and stepped into the vehicle first. "Auburn or flame-coloured are the words associated with Honey's hair. Not ginger."

Tammara stood a little straighter. "Sorry."

Honey dismissed the chastisement with a smile. "How was the party?"

"Great, thank you. Did you have a nice evening?"

Honey studied Tammara's smart outfit and tight bun. "I did thank you, very productive." She smiled. "You should wear your hair down more often. You looked lovely yesterday."

Liza's voice sounded from the back seat. "Not at work she shouldn't and stop with the chit-chat; we're on a schedule. I've spoken to you about this before, Tammara."

Honey spotted the anxious look in her driver's eyes. This was the third time they'd changed car companies in two years with Liza sure the spate of leaks about Honey's whereabouts could only have come from an indiscreet driver tipping off the paps in exchange for a fee. The fact that the paparazzi were always everywhere regardless of Honey's mode of transportation wasn't enough to appease Liza's suspicions.

"Sorry," said Honey, "it's always the schedule." She stepped into the car and whispered over her shoulder. "But you should wear it down, and don't worry, I know my hair's ginger." She saw the smile appear as the door was closed then reappear once more from the front of the car as the glass divider buzzed down. She handed over her iPod. "Can you put track one on, please, Tammara?"

Liza snapped her seatbelt into place. "We haven't got time for that. Put the divider back up so we can run through the day."

Honey waited until the music player had been taken before leaving the glass down. She had absolutely no interest in cars and would probably just describe the one she was travelling in as executive and black. Yes, it was nicely luxurious, but it wasn't a limo. Such extravagance for two people making the short journey into central London seemed preposterous to Honey, if not rather pompous, and she'd always decline the suggestion of anything more showy. Liza often made a point of highlighting the other *Britain Sings* judges' modes of arrival, which could include helicopter and Hummer, but Honey stood her ground and said she was happy. This sort of car was professional and appropriate. Its sound system was also top notch.

She smiled at her strung out PA. "We've spent the whole morning running through the schedule. Sit back. Relax. Listen to my song. It's only a short drive to the auditions."

Liza tapped into her PDA. "No, I still need to slot in three rehearsal sessions for the film score."

"I've not even seen the full script yet so I won't be rehearsing anything anytime soon."

"You're getting the songs and script at the meet and greet tonight... after the Live Lounge... after auditions." She paused. "I've told you all this already, Honey."

"Okay, but we're going to Apple Road afterwards."

Liza gasped. "Do you deliberately do this to me? We haven't got the time or the space to fit a new song on the album. Picador would have an absolute fit."

Honey fastened her seatbelt and smiled. "It's a good one. Just listen. Play it loud, Tam. Number one."

Honey ignored the nervous eyes in the rear view mirror and reinforced the instruction with an encouraging nod. Yes, Liza was sharp and direct, a somewhat powerful force to be reckoned with, but ultimately Honey was the boss, and Liza, through all her huffing and puffing, would always eventually succumb.

The a capella track started to play as the car headed out of the estate with the lyrics singing loud and clear.

What does it matter where I lay my head?

Liza's ears visibly pricked up. She wagged her finger. "Oh no."

Who cares if it's in a boy or girl's bed?

"No." The wagging got wider.

There's so much more to my personality.

What's the importance of my sexuality?

Liza's head joined in the dismissal. "No."

"Do you like it, Tam?" asked Honey.

"Oh my goodness, I love it!" came the excited reply.

Liza's shaking was now in overdrive. "Just stop."

Honey harmonised with herself on the chorus. "*Love who you love. Be true to your feelings. Who cares who's tugging at your heartstrings?* Just imagine the bass, Liza. *Love who you love. Be brave with your choices. Those who matter will accept our true voices.*"

"Bass? Bass! You can't!"

"It's fab, Honey," said Tammara. "So different."

Honey smiled. "Turn it up!"

Both driver and passenger lost themselves in the edgy song, ignoring Liza's objections entirely.

When silence finally returned, Liza made a point of pulling her jacket tighter around her body and clearing her throat. "No," she said, with a final point of her finger.

Honey turned to her PA. "You didn't like it?"

The voice was more forceful. "No."

"Look at me, Liza. You liked it."

The eyes stared forward. "I didn't."

Honey smiled. "You did! I know you did. It's exactly your type of song."

"It's not."

"It is!"

Liza gasped, finally spinning herself around. "It's just so... so..."

"So what? Yes, it's not quite my normal ballad style, but who says Honey Diamond can't be edgy or sassy or—"

"Not quite your normal style?! Honey, those lyrics are ridiculously controversial!" Looking away, Liza squeezed the edge of the leather seat before rubbing the corners of her mouth as she tried to find the words. "And it's so... it's so..."

Honey lifted her shoulders. "It's what?"

Liza spoke loudly. "Tammara, put the divider up please."

"No, Tammara," said Honey, shaking her head, "keep the divider down."

The eyes in the mirror looked torn, the voice hesitant. "I'll..."

"You'll keep it down." Honey was firm. "Liza's been snappy all morning. It's Sheila, isn't it? That's what this is about. You're always worse when she's—"

"No, it's not bloody Sheila!" Liza lowered her voice. "It's the hypocrisy of it all."

Honey raised her eyebrows. "Excuse me?"

"And you can't even pass it on to someone more appropriate like Jessie or Nicki because your name would get writer's credit."

"This is my song, Liza. I'll be the one singing it."

"Oh, Honey."

"What?"

"You really want to do this? Here? On the way to auditions in the back of the car dressed as a 1920s flapper girl with your driver listening to every word we say?"

"Tammara's my friend."

Liza almost snorted. "She's not your friend!" Clapping her hands she signalled to the front of the car. "Tammara, tell Honey you're not her friend."

The anxious eyes were back. "I'm... I'm..."

"Oh just spit it out, Liza! Is it really that bad?"

"You can't release a song that's all up front about sexuality."

The look was one of sheer confusion. "Why not?"

Liza inhaled deeply, paused, then let rip like a little Jack Russell. "Because you're well and truly in the closet at the back of the warehouse with the door shut, packaged up for some secure shipping container to shunt you out to the back of beyond."

Honey actually laughed. "I am not."

"It's hypocritical. You're so far in the closet Narnia's your holiday home."

"Oh stop it."

"And you do care where you lay your head."

"No, I don't." Honey was the one now waving at her driver. "Tammara."

Tammara gripped the steering wheel even tighter. "Umm, yes?"

"You know I... I... well what would you call it? I'm fluid?"

Tammara's response was shy. "Umm, I assumed with your chatter about Betty that..."

"Exactly." Honey turned her attention back to her PA. "And you Liza, of all people, know who and what I like."

"But you're not out!"

"I don't need to come out. I live out."

"You don't live out!"

"Because I'm single?" Honey turned to the window and shrugged. "I'm just busy." She stayed silent for a moment as the world passed her by. "But there have been some... some *loves*."

The Jack Russell was back. "As if! You're like a lone penguin lost on an iceberg at the north bloody pole."

"I didn't say I'd been *in* love. I said there had *been* loves. You know this. Mother knows this. There doesn't need to be any official announcement. And everyone's fluid nowadays anyway."

Liza snorted. "Your mother's still hoping you'll meet your James Dean! Listen to yourself. You can't even say the words. Women. Lesbians. Gay."

"I don't need to. It's private. It's personal. Labels aren't necessary."

"So you see my point? Singing this song will open the closet door. You can't go from your current white-wash to this sudden declaration of whole-hearted lesbianism."

"What white-wash? And it's not a declaration of anything. It's just a song saying so what, who cares, it's not important."

Liza flung her hands into the air. "So not important that it's written into every single interview screening sheet. Every single staff contract. Don't ask Honey about her sexuality. Don't engage in—"

"What?"

"Oh come on, Honey. Even you can't be this naive."

"People can ask me what they like."

"Not if they want to secure the interview they can't."

"I thought your whole confidentiality contract thing was a joke?!"

Liza let out a huge exasperated breath. "Do you realise how many balls I'm juggling? Your record company, your talent agency, your PR group, your security men, your lawyers, your mother."

"I don't have a PR group."

"No, in your eyes you have me, and I sort it. I sort everything, but I can't be dealing with this backlash."

"What backlash?"

"Oh Honey, there are so many vested interests in you. So many agencies involved. It takes a great deal of work to make it look as simple as little old me and my PDA. But that's what your mother wanted."

"My mother can't even remember your name."

Liza laughed. "We have weekly meetings! You were a child when I took on the job."

"I was seventeen!"

"Still not able to take full legal responsibility. Honey, this industry's brutal. Your mother wanted you shielded so you could focus on doing what you love. You know this."

"I don't."

"Writing songs, singing songs, performing, appearing."

"And doing interviews with people who are essentially gagged?" Honey laughed at her own stupidity. "You know what? I always thought people were just really polite or maybe they didn't really care. Like you, Tam. You rarely encourage me when I talk about Betty Big Boobs."

"I'm not meant to gossip."

"Says your contract? That's ridiculous. We're friends."

Tammara looked apologetically into the mirror. "I'm... I'm not meant to be too familiar."

"She's new, of course she's not."

Honey gasped. "She's been with us six months!"

Liza reached out and rubbed Honey's knee. "You're always so busy. You haven't come up for breath once since I've known you. You don't need the added stress of paperwork and politics."

"Maybe I do!" She shook her head. "Fine, this bubble protects me, but it also prohibits me. It stops me living a life."

Liza laughed. "You're never going to live a life. Not a real one anyway. You're Honey Diamond."

"Is it Picador? Or the agency?"

"You've been managed from an early age. It's just happened."

"My mother's PR company then?"

Liza shrugged. "It's like you're the Queen. No one asks the Queen about her private life. No one gets overly familiar with HRH."

"Actually it's Her Majesty, not HRH, and I'm not the Queen and I bet the Queen's actually got more going on than I have!" Honey shrank back into the seat, staring into nowhere. "You know what actually annoys me more? The fact you hated the song."

Liza sighed. "I didn't hate the song. You just caught me off guard." She tilted her head into Honey's line of vision until their eyes connected. The smile was genuine. "At the end of the day I'm your PA, Honey. I'll do whatever you need me to do."

"You will?"

"You know I will. I play at being boss but that's all I'm doing. Playing. You're ultimately in charge. I can advise and recommend, but if you're adamant about something then I have to take it on board." The same smile was back. "You do know it was me who got the 'don't ask about drugs' clause out of the interview screening contracts, don't you? Fine when you were younger but it seemed silly as the years went by knowing you never had and never would do drugs."

Honey laughed. "And look where that got us! I assume the 'I love Meth' beat-box is still doing the rounds?"

"Sure is." Liza paused before nodding. "If you really want to take hold of the reins maybe now's the time to increase your online presence. There are some great..." She stopped at the frantic shaking of Honey's head.

"That's always been me, not mother. I'm the one who hates the internet. Always have, always will." She sighed. "In fact, it was those nasty online trolls who inspired that song." She looked out of the window as the television studio loomed into sight. "Oh, this is so confusing, isn't it? If it's no big deal then I shouldn't make it a big deal. But if people think I'm hiding my true self then I need to tell them I'm not." Honey laughed. "But then there's never been anyone serious so it's not like I've got anything significant to say so I should stay quiet."

"There was Sheila's friend, Mandy."

"Oh, don't!" Honey cringed. "Take things back to how they were! I'm not ready to talk about that yet!"

Liza nodded. "And yes, sociopath Sheila is back on the scene and probably the reason I'm ratty. So I'm sorry. Everyone, I'm sorry. Tammara, I'm sorry. Honey, I'm sorry." She shouted upwards towards the gods. "Diana Diamond, I'm sorry!"

"Why are you apologising to my mother?"

"Because I'm encouraging this."

"Are you?"

"You need to follow your heart." She reached out and held Honey's hand. "Right here, right now. What does your heart tell you to do?"

"My heart tells me to sing."

"So sing. Sing your song. I'll deal with the rest."

Honey smiled as the crowd outside the studio started to cheer. Raised banners were flapping and placards were bobbing up and down as the fans realised a judge was about to appear.

Tammara stopped the car and twisted in the front seat. "Is now a good time to tell you that Betty Big Boobs has the hots for you too?"

"No, it bloody isn't," snapped Liza, straight back in work mode. "Just open the door, Tammara, and keep your head bowed."

Honey laughed feeling the warmth of the cheers and the pop of the flashes as the crowd erupted into a frenzy of screams and whoops. She waved and smiled. Determined to do things her way. "Liza, I'll be taking my time before I go in."

Liza joined her on the red carpet placing her hand at the base of her back, gently guiding her towards the entrance. "You're needed inside."

Honey stepped away from the contact and nodded. "I said I'll be taking my time." She walked towards the railings and the group of young girls who had been screaming the loudest. "Hi," she said, "would you like a few photos?"

CHAPTER SIX

Two months later:

The wine had been poured and the takeaway delivered with five minutes to spare. Saturday night and flatmates Meg and Jo were settling down, like most of the nation, to watch the latest episode of *Britain Sings*. The talent show hadn't gone live yet and was still playing the pre-recorded auditions with tonight offering up the best and worst of London's wannabes, some praised, but most dismissed, by the show's four famous judges. Everyone knew they were on the run-up to Christmas when *Britain Sings* returned to their screens, with the winner almost guaranteed the much coveted Christmas number one single spot.

Moving the clutter of magazines, books and blankets off the couch Meg sat with her legs curled up, curry bowl on lap, phone ready and waiting beside her. It was all she needed to enjoy the show to its fullest: good food, good company and Twitter's *Britain Sings* hashtag adding an extra dimension to the experience, with the whole nation in the room commenting on contestants in real time. She looked down at her flatmate, hoping the company would indeed be good for the evening. It was always hit and miss where Jo was concerned, her love of a quick tipple often turning into a full-on drink fest, bringing on the ugly side of her Jekyll and Hyde persona. Meg smiled at the long blonde hair. Things should be different now though; a recent more serious episode in the local A&E would have been enough to put the frighteners on the most seasoned of drinkers.

The blonde flatmate had opted for the floor claiming it gave her easier access to the coffee table and her half share of poppadom and paltry tear of naan, which had been laid out with precision to see her through the night. Meg knew from experience that Jo's frequent sips of wine were less visible from that low down position. "Come and sit up here with me," she said.

"No, and only read out the funny tweets this time." Jo tore a tiny piece off the bread. "No one wants your usual running commentary of waffle."

"It's only us here."

"Pia's in the bathroom, still trying to pull your wad of black hair from the plug."

"She is not. Stop being so cruel."

"I watched her earlier. It was like a tug of war competition. Her wrestling your hair out of the sewers." Jo dabbed gently at the mango chutney ensuring she got a graze of flavour rather than a chunk of calories. "You're moulting, Meg. And that floor by your dresser..." She shook her head as she popped the bread into her mouth. "Well."

"Well what?"

She spoke through the tiny portion. "Well it looks like a shag pile rug."

"It does not!"

"It does. The amount of hair there's just ridiculous. Is it a lesbian thing? Moulting." She pointed her fork towards the television. "Look, here comes Honey. She's not a lesbian. Her hair's too thick and coiffured."

"Her hair's gorgeous and I love that headpiece."

Jo glanced over her shoulder at her flatmate. "Says your scary eye bags. Seriously Meg, they're frightening. You need vitamin D for your hair, vitamin A for your bags, vitamin C for your..." The criticism stopped as the camera panned away to reveal the judges' outfits. "Oh no, what the bloody hell's Honey wearing? She looks like a tap dancing peacock from a feather factory. Gwen's definitely won best outfit tonight."

"What have my frightening eye bags got to do with her thick hair? Maybe if you ate more and drank less you wouldn't be so cruel. I thought you were taking it steady tonight."

"I am."

"Is there anyone you actually like?" Lifting her phone, Meg typed in the Honey Diamond hashtag.

"I like you. And it's not cruel. It's tough love. You've been in her company before, you'll be in her company again. You need to create an impression."

"Since when have you indulged in my Honey Diamond fantasy?" Meg scrolled through the tweets. "And I've only ever seen her from afar. She'd never notice my eye bags."

"Oh, she'd notice them alright. They're like dark hollows sucking your face back in on itself."

"Thank you."

"Seriously, let me give you that makeover. How many years have we been planning it for? Ten?"

"You've been planning it, and according to Twitter Honey's wearing a 1920s style flapper dress by Thierry DuBon, and it's mostly receiving positive mentions." Meg left the phone on the cushion and made a start on her curry. "And stop being so concerned with my style. This is me. I'm happy."

"Using the word 'style' loosely there, aren't you, my lovely?" Jo reached backwards and found Meg's knee, giving it a tap. "And you're not. You're miserable. You're working too hard. You're playing too little. Look at us. Saturday night, stuck in watching *Britain Sings*. Get rid of your geeky-journalist female-Clark-Kent look and you never know how your horizons might change. There's a chance you could pull someone other than a moody, mirror-image, chip-on-their-shoulder grungy lesbian." She smiled. "And if I indulge in your incessant Honey Diamond obsession you might realise you want someone more girly."

"I don't have a chip on my shoulder, I'm not grungy and that one date with that grungy girl you're so fond of recounting occurred over three years ago."

"That was a girl?"

"Oh stop it."

"Fine, you're not grungy, you're just serious looking with your chunky glasses and unintentional bed hair. But you do have a chip and that's why you're so jealous of Honey."

"I'm not jealous of Honey." Meg sighed. Her flatmate went through a cycle of being bearable, quite funny, far too much, then utterly inappropriate and offensive every time she started to drink, never seemingly growing out of that university phase where trips to the hospital to have your stomach pumped or your wounds sewn up were laughed about and worn with a badge of honour. Jo was a nasty drunk and even though she'd behaved unforgivably on many different occasions Meg always accepted the apology and moved on; life was short and people weren't perfect. Plus Jo needed her. Every time she was propped up in a hospital bed looking so vulnerable and lost she'd call for her. Jo would recount stories of her mother and her childhood, booze the ultimate cause in her mother's downfall and her own placement in care. What friend would give up on someone like that?

"What is it then?" said the blonde, not letting it lie.

Meg thought carefully. It wasn't jealousy, and it wasn't an obsession. She debated, as she had many times before, trying to place exactly what it was that she felt for Miss Honey Diamond, because there was definitely something. She'd first seen her performing in 2006 as Elphaba in the West End production of *Wicked*. Honey was eighteen and stealing the show; singing with a power that sent shivers down her spine and goosebumps up her back; singing with such a strong sense of ownership and pride and determination. She had it together. On stage, not much more than a kid, defying gravity. And there was Meg, also eighteen, sitting in the audience defying nothing much at all. A disappointing batch of A-Level results leading to an offer from her third choice university. A family now knowing they were right to be wary of the hair-in-the-face, hunched over, gothic-looking friends she'd selected, obviously a founding factor in her newly declared lesbian lifestyle, a phase that would hopefully pass.

Meg smiled. She'd been wowed by Honey, encouraged by Honey, and yes, maybe slightly enamoured by the beautiful actress with a rumoured singing career on the horizon, following in her mother's footsteps to become one of the nation's new favourites no doubt. She'd certainly become one of Meg's new favourites, but the disappointing internet search had only fuelled her quest for more insight. Where was her website? Her MySpace? And Twitter? All the celebs were crowing about Twitter, a new platform where you could talk to your fans, tell them your likes, keep them informed. But no, Honey had nothing, yet she'd been around for so long.

One page had informed Meg that Honey's career had begun almost ten years previously with stage performances and bit parts on screen. So why the blackout? Yes, there were fansites set up displaying the latest pictures from the papers or the shots from red carpets, and as Honey's fame increased so did these pages, but none were authentic, none came from Honey herself. Her record label set up a website and tried to make it look personal, but as Meg progressed in her own media career she realised nothing at all came from Honey. So when there *was* an actual interview or talking appearance she'd devour every last word, every last look, hunting for clues, desperate to know Honey and who really was behind those shy eyes. And of course she found her beautiful. Of course she'd imagined a meeting of lips, a connection of hearts, an understanding between them that they were somehow connected.

Meg dipped a chip into her curry. Maybe she *had* soured with age. Upset that Honey hadn't noticed her in the crowds at the shows. Hurt that Honey hadn't replied to her interview requests. Embarrassed that Honey hadn't seen her raised hand in that press-conference where she did finally have a credible reason to be in her presence, a lanyard granting her access, not realising there were two hundred others like her, the PA only choosing the faces she knew. And that was the next knock. Liza Munroe with her pixie haircut and androgynous style, appealing to all sorts of women; of course she'd appeal to her boss. Well known on the lesbian scene for her love life disasters, always using her hectic lifestyle as PA to the world's most famous woman as the excuse. But on the scene there were stories. With everyone connected in some sort of way. Liza Munroe seemingly connected in more ways than most.

Of course Meg had never actually witnessed Liza on the scene, but others had, and stories were shared by women who'd been in her presence. The presence of the woman who was in the presence of *the* woman they all wanted to know. Because it wasn't just Meg's obsession. 99.99% of the lesbian population needed Honey Diamond as their gay. Kylie was the obsession in the 80s. Britney in the 90s. Bette, Barbara, Liza and Dolly lifelong favourites no matter the decade. But Honey was different. She actually gave off the signs. Meg dipped another chip. Well she gave them to her anyway. No confirmed boyfriend. Lyrics open to interpretation in a number of ways. A look in her eye. That's what it was. That look. That look of longing. Of hurt. Of desire for someone like Meg to come and fulfil all of those hopes and dreams. She'd seen it at The Muse when Honey had walked in. Alone. Aware of the gazes. She needed someone like Meg to protect her, to provide for her.

Meg stopped herself, hating where it always went. The daydreaming, the romanticising, as if that would ever happen. She shook her head, remembering how she'd reacted when Honey Diamond walked up those stairs at The Muse. She'd shrunk so far down in her chair that her dinner guest, a well-known sculptor she'd been interviewing for an arts piece, had asked what was wrong. She could hardly tell him she was hiding her scary eye bags that sucked her face inwards from the crush of her life. The woman of her dreams.

Maybe Jo was right? Maybe the occasional post on her SlebSecrets site was her way of feeling close to what she knew she'd never have? Looking down at her flatmate, Meg opted for a change of focus. "You had sex, didn't you? You're always like this post-sex, all cocky and confident, setting the world to rights because yours is so perfect."

Jo wiggled her bottom on the floor. "Gavin Grahams."

"Again?"

"Yep. It's been two months since the auction, and two months of shagging means I'm officially a London Town lady." She turned and spoke seriously. "But it's not exclusive. I'm still spreading the love."

Meg grimaced. "Nice."

"Oooh look, this contestant's pretty." She nodded towards the television. "You should try going for someone like her."

Meg watched as the feminine woman hit the heart-pounding high notes in the beautiful ballad. "She's too young."

"She is not. Look. Honey's blushing. Oh good, they're getting her feedback first."

Both women watched as Honey Diamond judged the performance, praising the emotion and tenderness behind the song, a small tear forming in the corner of her eye.

Jo laughed. "She likes her."

"Of course she likes her."

"But you look nothing like her."

"So?"

"So if you want someone like Honey to like someone like you, you need to ease up on the dark grumpiness."

"Oh god, Jo! You just don't get it. I don't want someone like Honey to like someone like me. I want someone like Honey to be honest, to come out, to show the world it's okay to *be* someone like me."

"It's not okay though. You're hiding your beauty under that messy hair and those awful glasses."

"And she's hiding behind the pretence of heterosexuality."

Jo shrugged as she grazed some more naan across the chutney. "Why do you get so het up?"

"Because she's a lesbian! I just know it. It's like a sixth sense. I see it in people. I see it in her."

"So you're reverting to the playground and teasing the one you love by posting mean gossip about her?"

"It's not mean."

"You're trying to out her."

"You supported me when I started SlebSecrets, so what's stopping you now?"

Jo pulled herself onto the cushion next to her friend. She touched the folded knee and squeezed. "My lovely, in the beginning you were aggressively propositioned by that multi-media mogul Eddy – what was his name – Elroyd. Not enough to warrant police intervention, but enough to expose his sleazy nature. You researched, you wrote a piece, you found other women like you. No one wanted it. No one would publish. So you alluded to it in your first ever SlebSecrets post, and it went viral, because it was true. You then got a taste for the thrill, posting more and more salacious gossip until you grew up, got a proper job and realised people were free to live their lives as they pleased."

"It's not that. I have a duty to right the world's wrongs with my site."

Jo lifted a finger. "Shush, my lovely. I'm in full flow." She flicked her blonde hair and continued. "Your site's your baby. It's grown with you. You don't want to let it go, so you keep it ticking over, now only posting indiscretions, as you put it, that need to be outed. Admirable? Maybe. But only…" she raised her voice, "if they're true!"

Meg pushed her sideways. "Go back to your piddly pieces of bread."

"No." Jo picked up the phone. "Read your precious tweets. All the Honey Diamond hashtags are nice." She paused at a tweet that read *#HoneyDiamond looks like a peacock.* "Well mostly. And yes, there's the odd mention of hashtag contestant girl crush, but no hashtags declaring that Honey, in her tap dancing flapper gear, likes fanny." Jo paused. "Oooh hashtag leaked song."

Meg grabbed the phone. "Where?"

"There. One second ago."

Meg read the tweet from @StudioBoi1992. *#HoneyDiamond #LeakedSong ow.ly/Xghdn*... She spoke quickly. "StudioBoi 1992. Four followers. Two tweets. The account's new."

"Click the link then."

"Alright, alright." Meg fumbled with her phone, expanding the webpage as she looked for any sort of arrow that would play the hidden MP3.

"There!" said Jo, pointing at the text before grabbing the remote to mute the television.

Meg held the phone between them and pressed play. Artists' songs were leaked all the time, sometimes a PR stunt, but mostly a breach in production with someone recording on a mobile from the back of the studio. The track started to echo. "Definitely a breach in production," said Meg.

Jo nodded. "It's upbeat."

"Shush!"

"It won't be Honey's. Hers are never upbeat."

"Shush!" Meg lifted the phone higher as the lyrics started to sing.

"It's Honey!" declared Jo.

"Listen!"

The big blue eyes were wide. "Sexuality?! What?"

"Shush!"

"She's outing herself!"

"Shush!"

Jo jumped up. "Honey Diamond's outing herself!"

Meg listened closer. "It's definitely her."

"Of course it's her. She's got such a distinctive voice and here she is singing about sex!"

"It's not about sex. It's about..." Meg kept listening. "She's outing herself."

Jo nodded. "Get your laptop, goddamnit!"

"Why?"

"You need to post this!" She grabbed Meg's curry bowl and started to guzzle, excitement getting the better of her. "It's proof!"

Meg played the track again. "I can't post this."

"Why the hell not?!"

"Will you just calm down? You'll get indigestion."

"Me? You should be losing it! This is Honey Diamond, laying her head in different beds!" Jo gasped. "Oh god, this curry's so good."

"Sit down. Let's think. It might be for someone else. Or for that new film of hers."

"Doesn't matter. She's singing it. It's on the web. It's live. Don't post the actual song, just post a link to the link. This is big, Meg. When people get a whiff of it they'll come straight to your site. They'll expect you to know. Let me do it then. You check Twitter. I bet it's trending already."

"The host site will get pulled."

"Refresh it. There. It's still live."

"I can't. This is too far."

"This is a scoop!" Jo jumped up and grabbed Meg's laptop, opening the SlebSecrets admin page.

"What are you doing?"

"I've got it. I've watched you do this god knows how many times."

"Wait. I need to debate. Is this an intrusion too far? Speculating about her sexuality's one thing, but leaking a song?"

"You're not leaking it, it's already leaked, and this gives credibility to your previous speculation. This does you a favour. This shows you're not just a hard-hearted gossipy bitch. This proves you were telling the truth."

"I was."

"So do it."

"You're right." Meg keyed in the code and typed quickly. "Which sparkling treasure's recorded a song about sexuality? Sing it sister!"

"Sing it sister?"

"Like *Britain Sings* and sisterhood for us gay girls." Meg pushed up her glasses. "Can you think of anything better? No, thought not." She copied the link from her phone. "There. Posted. It's live."

Jo flopped onto the sofa. "Honey Diamond, you minx."

"You think she'll release it?"

"The song? No chance, but she sang it, and she sang it with heart."

Meg stared at the television and the silent close-up of Honey. "I knew it. I just bloody knew it."

CHAPTER SEVEN

The door to the Holland Park mansion was opened with the pomp and circumstance to rival any royal visit at any regal palace. Diana Diamond's head butler had bowed, called Honey ma'am, thanked her for gracing Velvet Villa with her presence, (Velvet Villa being her mother's bizarre chosen name for this latest London property), before the procession of staff swept her through the house with offers of drinks, sundries, beauty treatments, a hydro session and a hypnosis consultation.

"I'd just like to see my mother, please," said Honey, grounding herself under a huge chandelier, the ridiculous attention doing nothing to lighten her mood. She turned to the butler. "And Philip, please don't behave like you've never met me before."

"Sorry, ma'am." He bowed.

"It's Honey."

"Yes, ma'am."

"Oh for goodness sake." She spoke to the cluster of bodies. "Could we have a moment please?"

The head butler nodded to dismiss the staff before turning to Honey. "Your mother's in the front room."

"Who *are* these people?" she asked, softening somewhat as their departure refreshed the sheer scale of the mansion's reception area, allowing her to breathe more freely. She looked up at the décor. The place was extravagant, garishly so, and in keeping with her mother's habit of buying up properties and decorating them in certain themes, before declaring them out-dated and impossible to live in. Velvet Villa, with its fabric-covered walls and over-the-top bling, had a potentially shorter life span than most.

"That was your mother's new health and wellbeing consultant, her snack chef—"

"Sorry? Her what? Her snack chef? In addition to her actual chef I'm guessing?"

"Seven work in the kitchen now, ma'am."

Honey shook her head. "Oh Philip, don't you get tired of this?"

The man stood firm. "Never. I love your mother dearly."

Honey smiled, fully aware it was this man's stoic loyalty that had kept him in position for over thirty-five years. Other staff came and went with the wind, her mother hiring and firing as one fad went out of fashion and another came into force. But when someone was loyal, she treated them well. Just like Sofia: taken on as housekeeper, promoted to nanny once Honey was born and so well trusted that she'd earned the honour of godmother alongside Gerty and Dot. Trust was paramount in her mother's life and Honey knew what was coming.

"How bad is it?" she asked.

The butler lowered his voice. "She's called Mark the yoga boy in to work on her while she watches the show. She says she'll need his stretches to get her through it."

"In the front room?"

He nodded. "Gerty and Dot are downward dogging too."

"Aren't they always?" said Honey dryly as she made her way across the hall.

Philip caught up and overtook. "I have to announce you."

"You don't."

It was too late. Philip was at the padded velvet door. He knocked sharply, eliciting no sound from the fabric, so he twisted the handle, standing in position as he announced the arrival of: "Miss Honey Diamond for you, ma'am."

"Mother, it's me," said Honey, entering the room, immediately taken aback by the set-up in front of her. Her mother, Gerty and Dot were all kitted out in matching velour tracksuits, headbands and yoga gloves. Their heads were down and their arses were up as the three young men standing behind them massaged forwards and backwards up and down their spines. Honey grimaced. The pneumatic motion of thrusting was too much to ignore. "Good god, Mother."

Diana Diamond pushed herself to standing, her red cheeks and upright messy hair only half caused by her previous downward dog position. "Don't you good god me, my darling."

Honey stood her ground, ready for the onslaught.

"Can't you see I'm stressed? Look at me! Look at my hair! It stands up when I'm worried. I've had hydrotherapy, hypnotherapy, even Mark's manipulation can't calm me through this. Gerty and Dot are the same."

Honey looked towards the two white-haired women who had slumped out of their poses and onto their bottoms, both smiling as their well lubricated sherry glasses were topped up by the eager-to-please young men. "Appropriate post-workout drinks I see, ladies."

The old women laughed. "There's never a wrong time for a sherry," said Gerty.

"Croft Original," added Dot. "Would you like a glass?" She clicked her fingers at the man who'd been thrusting behind her. "Tyrone, pour Honey a tipple."

"No, Tyrone," snapped Diana, "you toddle off with... with... whatever your friend's called," she turned to the lead yoga instructor, "and Mark, I may need you later, but for now I'll have a moment with my daughter."

Gerty and Dot tried to pull themselves off the floor without spilling any sherry.

Diana waved them back down. "Not you two, you're fine." She looked around the room. "And Liza; where's Liza? She's riding this storm alongside us."

Honey rolled her eyes. "It's not that bad, Mother."

Diana Diamond waited for the yoga boys to leave the room. "Not that bad? Not that bad? You're all over the news. You're everywhere, and not in a good way!"

"I liked the song," announced Gerty, taking a large sip of Croft Original.

"Me too," added Dot, trying to remember the first few lines as she started to sing. *"Doesn't matter who plays with my head. Just as long as you get in bed."*

Honey laughed. "Better lyrics than mine."

"Stop!" screeched Diana. "It's not about *liking* the song, it's about the damage the song's leaking has caused. Eight o'clock last night and the nation was sitting down to watch you on *Britain Sings*, to adore you." She paused and softened her voice. "That tear rolling down your cheek during the young girl's ballad was genius, Honey, pure genius." She straightened. "But still."

"It wasn't a gimmick, Mother. I was genuinely moved. We filmed those auditions two months ago and I still get goosebumps when I think of her song."

Diana threw her hands in the air. "Oh well goody for you! Beats the heart attacks we're all getting when we think of *your* song, leaked last night onto the worldwide web!"

"It's got a great beat," said Gerty once more, lifting her glass in a toast. "To Honey and—"

"Stop!" Diana Diamond guided her daughter to the velvet sofa and tried to look calm. "Honey, my darling, we spoke about this. I trusted you'd do as advised."

"I did."

Diana cleared her throat, trying desperately to control the rising tone of her voice. "So why's the song out there?"

Honey shrugged. "I don't know. I've been busy these last two months. Liza's still in the car on the phone to Picador. There must have been a breach at Apple Road. I did exactly what you said. I played them my song. We recorded some versions and the talks are ongoing. Do I release it? Do I sell it? If so when?"

"Well it's too bloody late now!" snapped Diana, frantically running her fingers through her spiked hair. She looked at the clock and gasped. "It's time. Gerty, turn on the telly."

The old woman handed her glass to her friend and crawled clumsily across the yoga mats to reach into the velvet footstool for the remote. Within seconds the padded wall cabinet had opened up to reveal a huge jewel encrusted television. "And we're on," she said, nodding at the screen.

Honey watched as the talk show host introduced the next feature. "Up next we have what you've all been waiting for. An exclusive with Honey Diamond's step-siblings, Nick and Nadia Diamond."

Diana lifted her hands in the air. "They are just incorrigible! I was married to their good-for-nothing father for less than a year and they take my name, all of them take my bloody name, using it once again to reminisce about life in the dynasty."

The host started her pre-amble, discussing the facts surrounding the leak. "The internet's going wild with speculation. Record company Picador have confirmed the song was written, composed and performed by Honey, but have yet to explain what it's for. Rumour has it she's got the lead in a new Hollywood musical. Could this song be for a character?"

The co-host joined in. "Playing the part, or coming out loud. What could it possibly mean? We're lucky enough to have Nick and Nadia Diamond in the studio. Honey's step-siblings. Can you give us an insight? What's this song all about?"

Nadia spoke first in her nasal voice, the result of one too many nose jobs. "We prefer to call her sister."

"Sorry, your sister, Honey. What has she said? Was the leak deliberate? Surely she doesn't need any more publicity?"

Nick took over. "Young Honey was a quiet child." He spoke with his lip curled. "We've often wondered, haven't we Nadia, if our sister was hiding some big secret, some hidden angst."

Nadia shared the private laugh. "We have, and I remember once, when we were playing dollies," she paused for effect, "she would always make the two dollies," she paused again, "...kiss."

The host spoke seriously. "Female dollies?"

Nick nodded gravely. "Female dollies."

"Oh just turn it off, Mother," said Honey. "This is nonsense." She thought back to last summer and the reports of Nick and Nadia in the *Celebrity Big Brother* house, regaling viewers on a daily basis about their lives as Diamonds, even though they had lived with their own mother for the duration of their father's short-lived dalliance with Diana. His custody visits were restricted to one weekend a month, meaning Honey and her step-siblings were only ever in each other's presence on a handful of occasions, the most notable being the actual wedding. Hundreds of photos had been taken of celebrity guests, notable foreign royalty, a wedding cake big enough to feed the five thousand; yet there was one shot of the bride, groom and their offspring that had, over the years, featured more than any other. One photo. One photo that Nick and Nadia used as proof at every given opportunity. Proof they were close. Proof they had influence. Honey Diamond, age eleven, flanked by her two teenage siblings. Big brother and sister to what was soon to be the nation's most famous singer, quite possibly their guidance and support the major factor in her success.

"What could I have seen in their father?" asked Diana.

Gerty slurped some sherry. "Your next one was worse."

"At least he didn't have kids, and that was only an engagement." She looked back at the television. "But their good-for-nothing father said he didn't have custody. Said the kids would be seen occasionally but not heard. And look at them now, yapping away."

"Mother, they've always used your name." Honey lifted herself from the sofa and found the remote. "It's nothing new."

"It is! No one's touched you before and two months into your 'I want to take charge of myself' initiative and we've got prime-time television discussions about your sex life." The screen went blank. "Turn it back on, Honey."

"It's Channel 5. No one watches Channel 5."

Diana jumped up. "Everyone watches Channel 5 and everyone reads news on the web. Your leaked song's everywhere! Speculation's everywhere." She started to pace.

"Speculation was always there, Mother. Maybe not mainstream, but it was there, on the web. I found it." She watched the hair become static. "Are those velvet socks? On a velvet carpet? No wonder your hair looks like it does."

Diana fingered the spikes. "The speculation was so well hidden that even my Benedict and his tech team couldn't trace the owner of that site."

"I thought you got it shut down?"

"The forum threads on the L Chat site, yes, even though they've just started up all over again, but that SlebSecrets site, no." Diana shook her head. "And Benedict told me that site was the first bugger last night to point everyone towards the leaked song."

"So sue them for breach of privacy."

"We're working on it! And we'll find them. My men won't let me down." She paused. "But my darling, I don't think you get this. This is your reputation. This is your character. I have my crisis team in the kitchen working on a way forward as we speak."

The crisp voice was loud. "Miss Liza Munroe for you, ma'am."

Liza marched into the room. "Picador think it was a runner. Their lawyers are shutting down the host site."

"My lawyers are working on that," said Diana.

"Lots of lawyers then; doesn't matter, it's happening."

Honey nodded. "And the SlebSecrets site?"

"Clever enough not to repost. They're just pointing people in the direction of the song. Like torrents. They'll pull the story when they realise the link doesn't work."

Diana licked her fingers and tried to flatten her hair. "People have downloaded it. There'll be another link. We're like Beyoncé trying to chase that ugly picture off the web. Think ladies, think. Liza, what are your thoughts? I want to go into the meeting prepared with a good grasp of the options."

Honey took a deep breath, ready to relay the words she'd rehearsed. "Sorry, didn't I mention? That's what I came round for."

Diana nodded. "Yes, the crisis meeting."

"No. To tell you there is no crisis meeting. This isn't a crisis. A song I wrote leaked onto the web. Yes, I'm annoyed, but it's not from the album; it wasn't set for release."

"But the speculation!"

Honey slowed her words. "I'm getting ahead of that."

"How?"

Turning to her PA, Honey nodded. "I'd like to do an interview, with someone you trust. Someone who won't sensationalise. Someone who'll debate fairly whether there's any need in this day and age for celebrities to come out."

Diana gasped. "We're a good ten years away from that, my darling!"

Honey ignored her. "Liza, who do you know?"

Liza paced with little legs, swiping through her PDA as if it had the answer to all of life's questions. "It has to be *The Beacon*. Old school. Upmarket. Thoughtful. I know the Arts and Entertainment correspondent. Been there for centuries. Won a Pulitzer Prize a few years back. An old dyke herself." She corrected her words. "Crude, sorry, I'm thinking fast. I meant she'd be sympathetic. She interviewed Eton Myers when he went public about the surrogacy, and David Johns when he came out as gay. She's got stature. She'll sell a good story."

Honey shook her head. "This isn't about selling a story."

"Sorry, no, you're right. I meant she'll do a good job."

Diana's hair was electric. "Have you two planned this? You just spill the beans for some broadsheet?"

Honey shrugged. "There's nothing to spill." It had been an easy decision when the first call came in last night. Liza and her ever-efficient PDA alerting her to the leak, then her mother and Benedict's ever-pinging notifications, panic from all quarters; nothing worse than an ill-prepared, uphill PR battle. Yet strangely, all Honey had felt was relief. She'd never been questioned before. She'd never known there was interest. Now whether that was due to her mother and Liza's stranglehold on affairs, or just a genuine level of respect from the media, she didn't know. But reading those whispers in those well-hidden chat rooms and that speculation on the SlebSecrets site, she'd felt uneasy. Like she'd been lying. Like some dirty little secret was being discussed. There was no secret. She never had any secrets. Honey let her mind wander. If only there was a secret. Some private lover. Some person to hold. She pulled herself together and nodded. "I'm doing the interview."

Gerty lifted her glass. "Brilliant. That's decided then. Let's have a toast."

"Oh lovely, a toast," giggled Dot, finding her way to the bottle and filling her glass to the brim. "We've been getting quietly sozzled over here."

"There is no toast," said Diana. "This isn't happening."

Gerty cheered the room. "To Honey and her Honeybunnies!"

Honey sighed. "If only there were."

CHAPTER EIGHT

The loud, authoritarian knock sounded again. "Pia!" screeched Jo from her expert elbow-balance on her cluttered dressing room table. "The door!"

The little woman appeared in the messy bedroom, polish and duster in hand.

"The door," said Jo, adding a precise flick to her winged eyeliner.

Pia stood still, smiling politely.

Jo made a knocking gesture with her left hand and pointed at the door. "Could you answer it please?"

The cleaner smiled and nodded. She turned to the bedroom door and started to polish the panels.

"Pia! The front door! Someone's knocking! Oh for god's sake." Jo left her make-up where it was and stepped over the discarded clothes strewn all over the floor. "Now I have to open the door looking like David bloody Bowie." She edged past her cleaner. "Meg told me you're part of a posh cleaning company, but I've never seen the paperwork."

"Yhesh, yhesh," said Pia.

"You don't understand me, do you?"

"Yhesh, yhesh," came the smiling reply.

Jo crossed the hall and yanked open the door. "Yhesh?" she snapped at the two suited men, one bald and staring, the other moustached with a clipboard. "I mean yes." She looked at them carefully and changed her mind. "Actually no, thank you," she said, quickly closing the door.

The knock came again. "What?" she snapped, yanking it open once more. "I'm halfway through my make-up and you're meant to use the buzzer downstairs. Who let you in?"

"How long have you lived here, ma'am?" The man with the moustache was the first to speak.

"Ma'am? Why? What are you? The TV licensing people? We pay it, and if we've missed it just read me my rights. We've had this before. We'll get it sorted."

"We're trying to trace the occupants of a flat in Lewisham. Flat 214, Brickworks Way."

"We definitely paid it there! I remember the stand-off. You lot in that bloody van of yours trying to catch out us students." Jo laughed. "Ha! Those were the days, and this might only look like a crappy two bed above a discount store in Clapham, but it's a long way from Lewisham."

"And you are?"

She paused. "Why? We paid it."

The man spoke again. "We're not from the TV license company. Can you confirm you lived at Flat 214, Brickworks Way in Lewisham?"

Jo shifted her weight onto one hip. "Might have done."

"Ten years ago?"

"Maybe," she fluttered her eyelashes.

The men shared a glance. "May we come in?"

"Depends on what for." The smiles usually came faster than this. Jo tilted her head to the side and looked up. Her tried-and-tested female manipulation skills were able to pull her out of almost any situation.

The man nodded at his companion who pushed open the door and stepped past her into the lounge.

"What are you doing? Get out! Pia! Help me! There's a bald man in the flat! Pia!"

The man with the clipboard scribbled down the name and stepped inside too.

"Pia!" Jo tried to shoo them out. "This is private property, we rent it, so it's ours. You can't just walk in here." She paused. "You're not the landlords are you? That hole in the wall was an accident, we had a party, I got a bit drunk, but we've filled it now and we've got a cleaner, and we know we're not allowed parties, so we're not having any more." She shouted over her shoulder. "Pia, will you just come here and show them your duster!"

The maid appeared in the melee, nodding her head. "Yhesh yhesh. My company have visa."

The moustache twitched. "Does Pia live here?"

"Of course she doesn't bloody live here! Look at her! I didn't even know she could speak English!"

The bald man smiled. "Pia, does anyone else live here?"

"Yhesh, yhesh. Two girl. One nice. One not."

Jo pointed to the door. "Right, out, I'm calling the police."

The bald man walked around the apartment, lifting notebooks and papers as he went.

"Pia, get my phone." She pointed towards her bedroom. "It's on my dresser."

Pia stood still and nodded.

"Oh for god's sake," gasped Jo, shouting into the stairwell instead, keeping the front door propped open with her foot. "There are men in my apartment. Somebody help me."

"The gentleman from the other flat's gone out; he let us in."

Jo shouted again. "There are men in my apartment!" She turned back to the action. "I'll go downstairs onto the street then. Pia, can you please go and get my phone?"

Pia nodded. "I have visa."

"Well woopty-doo for you! Just do something would you!"

Pia smiled and nodded, lifting her duster to polish the lounge mirror. "Yhesh yhesh."

"Got it," said the bald man, taking the clipboard and copying the names from the paperwork he'd found. He handed it back to his partner and stood with a smug smile, waiting for the action to unfold.

The man with the moustache presented the document. "For Miss Jo Tustin and Miss Meg…" he paused, "what does that say, Bob?"

"Bob! Haha! You just said his name!" Jo was pointing. "I've got you now, Bob! Bald Bob and…"

"I'm Charles. Here's my card. You have a nice day now, ma'am."

"And I'm Bob," said bald Bob, reaching into his jacket pocket so he could present his business card too. "You read that document carefully now, love," he said, sidestepping past her and out of the flat.

"I'm not your love," said Jo. She leaned forward to shout down the stairs at the man with the moustache. "And I'm not your ma'am either." Kicking the door shut, she looked at the document and cards. Catching sight of the header and crest Jo gasped.

Pia nodded. "My visa all good, yhesh? My visa all good?"

CHAPTER NINE

"I'm nervous," said Honey.

Liza reached out to adjust the sweeping fringe. "Exactly why I should stay." She was studying the lack of make-up. "And let me call the girls. There's still time."

Honey pulled herself away from the fussing and moved to the sofa. "No. This is meant to be natural. You said it yourself: a private interview, just me, my home, my words." She nodded, smoothing out the cushions either side of her. "No cameras. No paps. No production. Just a chat about life, relaxed in my lounge."

"Remember what I said about Diana in the Bashir interview. The way she used her eyes."

"I'm not trying to seduce the old woman!" Honey jumped back up and shooed Liza away. "Go. You're making things worse."

Liza spoke over her shoulder. "She has to like you and she's a stickler for manners."

"And I have to act for that?"

"There's always a bit of acting when you meet someone for the first time."

Honey's finger was pointing. "Go. They're expecting you."

"I haven't got time for a spa. I need to sort out the photographer." She tapped into her PDA. "They'll want at least one exclusive image."

"Sort it at the spa. Sofia, Gerty, Dot, Mother. You complete the Golden Girls gang."

"I'm thirty-eight, Honey."

"Just go." She bustled her PA to the front door and nodded. "I've got this."

Liza paused. "Really?"

"Really. I'll call when I'm done."

"Right, well...." Stepping onto the porch, Liza cleared her throat, opening her mouth as if to find one further objection.

"Go. Relax." Honey motioned for her to move. "That's it. Keep walking." She watched as the brogues crunched across the gravel. "Off you go; join the other OAPs." Honey smiled as the first step transformed into an actual walking pace. A left at the end of the drive would lead Liza onto the private road that wound its way through the estate to The Alderley's main hub.

The paused PA made one final shout. "You're sure you've got this?"

Honey nodded back. "I've got this." She waited until Liza disappeared from view before closing the front door and crumpling against the hall wall. "I've not got this!" she cried.

Lifting her hand to her mouth, Honey realised she was terrified. She hated interviews, doing her best to avoid them at all costs, only taking part when deemed absolutely essential. The idea of celebrities courting the press or encouraging the attention still seemed foreign to her. Maybe because she'd always had it. That fame. That stardom. Or maybe because she disliked it so much. That scrutiny. That judgement. She sang. She performed. She didn't ask for column inches or fan sites. Being the centre of attention wasn't something she craved. It was a by-product of her chosen career, an inevitable consequence of her Diamond heritage. Being on stage under the spotlight was different. She could get lost in the starlight. Lost in her world. A world that made sense, singing lyrics that came from the heart.

She pulled herself up. This would be the first time she'd used the press for a personal purpose. Spinning a story, as Liza had put it. She started to pace as the doubts came flooding back. Was there really any need to discuss this? Weren't the lyrics in the song enough of an answer? It didn't matter where she lay her head. Who cared if it was in a boy or girl's bed? She stood still and laughed at herself. Honey Diamond, the singing Don Juan. If only people knew. A sexual preference never fully explored. Physical interactions you could count on one hand. She sighed. Never that pull of total wanton desire. Never that obsession to know someone's soul. Never that all-consuming feeling of love. That first waking thought and that last late-night dream. Never the fairytale.

It would come when she was least expecting it. Wasn't that what they said? And she'd been busy. She was always busy. It wasn't a priority. Love. Desire. Being liked by someone. Someone who wanted to know her. The real her. Not the famous celebrity they hoped for. Honey checked the clock on the wall. What if the journalist didn't like her? What if she went off topic? She started to panic. Of course she'd go off topic, it was a no-holds-barred interview. Honey paced faster. She'd offer tea and coffee on arrival. Or should it be wine? No, that would just create the impression of an alcoholic diva. She raced into the kitchen and checked for chilled bottles, just in case.

The chrome fridge door displayed her wobbled reflection. Honey looked down at her clothes. Maybe she should change? Maybe jeans and jumper wasn't the right vibe? Relaxed, yes. Serious, no. And this was serious. This was seriously the most serious public discussion she'd ever had to have. Honey raced out of the kitchen. She'd change. Skidding to a halt at the hall mirror, she checked her hair. What was wrong with her hair? She zhooshed it as much as she could, but it laughed back at her, her fringe flying free, layers all loose. Liza was right! Why hadn't she listened? Why hadn't she said yes to Heidi and the girls popping over for a quick pampering session? She checked the clock. Was it too late?

On hearing the doorbell, Honey shrieked. It was too late! The woman was here! What was her name? Margaret Rowley? Or Rowland? Or Rostrand, or something like that? A battle-axe type Miss Marple was the picture Liza had fashioned. The bell sounded again. "Oh, damn it," Honey yelped, pulling open the door in an overly enthusiastic fashion. "Hi there!" she said, feeling her cheeks fill with colour as her fringe fell out of place.

The woman lifted her hand. "Margaret Rutherton."

"Margaret, hello!" Honey realised she was shaking the hand too forcefully. "There's wine in the fridge!"

The woman raised an eyebrow. "Wonderful."

"Sorry, I…" Honey paused. "Do come in." She looked at the journalist standing in front of her, surprised by the pleasant features and enquiring eyes, not at all what she'd been expecting.

Margaret coughed. "May I?"

Honey realised she was blocking the door. "Yes, sorry." She shuffled to the side. "You're not as old as…." How could she say the old bag Liza had fashioned?

The journalist smiled. "Have you started on that wine already?"

"Yes. No! Well, maybe I should. Or we should." She nodded. "Shall we?" Throwing her hands to her face, Honey shook her head. "Sorry, can I begin again?" She paused and took a deep breath. "You won't write all this down, will you? I'm not used to hosting events by myself. Not that I can't do things by myself. I'm not managed. Well I am, but I'm very normal." The reassuring smile stopped her.

"Maybe we do need that wine."

"Really?"

"Your home, your way."

Honey narrowed her eyes. "Is this a trick? Are you monitoring my every move to use later as evidence against me?"

Margaret laughed. "We can chat. I'll make some notes." She smiled. "You can vet the article before we publish. In fact, I'll send it to you before I send it to my editor. You've got nothing to worry about, Honey. I've got the brief. I'm on your side."

"Luring me into a false sense of security?"

"No." The laugh came again. "Trust me."

There was something about the smile and searching eyes that made Honey do just that, trust her. The woman was kitted out almost identically in jeans, jumper and boots, which had immediately put her at ease. "So, Margaret, may I welcome you in?"

"I was hoping for that five minutes ago."

Honey's lips turned at the corners. "You don't want to do the interview on the doorstep?"

"Doorstep, drive, back up near those security gates, you name it, I'm there." Margaret spoke sincerely. "We're honoured that you chose *The Beacon*. And I'm thrilled to meet you in person. You're famous for shunning the press, so this was quite a surprise."

"I'm not famous for my singing?"

"Yes yes, of course you are. Sorry, you're endlessly talented. Your singing, your songs, your…" The journalist spotted the smile. "Clever. Making me nervous as well."

Honey pointed towards the kitchen. "Shall we start with that wine?"

Margaret nodded. "Sounds perfect to me."

****

Liza huffed as she pulled the blue plastic covers over her shoes. So much for accommodating. The Alderley was famed for its pledge to meet all of your wishes, to make all of your dreams come true. But walking past the pool and into the sauna without any kerfuffle? Too much trouble. She snapped the plastic around her ankles and smiled sarcastically at the spa attendant, who had politely requested she remove, or cover, her brogues.

"Thank you," said the young man, "I hope you understand it's a health and safety issue."

Liza snorted. "I bet they're all sipping sherry in the sauna, aren't they?"

"The residents of The Alderley don't mind alcohol in the spa, but they do mind muddy shoes by the pool."

"My brogues aren't muddy. But fine. I'll have a crème de menthe."

"In the sauna?"

"Yes."

"In your three-piece suit."

"Yes!" Liza snapped. "I'm on Honey Diamond's guest sheet! You should be granting all my wishes."

"Sorry, of course. I'll be right with you."

Liza nodded, finally feeling The Alderley's renowned air of importance. She looked at the heated pool, bubbling Jacuzzi, padded loungers and soft lighting. No bugger was even here. So much for appeasing the health and safety conscious residents. Marching to the sauna, she pulled open the door and was immediately hit by a wall of heat and alcohol. Diana, Gerty, Dot and Sofia were steaming, in more ways than one.

"Shut that door!" cried Diana, sporting a leopard-print swimsuit complete with upright neck collar. "You're letting the heat out."

Liza edged inside the wooden furnace, noticing Gerty and Dot's bare breasts mottled with drops of perspirations. "Hello, everyone," she said, to no one in particular, trying to act as casually as she possibly could in the rising temperature.

Sofia laughed. "Oh Liza. You've surpassed yourself this time. Honey sent you here to relax."

Edging herself onto a wooden slatted bench, Liza nodded. "And here I am, with a crème de menthe en route."

Sofia stretched out on the highest bench, smiling through the mist of alcoholic warmth. "You're wearing a three-piece suit. In a sauna."

"At least those bloody awful brogues are covered," added Diana, pointing at the blue plastic bags as she sipped from her flute.

Sofia lifted her head up. "Go and borrow a costume."

"Or get nuddy-duddy like us," added Gerty, toasting her glass against Dot's too forcefully, resulting in an unexpected breast-led Mexican wave.

Liza breathed in the scorching air, realising she'd have to loosen her collar any minute. "I shan't stay long," she croaked, thankful for her short haircut.

"You shall," said Diana. "We're under strict instructions to stay away. Give Honey some space. Let her do what she needs to do." She leaned forward and pressed the button that would summon the spa attendant, because residents of The Alderley were wholly incapable of adding more water to the sauna rocks by themselves, or in this case ordering more drinks.

"It's cost me ten thousand pounds in therapy over the past two months to say that sentence." Diana inhaled for three and exhaled for four. "Let her do what she needs to do." She repeated the breathing technique. "Let my daughter roam free."

Sofia shook her head. "She's hardly roaming free. She's just showing a bit more initiative."

"Our little girl's growing up, isn't she Gerty?" said Dot.

Diana spun round on the hot wooden slats, breathing forgotten. "She's *my* little girl and I've spent my whole life protecting her. And so far it's paid off." She pulled on her collar. "Oh stuff the therapy, I was right all along. She's had no scandals, no—"

"Not like you in your day," interrupted Gerty.

"Different times." Diana composed herself. "And as I was saying, no scandals, no—"

Dot took over. "Remember that picture of you, Heath, and... what was Heath's friend called? The one with the Elvis hair?"

Gerty nodded. "Norman."

"And Norman, in a field, not an ear of corn between you."

The two crowns of curly white hair giggled. "Cost you an arm and a leg to keep that out of the papers, didn't it, Di."

"Exactly my point! Honey's lived her life unscathed. I challenge you to name one other child star of her calibre who can claim the same."

Sofia spoke up. "There's no one like her, but she's hardly living her life. She's working."

"And she'll keep working, so there's really no need for this sudden outpouring of personality."

No one had noticed Liza slowly wilting off the bench until she wheezed from the floor of the sauna. "We agreed… she needed the reins."

Diana was sharp. "Will you get up, woman?" She banged the button once more. "And where the bloody hell's that pool boy? He's probably gone off site to find your bloody crème de menthe." She tilted the flute and shook it over her outstretched tongue, trying to drain the last few drops of Champagne. "I mean, for god's sake, who drinks crème de menthe?"

Liza struggled to breathe as the sweat began to seep through her suit. "I'll go and find him." She started to crawl.

"Oh no you bloody won't. It's your fault we're here. You've pushed this new found independence. You've given Honey the confidence to take on the world. You were meant to show her how hard life is."

"Hard how?" Liza started to rock in a weak attempt to aerate her jacket.

"For a woman like you. I employed you. I gave you the role of PA."

Gerty laughed, tits out, enjoying the show. "You and your master plans never work, do they, Di?" She looked at Liza. "You okay down there, big girl?"

Liza's voice was laboured. "Honey employed me."

"I made sure the other candidates were useless. I wanted her to have access to your world if she needed it," she turned to her friends, "because we can't deny we all saw signs in young Honey, didn't we ladies?" She nodded and turned back to Liza. "But she also needed an up close and personal example of how hard your world truly was."

Liza wiped the sweat from her brow, still on all fours, as she struggled to swallow. "My world's not hard."

"Life for lesbians is! Gay men do well in this industry with their utter fabulousness, but lesbians? No. And Honey's sympathetic. She likes the gentler things in life." She sniffed. "Don't we all on occasion?"

Gerty toasted her glass against Dot's once more. "Hey, Di, remember old Fonda's pool parties back in the day. All us having a piece of her pu—"

Diana interrupted. "But Honey's not ready for the media glare. We've had things in place. It's worked."

Sofia added to the chorus. "She's hardly living the lascivious life of a loose lesbian."

"Exactly," nodded Diana, "so there's no need to utter those words."

"Chin, chin," added Gerty and Dot.

Diana slammed the button once more. "We need more drinks so we can toast to no lesbian labels."

Liza, unable to handle the heat any longer, edged the short distance to the door and was greeted by a sudden cool blast of air as the spa attendant entered the sauna.

He crouched down. "Your crème de menthe."

Liza took the glass but wrinkled her nose at the smell. "Water," she gasped instead, trying unsuccessfully to hand it back.

"And champers," added Diana. "Bring the bottle."

Liza watched with horror as the door shut once more, trapping her, her three-piece suit and her ill-chosen liqueur back in the furnace. "I need to…"

"Get nuddy-duddy!" wailed Gerty.

"No, I need to…"

"You need to hand round that bloody crème de menthe," said Diana, grabbing the glass and lifting it in a toast. "To Honey, not using the lesbian label."

"No need for lesbian labels!" cheered Gerty and Dot.

Liza felt her arms and legs weaken as she flopped flat out on the floor.

"And the suit is down!" said Diana, prodding Liza with her toe. "Get some air and head back to the house. Check Honey's singing from the same hymn sheet. Get her to use the word fluid, or modern, or progressive. She has a progressive sexuality not defined by pigeon-holed labels." She prodded once more. "Liza? Oh dear lord, the suit's gone and fainted."

****

Honey nodded as the journalist re-read her previous statement. "Yes," said Honey with authority, "I'm fine with the lesbian label."

CHAPTER TEN

Margaret Rutherton looked at the woman sitting in front of her. They were half an hour into the interview and she was smitten. There was something about Honey's innocence that put everything she had recently heard and everything she had recently read to rights. Honey's leaked song didn't mean she'd been playing a game. She hadn't been hiding her sexuality. Her only crime was naivety. She hadn't previously courted the press, or encouraged them to jump to conclusions when pictured with male friends. She'd stayed quiet. And while some could cite this as guilty by omission, Honey's case for the right to privacy was sounding more credible by the minute.

"It's in my contract to promote my music and my shows," said Honey, "not my private life. But if there was something," she smiled, "*anything*, in that realm worth talking about, then I might have talked, but there wasn't, so I didn't, and that's why I haven't."

"But you're okay with me labelling your sexuality?" Margaret watched the quiet confidence with interest, wondering just how far she could push her subject without overstepping the mark. Both had glasses of wine in front of them, mostly for reassurance, but something caused her interviewee to reach forward and take a sip. "We can always allude to it instead," she added, "if you'd prefer?"

Honey visibly swallowed before nodding with decision. "I prefer women to men. If lesbian's the word for that, then lesbian's the word for that. I can't shy away from a word. But I'll be honest, I'd rather there was valid reason for that labelling. For example, Honey Diamond to wed the princess of her dreams, or Honey

Diamond whisked off her feet by kind, clever, somewhat quirky, but definitely funny, independent woman who loves Honey for Honey, not for who she thinks Honey is, or who she thinks she'll become when she's with her." She rolled her eyes. "Honey Diamond celebrity extraordinaire."

Margaret could feel herself melting at the cuteness, yet sadness, of it all. "Don't we all want that?" quickly adding, "…not that I think anyone could become someone from being with me."

"Pulitzer Prize-winning journalist, I bet they could."

Margaret laughed. "I must convey your humour in this piece."

"I'm serious." The shy eyes dropped away but the voice continued. "You look like a lovely catch."

"My chance of winning a Pulitzer—"

"With this piece?" The eyes were back. "It's awfully dry, I know, I'm sorry. I wish I could be more exciting but I'd have to make things up." Honey shrugged. "Yes, I've had the odd date and liaison, mostly with Liza's friends, but nothing's ever lasted. In fact, she probably vetted them first. I bet she got them signing non-disclosure agreements before she scheduled them into her PDA on a half-yearly basis; you know what she's like."

"Your PA?"

"Liza, yes. She says you go way back." Honey took another sip of wine. "So, there *was* a slight romance with a well-known female pop star." She smiled. "*Very* well known." The pause was thoughtful. "But she's married now, to a man, and I was young. Crushing no doubt."

Margaret watched the insecurity with interest. "I'm sure she liked you too."

"Maybe." The eyes twinkled. "Off the record, do you want to know who?"

Margaret's inner hack screamed. Of course she wanted to know, but the temptation to snoop, dig and find similar stories would be too great. "It's better if you don't tell me."

Honey cringed. "Right. Sorry. I'm being too familiar."

"You're not. It's me. I'm not quite in the zone." Margaret released the breath she'd been holding from the moment she'd arrived on the doorstep. She looked away. The front too hard to maintain. The idea she could converse with Honey Diamond and ignore the fireworks going off inside her, the thrill coursing through her veins, the rush of adrenaline that – far from subsiding – had grown with each moment. Moments where she'd stared with a straight face, but gazed internally with longing, with desperation, with a long-standing desire to know more. "I think you threw me with your wine and friendly chit-chat."

"Were you expecting some straight-laced, poker-faced bitchy beast? An entourage? A list of demands?"

"Maybe." Margaret looked at the woman sitting in front of her, whose beauty was radiating from every honest word she spoke. "Just not this."

"Nor me," said Honey, smiling. "I was expecting the straight-laced, poker-faced bitchy beast."

Margaret laughed. "Maybe I should tune into that vibe as I'm completely lost. I have no line of questioning. No desire to poke and prod."

The glint was wicked. "Really?"

"Well, I…" Returning her eyes to her notepad, Margaret flicked quickly, as if the answer could be found somewhere in the empty pages. She needed to focus. This was beyond a joke. A few endearing comments and she was bewitched, absorbed by the beauty, lost in the confident innocence. "Right," she finally managed, "let's do old school quick-fire Q and A."

Honey nodded. "I'll start. Why are you thrown?"

Margaret couldn't help but laugh. "Are you always like this?"

Honey's smile was natural. "I'm never like this. I don't get the chance. I'm always busy. It's so hard to meet people organically. Not that this is organic. This is far from organic, but we're two women, alone, with wine, and a promise," she reached out and tapped the notepad, "a promise to *only* publish what I okay." She smiled. "So my guard's down." She lifted her wine. "Is your guard down?"

Margaret winced. "I'm the hockey player standing in goal, kitted up with full body armour and helmet."

"You're not!"

"I am! You're Honey Diamond!"

"So?"

"You must be aware of the effect your presence has on people?"

"Not for a seasoned journalist like yourself."

"Seasoned?"

"Sorry, I didn't mean that in a 'you're old' way. That's what struck me when I saw you. Your age. You're younger and more, more..." She smiled. "You're better looking than I was expecting." Lifting her glass, Honey took another long sip. "Sorry, now it's me losing my train of thought. Shall we do the quick-fire Q and A?"

Margaret tried to ignore the fast beat of her heart. "Okay," she said, keeping her eyes on the empty pages. "Question one. When did you know you were gay?"

"Jump right in there, why don't you?"

Margaret fanned her face. "I don't know why I asked that. I'm being nosey, sorry. This is going so badly. I won't even be using that storyline in the piece."

"You already know what you'll write?"

Margaret nodded. "I knew within five minutes of meeting you; that's why I'm struggling for questions."

"Go on."

"I'll write about your music, your success, your constant, non-stop, never taking a breath work ethic and your desire to lead a private life." She nodded, confidence returning, always able to sell a good story. "Now, unless I'm mistaken, that doesn't mean you've been hiding your sexuality for fear of exposure, or shame of labelling, but simply because the two worlds haven't collided. And you're right. There's been next to no mainstream speculation until this point, whereupon you've addressed the rumours and come out."

"And you'll examine whether coming out warrants column inches?"

"Yes, and I think the conclusion will be that it does. Celebrities, whether they like it or not, are role models. People aspire to be like them. Showing the world you're proud of who you are gives others the confidence to do the same."

"And I'm proud of my music, I'm proud of my shows. Like I said before, if there was someone special I'm sure I'd be proud of them too."

The passion in Honey's voice confirmed the truth for Margaret. "I know you would."

"And I was seven. A crush on one of my mother's glamorous friends."

"You don't have to tell me. You've successfully, and quite rightly, kept your personal life out of the press. I'm not going to ruin all that with one sensationalised piece."

"Let me answer for you then."

"For me?"

"One gay woman to another."

"Am I that obvious?"

Honey smiled. "Liza told me. She said it would be good to keep this in house." She paused. "A change of scenery though."

"Where are we going?"

"The green. Do you have a coat?"

Margaret nodded. "I always have a coat."

****

Buttoning up her warm duffel, Margaret reached into the car for her scarf, feeling the eyes of Honey Diamond on her shoulder. "Sorry, I won't be a minute."

"Why didn't you drive up to the house?" was the question.

Margaret closed the door to the Mini Cooper and turned, lifting her eyebrows. "For all I knew, you had five Porsches in your drive."

"So you parked behind the hedge and walked up to the house without your coat? In winter?"

Margaret laughed. "Very out of character, I must admit," she smiled at Honey's hat, gloves and over-the-top layering, "and I'm glad I've met a fellow wrapper-upperer, but I needed the breeze to calm me."

"And you're calm now?"

"No. I have Honey Diamond on my shoulder judging my 2002 Mini Cooper."

"At least you can drive. I've never learnt. And I never judge. Come on, this way."

Margaret felt the hand on her back, guiding her away from the car. "How far to the green?" she asked, totally unsure of the protocol. Should she step away from the contact? It looked like one empty road, gently winding in front of them to the estate's centre, no doubt. There really was no need for the physical escort. She paused. Should she link arms? She gasped at herself. Of course she shouldn't link arms. This was Honey Diamond. This was her turf.

The celebrity smile was wide. "Okay?"

"Yes fine, thank you." *God no I'm not okay! I'm strolling down a deserted road with Honey Diamond's hand on my back. And the air's crisp. And the sun's all wintry. And the view's really quite gorgeous.* Margaret kept her eyes forward. If the hand shifted slightly, Honey would have her by the waist. Side-by-side. A close companion. A lovers' walk. The hand dropped away.

"If anything I'm jealous," continued Honey, completely unaware of the ripple effect that her touch had created. "The thought of jumping in a car and driving to anywhere. To nowhere. Just driving without a purpose, or a place to be. Just enjoying the moment."

Margaret laughed. "Now that's low maintenance. A drive down the M25 in a Mini."

"Maybe somewhere slightly more scenic."

"The M1?"

"As long as there's a roadside café. Or the services. Hanging out in the services always looks like fun."

Margaret could feel her walls crumbling inside. The sweetness of the simple request was so endearing, so moving, so downright sad that the temptation to scoop Honey up and take her, via 2002 Mini Cooper, to the services, right now, was simply overwhelming.

Honey continued. "On long trips the tour bus stops and Liza will often go in, but the fuss it causes if I *do* choose to get off... well, it just isn't worth it."

"Why could you possibly want to hang around the services when you've got all of this right here on your doorstep?" Margaret lifted her hands to their surroundings. "It's beautiful. It's picturesque."

"It's like *The Truman Show*."

The comment made Margaret laugh loudly.

"But not as many people. Come on. Count the cars that pass as we walk to the green. In fact, just stand still and listen. Tell me what you hear."

Margaret closed her eyes. There was the low hum of traffic from outside the estate, a very distant siren and the wind. She could hear the nipping winter wind blowing gently against her collar. "People pay thousands," she smiled, "millions for this."

"You can't hear life."

"It's worth billions then."

"Sometimes I want to hear life. I want the hustle and bustle, the pushing and the shoving."

"I'm sure you get pushed and shoved all the time moving from venue to venue, or getting through groups of fans?"

"Yes, but they're pushing and shoving so they can gawp and gape. I want to be pushed and shoved by people living their own lives, people barging past on the tube, or at the fast food counter, places to be, people to see."

"Right. So, Honey Diamond's ideal date, a drive round the M25 followed by a trip to the services and some argy bargy at the McDonald's counter."

Honey laughed. "Can we do it tomorrow?"

Margaret looked across at the twinkling eyes, teasing yes, but also quite telling. "If we carry on like this I won't be able to give *The Beacon* enough of a story, so I may indeed have to return tomorrow."

"Good. I'm not answering any more of your questions." Honey linked her arm with Margaret's. "Come on. Let me show you my life."

Margaret felt her heart quicken at the contact. The lovers' walk. So strangely surreal. Bizarre in fact. She looked around, desperate to focus on something, anything, other than their locked limbs. Turning to her surroundings, she smiled. Honey was right. It was like *The Truman Show*. Staged somehow, and so far cut off from reality that reality no longer felt real. There was no movement, no shouting, no beeping of horns, all of the things she associated with her own street, her own living neighbourhood.

Walking in silence, they passed huge houses set back from the road, all of which appeared empty, the odd flash car in the driveway, but no sign of life inside. "There!" gasped Margaret.

Honey jumped. "What?"

"A grey squirrel. There! It ran across the road."

"You scared me."

"Sorry, it was a sign of life. The first one we've seen. I was excited."

Honey laughed. "It's not that bad. Look," she pointed over a grassy bank towards a cluster of tall bushes, "Tony the handyman."

Margaret squinted, finally spotting the camouflaged fence behind the bushes. A man was up a ladder. "Security camera?"

"They're well hidden. Oh," she grimaced, "and he's waving."

"See, that's friendly. You wouldn't get that on my street."

Honey nodded back at him. "I'm not meant to engage. He two-timed my godmother Sofia. Seventy-three, living the life of a teen. Now she's dating Peter the gardener. If he bites the dust she says she'll switch it up and try old Sal from security."

"Sofia sounds fun."

"She is. You should meet her."

Margaret looked at the woman locked into her shoulder, their walk perfectly in sync. "I'm just a journalist, doing my job."

Honey gently untangled the arm, her eyes dropping away.

"I didn't mean to say that out loud. It came out wrong. I'm sorry. I would love to meet your godmother. I'm having a lovely time."

"Doing your job."

"Yes, but in my head I was thinking about why *you're* being so nice to me when I'm only a journalist, doing my job."

"I am nice! I told you before, I can meet a hundred new people on a daily basis, but we only ever interact for a purpose, and I know this interaction does have a purpose." She took a deep breath, "To address the rumours caused by my song, but unless I'm mistaken," she exhaled slowly, "this feels a bit more than that."

"In what way?"

"You're not the typical journalist. No recorder. No notes. No sit-down structured interview. You're easy to talk to."

"I'm new to this."

"What, a no-holds-barred, access-all-areas Honey Diamond interview? So am I!"

"No I mean—"

"Look," she pointed, "more life. Over there on the green. It's Jackie Laurent and her children."

"Louis Laurent's wife? They live here?" Margaret shook her head. "I had no idea."

"Let's go say hello. She's really lovely."

"No, no, I can't."

"Starstruck?"

"You're right. I've not been professional. I've not handled this interview well at all." She spoke quickly, struggling to find the words. "We should get back and sit down. I could do with some more detail about the hours you work each week."

"It's non-stop, all day every day, we covered that at the start. Come on." She linked Margaret's arm once more, pulling her towards the open expanse of grass. "I need to fill her in on the latest."

Margaret was almost jogging to keep up. "The latest?"

"Yes, there's this godawful site on the web. SlebSecrets. Spreads horrible rumours. Have you heard of it?"

"I don't think so."

"You must have? Apparently it's the go-to place for gossip."

Margaret shook her head. "Doesn't ring any bells."

"They speculate about me."

"Doesn't everyone?"

"Possibly, but it's the first time I've actually seen it online. I hate technology and I try and stay as far away as possible, apart from my music studio bits and bobs obviously." She slowed their walk as they approached the green. "But they've really upset poor Jackie." Lifting her hand she waved. "Jackie, hi!"

The heavily pregnant woman threw the three soft balls with as much effort as she could muster. "Go fetch!" She turned and shrugged. "Awful of me, but they love it."

Margaret watched the three children, all under five, racing off to retrieve the balls.

"I just wish I could throw further," she continued. "They're back almost as soon as they're gone."

Honey smiled. "Jackie, this is—"

"I recognise you. From the paper. Margaret, isn't it? You interviewed Louis a while back. Great piece. He was really pleased with it."

Honey turned, raising her eyebrows at Margaret. "Oh I see. You're shy."

"No, I..." She turned her attention to Jackie. "How old are your boys?"

"Two, three and four," she patted her bump, "and another on the way."

"Boy?"

"Yep. Good old Louis and his testosterone." She blew out a puff of air. "The bane of my life."

Honey nodded. "I was telling Margaret about SlebSecrets. Mother's on the case. Apparently they've found an old address where the site was registered. Her men, as she calls them, are close."

Jackie held out her hands for the balls and threw once more. "I'm not angry because it's untrue. God knows what Louis gets up to, and look at me, who could blame him, but I'm angry for them." She paused and smiled at her three children scrabbling around for the balls. "Those little people. They'll read it one day. And no relationship's perfect. Most men have affairs. But why should his be spread all over the web for everyone to see? We're not a perfect couple, but we try, and we'll always try for our children. The last thing we need is the added pressure of every Tom, Dick and Harry knowing our business. Louis is closed off enough as it is. Stuff like this makes him worse, seeking solace in whichever pert bosom is closest." The eyes dropped to her own breasts. "Oh and now I'm leaking. It always happens when I'm emotional. I'm like a milk machine offering free samples wherever I go. Ladies, I'm sorry, the last thing I need is these wet paps getting papped. I'll speak to you soon Honey, and keep me informed." She smiled at Margaret. "Nice to meet you. It's not often Louis has something positive to say about journos."

Margaret nodded a thank you and watched as the woman threw the balls in the opposite direction, heading, most likely, towards home. She turned to Honey. "You get papped out here?"

"Never. She's embarrassed."

"About her breasts?"

"Jackie Laurent embarrassed about her breasts?" Honey smiled at the suggestion. "No, about Louis. Yes, he's apparently a bit of a toe-rag, but they're a family, they make it work."

"But if he's cheating…"

"Then it's their business. And I've no clue who these clean-cut, mightier-than-though, internet people think they are. Rubbishing strangers' lives. Criticising and condemning. They're damaged. They must be. Sadistic psychopaths who get a kick out of abusing people online. And she's right. Those children didn't ask to be born into that family. They've got as much right to privacy as anyone else." Honey shrugged. "They need at least half a chance at a normal life."

Margaret spoke quickly, wanting a new direction, the peaceful walk shattered by the encounter. "Did you want a chance at a normal life?"

Honey smiled. "Maybe for a day."

The thought was fast. "Let me take you."

"Where?"

"To the services. In my Mini."

"I wish."

"I'm being serious. I know what I'll write, we've got an hour left of the interview." She smiled. "And I've got a bigger hat in my car."

"A bigger hat won't disguise me and my security won't be prepared." Honey stopped. "Sorry, that sounded so spoilt."

"Come on, we can try." Margaret was now the one with her hand on the back, guiding Honey away from the green.

"It gets scary sometimes."

"I won't stand there with a sign saying – here's Honey Diamond, come for free hugs."

Honey laughed. "Oh, I was hoping you would." She paused. "I guess it wouldn't hurt, would it?"

"No."

"And I've always wanted to be spontaneous and uninhibited." She sucked her lip between her teeth. "You really think we can do this?"

"Be uninhibited on the M25? To an extent."

"You're funny!" She smiled. "We're bonding. Actually, no, we bonded over that wine; this is the next phase of our growth. I've always been interested in psychology, particularly human dynamics and human behaviour," she paused, "but don't write that in the piece."

Margaret puzzled. "Why not?"

"I rarely get time to read so I don't want to overstate my talents. It's more about me sitting back and observing others. There are lots of times I'm in the chair, the supposed centre of attention, when actually the interesting things are happening all around me. I like to observe. I see friendships formed, niggles starting," she sighed, "but I'm never part of it." She clapped her hands. "You could be my portal."

Margaret coughed. "No one's talked about my portal with such enthusiasm before."

"Ha! We've got it."

"Got what?"

"That shared wavelength. Let's do this. Let's go crazy."

Looking into the excited eyes, Margaret lifted her shoulders. "If that's what you want."

"Yes! I've always dreamt of random adventures, running wild, lost in the crowds and if I'm honest the idea of free hugs sounds quite appealing."

"Right then. Let's give it a whirl."

Honey's eyebrows rose wickedly. "So, lead on to your portal."

****

The commotion occurring at The Alderley's hub was farcical to say the least. Four ageing women, the most glamorous clearly the leader, now trussed up in white robes and slippers, hauling a brogue-wearing suit out of the spa. The young attendant had returned with Champagne before squealing and running for help. Diana had realised they needed to get the now-disorientated PA out of the heat, so with a swift neck of her refilled flute she'd summoned her troops. The first lift had been the hardest with Gerty and Dot's sweaty breasts slapping into each other as they leaned over the body, but once outside the furnace, with towelling accessories in place, they'd got into a good rhythm: two steps forward, their cargo trying to force every other step back.

"Please release me," said Liza, unable to avoid the gape in Gerty's gown.

"No, this is perfect," said Diana, encouraging the forward brigade. "The pool boy's calling my people. I have a whole new holistic team. They'll take care of you."

"Really, I'm fine. This friction's making me worse." She pushed the towelling dressing gowns away from her face, inadvertently exposing more udders. "Please, I need to check on Honey. Check she's singing from our hymn sheet."

"We'll vet the article later. This is much more important. I've got a hydrotherapist, a hypnotherapist, a physiotherapist, a cryotherapist, a psychosexual therapist, a—"

"I fainted!"

"And they'll find out why." She stopped at the ringing in her pocket. "The van must be here. Gerty, set her down over there." She signalled towards the lounger.

"The van?" gasped Liza. "You're taking me away in a van?"

"Sit on her," said Diana firmly. "Make sure she can't move."

Sofia stopped walking. "Is this really necessary?"

"Yes, and you're in charge of the schedule. Take Liza's PDA, check on Honey's itinerary."

"No one takes my PDA!" shrieked the thrashing suit.

"Hello!" giggled Diana into her phone, thrilled to finally make use of her people. "Oh, it's you." Putting her hand over the receiver she mouthed to the struggle on the lounger. "*It's my OTHER men.*" She paused. "You have their names? Women? Never? And you gifted the letter?" She straightened as she listened carefully to the details, trying her best to ignore the wrestling behind her. "Everything. Find out everything. Where they work, what they do." She paused. "We'll destroy them with this. Present me with the particulars tomorrow. I'm busy at Velvet Villa tonight. We have a patient." She looked back to the lounger. "Who may need the full works."

****

Margaret smiled at the woman slumped in her passenger seat. She'd always imagined this car would bring stature. Not in a Range Rover Vogue type way, but in a quirky, I'm an independent woman and my life's in order type way. And here she was now, with the woman to end all women gazing up at her with excited eyes, almost hidden under the oversized beanie. A woman who'd talked about her portal. Hers, Margaret Rutherton's, and that certainly hadn't happened in a very long time. It was as if the hunted had become the hunter. Honey must have hundreds of fans trying to contact her on a daily basis believing they were soul mates, or even worse, stalkers embodying the Stan character from the infamous Eminem song, yet it was Honey being forward, Honey daring to flirt, Honey discussing a connection she'd like to take further. Margaret nodded, and all of that was extremely fine with her. "Sorry about the stereo," she said, holding the steering wheel with pride. "It can be a bit tinny."

"I can't hear it through this hat," said her companion, "but I *can* feel the bumps. Has this car got suspension?"

"It fell off a couple of years back." The white bonnet stripes and white roof were two of the few things still intact on the little red car. Margaret squeezed her knuckles even tighter. She didn't care. This car had housed Honey. Honey Diamond in *this* little car. A car that had seen her rise in her work life, her social life now catching up, catching up to this pinnacle, this day that would never be beaten. "Top of the range back in the day."

Honey laughed as she peeped out of the window at the traffic haring past them. "Even the motorway seems more alive. The cars I travel in must be well sound-proofed."

"That's the back window; it doesn't close properly."

Honey laughed again. "I can't remember the last time I felt this free. Yes I can. My summer with She-Ra."

Margaret gasped. "She-Ra the singer?"

"How many other She-Ras do you know?"

"He-man's?" Her eyes darted away from the road to her passenger.

"She was my crush."

"She-Ra?!" Margaret straightened in the driver's seat trying to refocus on the traffic. "No!"

"We did some tour dates together. I was eighteen. She whisked me away to a late-night Leicester Square cinema showing. Back row. No one else there."

"She-Ra?!"

"Yes, She-Ra. Keep your eyes on the road."

"She likes women?"

"She did. Still might. Our paths haven't crossed for a while."

Margaret squeezed on the steering wheel. "I *knew* her husband looked gay."

Honey nodded. "It's called bearding. I learnt that from the dreadful SlebSecrets site. A beard is any opposite sex escort taken to an event in an effort to give a homosexual person the appearance of being on a date with a person of the opposite sex."

Margaret's eyes were back where they should be. "How far shall we drive?"

"Don't you want to ask if I've ever bearded?"

"Should I?"

"You're an uncharacteristically quiet journalist, Miss Rutherton." Honey spoke with a smile. "It's intriguing. Very intriguing. I thought you lot were meant to dig around for that extra titbit? That unanswered question." She paused. "But no. I haven't. I attend premieres and functions and charity dos and that sort of thing with male friends and acquaintances, but I don't do it to look straight. I do it for company, and if I'm honest I don't have many female friends. I've tried to ask my stylists and hair dresser along but they always refuse. Now whether that's another one of Liza's 'don't get too close to Honey' rules, I'm not sure. Or whether they just feel uncomfortable, or whether they just don't fancy it, I don't know. But sometimes it's easier when Liza suggests the arm of another well-known celebrity. They know how it works, all the protocol of the pictures and the smiling and the polite chat with reporters on the red carpet." She smiled. "And then you both leave at the first given opportunity without having to explain yourself."

"I've seen that happening before, as soon as the cameras are gone the celebrities leave."

"It's work. People outside of the industry don't understand. Yes it's a party, yes it's an event, but you're always on the job, wherever you are. You're protecting your brand. Never off guard. Never letting the mask drop."

Margaret looked down at the cosy bundle on her passenger seat. "I can't see a mask."

"I'm relaxed. I feel carefree for the first time in ages. Sounds strange given the fact I'm hiding out in a micro mini."

"This isn't a micro mini. This is a..." Margaret smiled. "Look at me trying to impress Honey Diamond with my 2002 Mini Cooper."

"You *can* just call me Honey. You don't always need the Diamond bit on the end." She peeped up at the window and pointed at the sign for the services. "Oh goody. Come on, indicate left. Can I call you Maggie?"

"The services? You're sure? And no, I'd rather you didn't."

"Yes I'm sure, and fine, *Miss Rutherton*. Let's see how far we get. If we get to the door we get one point, the shop at the entrance is two, the toilets are five and a sit down drink in the café is ten."

"We'll get the full house."

Honey lifted herself properly into her seat as the car came to a stop. "Will we?"

"Yes, come on." Jumping out first, Margaret suddenly wondered if she should go round and open Honey's door. That's when she heard it. The first shout.

"Is that Honey Diamond?"

Honey was one foot out of the car.

"Yes it is! It's Honey Diamond!"

"Honey!"

"Honey!"

The shouts got louder. "Honey Diamond! It's Honey Diamond!"

Margaret watched in frozen fear as the swarm of people picked up their pace. It was like a scene from *The Walking Dead*. They were everywhere. Coming from all directions. "Back in, back in," she shouted to Honey, who was already seated, door shut, fastening her seatbelt."

"Go!" Honey was trying to move the gearstick as Margaret threw herself back into the front.

"What are you doing?" she gasped, strapping herself in and starting the engine. "You don't just push that stick and we start."

"I thought it would help. Oh quick! They're here!" Honey smiled and waved politely through the window, talking to Margaret through gritted teeth. "Any time today, this one's going for the handle and my security have no clue we're here."

Margaret revved the car and reversed, missing the gears as she jerked away. "Where's the Porsche when you need it?"

Honey looked over her shoulder at the crowd. "How many points do I get for one foot on the tarmac?"

"I am so sorry," said Margaret, finally picking up some pace. "This is all my fault. What a ridiculous idea. I should have known better. Of course you can't just get out and wander around the services."

Honey shrugged. "That's my life."

"I know." Margaret was shaking her head as they sped onto the slip road. "I've no clue what I was trying to prove. I have a very, very poor portal."

The smile was wide. "The first time's always the hardest." The eyes glinted. "We could always change it up and try something new?"

CHAPTER ELEVEN

"Where the hell have you been?" Jo was in the doorway of the two-bedroomed flat, arms flailing, voice shaking, ready to regurgitate the rant that had been churning and smouldering inside her for the past few hours. "I've lost a day's pay. I've been traumatised, victimised, almost frickin sodomised in my own frickin flat. And all for you." She snorted air through her nostrils. "And what the hell do you look like? Where are your glasses? You have absolutely no idea! The drama I've been through! And here you are, turning up with a makeover. A makeover that I was meant to give you. Bloody hell, Meg. Ten years I've been going on about this." She raised her voice. "Who did it?"

Meg edged past the shouting banshee and into the flat. "My dash of mascara's traumatised you?"

"No! Well, yes!" Slamming the front door she followed Meg in. "And where the hell have you been? Your phone was turned off. Your phone's never turned off. Obvious now though. You were getting styled up by someone you trust more than me."

"I was working."

"On your sass, clearly!" She screamed in annoyance. "Oh damn you, Meg. Why do you look so good?"

"That's a bad thing?"

Jo was pacing around the coffee table. "Yes! I'm angry!"

"I had a trim yesterday. I put my contacts in today, and I finally opened that make-up set you bought me two Christmases ago. No one's *done* me."

"That makes it even worse! You're a natural. Crikey, with my makeover you'd blow the roof off."

Meg sat on the sofa, patting the cushion next to her. "What's happened? Why's the place still a mess? I thought Pia was here today? Oh god, Jo, is that bottle yours?"

Jo continued to pace, ignoring the almost empty bottle of chardonnay. "I fired her."

"You did what?"

"She was useless."

"At polishing?"

"At saving me from the sodomisers who strolled in, strutted around, searched through our stuff before serving up their snotty-nosed papers."

"Whoa, back up a minute."

Reaching down to the coffee table, Jo shoved the documents towards her flatmate. "Head on a platter. Baying for blood. The Diamonds have got you for dinner."

CHAPTER TWELVE

"I've invited her for dinner." Honey was smiling into her coffee cup as she sat opposite her godmother on one of the tall stools at the kitchen's breakfast bar. The day had been so full of surprises. The interview she'd been dreading turned out to be the most natural meeting of minds. That feeling of knowing someone a lifetime. Somehow you connect. You click. You get on. You relax in their company. You experience their energy. There's that buzz. That knowing. Honey smiled to herself. It was the knowing that meant the most. Knowing they felt it too. That invisible pull. That draw of desire bringing you together time and time again. Desire to know more. Desire to grow. Desire to see where things went. And she hadn't paused; Margaret, when she'd asked her, hadn't paused. "Yes, I'd love to come back for dinner," she'd said, like it was the most natural thing in the world. Like two old friends extending their day, not wanting the experience to end. She was awkward, incredibly awkward, but that had only endeared her further. She was special. Miss Margaret Rutherton had something special.

"Shouldn't you check with Liza first?" said Sofia, pulling Honey's focus back into the room. "Skeletons in the closet and all that." Her eyebrows wrinkled into a wince. "And I feel bad saying this because you seem so excited, but Liza described her as a bit of an *old hand*." She shrugged. "And I don't want you getting hurt, dear."

"It's only dinner, and Liza's description of women is always way off."

"She called her a dusty old dyke."

"Exactly! She's far from it. She's interesting and intriguing." Honey's smile was wicked. "Plus Liza's holed up in some top-of-the-range holistic therapy room at Velvet Villa, so she's best kept out of it."

Sofia laughed. "Your mother was thrilled when she fainted, a chance to finally use some of her staff." She shook her head. "Did you know she has a special vehicle for medical emergencies?"

"I did not."

"It's a cross between the A-Team van and a high-end SUV, complete with red medical stripe down the side."

"Oh dear me."

"She called it up, dragged Liza inside, kicking and screaming, claiming that a night in her therapy room would cure all her ailments."

"Is she okay?"

"She was. I doubt she will be after a night with your mother." Sofia reached out and rubbed Honey's hand. "It will be nice to have you all to myself, dear."

"I've got a meeting at the studio this afternoon."

"I know. I'm coming with you. I promised I'd keep you on schedule. Tammara's coming at four. Alan or Andy or whichever of them is on duty today have said they'll be there."

"Fine, as long as we can make a menu on the way and stop for ingredients on the way back. I'll ask Tam to run in."

"You're cooking for her?"

"I'd like to try."

Sofia's smile was wide. "Oh Honey, dear, tell me once more what she's like."

****

Sitting at home, back in her world, Margaret stared at her screen. The cursor key was ready to go, but the words just weren't coming. The day was too much to process. Was it shock? Infatuation? Adoration? Worry? Something was stopping the writing. Some block was halting the words. The piece was easy. Honey was a hero. A heavyweight role model in the way to do fame. She hadn't played the press or, equally, hidden the truth. She'd lived her life as best she could, rising to the occasion when called. And here she was now, standing tall, a beacon of pride and acknowledgment. Some people were gay and got on with it. It didn't need a big announcement, a big discussion about what that now meant. It was an insignificant aside, just like the colour of her kitchen, or the fact she didn't drive. Things of slight interest that should be noted and left. None had any bearing on her skill, her talent, her vocation, her life's work. Margaret smiled. Her voice.

A soft soothing voice with a hint of intrigue. A voice that spoke like a smile. A secret smile. A smile that had been directed at her. Margaret slammed the laptop closed. This was no good; she knew what had to be done.

CHAPTER THIRTEEN

Rushing back to the smoking pan, Honey waved her tea towel over the spices. Toast the spices, it had said in the Indian cook book. On a hob. In a pan. That's what she'd done. She flicked back to the first page of the recipe. Nowhere did it mention the plume of black smoke that would rise up and fill the kitchen, choking anyone who dared try and breathe. She darted back as another cloud of stench rose up, like one of those fireworks gently puffing every couple of seconds but without the pretty colours and wows of awe. Nothing impressive about this display. Turning off the heat, she removed the pan from the hob and crouched, squat-walking towards the door, vaguely remembering something about staying low during a fire to avoid the smoke. The top of her head suddenly felt warm. *Brilliant*, she groaned, quickening her pace as best she could with burning thighs and an outstretched arm. Her hair would be stinking of spices; what a lovely start to the night.

Reaching the front door, Honey dumped the pan on the step, relieved as the fresh air hit her hard. Gosh, what a disaster. At least her guest wasn't due anytime soon.

"Honey, hi," said the voice from above.

Honey looked up from her squat position. Margaret, or a more angelic version of Margaret, was standing on her doorstep next to her burnt offering.

"Are you okay down there?"

Honey continued to stare. The glow of the driveway lights behind her guest was having a halo effect with the winter breeze moving Margaret's hair like a carefully placed wind machine on a modelling shoot. Honey used the door handle to pull herself up in as ladylike a fashion as she could muster. "Wow, you look incredible," she managed, leaning forward in greeting and immediately noticing the way Margaret's nose jolted out of the way. "My hair stinks. I'm so sorry. It's these spices. I'm cooking you a curry. Apparently you toast the spices to coax out their flavour. The dry heat transforms them into..." she looked down at the smoking black pan, eyes drawn instead to the flash of bare skin at the ankle, "...into charcoal it seems." She coughed as her eyes rose back to her guest. "Maybe I should bury it in the back garden? And you haven't smelled the kitchen yet. I really am sorry, and I can't believe it's that time already. Damn it, here's me thinking I can cope without being managed but, no, it's all gone to pot, or soot, or whatever. Sorry. Come in, come in. Look at me leaving you on the doorstep again."

"I might be better off out here."

"Don't you dare, I've been working on this all evening." She smiled at her guest who was clearly holding her breath. "You really do look sensational, Margaret. Ignore the smell, relax and come in." Honey shut the front door before fumbling with the knot at the front of her apron, the messy bun on top of her head suddenly falling forward.

Margaret's voice was shy. "You look lovely too."

"Liar," laughed Honey, swiping her auburn fringe to the side and watching her guest's surveying eyes. Honey followed the searching stare. "You're not relaxed, are you?" She shook her head. "You're still not relaxed. You have stiff shoulders. I can see them under your coat."

The pause was anxious. "You really want me here?"

"Of course I want you here."

"This isn't a set up? Hidden cameras?"

"Of course not! What's changed? You seemed so eager to come this afternoon. You said yes instantly – really instantly. I thought you were thrilled. I thought you were happy." Honey stopped. "Have I got this wrong?"

The eyes darted around one final time before coming to rest on their host. "You haven't. It's me." Margaret sighed. "Oh, I don't know. Sitting at home, trying to write this story, realising how," she signalled to the space between them, "how extraordinary this is." Shaking her head she continued. "Ignore me. It's the smell making me dizzy."

Honey flicked her apron against Margaret's shoulder. "It's not that bad! Come on, just relax and give me your coat." She reached out to help slide the duffel from Margaret's arms, gasping as the beautiful dress was revealed, her fingers dancing on the delicate silk. "Wow."

"What?"

Taking a step backwards, Honey appraised the vision in front of her. The dress was in the kimono style, blue and white, unlined with short sleeves, a matching belt accentuating the waist to create an effortless chic and fashionable look. "Where did you come from?"

"Clapham."

Honey laughed. "Go and make yourself comfortable in the lounge." She tapped the apron and coat. "I'll get rid of these."

"Can I give you a hand in the kitchen?"

"It's fine. The curry's in the slow cooker. Those spices were meant to be the final finishing touch." Pointing her guest towards the music, she nodded. "Go and relax. You know why you're here."

Margaret lifted her eyes. "Do I?"

"Yes." Honey kept the connection. "I like you, and I think you like me too."

A silence filled the room.

"Right," said Honey, breaking the hush with a nod. "There's Champagne in the bucket. I'll be there in a tick." She walked to the kitchen. *There in a tick?* What was she? Some kind of 1950s housewife welcoming her husband home? And what was with the early declaration of emotions? She cringed at herself before heaving as the smell hit her once more. She knew Margaret felt something too, but she didn't need to force it to the forefront the moment her guest set foot in the door. She was clearly a nervous creature herself.

Act calm, act casual, she chanted silently, swapping the coat and apron for a tea towel and wafting the smell away with vigour. She thought back to her other option. She could have waited for the interview to go live before trying to decipher if there were any nuggets of code suggesting Margaret had liked her too. But then there'd be to-ing and fro-ing about who should call whom. No, Honey threw the tea towel on the table, this was the best move. A nice meal. Some more chat. Some possible contact. She held on to the back of the stool and quivered. Female contact. The soft touch of skin on skin. The tingle of anticipation.

The cough and clink of glasses was staged. "Sorry, I thought I'd bring the Champagne in here. You're wobbling. Are you okay? Is it the fumes?"

Honey spun around, holding harder on to the stool with one hand, trying to look as casual as possible. "Just taking a moment."

"You were shaking."

"Was I?"

"Yes, and it looked like a full body shake."

Honey shifted into another equally awkward position. "Someone walked over my grave."

"Does that happen a lot?"

"Not nearly enough," she said, forcing a smile. "Please, go back and relax."

"I can't sit in Honey Diamond's lounge while Honey Diamond slaves over a hot stove for me. I'm just a journalist. I feel unworthy."

"Stop saying that. You're more than just a journalist. You're my friend."

"Your friend?"

Honey took a deep breath. "Well probably not in the dictionary definition of the word, but we've connected. We've bonded. We've made that conscious decision to take this past work and into this new, albeit slightly awkward, place." She sighed. "You know my life's crazy. I have to grab moments otherwise I morph from one event to another without actually having the time to experience what life has to offer... and I understand this may sound full-on to you, but I rarely get chances like this, chances to meet someone genuine." She smiled. "Could we blame the smell for making things strained?"

Margaret smiled back towards the lounge. "Let's get out of this cesspit."

"Deal. We'll eat in there."

"On our knees?"

Honey paused as a flurry of rude innuendos raced through her mind. She studied her guest, imagining what she'd look like on her knees. "Perfect," she finally managed.

****

"We've got 'em!" said Diana, flapping the paperwork in the air as she pushed her way into Velvet Villa's holistic medical suite. "Turn down the chiming, Svetty."

Liza lifted her head from where she lay prostrate on the trolley only to have it pushed back down by the heavy handed Russian woman wearing white slacks, white bandana and medical face mask. An outfit devised by Diana, no doubt. "Got who?" she managed before looking at the woman. "And I thought you were called Sokolova?"

"Sokolova be last name, boss allowed to be using the first name, Svetlana. Boss call me Svetty."

Diana flapped her papers once more. "The gossips at SlebSecrets. We've got them. My men delivered the cease and desist letter. I've got their names. More details coming tomorrow. They have forty-eight hours to remove the site or we'll commence legal proceedings."

Liza tried to lift her head once more, forcing the allegedly well-qualified holistic healthcare practitioner to strap it into position with a Velcro tie. "Is this really necessary?" she asked. "And no one wants a holistic therapist called Svetty."

"Yes, it is necessary." Diana retorted. "And Svetty, you're doing a great job. Try that new colonic irrigation machine we bought last week and then do the ear candling. We'll get you right in no time."

"Diana really, there's no need." Liza strained against the Velcro. "I could get up and help you with that. We could Google the names. See what else we can find."

Diana lifted the papers. "No. My men are ex-army. No stone unturned. They'll get me photos, work history, life story. Honey's asked me to help. I'd never usually get so involved, but this is the perfect opportunity to show her what good staff can do." Diana nodded. "She needs more staff. Maybe this will convince her. You lie back and heal. You're Velvet Villa's first official in-patient."

"I'd rather not be."

Diana walked right up to the trolley where her daughter's PA was reluctantly horizontal. "You encouraged Honey's freedom, so now you have to accept Honey's freedom." Lightening her tone, she danced away. "Relax and recuperate."

Svetty Sokolova cracked her own knuckles before rolling her shoulders and kneading a selection of her own joints in what looked like a more vigorous version of the haka. "Svetty heff permissions to start, ma'am?"

"Looks like I should leave you to it," said Diana as the holistic chiming rang out once more.

"What about Honey? What about—"

"Honey's fine, Sofia's in charge. Enjoy the treatments. Let Svetty work her magic."

Liza's eyes widened at the sound of the large colonic irrigation machine coming to life. "Fine, you win," she said, reaching up to remove the Velcro head strap. "I'll stay the night." She rubbed her face. "I'll relax. I'll have the massages and the acupuncture. Maybe even the cupping. But the colonic and the ear candling, no."

Diana Diamond smiled. "And you'll always support me in future?"

"Always."

"Always what?"

"What?"

Diana nodded. "Always what?"

"What do you mean always what?"

The collar was straightened. "Always ma'am."

"Oh for god's sake, Diana, I'm not calling you ma'am."

Diana turned on her heel. "Well then. Svetty, it's over to you."

****

Margaret rose from the sofa as Honey came into the lounge with their plates. "Here, let me help you," she said, relieved to have something to do, having been banished from the kitchen and forced to relax in what was quite possibly the largest front room she'd ever been in. A front room that reminded her of a show home, or an area of an upmarket department store showcasing what your front room could look like if you filled it with their furniture, wallpaper and ornaments, none of which you'd relax in, but would instead creep around gently to ensure you didn't knock anything out of place or leave any evidence of your presence. Margaret took the plate and made her way to the large shag pile rug lying in the centre of the room surrounded by dark wood flooring. She looked again. It wasn't just a rug on the floor, it was encased by the wood. It was a whole other type of flooring built into the centre of the room. She sat carefully and crossed her legs, adjusting her kimono to cover her modesty.

"What are you doing sitting in the middle of the room like that?" asked Honey with a laugh.

Margaret looked up at her host, still standing there with her plate. "I thought we'd agreed to eat on our knees?"

"Yes, on the sofa. The coffee table's here too so it'll be easier."

"Don't," gasped Margaret, unable to watch as the clearly expensive oak table was pulled, one handed, across the floor. "It'll scratch!"

"I *have* moved it before."

"Have you?"

"Well no, but we can't sit in the centre of the room like two little Buddhas."

Margaret patted the soft pile next to her. "Yes we can. That sofa looks like it's made of white mink and this curry will stain. Where do you usually eat?"

"In the kitchen, on the road, in the studio." Honey gave up and joined her guest on the floor. "Sofia's a great cook. She prepares most of my meals no matter what time I'm due out or in. She's always ready, and it's always delicious."

Margaret scooped up some of the sauce and rice. "And I'm sure this is too." She lifted it into her mouth, quite unsure what hit her first. Was it the strong smell of garlic or the rancid taste of rotten eggs?

"How is it?" asked Honey, watching eagerly for approval.

Margaret's eyes started to water as her nostrils widened, trying desperately hard to chew confidently as she masked her utter disgust. She nodded as keenly as she could. "Mmmm," she managed.

"Oh good. I've not cooked it before, but I've seen Sofia do it a number of times and aside from the burnt spices I think it's a success. I added the boiled eggs at the last minute to give it some bulk."

Margaret almost baulked. "Did you boil them earlier?" she asked through the mouthful that wouldn't go down.

"No, Sofia always has some ready in the fridge. Here, let me grab us more drinks." Putting her plate onto the rug Honey rose up and headed back into the kitchen.

"Shit," cursed Margaret, lifting her plate as high as she could before working the contents of her mouth out with her tongue, quickly using her fork to bury the mush. She left her tongue hanging there and exhaled heavily, panting like a dog to rid her taste buds of the putrid flavour.

"You're really getting into that, aren't you?" said Honey, smiling at the scene in the centre of the room.

Margaret looked down at her position. She appeared to be plate up, mouth open, guzzling away. "Sorry, us journalists are known to wolf down our food then abandon it as we head off on one lead or another." It was a total lie but it was all she could think of. "So don't be disappointed if I forget all about it."

"You're not going anywhere are you?"

"No, I..." She lifted her hand for her glass. "Thank you, it's got quite a kick."

"I think I may have confused bulbs of garlic with cloves of garlic."

"Right."

"It's not too bad though is it?"

Margaret coughed slightly. "Try a bit with some egg."

Honey eyed her suspiciously. "Feed it to me?"

"Really?" She watched the smiling eyes. "Okay then, here goes." Margaret scooped up some sauce making sure she stabbed a large chunk of fermented egg as she went. "Open wide. Shall I do the choo choo?"

"I was thinking of something more sexy."

"I'm not sure this will be sexy with or without the choo choo." She lifted the curry to Honey's mouth. "Enjoy."

Honey slowly closed her lips around the fork. The splutter came first, then the choking. "What in god's name is that?" she gasped, flicking the food out with her fingers. "That's horrific! It's off! Something's off!" Gulping from her glass she continued to finger her tongue. "It's burning!"

"That's the garlic. Has the egg hit you yet?"

"If it's responsible for that decomposing putrid taste then yes!" She slugged the Champagne and growled. "Oh Margaret, I'm so sorry. I've been tasting it as I've gone along and I thought it needed more garlic, hence my confusion about the bulbs versus cloves, so

I've obviously gone and put too much in, and those eggs are just horrific. They must be off. Sofia usually leaves them on the middle shelf for me in the fridge, but these were on the top shelf and I thought they'd be fine. I'm so sorry. This really is revolting, isn't it?"

Margaret lifted her fork to scoop a bit more. "If I avoid the egg it's fine. You've got some good flavours coming through."

"You're lying. It tastes of death."

Margaret laughed. "It's okay."

"That's sweet, but it's not." She reached for the plate. "You top us up; I'll throw these away and grab us a toothbrush."

"It's not that bad."

"It is. The Champagne's over there."

Margaret rose from the floor, masking a burp that made its way into her mouth, reigniting all the vile taste sensations. A toothbrush? Why was Honey grabbing a toothbrush? This whole experience was bizarre enough as it was. Equally as unusual as the interview and the services trip. Was she uneasy? Was she holding back, being stiff? Honey certainly wasn't. Honey was beautifully at ease. An innocence that made the whole situation even more shameful.

"Right. I have a new toothbrush for you, some toothpaste, a bottle of water and a bowl."

Margaret looked at the offering. "You want me to clean my teeth in your lounge? And spit into a bowl? In front of you?"

"I've got mine too."

Margaret smiled. "This is a sign."

"What sign?"

"A sign that you're different. Someone obviously brings you bowls and toothbrushes like it's a normal thing to do."

"I thought this would be less weird than standing side-by-side in my bathroom like you're staying the night." Honey blushed. "And I'm not saying that you staying the night would be weird, I'm just saying..." She paused. "Oh, just take your toothbrush and scrub that stink off your tongue."

Margaret took the brush, bowl and water towards the window and rested them on the sill. She dipped the toothbrush and stared out across the wide driveway, wondering if it ever got lonely living so hidden away. She brushed her teeth quickly. It was now or never. "Listen, Honey," she said, not turning around. "I need to—" She stopped at the fingers that were touching the back of her neck, parting her hair. "I need..." They were moving up and down with a devastatingly arousing effect. "I..." Honey was behind her, her body inches away.

"I'm sorry about the curry," came the whisper.

Margaret slowly edged herself around, trapped between Honey and the window. "It's fine."

"Can I make it up to you?"

Feeling the hands move slowly around her back she gasped. *Shit.*

"I like you."

The lips were brushing her cheek. *Oh. My. Good. God.*

"And I think you like me too."

The mouth hovered over her own. *What the hell's going on?*

"Liza's known you for years," Honey was pulling herself closer, "and that's good enough for me."

Margaret couldn't reply. Their mouths had connected. She had to stop this. She couldn't stop this. Honey was hungry. She was forceful. She was pushing her onto the windowsill, parting her legs with her body.

Margaret snapped her legs closed and slid down. "I'm so sorry, I can't do this. It's too soon."

Honey shunted backwards, pressing her hand to her mouth. "Gosh, I've misjudged this. My life's so busy. I have no time for spontaneity. I thought I'd try and snatch it, but I've snatched it too hard and too fast."

Margaret felt her insides weaken. She liked it hard and fast. Damn it, she liked Honey. So much. Too much. She'd never said no to a woman, she never had the chance; they were always so few and far between. And here she was with Honey Diamond, saying no. Stopping what would no doubt be the experience of a lifetime. She thought fast. "Tomorrow? Start afresh? Take our time?" She paused. "I'm not the woman you think I am." She thought back to the Liza comment. "Maybe quite literally. But I'm worth knowing, and I'll explain. I'll make things right."

"I'm the one who needs to make things right. Look at me. I'm a sex pest. I have no clue what came over me." She shrugged. "Well I do, it was the sight of you in your kimono. But I know I can't just take what I want, and I don't want you thinking I do. I never do. You're right, we should slow it down." Her cheeks were flaming. "You should go. I'm embarrassed."

"Tomorrow then? I'll take you out."

"I'm at the studio tomorrow."

"Postpone it."

"I can't. And where would we go? People will see me. You remember what happened at the services."

"You have make-up artists."

"So?"

"Contouring."

"But—"

"Please, Honey. I need to get my head straight. I need to start from the start. If this is more than just work then I want to do it properly. A date."

"Look at us. We're both in a tizz. We're ridiculous." The eyes dropped. "This is ridiculous."

"I think me brushing my teeth at Honey Diamond's lounge window was the pinnacle."

The laugh was quiet. "Okay," said Honey, "I'll spend tomorrow with you, but only if you promise to spend the next day with me. I'll live your life if you live mine. Now leave me alone before I change my mind, or before I internally combust with embarrassment."

"It'll probably be those fermented eggs."

The laugh was louder. "Actually stay, let's start this again?"

"I can't."

"You're right. Look at me. Always pushing. I'm useless."

"Trust me, this is all me. My fault. My mess." Margaret shrugged. "My car's by the hedge."

"You drove? You had no intention of drinking?" Honey led them out of the lounge towards the front door. "Well you *were* drinking, so that means you thought about staying?"

"I didn't know what I was coming round for."

Honey opened the door and shook her head. "Earlier today you said you were suited up like a goal keeper with full body armour and kit. You weren't lying were you?"

Feeling the cool breeze on her cheeks, Margaret stepped into the shadows. "I don't want to hurt you." She crunched onto the pebbles. "I…" The words just weren't there.

Honey followed her out onto the drive, moving towards the lights. "Am I way off the mark?" she asked as they walked.

"Not at all. You're wonderful. You're…"

"I'm what? Because you can't get away from me quick enough."

Margaret sighed. "You're perfect."

The voice was soft. "So show me."

Looking down at the arm now resting against her own, Margaret paused, unable to control the conflict in her mind. "You don't know me." They were at the car; she should get in and go.

"But I want to." Honey's lips were back, kissing gently, kissing kindly.

Margaret moaned, quickly losing herself to Honey's demands. "Wait," she gasped, hearing the footsteps behind her.

Honey pulled away and looked over the shoulder at the person coming their way on the pavement. "It's fine. It's one of the contract cleaners from the hub. They have to sign non-disclosure agreements to work here. You don't need to worry. Oh and I know this one, she's lovely." Honey waved. "Pia, hello."

Margaret span around and looked at the woman.

"Yhesh, yhesh, Miss Diamond."

Hunching her shoulders, Margaret tried to hide against the car.

"Pia, this is my friend, Margaret. Margaret, this is Pia."

The little woman inclined her head to get a better look. "Meg, what you do here?"

Honey frowned. "Meg?"

"Yhesh, yhesh, Meg nice girl."

The journalist's voice was quiet. "Meg's the shortened version of Margaret."

CHAPTER FOURTEEN

Keying in the code next to the battered shutters of the discount store, Meg granted herself access to the stairwell. The drive home had been peppered with half swerves into side streets, a decision to turn around and explain quickly discarded and corrected by the analytical part of her brain. The part that always won out. Hence her position now, trussed up in Jo's ridiculous kimono, trudging back up the stairs to her flat. No new truths had been told except for the fact she was sometimes called Meg. Shoving the key into the lock she mouthed to herself. *You're always called Meg, you liar*. This whole Margaret bollocks was recent. Apparently the prestigious role of Arts and Entertainment correspondent at *The Beacon* required her full name. The horrible old-fashioned gift from her parents: Margaret Audrey Joyce Rutherton. Yes, she could just about manage to introduce herself as Margaret, but including Audrey and Joyce in her byline, no.

The paper's proprietor had claimed that good old stalwart, Margaret Rutland, admired and adored by all, couldn't possibly be replaced by some young upstart called Meg; bad enough she'd joined them from HotBuzz, but a Meg who wasn't embracing the fact she could follow in her predecessor's footsteps by name, if not by constitution, just wasn't okay. So she became Margaret at work, and if she was honest it did help. People who were expecting Margaret Rutland were somewhat appeased that this new woman had a very similar name.

Meg shoved open the door. She should have corrected Honey at the first opportunity. Thinking back, she couldn't even remember when that first opportunity was. She'd assumed Honey's Pulitzer Prize comment had been a joke, but no, good old Margaret Rutland won it back in the 80s. She paused. Just how old did Honey think she was? And all this chat about Liza. She should have said: I'm sorry, I don't know her. I know *of* her; so many stories from the scene... She stopped herself. It was like that moment someone says your name wrong and you don't catch it until a couple of seconds later but by then it's too late. She slammed the door behind her. None of this mattered anyway. This wasn't the exposure she was expecting. She was expecting a set-up by Honey, luring her in before throwing Diana Diamond's findings right in her face with the full force she deserved, revealing what a low life creature she truly was.

Meg flopped face first onto the sofa. But Honey hadn't known, and maybe she'd never know. Maybe the letter *had* just come from the family's matriarchal dictator, Diana, puller of strings. The hidden force behind a highly successful media whitewash. Maybe the cease and desist was standard. Maybe the men were employed full-time to rid the internet of negativity. Meg felt a crushing realisation of what she'd done. Sitting across from Honey at the interview and then staring at Jackie Laurent on the green had both served to flick that switch, to confront her thoughtlessness. These were real people. She'd hurt real people. And now someone knew. Someone knew it was her. She was exposed. A silly, stupid hobby suddenly of so much importance, so much consequence. She'd never got it before. She'd never made that connection. Celebrities were untouchable, weren't they? It didn't matter with them.

That's why she'd frozen. That's why she needed to think. She was about to tell Honey when she'd been kissed. She needed to get away, clear her head and formulate a plan and, yes, maybe she'd been saved by that kiss. Maybe there was no need to tell the truth, or to go back and confess something that may never come to light. Honey didn't know. A simple misunderstanding about which journalist was doing the interview was one thing, but finding out about her links to SlebSecrets? Well, that was a whole other disaster. Yet it was this fear which had caused her to run from their contact. To pull away from the come-on. Honey liked her. For some unknown reason, she liked her. Damn it, she'd even kissed her, with such want, such desire.

Meg sat back up. The site was down. She'd done what was asked. Yes, it had taken the writer's block this afternoon to finally convince her. The realisation that she had, for the first time, the chance to write about Honey from an honest, informed and enlightened position, instead of her usual chip-on-the-shoulder guesswork. The acceptance that she'd been theorising, and while her theories had in most cases been correct, they weren't her truths to tell. They were Honey's.

Shaking her head, Meg sighed. She'd felt guilty. It wasn't the threats in the letter, it was the regret. Trying to write those real words, those informed observations, those truths that Honey had trusted she'd tell, well... they'd made her feel sheepish, wicked even. Maybe she *should* have gone back and explained? Maybe she *should* have told Honey the truth? She wasn't shying away from Honey because Honey didn't know the shortened version of her name, or that she'd taken over from old Margaret Rutland. She'd shied away from her because of the guilt. The sin of who she'd been, what she'd done. Meg stopped herself, the analytical part of her brain firing up once more. Was there really any point in coming clean? It was the same as the husband having an affair and telling his wife just to relieve himself of his own burden. She shook her head. If they won't find out, don't tell them. Don't hurt them. And the chances of Honey being involved in the internet side of things was slim. She despised technology. She hated social media. Crikey, she didn't even have her own mobile phone. Meg paused. But she'd heard of the site. She'd announced an address had been found. Would she want to give Jackie Laurent a name, or just the knowledge the site was no more? Biting the inside of her lip, Meg shouted. "Oh god, Jo, where are you?"

"You're back?!" The body flew out of the bedroom at speed.

"Didn't you hear me?"

"Obviously not or I'd be out here finding out what the hell happened! You're back early! She knew! She's telling the papers! You're fired! Can you make the rent if you're fired? You'll be unemployable, I bet. Like those journalists with that phone hacking."

"She kissed me."

The mouth dropped open. "What? Was she desperate?"

"No she wasn't desperate! And you said I looked great."

"A kiss from Judas Iscariot then? For the one who needs to be killed? An act of kindness before she kicked you to the curb?" Jo started to pace. "I knew there was a reason for the invitation. I'm not being funny, Meg, but why else would Honey Diamond invite you for dinner?"

"She likes me."

Jo stood still. "As if."

"She does!"

"She obviously doesn't know you're the founder of SlebSecrets then?"

"That doesn't change who I am."

"Of course it bloody does!"

"Not in terms of what drew her to me."

"What? Your hot looks and riveting personality?"

"I think we're quite similar."

"You and Honey Diamond?" The snort was mocking. "In your dreams!"

Meg folded her arms and slumped back into the cushions. "She thinks I'm Margaret Rutland."

"That old bird you replaced?" Jo laughed. "Well there's a compliment for you."

"I'm there worrying she knows about the site, worrying that her mother's going to pounce and confront me, so much so that I don't fully comprehend what she's going on about when she says I know Liza. And I'm confused, not because she doesn't know I replaced Margaret, but because she doesn't know I'm Meg Rutherton of SlebSecrets, and this piece of paper *does* know I'm Meg Rutherton of SlebSecrets." She reached out and grabbed the document. "*No one* knows I'm Meg Rutherton of SlebSecrets."

"They do now." Jo sat down next to her flatmate. "But you said it yourself, it's just a piece of paper, it's just a threat. They don't know for sure who's behind the website. Now obviously if you hadn't used our student flat address—"

"I had to pay for the hosting. I used a fake name, but maybe my online payment account was registered there."

Jo was frowning. "Were we even on the electoral role? Wasn't it that really crappy place we sub-let off that fourth year weirdo? They've probably traced so many students from there." She clapped her hands as enlightenment struck. "They didn't know our names! That's why baldy was sifting around through our post. I bet they've handed letters to everyone who's ever lived in that shit hole hoping they'd strike lucky and somehow the site would shut down."

Meg shook her head. "They've got me. However they've got me, they've got me. I can't sit here clutching at straws. They were probably just confirming our names before they handed over the letter. Making sure it ended up in the right hands."

"What do you mean *our* names?"

Meg flapped the document. "It's addressed to both of us."

"Oh no. Oh no no no no no."

"What?"

Jo's head was shaking violently. "No, you don't."

"Don't what?"

"Involve me. I'm not taking the blame."

"I haven't shut down the site because of this letter. I've shut down the site for Honey."

"Try telling her that."

"She may never find out," the slow pause turned expectant, "but if she did…"

"What?"

"Well if she did…"

"What?"

Meg's eyes were wide and encouraging.

"What? Just say it. I take the blame?"

"Oh listen, Jo, this letter's only a cease and desist. It's a demand to halt purported unlawful activity. *Purported*."

"And what the fuck does that mean? Stop talking to me like I'm stupid."

"It's a threat. They don't like the site so they're trying to get it shut down."

"I thought you shut it down?"

"It's offline, but anyway, they'd have to take me to court and prove the site was unlawful. I don't name names. It's not slander. It's just gossip. I'm not sure they'd win. But the fact they have my name means they've already won. I don't want to be exposed. Well, maybe I wouldn't care if it wasn't for Honey." She paused. "But Honey's in the picture now and I can't have her finding out it was me. It would ruin everything. Oh, I've been such a fool, Jo. I thought I was doing the right thing trying to out the sleazeballs and the secretly gay. We need good role models, people who are honest and true to who they are, and Honey *will* be that role model; she *wants* to be that role model. I had no right to try and rush that. It would have happened with or without me."

"Would it?"

"Regardless, I'm the one in the wrong and, yes, while the letter could be standard procedure, I'm not sure I can take that risk."

"You can't tell her, Meg."

"So what do I do? Ignore it and hope Honey never gets given my name?"

"Why would she? Honey's lawyers, or Diana's lawyers, or whoever those men answer to, wouldn't realistically bother her with paperwork and names would they? Surely they'd just inform the Diamonds that the site's down?"

"Do you think?"

"SlebSecrets was nowhere near as offensive as some things out there. I'm sure the Diamonds have enough on their plates without worrying about little Meg Rutherton's gossip column from Clapham."

"I just want a chance to show Honey who I truly am."

"Wait a second, you're seeing her again? You don't tell me about the interview and now this?"

"I've been trying to tell you. I've been trying to tell you she kissed me. And the interview was last minute. You weren't around."

"Not so last minute that you couldn't get your hair cut or switch in your contacts." Jo shook her head. "And what do you mean she kissed you? She *actually* kissed you? *The* Honey Diamond kissed..." she frowned, "...*you?*"

Meg bit gently on the inside of her lip as the sweet sensations came flooding back. "I really like her."

"Well, let's hope she never finds out."

The huff came quickly. "I didn't take the site down because of the threat of exposure. I took it down through personal guilt. The site would be offline now with, or without, this letter."

"Like I said, try telling her that."

CHAPTER FIFTEEN

Diana Diamond's mouth was wide open, staring in shock at the vision in front of her, the low-lighting and chiming music doing nothing to alter the scene.

"Do it again, Svetty," giggled Liza, lying face down on the massage table, naked from the waist up with six small glass cups sucking on her skin.

Svetty Sokolova, whose white uniform had somehow come loose at the collar, plumped up a substantial bosom that was now out in full force. "Svetty be rough this time."

"Oooh yes," came the muffled giggle.

The bandana was tightened before the big hands banged together, a mini haka performed before the forward thrust of breast and yank of cup, pulling it free from the skin.

Liza's moan was feral.

"You like Svetty be rough?"

The PA growled. "Liza like Svetty be rough."

"Svetty be fired," said the loud voice filling the room, "if I find out this isn't how the ancient art of suction cupping goes down."

The holistic therapist stepped away from the table. "Ma'am."

"Ma'am!" gasped Liza, rolling off the bed and crouching behind it as if she was hidden, a difficult belief given that she looked like some kind of prehistoric reptile with bulges and bumps and half of the glassware cupboard stuck to her back.

"Oh don't you ma'am me, Liza. How can you be locked away in here and still cause such a commotion?"

"Was I growling too loud?"

"No, you weren't growling too loud," yelped Diana. "Your highly recommended, we can count on her, she's perfect for the job journalist from *The Beacon* has only gone and snatched Honey's heart."

Liza shot straight up, the glass cups chinking, forgetting about her bare breasts. "What?!"

"Svetty! Will you please cover those!"

The Russian woman lifted her large hands to shield the offending bosom.

"With a towel!" Diana screeched.

The nod came quickly. "Svetty getting towel."

"And get those bloody cups off her back."

Liza lifted the proffered towel to her chest as the holistic therapist tugged on the glassware.

"Focus, woman!" said Diana, noticing the way Liza's eyes rolled erotically each time a cup popped away from her skin. "*Your* journalist! She came round for tea! She could still be there now! Sofia's at the spa; I phoned to find out how the afternoon had gone and she told me. She said Honey cooked. She cooked! She never cooks."

Liza's head was shaking. "Maybe they needed more time for the interview?"

"All done and dusted apparently, so much so that they nipped out on a jaunt in the journalist's car while we were all busy dousing you in smelling salts."

"She's too old for Honey."

"I don't care if she's Zsa Zsa bloody Gabor reincarnated. It's unprofessional. Plus we're only day one into this public personality outpouring and here she is with a girlfriend."

"I very much doubt that, Diana."

"Why? What makes you, standing there in your towel, titties and cups, the fountain of knowledge?" The spiked hair was vibrating. "Sofia said she was enamoured, full of it, impassioned by this woman."

"She's sixty-five."

"Oh don't exaggerate."

"At least." Liza shuddered. "And the moles. So many of them. Like rough terrain on her face sprouting hairs."

"Wonderful. The pictures of my daughter and her first girlfriend sound perfect. I wonder how much *Hello!* will pay for the wedding? The princess and her wicked old bag of a wrinkled, stinking hunchback witch."

"She hasn't got a hunchback."

"Will you just sort this out!" shouted Diana.

"I'm free to go?"

"Of course you're bloody well free to go!"

"Oh." Liza glanced at Svetty. "We were moving on to the hard water spray next."

The therapist's large hands came together in front of her even larger body, grasping themselves around an imaginary hose. "Svetty Sokolova spray water hard, very hard."

Liza quivered. "I should stay the night. You were right. Who knows why I fainted."

Diana lifted her chin before turning on her heel. "I'll be at Honey's tomorrow evening. I need it sorting by then."

****

Sitting on the sofa in her lounge, Honey brushed her fingers across the fabric. Margaret had laughingly suggested it was white mink, whereupon her carpet Buddha pose had taken shape. She smiled, remembering the image before leaning back into the cushions and turning to her godmother, now returned from the spa and insisting on a full rundown of the evening. "She was breezy in lots of ways," said Honey, thinking back to Margaret's wonderful handling of her godawful curry, "yet uptight in others," she added, unable to ignore the anxious arrival and awkward departure. "As if showing me glimpses of her true self, before recoiling into the safety of her professional persona."

"Probably just nervous, dear."

"Of what? Of me?"

"Your mother thinks it could be deemed somewhat unprofessional, taking you out in her car, accepting your invitation for dinner."

"Oh Sofia! You're telling tales on me? You're meant to be on my side. And we both know mother would be fine if she were a he."

The older woman reached out to rub Honey's hands. "I'm always on your side, dear, you know that. It just slipped out. I was happy for you. There you were, cooking, all carefree and—"

"Crap. My cooking was crap." Honey straightened. "Maybe that's why she dashed off. Maybe it didn't agree with her?"

"The curry?"

"It really was pungent. You hear of these things don't you? Dates ruined by sudden... sudden *urges*."

"It can't have been that bad."

"Oh, it was."

"Maybe it was a sudden urge for you? Maybe she didn't want to rush things, so she made her escape before crossing that line?"

Honey shrugged. "She didn't even tell me her real name, well not her real name, the shortened version of her name." She lifted her eyes to her godmother. "You know Pia, the cleaner at the hub?"

"Yhesh, yhesh."

Honey laughed. "Well she cleans for Margaret too. And if Margaret lets her cleaner call her Meg, then why didn't she tell me I could call her Meg? We'd even had a conversation about nicknames," Honey sighed, "and she wasn't worried about crossing that line. She saw me step over it first. In fact I jumped. I bounded forward, leapt and lunged myself right onto her side of the line."

"You kissed her?"

"I tried to, but you know how useless I am at things like this. Something was wrong. She wasn't comfortable."

"Could it have been the lunge, dear?"

"I thought she liked me. I'm sure she liked me. I caught glimpses; I saw..." Honey's voice tailed off.

"Find her for me." Sofia reached into the arm of the sofa and took out the iPad. "I'm a good judge of character."

"Her picture?" Honey took the tablet and started to type. "Margaret Rutherford? Rumerton? I'm so useless with names."

"Just go to *The Beacon*." Sofia pointed at the screen. "Arts and Entertainment correspondent. There. Margaret Rutherton."

Clicking on the link Honey enlarged the photo of the journalist. "She wasn't wearing glasses today." The nod was decisive. "Her eyes look better without glasses."

"Yes, she is younger than Liza described." The nod was approving. "She's certainly got a bold, capable look."

"And her hair's a bit shorter and neater now." Honey squinted. "That's not the best picture."

"She looks nice. Strong."

"She's the same height as me."

"In an intelligent way."

"Oh Sofia, do you like her or not?"

"Of course I do." The pause was thoughtful. "Possibly not quite the exquisite princess your mother was hoping for, but she's interesting."

"I think she's very good looking. Striking. And her smile's so naughty."

"This woman here? She gave you a naughty smile?"

"That's obviously just her professional pose."

"Read her bio, dear. Tell me more."

Honey warmed at the interest. Sofia was always there, by her side, listening, encouraging, paying attention. She was the one who'd spent endless hours playing the new board game at Christmas. She was the one who'd sat for weekend after weekend watching class after class of singing, dancing and acting. She was the one who'd read every single night at her bedside. She was the one who was always there.

Honey scrolled back and cleared her throat. "Margaret Rutherton is *The Beacon's* new Arts and Entertainment correspondent, taking over from Margaret Rutland earlier this year." She lifted her head. "Wait, what?"

"Carry on, dear."

"She's not been there for years?"

"Carry on."

Honey struggled to find her place. "Joining us from HotBuzz, Margaret brings the passion of..." She stopped herself. "Wait, *what*? Liza said she was... she said she was..." Honey shook her head. "She obviously thought she was Margaret Rutland. The old one." Clicking on the other name Honey gasped.

"Wow!" said Sofia. "Who's that?"

"That's Margaret Rutland."

Sofia grimaced. "Slightly difficult to look at."

Honey stared at the old and moley Miss Trunchbull look-alike. "We need Liza on the phone. Poor Meg. This all makes sense now! No wonder she was hesitant. There I was going on about her Pulitzer Prize and what a seasoned journalist she was and it wasn't even her. She obviously felt inadequate. Filling this woman's shoes must be hard enough without people like me comparing them, or even worse, assuming they're the same person. Oh, I'm so foolish. This explains everything. I need to apologise. I need to let her know that I know."

Sofia tapped her mobile to life. "Didn't she correct you?"

"I got confused with the names. Liza had obviously told me she was called Margaret so I didn't directly call her this old woman," Honey shook her head remembering, "but I went on about her age. I've obviously confused her. She must think I think she's this moley old... Is it ringing?" She took the phone from Sofia. "Liza? Is that you? Where are you?" The pause and grimace were severe. "Svetty who? A deep tissue what?"

Sofia patted her hand. "Put her on loudspeaker."

The holistic chiming music loudly filled the lounge. Liza's voice was slow and groaning. "I'm having a deep tissue massage. Svetty's using her toes."

"Who's Svetty?"

"Svetty Sokolova. Your mother's," the groan came again, "holistic, oh yes, therapist."

"Who wants a holistic therapist called Svetty?"

"That's what, oh yes this is good, that's what I, mmmm, what I said, but, but she's good." The groan turned into a lust-filled giggle. "Aren't you, Svetty?"

Honey strained to hear the deep Russian voice in the background. "Svetty be freaky. Svetty be pervert."

Liza's voice came through firmly. "Pervert's the wrong word; use risqué instead."

"Excuse me for interrupting, but this journalist you sent me."

"Oh yes, it wasn't Margaret Rutland. She retired earlier this year. Sorry Svetty, hang on a minute. That's it. Take your toes out for a second."

"Liza!"

"What? I'm with you. Sorry, yes, right, your mother told me. Worried to high heaven about you dating that crumple-faced old bag. I phoned *The Beacon* after my hard water spray." The moan came again. "You really should try your mother's—"

"Focus!"

"Sorry, yes, they admitted their error. Well, it wasn't really an error. I'd asked for Margaret Rutland and there was no way they were going to pass up the chance of a Honey Diamond exclusive, so they said yes, no worries, but sent their new girl instead. She's very good apparently; well, I guess you know that if you invited her to dinner. And they might have been right. I'd possibly have cancelled the interview had I known the old correspondent had retired."

"You're not up in arms?"

"No harm done. As Svetty says: Life be short."

The distant voice was gruff. "So Svetty be spicy."

"Liza, I'm leaving you to whatever it is you're doing."

"I'm not doing anything and it's wonderful."

The growling voice was louder. "Svetty be working. Svetty be pumping."

Honey coughed. "Right. I'll leave you and your traction engine to it."

"You don't need me at the studio tomorrow, do you? You're just singing the songs from the script?"

"Actually, I was thinking of..." Honey stopped herself, deciding to keep the plans private. "That's fine."

"Good, Svetty says—"

"I'm going." Jabbing at the off button, Honey turned to her godmother who was clearly in an equal state of shock. "Can you believe that was Liza? Have you ever heard her so out of it?"

"I think I might need a bit of Svetty Sokolova if she works wonders like that." The smile was wide. "So you're doing it, dear?"

"I told her I would. I agreed we'd start afresh tomorrow. And I'll apologise. I'll make sure she feels equally as worthy even though she's not the veteran Pulitzer Prize-winning journalist I made her out to be." Honey smiled. "I *knew* there was something. This explains it all. I'm excited." Taking her godmother's hands, she squeezed. "I'm really excited, Sofia."

"And where is this wonderful woman taking you?"

"I don't know. We agreed I'd spend tomorrow with her as long as she spends the next day with me. Living each other's lives. I've asked the girls to come over and disguise me. Apparently contouring can make you look like a whole other person."

"Can it?"

"I don't know, but Margaret, Meg, I don't know what to call her now, well she's been given a few days to write my piece so time off isn't an issue," Honey shrugged, "for her at least. I'll make up the time in the studio, I'll work through the night if I have to."

"Oh Honey, I know you will, but you deserve some time off, and I'd like to meet her, this woman who's made you see sense."

"I've asked her to pick me up." The smile was knowing. "I knew you'd want to give us your blessing."

"Anyone who makes you happy makes me happy."

"And Mother?"

"You leave your mother to me, dear."

CHAPTER SIXTEEN

"The door!" wailed Honey from the chair in the centre of the kitchen. "She's early!"

Hair stylist Heidi nodded towards the wall clock. "You said ten. It's ten."

"Then why aren't we ready?!"

Louisa the make-up artist squeezed the sponge across Honey's cheek. "Contouring, with the purpose of looking like a whole other person, takes time."

Heidi spoke again. "Plus, we're missing Liza."

"She does snap you girls into shape," agreed Sofia, getting up from the breakfast bar and heading out of the airy kitchen.

"Wait! She can't see me like this!"

"I'm not leaving her on the doorstep."

"At least warn her before she comes in."

Heidi's wince was teasing. "That you look like Snoop Dogg? You should have listened to me: black bobbed wig, baseball cap."

"I only showed Louisa that picture of Snoop Dogg as an example. The contouring disguise tutorial on YouTube had the woman looking like a whole host of celebrities."

Louisa stroked her shoulder. "You don't look like Snoop Dogg. But Heidi's definitely given you poodle hair."

Heidi nodded. "A faux perm that we'll tie into a pony. You'll look like an everyday run-of-the-mill school run mum."

"And with this cagoule," said clothes stylist Caitlyn, "no one will notice you're there."

"Oh wonderful. Just the impression I want to create: fuzzy hair, boring clothes, a face-full of thick brown foundation..." Her voice tailed off as the journalist entered the kitchen. "Wow!" Honey gasped, unable to hide her shock. Last night it was the kimono that caused her eyes to widen; today the whole package was bringing light to the room. The outfit, the hair, the striking features. She was glowing. She was gorgeous. "Margaret," she finally managed, "you look—"

"Meg, please."

"Yes Meg, you're, you're..." Honey slid off the stool, moving towards her guest. "You look..." She realised she was doing a great impression of Danny from *Grease*, seeing Sandy for the first time at the pep rally before realising all his friends were watching. She turned around. "Stop staring you lot. This is Mar—, this is Meg, and she looks amazing!"

"Hi Meg," came the chorus.

The voice was shy. "Hello."

"Wow! Look at you and then look at me! What a let-down. I'm like a dirty-faced old bag lady."

The anxious eyes stopped scouting the room, focusing instead on Honey. "You're not. You just look totally different. Great different. Maybe a bit like... like Cher."

"Cher?"

"With all the curly hair. Or Baby from *Dirty Dancing*. With the perm. Jennifer Grey?"

Louisa interrupted. "See, you don't look like Snoop Dogg."

"Oh yes, him too." Meg's hand flew to her mouth. "Sorry, no. I mean you look famous somehow, just not famous like you." She tilted her head. "Are those wind trousers?"

Clothes stylist Caitlyn took over. "Yes, and paired with this brown polyester cardigan and storm-proof cagoule no one will give her a second glance."

"I will."

"Oh, she's a sweet one!" gushed Heidi. "And I do like your hair. Who's your stylist? The choppy unravelled look suits your face shape."

"Flared capri pants," added Caitlyn. "Very in season."

"Your lip colour suits you too," said Louisa. "Maybe just a touch more mascara to bring out the depth of your eyes, but overall your make-up's well thought through."

Sofia, who had been standing in the doorway watching the scene, clapped her hands. "We approve. Right. Welcome, Meg. Can I get you a drink?"

"Something strong?"

"Ha! I told you she was funny," said Honey, smiling at her guest, trying to reassure the wide eyes that were still prone to sudden darts around the room. She stepped in closer and lowered her voice. "I need to apologise."

Meg's head started to move from side to side. "I do. You thought I was—"

"Margaret Rutland. That's who Liza asked for."

"She retired."

"I know. I'm so sorry. It must have been horrible for you."

"That she retired?"

"No, that you thought I thought you were her."

"I didn't know you thought that until…"

Honey turned to the staring women. "Give us some space, would you!"

"No, we're not finished." Louisa patted the stool. "And even though you two look so cute standing there in your little huddle, whispering your sweet nothings, we need to get finished."

"They tease me," said Honey, secretly relieved for their support and presence, helping to make this encounter a lot less nerve-racking, even though she looked so utterly ridiculous. She stopped herself. Was the disguise actually helping? That extra layer of make-up, protecting, giving confidence? Or was it simply because Meg looked so gorgeous? Smart, chic, well put together, but mostly gorgeous in a strong and striking kind of way. Maybe she was relaxed because Meg was here? Relieved? Pleased? "You really do look lovely," she added.

"And you look great, and different."

Louisa interrupted. "Would you recognise her?"

The journalist shook her head. "No. Certainly not from a distance."

"And not once I've got that frizz in a pony," said Heidi, summoning Honey back to the seat. She pulled on the hair and fluffed up the fringe. "So tell me... where are you two love birds heading off to?"

Meg took a deep breath. "We're heading off to Ikea."

****

Closing the passenger door to her Mini, Meg felt the same mixture of nerves and anticipation she'd had the first time she'd arrived at The Alderley. The knowledge she was about to spend time with Honey Diamond, the woman she'd known from afar for so long, the woman who'd entered her thoughts time and time again, the woman who, through no fault of her own, hadn't been aware she existed. *Well now was her chance*, she thought, hurrying back around to the driver's side. She wouldn't usually open the passenger door for a friend, but Honey would no doubt be used to the fuss. She'd have that level of expectation, that standard of need to be met.

"Oh," the voice was sighing. "I had high hopes for you, Meg."

Meg closed the door and pulled her seatbelt across her lap. Did she know? Had she been saving the announcement until they were alone? Teasing her with the hope of a day trip before ripping it away with one swipe. There hadn't been any signs that anyone knew. No signs in the house that her name was being bandied around as some, some... what was it Honey had said? Internet troll? And she'd been looking. She'd been looking carefully. Just as she had last night, arriving for dinner, waiting for Diana Diamond to swan into the hallway brandishing the documents that would no doubt signal the end of everything.

Meg stopped fumbling and lifted her eyes. She could tell her. Of course she could tell her. Crikey, she'd been about to tell her last night, but the come-on had stopped her. Honey's come-on. The very idea that this incredibly talented, utterly gorgeous woman might like her. Why ruin it with something that might never come to light? Why not give Honey a chance to see who she truly was, not the chip-on-the-shoulder person she'd been. Maybe Jo was right. Maybe it had been some weird infatuation that morphed somehow into an envious sort of jealousy. "Sorry," she managed.

"You don't need to open my door for me, you dafty! I thought you were different. The girls loved your Ikea idea, and it sounds like so much fun. Don't spoil it with special treatment. My security are allegedly staying away so I want this day to be lived as normally as possible."

"I'd open a taxi door or a restaurant door for my date."

"Would you rush around to the other side of a car you were driving, curtseying and bowing in the process, as you opened your date's door?"

"Well, no. But I've never been on a date with Honey Diamond before; in fact I've hardly ever been on any dates with anyone, let alone someone as beautiful and as talented as you."

"Honey! I'm just Honey, and you're Meg, and we're off to Ikea looking like bag-lady mother and daughter." The correction was quick. "Not that you're looking like the daughter of a bag-lady. I'm the bag-lady. You're the daughter who's somehow managed to escape bag-lady life, head off to university and get your act together. More than get your act together. You're like a model."

"I am not!"

"You are. You've got those brooding, interesting features."

Meg focused on the eyes, the only thing reminding her it was indeed Honey Diamond sitting once more in her car. "You're really kind," she said, "but it's quite possibly false advertising. My flatmate gave me a makeover. I think she called it a full body and personality overhaul, but she did me. This isn't a common occurrence." The pause was thoughtful. "And if I'm honest, I'm most happy in jumper and jeans."

"Oooh, me too. Or soft-touch tracksuits. Not the velvet ones my mother wears with ridiculously high collars, just the ones you pull on when you're home and finally able to relax."

Meg felt a wave of nausea rise from the pit of her stomach. She had to know; she couldn't keep second guessing. Yes, she'd seen them dining together at The Muse, but maybe it was a twice-yearly thing. She couldn't not ask. "Just how often do you see your mother?"

"Too often! No, sorry, that was unfair. She's coming over this evening. I'll introduce you if you like?"

The panic that swelled inside Meg was one of all-consuming dread. It was that horrible sickening feeling. Gnawing worry. What choice did she have? What path could she take? If she told her now the day would be ruined and Honey wouldn't see the person she could be... the person she wanted to be... the person deep down she knew that she was. Meg nodded. She'd made a mistake but she'd rectified it – the site was offline. She'd been thoughtless, but now she needed to be thoughtful. Banging the car's steering wheel she made a fist. There was only one way to play it. "Honey, I'm going to give you the best day of your life."

"They closed Harvey Nichols last year so I could do some Christmas shopping in peace. Is Ikea a similar sort of store?"

"Like Harvey Nichols?" Meg sucked on her lip and spoke through her teeth. "Umm, it's not *exactly* identical."

****

Pulling off the main road, Meg followed the signs for Ikea. "Okay. So you said you wanted a normal life. You said you liked the idea of hanging around the services. You said..." She shook her head. Just who was she trying to convince? This idea, which had seemed so cleverly ingenious and imaginative at the time, had slowly deteriorated from inventive to just plain ridiculous the nearer they'd got to the junction. Yet, it had all seemed so perfect when she'd thought of it. Giving the celebrity who has it all, who's seen it all, who wants for nothing, giving them real life. Of course she could have taken her to a posh restaurant, or a theatre, but Honey would have done all those things, time and time again. Meg nodded to herself. She'd thought outside the box. She'd used her initiative. She had one chance to give this sensational woman a great time. A memorable time. An experience. Meg's confidence grew as she remembered the mantra: be with someone who makes a trip to the supermarket good fun. "It's the world's largest furniture retailer," she said with gusto, "but there's so much more than just furniture. I thought we could look around, have some lunch."

"Oooh, they have restaurants. How lovely."

"Not quite."

"A food hall then?"

Meg turned the steering wheel. "More of a café."

Honey's gasp cut her off. "Is this it?!"

Meg glanced at the eyes that were focused on the huge blue corrugated iron building, the yellow sign screaming IKEA and the flags waving proudly in the wind. "You've really never been?"

"No!" Honey's head wobbled with excitement. "Are we near an airport?"

"I don't think so, why?"

"All these cars! Or is it a car supermarket? I saw an advert for one once. It was a bird's eye view of this place you could just stroll around with thousands of cars waiting there for you to simply pick the one you wanted and drive away."

"This is the car park. All these people are inside."

"Inside Ikea?"

"Yes." Meg questioned her choice once more. Ikea with the piled up products. Ikea with the build-it-yourself bedrooms. Ikea with the café. "You said you liked the idea of being pushed and shoved, of being part of a crowd of people busying themselves with their everyday lives. Ikea's the perfect place for that."

The smile was wide. "I can't wait! Let me at it! There! Park in D4. Right next to those trolleys. Are you sure this isn't an airport? Those are airport trolleys."

Meg pulled on the handbrake. "It's for the furniture."

"You can take the furniture away on the same day? No ordering?" The voice was quivering with excitement.

"I'm not sure we'll be needing a trolley."

"Oh, we will. I had an interior designer do my place, but I wish I'd been more hands on."

Taking a deep breath, Meg shook her head. This was going to be such a disappointment. As if Honey Diamond, A-list creative artist, would find something she liked in Ikea. "Let's just have a look, shall we? They have trolleys inside if you see something you really fancy." She turned to the woman sitting in disguise beside her. "Are you ready for this?"

"The world's largest furniture retailer? I sure am!" The sparkling eyes scanned their surroundings once more. "Is that the Swedish flag? Yellow cross, blue background? Ikea sounds Swedish. I love performing in Sweden; the people are so friendly."

"It is, but I mean *this*?" She lifted her hands to the stream of people making their way into the store.

"There's only one way to find out," said Honey, opening the car door.

Meg smiled at her gumption. Honey Diamond, recognised everywhere she went, about to enter Ikea, the place where the average person bumps into at least three second cousins, a past teacher from primary school, two next door neighbours and one ex-partner, now refurbishing a home with the new love of their life. "Wait for me," she said, catching up to the wind trousers and cagoule.

"I'm invisible," said Honey with a giggle. "Is this what happens when you hit middle-aged-mum? Worrying that people are laughing at your messy hair and thrown-on comfy clothes, when all they're doing is glancing at you, classing you as said middle-aged-mum and moving on."

"There," whispered Meg, eyeing the two men walking their way. "They're looking."

"At you!" said Honey with almost a wail. "Not one set of eyes has lingered on me. But they're widening for you, look!" Nudging Meg's arm she teased. "They fancy you."

"They don't. They're clearly a couple."

"They probably imagine you're my kind and well-dressed carer then."

"Oh stop it, you look lovely. Come on. If you couldn't tell by the sign, this is the entrance."

Walking under the huge yellow letters the women stepped into Ikea. "Bags ladies?" asked the girl on the other side of the revolving door, kitted out in blue trousers, yellow t-shirt, yellow cap and here to help breast tag.

Honey frowned. "Sorry, did you just call me a bag lady?"

"No. I asked if you would like bags, ladies." The girl pointed to the stack of yellow crates full of over-sized blue carriers.

"We're okay, thank you," said Meg, trying to guide Honey towards the escalator.

"I will actually," said Honey, taking one for each hand.

The woman was smiling. "Lovely, and there are toilets over there if you need to go before you head upstairs."

Honey nodded and moved away before hissing under her breath. "She thinks I need the toilet. She thinks I'm one of *those* women."

"At least she doesn't think you're Honey Diamond. Come on up; let's get this started."

Honey stepped onto the escalator. "This really is quite exciting. And look!" She pointed at the sign on the wall. "You get twelve months interest-free credit when you spend £500 in the store."

"Honey, you won't be spending £500 in the store and you wouldn't need the interest-free credit if you did, would you?"

"It looks like a good offer."

Meg frowned. "Are you teasing me?"

"No, I'm excited. I'm giddy. This is so totally freeing. I knew your portal had potential. I've never met anyone who'd think of taking me here. You're a breath of fresh air, Meg, you really are. Oooh, what's that lovely smell?" She stepped out as the escalator rolled to the upper floor. "Ten scented candles for 85p? And all these colours!" The eyes widened. "And cushions for £2.50!" She picked one up and squeezed. "It feels so good. This can't be £2.50, surely?" Opening the first blue bag, she shoved two cushions inside. "They'll look good in the lounge."

"On your mink sofa? Oh, Honey."

"What? Come on! Which way?"

Meg laughed at the enthusiasm. "You don't have to do this for me. I knew this was a bad idea. We could be sitting in some posh restaurant right now."

"And miss these desk lamps! No chance! £2 each, and they bend, and again so many colours." She lifted the red one. "Perfect for my study." Dropping it into the over-sized blue bag she squeezed the cushions once more. "I really do love those cushions, and I may come back for some of these candles too." She stopped to study the overhanging sign and its list of areas. "Living rooms or kitchens first?"

"You just follow these yellow arrows on the floor."

"It's like Dorothy and the yellow brick road. Come on! Here's one!"

Meg couldn't help but get caught up in the giddiness. Whether Honey was acting or not, her enthusiasm was contagious. And it wasn't that distant a memory back to when she'd been here for the first time herself. A trip to Ikea before university. Buying all those essentials: table lamp, cushions, candles. She smiled, remembering just how stuffed full her blue carrier bag had been by the end. Mugs with matching plates, bowls, cutlery. A picture to hang on the wall. "Wait up," she said as Honey disappeared into a lounge room setting.

"Sit, sit!" The blue bags were bulging next to the wind trousers and the hand was patting the sofa. "This must be Cath Kidston. My designer used Cath Kidston for Sofia's room."

"I don't think she's Swedish. And even if she were I don't think she'd display in Ikea." Meg took a seat and looked around at the floral walls, floral rugs and floral lampshades. They were in the first of many faux living rooms, set up in small pods to give the customer a feel of how your very own lounge could look if you chose said sofa, said rugs and said walls. "Look." Meg lifted the tag hanging from the arm of the sofa. "This is the KlitVik range."

"The KlitVik range? Really?"

"Yes, you get matching footstool, armchair and cushions."

"I have cushions."

"And they're Swedish. Everything in here's Swedish. Haven't you noticed all the Daim bars?" She pointed back out to the arrows where another wire basket was stuffed full of Sweden's most popular chocolate export.

Honey reached for the label attached to the coffee table. "This coffee table's called the LiaTorp."

"The lie atop? Really?" Meg grinned. "Come lie atop this coffee table?"

Honey smiled. "Who do you think lives here? Who do you think might lie atop this table together? Wait, I know. Lesbian teachers. Primary school teachers. This room's pretty. It's feminine." She turned her head to the large bookcase behind them. "Pretend it's us. We come home from work and put our books in there. You work at that desk in the corner."

Meg frowned at the small, white metal workstation. "Where do you work?"

"Here on this sofa, as I watch the TV. And look, we even keep our tea and coffee mugs in that cabinet over there. Fancy a living room having a sofa, desk, bookcase, shelving unit *and* a cabinet for kitchen cups. All very compact, but I like it. It's cosy. It's all you need." She stopped at the cough from the woman standing behind her, noticing for the first time the queue of people waiting to set foot in the floral room. "Sorry," she said, "lesbian teachers. We like this one."

Meg scooted off the sofa and helped Honey and Honey's blue bags out through the crowd. "Plenty more to see," she said to the waiting customers, before lowering her voice to Honey. "Lesbian teachers?" It was too late, she hadn't heard. She was already bottom down, wind trousers crossed on the sofa in the next pod.

"Welcome home, darling," said the voice. "How was your day in the city?"

Meg laughed. The banter was so light-hearted and refreshing, and Honey was funny, endearingly so, a playful personality to add to all the other positives she had going on. "I'm a banker now?"

"We both are. This black and white theme really suits us. It's classically edgy. See how we have CDs and DVDs on the shelves now, and tumblers for whisky in the cabinet. I can't get over all this really great storage everywhere."

"I'm not sure bankers would be sitting on an Ikea sofa."

"They would because this one's called the Svlasta. See, it even sounds expensive. Oh look! That black rug! It's gorgeous! Perfect for my bedroom." Honey dropped to her knees and started to roll it. "I think I may need a trolley."

Meg tried to halt the stealing of the shag pile. "Stop it!" she laughed. "You can't just take this one. Look at the tag. It gives you a location number. That's where all the rugs are kept. You take one from there."

"Like a treasure hunt?" The cheap shag unwrapped itself back onto the floor.

"This Svlasta rug can be found at 202.758.14 aisle 8 location 9."

"How am I supposed to remember that?" Honey bent back down. "I'll just take this one."

"Go and get a pencil and one of those sheets." She pointed towards the walkway. "You write down the list of locations you need to visit at the end."

"How clever," said Honey, wind trousers rustling away before she let out a squeal of delight. "Meg, look! I've got a paper tape measure too!" The thin metre-long rule was flapping as the rustling made its way back. "You're allowed to just rip them off!"

Meg's heart was melting. This woman was so loveable, her innocence so bewitching. There was nothing pretentious or pompous lurking behind the thick foundation. There was a natural purity shining through her eager eyes. A purity too good for someone like me, thought Meg, dropping her head to the yellow arrows and walking them into the next lounge, the weight on her shoulders becoming too much to bear. "This is more my sort of living room," she said looking around at the plain décor.

"No," Honey took a seat on the sofa, "this is too boring. This is a lounge for doctors. Wine in the cabinet. Journals on the shelves. You need something with a bit more colour, but not quite as floral as the lesbian teacher's lounge, just something with intrigue."

"You think I like colour?"

"I think you like the organisation of the banker's lounge. I sense a slight rigidity in you sometimes, yet there are definite sparks of colour, definite aspects to you that you wouldn't expect. Unpredictable maybe."

"Says the A-list celebrity loving life in Ikea." Meg smiled. "And our flat's actually quite messy."

"Really? But is it more your flatmate?"

Meg felt herself pulled back into that cloud of worry, that untold truth. "She…"

"You did say you had a flatmate, didn't you?"

"Jo, yes. She's been my best friend for ten years now. She's got her flaws, but then haven't we all?"

"I'd like to meet her one day." Honey paused. "My friendship circle's always been small. It's sometimes hard knowing who you can trust. Who wants to know you for you, not just for the story or the selfie." She put on a fake voice. "I met Honey Diamond; we did lunch."

"Do you do lunch a lot?"

"Not anymore. I got burned a bit when I was younger by social media and false friends. Throwing myself into work seemed the best solution. And I have Liza, and mother, and Sofia, and Gerty and Dot." Honey groaned to herself. "Oh god, they're all so ancient. I know I need to get out more, but that's so much easier said than done. That's maybe why I overstepped the mark last night. You arrived on my doorstep earlier in the day like some hot Lois Lane and we got on, we bonded. And we're similar ages, aren't we?"

"Twenty-eight."

"Exactly, and we talked, we talked about stuff outside of the interview. You seemed genuinely interested. You took me to the services. I liked you. I tried to show you by cooking for you and if that wasn't enough of a disaster on its own, I ruined everything by trying to kiss you. I wanted to seize the moment. I wanted to make friends. More than friends. I like you, Meg. You're not only gorgeous, you're interesting. You're unique. You brought me to the world's largest furniture retailer, for goodness sake. And it takes a really special person to do that."

The sharp cough from the same queuing woman interrupted again. "And there's a lot more of the world's largest furniture retailer to see," said the voice.

"Sorry, just two doctors relaxing in their lounge."

"I thought you were lesbian teachers?" The woman looked puzzled. "Do I know you from somewhere?"

Honey dropped her gaze. "I don't think so, apart from in that floral room down there."

"I'm sure I do. I am, in actual fact, a doctor."

The eyes were back. "Oooh, you'll like this room then."

"You look familiar. Definitely."

"I don't think so."

"I definitely know you. Yes. I do. You're familiar."

Meg took hold of Honey's waist, guiding her away from the enquiring eyes. "Sorry. It's time we tasted the meatballs. Come on, Iris, the café's this way."

CHAPTER SEVENTEEN

Sitting at the huge window with its panoramic view of the car park, Meg decided she had no choice but to confess her sins. Honey's behaviour had gone from charmingly endearing to heartbreakingly beautiful as they'd moved steadily through the kitchens area with her posing as a stay-at-home mum, cooking tea for the children in the cosy and compact show-pod. She was free. She was natural. She was loveable. So, so loveable. Meg looked down at her plate of meatballs. Honey had even found joy in the fact the Köttbullar meatballs were on special at £1 a plate. And the choice between meatballs or an all-day breakfast at £1.50 had been debated with such thought. There were no judgements about what sort of place would have a café with windows focusing entirely on the car park, or what sort of person would bring an A-list celebrity to such a place. She was loving the experience. Loving life. There was literally nothing to dislike about this woman.

Yes, if they made it to tomorrow, Meg realised she might see Honey in a different light, at home in her real world. Would entitlement creep in? Would self-importance show its face? Meg lifted her eyebrows. Probably not. The woman sitting in front of her was perfect. Too perfect for her. She didn't deserve to be cheated, to be lied to. If they were going to have a future of any kind, colleagues, friends, lovers, she just had to tell her. Meg felt her stomach lurch at the thought.

"You know that website," she said, somehow managing to talk without breathing.

"That godawful SlebSecrets one? I meant to tell you. Mother's found them. That's why she's coming round this evening. To present me with all the information. Oh goodness, these meatballs are fantastic." Honey spoke through the mouthful. "She'd usually just get her men to deal with it, but it's the first time I've ever asked to be involved, so she's letting me lead on this one. Sorry, look at me guzzling away. I must get Sofia to find out this recipe." She swallowed and popped one more into her mouth before nodding. "The site's down now, so whatever Mother did worked, but I'm interested to know what sort of sadistic psychopath would make a living from spilling secrets and lies like this. From taking pleasure in someone else's misfortune. They must get a real kick out of abusing people."

Meg carefully placed her fork on her plate. "Did they make a living from it?"

"I assume so. It was a popular site. Most sites have adverts don't they? You know those awful pop-up things. Website owners get paid for those."

"I don't think SlebSecrets had paid advertising."

"I thought you'd not heard of it?"

"I looked when I got home." *And there was another lie.*

"What did you think? I imagine they live in a dirty attic somewhere, surrounded by porn."

Meg didn't want to laugh, she didn't mean to laugh, but she laughed. "No lie atop furniture for them then?"

"Definitely not, and no Svlasta sofa or rug. They'll be the sort of person who hurt animals when they were younger."

Meg laughed again. "Really?"

"Yes. A narcissistic psychopath who has fun causing distress and feeds off other people's unhappiness. A one-time cat killer now turned savage nutcase."

Meg took her fork and stabbed a meatball. That was that then. Honey could never know. No amount of justification could compete with that character assassination. And maybe she was right, apart from the attic room and porn, maybe there *had* been a slight pleasure garnered from the spilling of secrets, but not in a narcissistic psychopathic way, just in a – who do you think you are lying to the public way. Celebrities were protected. They were shielded by their fame. Why should they get special treatment? Why should they—

"Would you like it if your secrets were spilled all over the internet?"

Meg chewed slowly before swallowing. "I think that's the mistake people make. They don't view celebrities as real people."

Honey scooped up another meatball. "I'm a real person."

"I know you are. I see that now. But you were so untouchable." She paused. "I tried lots of times to get an interview."

"You didn't!" The eyes widened. "Did you?"

Meg nodded.

The hand reached over the table for Meg's arm. "You should have said! I'd have given you an interview."

"How? I tried to contact you through official channels, and some not so official channels. I was at press interviews; I tried to ask questions but you never saw me."

"We've met before?!"

"I've seen you lots of times. But you've never noticed me."

"Oh, Meg!" The arm was rubbed with warmth. "I would have noticed you! I feel awful!"

"It's fine. I think it's probably the same for lots of people. That's why they believe you're untouchable. You mean the world to them, but to you... they don't even exist."

The voice was quiet. "I've never thought of it like that before." The eyes looked back up. "But that doesn't give people the right to be mean."

"I know. But maybe people don't realise they're being mean. Maybe they're just gossiping."

"Gossiping *is* mean."

"People do it. Everyone does it."

"I'm not sure I do it." Honey paused. "Maybe I've never had anyone to do it with." Speaking with a smile she squeezed the arm once more. "Meg, will you be my gossip?"

"Ha! I don't want to corrupt your innocence."

"Maybe I'd like you to corrupt my innocence." The eyes lingered. "Maybe I'd like to be bad."

On any other occasion Meg would have laughed at such a line but it was delivered in a fashion that made her shudder instead with desire. "I…"

"Tell me about the first time we met."

"The interview?"

"The first time we were in each other's presence."

"2006. I saw you in *Wicked*."

"No!?"

"Then 2007 in *Les Miz*, 2008 twice at your first concert tour. And 2009 in the audience at the Palladium, 2010 on your world tour, 2011—"

"Stop."

"I was a fan. I've always been a fan."

"And I've always loved my fans. I've always appreciated everything they do. Buying tickets, supporting albums, showing up at events. Oh, Meg. I'm so sorry I didn't see you."

"People often don't. I have one of those invisible faces. Not pretty enough to make you look twice, yet not ugly enough to make you remember."

"I'm looking now." The eyes were intense. "You're not invisible, Meg."

The lingering connection was rudely interrupted by the same sharp voice of the queuing woman. "I've remembered. You're that comedienne, aren't you? Catherine Tate. You're in disguise. Are you filming a sketch?"

Honey spoke with all seriousness. "Yes. You're right, I am. Would you like to be in it?"

"Of course! What do you need me to do?!"

"Go and buy a plate of meatballs and join us back here."

"Oh, how exciting!" said the woman, spinning around and racing off.

"And run," said Honey, giggling as she grabbed Meg's hand. "Bag each. I'm not leaving those cushions."

Meg felt herself yanked from her seat, head low as they scuttled out of the café. "You can't just leave her!"

"I can!"

"She'll be tweeting about Catherine Tate later, telling the world she's rude."

"Oh no, you're right." Honey stopped the escape. "I thought it was funny. Look at me! I'm no better than those trolls!"

"Trust me, you are." Meg took the lead. "Come on. Utilitarianism. For the greater good."

"What?"

"That interrupting woman left alone in the Ikea café with a plate of meatballs is the lesser of two evils. If she outs you, you're history. It would be like the streets of Pamplona at bull running time."

"You like philosophy and bull fighting?"

"Neither. I'm just waffling. Come on, in here." Meg pulled them into a bedroom. "Catch your breath, we need to get to the exit."

"Not just yet," said Honey, stepping forward and taking away Meg's space.

Meg held the connection. They were in a small corner bedroom pod decked out in stripes. People would pass by any minute. People would come in. People would... She lost herself to the lips, kissing back with as much passion as was given. She was melting, the connection so deep and meaningful. It was a meeting of more than just mouths; it was a meeting of minds and of souls. A meeting she'd dreamed about many times in the past, only the reality was so much more than she'd imagined, shockwaves of bliss lighting up all the parts of her she'd feared were lost, or unworthy. This felt right. She kissed deeper. This was right.

Honey eventually pulled away. "We've got it," she groaned before opening her eyes and gasping in fright. "Gosh, and you've got foundation all over your face!"

Meg focused, lazily pulling herself out of the moment before blinking quickly at the sight. "Me? Your right cheek's just fallen two inches. Come on." She took hold of the hand once more. "We better get out of here."

"But I like that picture!" Honey was pointing at the stripy design.

"We'll get it in the market hall." Meg led the retreat with as much decisiveness as she could muster. Her legs were all aquiver, her face was sticky with make-up and her heart was rising up against her head. Who cared about the danger of the situation? Who cared if she was about to be outed by Diana Diamond herself? This was her moment and she'd live it. "In here!" she gasped, pulling Honey into another vacant pod, this one decked out like a study with everything made from beige MDF.

"What?"

"This." Meg kissed the make-up without a care in the world, demonstrating her real feelings with her lips, bags dropped to the floor, hands pulling tighter as she tasted the true flavour of Honey.

"We need to go somewhere," came the groan.

"We've got to get out of this bloody building first," said Meg, eyes drawn to the smudged nose and chin. "Keep your head low; you look like you're melting."

"I am."

Understanding the meaning behind the smiling eyes, Meg followed the arrows leading them through the textiles area, the home organisation, the lighting and the clocks.

"That clock!" said Honey. "It matches my rug!"

"What rug?"

"The one we're picking up at location..." she pulled the piece of paper, pencil and paper tape measure from her cagoule, "202.758.14 aisle 8 location 9."

"Really?"

Grabbing the clock, Honey thrust it into the blue carrier. "Yes! Where do we go?"

"Down there." She pointed to the escalator.

Honey bent over as it took them lower. "Can't be right. Looks like a warehouse."

"It's the self-service furniture area."

The gasp was excited. "Wow! Like a cash and carry? I read once about cash and carries!"

Meg hurried them along the aisles of stacked-up brown boxes to find the random pile of rugs. "Here." She grabbed the top one and rolled it up as best she could. "Tills are this way."

"Why's everything boxed up?"

"You build it. Come on, hurry."

"What?"

"The furniture." Meg guided them towards the checkouts. "You build it. Everything in the show rooms is ready to assemble."

"No? That sofa in the lesbian teacher's lounge?"

"Over there, look." Meg pointed to the pile of cardboard boxes with the picture of the floral sofa on the front. "You build it. With just one Allen key. Right, here we are, the tills."

"Catherine! Catherine!" The now familiar sharp voice sounded loud behind them.

"Oh, Honey, let's leave this and go."

"No, that queue's only four deep and, wow, look! Here's a freezer with meatballs in it!" Honey reached in and grabbed a couple of bags. "I know supermarkets have sweets at the checkout, but this is a whole other level. Köttbullar meatballs. Three packs for £5." She shoved another into the blue carrier.

Meg looked over her shoulder at the woman racing their way, her speed somewhat impaired by the hot plate she was holding. "Honey, really, I think we should go. I don't want you to be recognised."

"But my stuff. My cushions. My meatballs."

"I'll come back for them. I promise."

"You promise?"

Meg watched the eyes falling as the two blue carriers were placed on the ground with the same heartache as if Honey were leaving a child she could no longer afford. "They're just cushions and meatballs. I'll get you some more."

"But I've never bought cushions and meatballs before."

"We'll make it a yearly outing. Come on!"

Honey fell in step with the fast trot towards the exit. "Twice yearly at least."

Meg laughed at the rustling coming from the wind trousers. "Let's just get to the car, you crazy lady."

"I'm trying, but I think these trousers might spontaneously combust."

"Is that a promise?" asked Meg with a smile.

"Well, they're certainly sparking already."

****

Diana Diamond was sitting on Honey's lounge sofa, brown folder clutched in her hand. She'd informed her daughter of her evening arrival, but the day's antics at Velvet Villa had become too much to bear. Liza and Svetty's growlings could be heard on the whole upper level and Gerty and Dot's downward dogs were far too giggly for her cracking headache, an after effect of last night's martinis, essential in surviving yet another TV special featuring Nick and Nadia *Diamond*. She spat the surname in her head. The Diamond name was precious. It was treasured. It was hers. She'd been the star that exploded from nowhere. She'd been the one building the empire. She'd been the one protecting the name from any chinks and cracks, ensuring the sparkle always shone brightly. And, yes, while Nick and Nadia weren't real threats – most people understood they were just leeches riding their fifteen minutes of fame for all it was worth – Honey could quite possibly tarnish the name with this ridiculous desire to come out.

That had been the focus of last night's program: the labelling of sexuality and the possible consequence of this new-found fluid society. Dropping the folder onto the coffee table, Diana closed her eyes. Most women were bi-curious, weren't they? And most would experience the softer side of love at some point or other. Lesbian liaisons were certainly common among the stars. They weren't hidden. They weren't whispered about. They just happened. Like cocaine. Everyone saw it, did it and enjoyed it at one time or another. If Joe Public found that titillating or gossip-worthy then it only showed what dry little lives they lived. Diana pushed her head further into the cushions. Maybe the cocaine analogy was too far.

"Oh, Di," said Sofia, entering the room with a tray of tea. "You look pained."

The eyes were open and narrow. "Honey's going to label herself as a lesbian and spend the rest of her life known as just that, the lesbian singer, not Honey Diamond the singer who happens to like girls. You know what the media's like. They're vermin. They raise people up just to pull them down again."

"They've never pulled you down."

"I've played them. I know how to work the system. You don't go around making big statements about your private life. She'll never be able to take those words back."

Sofia sat next to her friend. "She wants to be that voice."

"Why?"

"She's brave." Sofia handed over a mug and sipped from her own. "I think we should support her on this one, Di."

"It'll be a shit storm."

"The piece will be good. The journalist's lovely. She came across as very thoughtful."

"Journalists aren't lovely and that paper's got one hell of a fireball coming their way. Do you know they've employed the owner of SlebSecrets, that site Honey wanted my men to take down?" She nodded towards the brown folder. "It's all in there and this so-called lovely journalist of Honey's will know her no doubt, passing her titbits I bet. They're probably all in it together."

"Meg's not like that. She was very sweet towards Honey and she seemed shy, respectfully professional."

"You've read it?"

"Read what?"

"My folder."

"Not yet."

"You said Meg."

"She goes by Margaret in the paper."

"I know she does."

"I think they'll be really good together. Bringing out the best in each other."

Diana placed the mug back on the tray. "What *are* you talking about, Sofia?"

"Honey's date today, with Meg."

"The dusty old dyke? She's not called Meg, and anyway, Liza's told me she'll sort it."

"She's not old. They've got to be similar ages."

"Who?"

"Honey and Meg."

Grabbing the folder, Diana yanked a photo from the front page. "This woman?"

Sofia studied the picture. "She wasn't wearing glasses today but, yes, that's Meg."

"This is Meg Rutherton!" Diana hit the photo with the back of her hand. "Of SlebSecrets!"

Sofia was frowning. "You've lost me."

"They traced her. My men. They traced them both." She pulled another photo from the folder; this time a pretty blonde pouted back at them. "Her flatmate, Jo Tustin. Probably not involved. Not clever enough. A make-up artist on set at *Reality Rules*. She might possibly pass on information, but she's not got the brains to run the site or phrase the posts." Diana was shaking her head. "SlebSecrets is the work of *this* woman." She slapped the picture of Meg once more. "You're telling me this woman is out with my daughter? Right now?!" Diana could feel the steam rising from the top of her head. It had been bad enough believing Honey was enamoured by some old hack, but *this*. This was far more horrific.

"Who knows?" asked Sofia with real concern.

"Just me and my men. I'd usually have them deal with everything, heaven knows how many sites we take down each month, but this was on Honey's insistence. I wanted her to make the call. I wanted her to decide if it was enough for the site to be down, or whether she wanted to ruin this bitch's life once and for all. Tell her workplace. Tell her family. Expose her online. Good god, she's probably out there right now stealing all Honey's secrets. What a sly little sleazeball."

"I really don't think—"

"She's using my daughter. That bitch is using my daughter!"

****

Slamming the car door, Honey looked over her shoulder at Meatball Woman, still on their tail. She glanced at Meg who was frantically trying to get the key in the ignition. The mixture of nervous excitement, hilarity and desire was too much to ignore. "Come here," she said, giggling as she leaned towards her driver, planting teasing lips on her neck.

Meg turned into the embrace. "Meatball Woman," she muttered through the kiss, still fumbling with the keys.

Opening her eyes, Honey spotted the plate looming in the rear view mirror. "Damn it, just drive."

The engine started, Meg hit the pedal and the Mini sped out of its parking bay. "You're crazy!"

"Me!?" Honey laughed as she realised this *had* quite possibly been the craziest, funniest, most memorable day of her life, and a new favourite role in Iris the bag lady. Yes, there had been an element of camping up the excitement with some of the products, but those cushions... and that rug: they were fantastic, and so cheap! The whole place was incredible and if she hadn't been able to name a designer or an era she was drawn to in the past then she certainly could now. Ikea. She liked Ikea. Ikea was her style of choice.

Looking across at Meg, Honey laughed. Her neck was covered in brown make-up, as was her face, her hands and part of her collar. "If you look like that then I dread to think what I look like." Pulling down the passenger mirror, Honey gasped. "Michael Jackson in *Thriller!*"

"You can shake my bones any day."

Honey turned and frowned. "Does that work?"

"Probably not." Meg was laughing. "I'm not smooth."

Reaching for Meg's leg, Honey rubbed slowly. "Oh, I think you are." She took a deep breath and decided to brave it. Yes, Meg had shied away from her advances yesterday, but everyone knew lesbian relationships were like dog years: one full day-date the equivalent of three weeks in the straight world. "Shall we go back to mine? Mother's not due till this evening, and I can't really go anywhere else looking like this."

"I wanted to take you to a penny arcade."

Honey moved her wandering fingers higher. "I'd love that... just not now." She turned in her seat to stare at the intriguing woman driving beside her. So unexpected, and so freeing, to have someone suddenly come into your life and be the answer to all of your questions. The randomness of the day being exactly the structure she needed. Normality. Realness. Fun. "Right now, I'd like you to take me home," she said with a smile.

"So I can fill your slot?"

Honey laughed. "Again, doesn't quite work."

"Sorry, no, I was thinking of the penny arcade."

"I know you were; I get you." She smiled. "We've got it. That shared wavelength, that ability to build each other's banter." The smile turned wicked. "And now that you mention it."

****

"I can't not mention it!" cried Diana, off the white sofa and pacing the lounge.

"It might not be her."

"Of course it's her! They went all out with this one. I wanted to show Honey how good my men were. How much she could benefit from their expertise."

Sofia, who had so far tried to remain the voice of reason, took a different tack. "So tell her. Ruin her day. Spoil any chance of romance."

"Romance?! With that twisted troll?! Over my dead body! Get them all here: Gerty, Dot, Liza, even Svetty sodding Sokolova. I want this outing witnessed by all! This warning shall be heard far and wide." She pulled up her collar and snorted the words like fire from her nose. "No one dares mess with a Diamond."

CHAPTER EIGHTEEN

Pulling into the gates of The Alderley this time was a new experience entirely. Old Sal from security had recognised Meg's little car and its passenger as she'd rounded the corner into the estate and the gate had been opened without even a consultation of clipboard or request for ID. Meg realised that her driving was also rather different. Usually, she crawled along the winding road past the huge houses, not wanting to disturb, pulling up alongside the tall hedge, not wanting to impose. But this time she'd sped through, scooted down the road and swerved into Honey's driveway with the bold resolve of a woman encouraged. Encouraged to go faster, encouraged to cut corners, encouraged to pull right up to the door. Honey's fingers had done the talking. Exploring her neck, her shoulders, down her spine and back onto her thighs, which were now thoroughly relaxed, manipulated and aroused.

Upon feeling her seatbelt sweep across her chest, Meg realised that Honey had unclipped it. In fact, she'd not only released her, she was now leaning across her legs to push open the driver's door.

"Go," came the soft voice.

Meg looked down at the face peeping up from her lap, another brown make-up stain now smearing her trousers. "We're not in The A-Team."

"I just want you inside," explained Honey, giggling as she hauled herself from the car. "Come on!"

Stepping out onto the gravel, Meg felt the hand in her own, the warm fingers pulling her towards the door. "Isn't Sofia in?"

"I'll advise a session in the spa if she is." Honey lifted her thumb to the fingerprint lock, discreetly hidden under an old fashioned key cover. "Sofia! Sofia! Are you home?"

Following her host into the entrance, Meg didn't even notice the wide expanse of hall, the beautiful long mirror next to the door or the carefully colour co-ordinated accessories and ornaments. Instead, she was up against the wall, Honey's lips pressed hard to her own. It was frantic. Heated. It was that rush of desire packed into one moment where nothing mattered but the emotion rising from inside, bursting out in the power of the kiss.

"Let me take you upstairs," came the groan.

"Not before I take you to town!" came the sudden snap from a suddenly present Diana Diamond.

Meg felt the shoulder squash in beside her, pressed against her own as Honey jumped into the same position, back against the wall, both women pinned there by the firing squad.

"Mother!" said Honey, hiding her face.

"Mrs Diamond," uttered Meg, aware they must look like two naughty children returning from a day in the mud.

"Both of you. In the lounge."

"Mother, that's not very polite." Honey stepped forward but kept her head low. "This is Meg."

"I know full well who she is. Lounge." A foot stamped sharply. "Now."

Lifting her eyes to Honey's, Meg shook her head. "I'm so sorry," she whispered.

"It's fine." Honey's voice was reassuring. "She'll no doubt tell us off for looking like this. And she might have a point. Can you imagine if I'd been papped looking this pooped!"

"Why are you laughing?"

"It's funny. Let mother have her moment." Honey signalled for them to follow her mother's rigid back view. "She likes to let off steam."

Meg stared back at the door. "I think I should go."

"Don't you dare! You'll win her over in no time. Trust me. Stay quiet. Nod respectfully and act like she's right." Honey smiled. "Just don't interrupt her. Ever."

"I really can't do this." Meg felt the sickness rising inside her, the taste of bile on her tongue, her legs betraying her in her moment of need.

"Mother's like this with everyone at the start. Setting her stall out, running through her ridiculous Diamond dynasty rules. She's possibly been on the slosh as well, so just roll with it."

Meg felt the fingers lock into her own, squeezing, guiding, moving her forward into the lounge. "Honey…"

"Shhh, It'll be fine." The gasp was one of genuine shock. "What? What's this?"

"Sit!" came the shout.

Meg lifted an eye to the room, full of people. There was Sofia, whom she recognised from the morning, sitting next to Liza, whom she recognised from Honey's events, who was squashed next to an unusually muscular woman who was spread across most of the sofa, causing the two elderly women to stand behind the group like long lost great aunties in a strange family portrait.

"Meg, this is Sofia; you know Sofia." Honey was talking quickly. "This is my PA Liza, and that's…" the voice tailed off. "I'm not sure who that is."

"Me Svetlana Sokolova. Svetty for shorts." The large lady pulled herself up and bowed with hands together as if ready for battle. "Yous heff been dirty bitches."

Liza interjected. "Wrong words."

"They be dirty. They be having the pom."

"The pom?" Honey frowned.

"The pom pom. The sexy time."

Honey continued. "Who is this, Mother?"

"She's my new holistic therapist and she's sensational. Look at Liza. Totally relaxed."

Meg followed all eyes in the room to the PA, famed for her strung out persona and brogues, neither of which were in evidence today.

Honey nodded. "Fine. Hello, Svetty." And lifting her hand to the back row she added, "Meg, this is Gerty and Dot. Mother's two very best friends."

Meg held her breath, no chorus of "Hi Meg," serving to relax her as it had this morning.

"Can I get anyone a drink?" asked Honey, continuing her bizarre introduction to a gathering she'd been given no part in.

"Just sit down and listen." Diana was pointing to the white pouffe, large enough to house another branch of the weird-looking family.

Meg followed with no option but to raise her arm and accept the lethal injection that was coming. This was it. This was the end. Her comeuppance. And all in front of an audience too. Studying the grain of the wooden floor encasing the room's central carpet Meg conceded her run had been good. Of course this was coming. She deserved what she got. Maybe Honey would forgive her? But to forgive she had to understand, and the more Meg thought about it the less she herself understood the reasons for her behaviour. Why *had* she thought it okay to spill other's secrets? Why *had* she enjoyed posting news first? Yes the motivation at the start had been the outing of the vile Eddy Elroyd. But she could have left it there. She should have left it there.

"You are gathered here today," the voice was preaching, "for two reasons. The first... is this." Diana Diamond pointed her finger towards the pouffe. "We cannot..." the collar was lifted, "as a collective..." the chin was raised, "have Honey..." the finger was pointed once more, "going out... looking... like... this."

Sofia cut in. "She looked different this morning. The make-up must have smudged."

"Yes." The Russian therapist agreed. "They be heffing the pom. The bonk bonk." The woman thrust forward in her seat. "They be doing the sex. The pervert."

"We have not been doing the sex!" gasped Honey. "And I am *not* a pervert."

Meg found it very difficult not to say *shame*. It would have been a funny comment had it not been for the family portrait, the lethal injection and the brown folder suddenly spotted on the coffee table.

"Svetty," Diana was back in control, "I appreciate your input, but I need silence." The long pause ensured all eyes were once again focused. "Honey needs our support. She needs our guidance. She needs to be told when it's *not* a good idea to slap on some ridiculous disguise, pull a sickie from work and take herself off to Ikea without her security. I've heard of this place. It sounds utterly dreadful." Diana reached for the document. "There is a fiend on the loose. A fiend who's taken great pleasure in pulling Honey down. In spilling her secrets for all to devour. In badmouthing. In shaming. In ridiculing her naive innocence. Imagine if she found out that Honey... the pervert... had been pomming."

Honey rolled her eyes. "Oh Mother, stop it. And what do you mean 'she'?"

"The owner of SlebSecrets." Diana narrowed her eyes and puckered her mouth. "She's a she."

"Really?" Reaching out for the document, Honey frowned. "Who was she?"

Diana clutched it tighter to her chest. "She was a lowlife cretin of the most repulsive form. A rat. A cockroach. A double-crossing snitch of a stool pigeon. Someone so sad that her little life stank with a stench worse than cat piss."

"Mother! Stop being so melodramatic."

"She was a gutter rat, a sewer shit, a friendless, heartless excuse for a human."

Meg could bear it no longer. Her eyes had been examining the same wooden knot on the floor during the spiel. She daren't look up, Diana's eyes sure to meet hers, pinning her with force, directing every insult right to her face.

"She was a nobody," continued the voice. "No friends, no life, no hope in hell of ever becoming someone herself, so she tore down the people who had. The successful. The righteous. But now her stinking little site's down." The bow was theatrical. "And there, ladies and Svetty, we've won."

Honey reached forward and grabbed the folder from her mother. "So who was she?"

Meg gasped. "No!"

The folder was opened. "It's empty." Honey shook it. "Mother, it's empty."

"I told you," Diana took a seat on the regal white armchair, "a nobody. An alone in the attic surrounded by porn sort of person. Called Sarah or something nondescript like that."

Honey stood up. "Well thank you all for coming. I'm glad we've seen the show and, fear not, I have no more off-the-cuff outing plans, so can we all go about our business now please."

The large therapist wiped the sweat from her brow. "What heff happens? This house heff pigeon or rat? Svetty Sokolova uncle do pest control."

Liza stood up. "Don't worry about it." She lowered her voice. "Even I was lost in that translation." The smile was suggestive. "Fancy a pom in the spa?"

The growl was deep. "Pervert pom?"

Liza's uncharacteristic giggle signalled the answer.

"We'll join you too," said Gerty and Dot, at last moving from their position behind the sofa. "And Di," said Gerty, "one of your more *out there* performances, but we enjoyed it all the same. Meg, nice to meet you."

Meg was sure she'd heard someone addressing her. Was she discovered? Was she exposed? The shock was all consuming, as if the movement of people around her was happening in another dimension where she was an onlooker, a mere observer. Her name again. She glanced up. Both elderly women were now peering down at her.

"We like the fact you got her dirty," said the one with the slightly fuller face.

"Dirty?"

"I'm Gerty," said the woman, "but yes, she's dirty. Our Honey needs some fun, so we'll leave you love birds in peace." The voice was lowered. "And ignore old Di. She does this every once in a while. Shows us who's boss. I'm sure Honey's told you to sit back and applaud. She'll be sharing sangria with you in no time. In fact, would you like a trip to the spa?"

"No, of course she wouldn't," said the other old lady. "She'll be wanting to get the rest of her inner thigh covered in make-up."

Meg glanced down at her trousers, indeed stained muddy brown. She lifted her eyes to the room, which was now slowly clearing. Liza and Svetty were limbs locked and guiding each other out of the hall with inappropriate fumblings and indistinguishable but unmistakably dirty words. Gerty and Dot had turned to shuffle behind them, leaving Honey to stand in front of her mother with arms folded and furious face.

Meg turned to Sofia who had been so smiley and warm this morning, but now seemed to be staring with what could be considered an air of displeasure. Or was she being paranoid? Meg tried to grasp hold of the situation. Did Diana and her crowd really not know? She tried to smile. Sofia stared back. Sofia definitely knew.

"Meg." Diana was talking loudly. "A word in the kitchen with me."

And so did Diana.

CHAPTER NINETEEN

Ensuring once more that the kitchen door was fully closed, Diana made her way, with purposeful hip swish, narrow eyes and high collar, towards the breakfast bar where Meg Rutherton was perched, rather uncomfortably, on one of the tall stools. It had taken just one sharp snap of "sit" to get her down, easy compared to how long it had taken to persuade Honey to let this odd-looking woman out of her sight. But her daughter had finally allowed it, for ten minutes only, conceding the time could be used to freshen up. Maybe that's what this Meg woman needed. A freshen up. Maybe it was the smudges of brown make-up making her look rather peculiar. Diana peered closer. Yes, she could *potentially* be pretty with some lashes and lippy and maybe a wave in her hair. She pulled back; she had just ten minutes to give this young upstart the fright of her life.

Meg spoke first. "How can I help?"

Diana's voice snapped with acidity. "Oh, don't you play the how can I help card with me! And how dare you talk first. Don't you know who I am? Don't you know where you are? Show some respect you sadistic little savage." Diana inhaled, relishing the red cheeks, dropped eyes and nervous fingers that were slowly shoved between the crossed legs on the stool. "You're Meg Rutherton. Meg Rutherton of SlebSecrets."

"Please." The eyes dared to lift in a look of repentant panic. "I was going to tell her. I've tried to tell her. I will tell her. Call her in now. I'll tell her myself. I can't live with what I've done. It's killing me. I need to be honest. Please, Mrs Diamond, I'm so very, very sorry."

Diana paused. She'd assumed the woman would try and lay blame with her flatmate, or deny culpability altogether. But no, here she was, fessing up. "Stop the snivelling. You're not worthy of sharing the same air as a Diamond. Do you know just how many creeps and psychos she has stalking her every second? I know. My men know. Honey, however, is completely oblivious, but they're out there, like you, thinking they know her, thinking they can have something with her, creating a fantasy world. You created your site but I've destroyed that, just like I'm going to destroy you: slowly, painfully."

"Please, Mrs Diamond, let me tell her myself. I'll tell her right now and I'll go. You won't ever have to see me again, and nor will she. I know I'm not worthy of being in her presence. She's the most remarkable woman I've ever met, and it's been brief, but I'll hold it in my heart forever. I know I don't deserve the moments I've shared, and it was selfish of me to try and steal them before revealing the horror of who I've been and what I've done, but she made me want to be a better person from the moment she opened that door – I knew; I just knew."

Diana wrinkled her nose in a mixture of disgust and puzzlement. "Oh, this is even worse. No one likes a snitch. Now keep quiet and listen." Lifting her collar she nodded; she'd assert her authority once more. "You're going to do exactly as I say."

"But it must come from me, it must—"

"Silence! Eyes down!" Pausing for the obedience, which happened quickly, Diana smiled at the power already held in her hand. This jumped-up excuse for a journalist would be in her pocket in no time at all. She stopped, taking a moment to look at the quiet repentance. She had to admit it was all rather admirable, the idea of honesty, but that wasn't the plan; the plan was much bigger than letting a silly cat out of a bag. Who actually cared that this woman had written a few gossipy posts? She didn't. God knows, she understood how the system worked: journalists being polite to your face but backbiting behind the scenes, employees doing the same, false friends selling their stories. No, this woman's crime wasn't horrific, especially compared with some of the things you'd find written online, and if Honey hadn't mentioned the site it certainly wouldn't have been one her men would have tackled. Slebsecrets was more showbiz than sleaze, a UK Perez, and everyone liked his barbed comments, didn't they? Diana focused herself. "So," she began, "I was ready to tell her, of course I was. I'm not having my daughter hounded by someone just after the latest scoop."

"It's not like that."

"Silence." She leaned forward. "You could be useful to me. To Honey. She's confused. She's naive." The pause was thoughtful. "She needs guidance."

The voice came slowly. "In what way?"

"This piece you're writing." Diana fingered her hair and paced once more. "Make it neutral."

"But Honey wants to use the lesbian label."

The staring face was back. "Make. It. Neutral."

"But—"

"Oh for god's sake, Meg. You know what this'll do to her career. There is absolutely no need for *any* label of *any* sort. Write the piece. Make her see sense." The smile was wide. "And that way our little secret will stay just that. Our. Little. Secret."

"But I've already written the article and I've already come to the conclusion—"

"You, you little upstart." The finger was pointing. "You don't come to any conclusions," the point got fiercer, "apart from this one." Diana straightened and nodded in decision. "She doesn't get labelled and you don't reveal your identity."

Meg frowned. "But your men, and whoever else you paid to hunt me down and expose me?"

"Oh, stop with the flapping. My men are already working on their next case. The only person you need worry about is me and, like I said, you scratch my back and I'll scratch yours."

"But I already—"

"Oh Mother, you're not coercing Meg into another of your PR stunts are you?" asked Honey, entering the room all fresh-faced with hair now tamed in a bun, soft tracksuit restoring her youth.

"You know me, dear, always looking for that outside opportunity."

"Don't listen to her," said Honey. "She already has a team of people ensuring she's papped at the places to be." She looked at Meg. "Would you like a shower?"

Diana answered for her. "*The Beacon* just called. They need her at work. Probably got wind she was cavorting around a furniture store instead of writing her article." She nodded. "Get going now, Meg. You don't want me to report you, do you?"

"Oh Mother."

Meg stood up. "It's fine. I should be making a move."

"Mother, really, what have you done?"

"Nothing," said both co-conspirators simultaneously.

Meg continued. "Honestly, I should head off. I need to finish my article. That way I'll be able to enjoy tomorrow without worrying about work."

"You're still coming? She hasn't put you off?"

"Of course I haven't," said Diana, reaching out to squeeze Meg's shoulder. "There's something special about this one."

Honey looked shocked. "Really?"

"It was lovely to meet you, Mrs Diamond."

"Ma'am's fine."

"Don't be ridiculous, Mother. Meg, you can call her Diana, and I'm thrilled you're getting along. I told you she'd set out her stall, didn't I? What was it? Don't hurt my daughter? Don't mess with the dynasty?"

Diana cut in. "I just told her she'd look better with a wave in her hair and maybe some lashes."

"Oh Mother, really! And Meg, you don't have to go. Freshen up here; let's go for some food?"

"Honestly, they've only given me three days to write the piece and I said you could check it first, so I really need to crack on."

"You'll bring it in the morning?" asked Diana. "I'll be here."

"No, you won't, Mother."

"Sofia and I have a day trip planned. I'll cast my eye over it too."

Honey gasped. "Why not have Meg read it aloud in front of the girls when I'm getting done up? I know! Let's ask Liza and Svetty Slick-A-Lik, or whoever the hell that woman was, to join the crowd too!"

"Sarcasm doesn't suit you, darling." Diana paused. "But that's not a bad idea."

Honey looked stormy. "It's *my* story and *I'll* have the final say."

Meg bowed her head. "So I'd better make it good."

"Oh, I'm sorry." Honey was by her side to escort her from the room. "I'm sure I'll love whatever you write, and thank you so much for today; I've had the most magic of times. I only hope tomorrow's day in the life of Honey Diamond can live up to the hype."

"Off you go then," said Diana, crowding them both at the door.

"Mother, please!"

Diana watched with interest. What on earth was her daughter's fascination with this woman? She was gazing with warmth, with longing, oh good god that looked like desire. Spinning on her heels, Diana marched back to the lounge. "Miss Rutherton, I'll see you tomorrow."

"She likes you," said Honey with a whisper.

"Don't count on it," came the matriarch's parting shot.

✳✳✳✳

Meg got back into her car dejected, once again leaving The Alderley with an awful feeling of torment. The same feeling she'd had after the interview, after the meal and now after the most perfect of days. Could Diana be trusted? Should she be trusted?

Meg sighed. She shouldn't even be entertaining this ridiculous plan, but what choice did she have? Diana was right. The lesbian label wasn't necessary, but she already knew this; it had become apparent last night as the words flowed from her fingers the minute she'd pulled the plug on her site. Her writer's block lifting the instant she removed her past sins. She'd been able to sit there at her desk writing words that were true to Honey's story without categorising her in a manner that would precede every further mention of her name. Lesbian singer, Honey. Gay girl gets gig. The papers would do this. Everyone in the industry knew they'd do this. She'd wanted to save Honey. So she'd written the article her way, the same way Diana had just so forcefully demanded, but now it would look like she was doing it to save her own skin.

Putting her car into gear, she pulled out of the drive. Could she tell Honey? If she did, she'd be telling two tales on her mother. The first that she knew her daughter was dating the sadistic sleaze, as she'd put it, from SlebSecrets, and the second that she'd deemed it more important to abuse this knowledge with manipulation than have her daughter in the know. Meg shook her head. She couldn't come between mother and daughter.

Passing under the security barrier and through the gates, she tried to smile at old Sal. This was all going too fast. Maybe this was a good thing. Maybe this took the dilemma out of her hands. Maybe she could finally be herself without constantly worrying the truth would come out. Diana had been the unknown. The ticking time bomb. But she was keeping quiet and she certainly looked like a woman of her word. She wouldn't want Honey knowing she'd used a situation to advance the march of her ridiculous Diamond dynasty brand at the cost of her daughter's integrity, would she? Because that's what it was: Honey's integrity. She deserved to know the truth.

Pressing down on the accelerator, Meg let the analytical part of her brain kick in. Utilitarianism. When in doubt, question what's for the greater good. Tell Honey about her past and she, Meg, would suffer. Diana would suffer too. Tell Honey about Diana's demands and Honey would suffer, and so again would Diana. Stay quiet and everyone's happy.

Stopping at a red light she suddenly remembered. Sofia.

****

Sofia had waited until they had the house at The Alderley to themselves before settling down next to her goddaughter on the sofa. This was a delicate line and she'd have to tread carefully. There had been many times before where she'd kept secrets between the two women: Diana her dear friend and Honey the daughter she'd always dreamt of. It was difficult not treading on Diana's toes and her loyalties were often hard to get right. She never wanted to come between the two women, but in her eyes Honey's happiness always had to take priority. If Honey wasn't aware of Diana's meddling and it had no real impact on her personal world, then she could let it go, but this was different, this *was* Honey's personal world.

"So," she said, "Meg."

The voice was gushing. "Isn't she just wonderful? Who'd have thought to take me to Ikea? Have you been? We must go. There's everything, absolutely everything you could possibly want and need to kit out the whole house."

Sofia laughed. "You sound more enamoured by Ikea than the journalist."

"Oh, she's much more than a journalist; she's my one."

"What?" The frown was deeply furrowed. "How can you say that, dear, after only one date?"

"Love at first sight. I believe."

"You've always wanted to believe, dear."

"If it was a simple want then it would have happened before. I see so many beautiful people in my line of work. I've..." the cheeks reddened slightly, "I've had so many come-ons from people wanting to use me to further themselves, or from fans thinking we're destined to find love with each other. I could easily have found love if that's what I was looking for, but I wasn't, it's just happened."

"What's happened, dear?"

"I'm falling."

"In love?"

"I'm falling in lust, in desire, in emotional connection, in intellectual connection and yes maybe in love. It happens, Sofia. I opened the door and I saw her, and she saw me, and neither of us have stopped looking ever since."

"Ever since yesterday?"

"Oh Sofia, you're mocking me."

"No, dear, I'm not. I'm sorry. You carry on."

"It's just that feeling of knowing. Knowing you want to be in their presence. Knowing you want to interact with them. To understand them. To complete them."

"And if you get to know her and don't like what you find?"

"Then I guess it runs its course." The eyes were wide. "But I don't think it will. People connect, Sofia, in many different ways, but sometimes, just sometimes, you find someone who sparks your soul. Someone who makes you want to live life by their side."

"Well dear," the words were honest, "if you think Meg's that person then you hold on with everything you've got."

Honey's arms reached out and wrapped themselves around the narrow shoulders. "Oh Sofia, I love you so much."

"And I love you, dear." She paused. "Just make sure this Meg loves you too."

"That's just it, it's like I'm the huntress, I'm the one pursuing her and the fact she's unsure makes me see her truth; this isn't about who she thinks she can become by being with me. I think she's scared, but maybe because she knows it could be something really special."

"Maybe."

"I like her, Sofia. She makes me happy and she makes me smile. I want to see where this goes."

Sofia nodded. That was all she needed to hear. "You have fun then, dear. You deserve some light in your life."

CHAPTER TWENTY

Standing once again in Honey Diamond's kitchen, this time in front of a crowd of people, Meg read aloud the article she'd poured her heart and soul into, knowing her words would be judged and dissected, yet confident she'd done the right thing regardless of any response. Honey had so desperately wanted to address the rumours about her sexuality, to show she wasn't hiding, but a direct labelling wasn't needed. Meg realised if she'd been honest with herself when writing those ridiculous posts for SlebSecrets it was simply her own vested interest that had been so determined to force Honey out. She'd wanted her own personal romanticising to have legs, to have potential, the first step knowing for sure that Honey was gay. Well she was, but that shouldn't be the screaming headline in this piece.

Diana, although going about it the wrong way, had been right; it simply wasn't necessary. But she herself had come to that same conclusion before yesterday's raging ultimatum. This is how she'd written the article the previous evening. These were her words. Not Diana's. All the community needed was visibility. Like Cara Delevingne pictured with her girlfriend, St Vincent. No lesbian labels were announcing their love. Likewise Kristen Stewart, dating women to see where things went.

Meg continued to read. She'd phrased the article in a manner that answered the questions without labelling the terms. There was no omission or denial, but likewise there was no declaration or affirmation. It was a well-written piece about Honey Diamond's personal life, a glimpse into her world; mostly work related, yes, but touching occasionally on that private desire to find love. Meg paused, holding everyone's attention before the final line. "Honey's the heroine of her story, and the magic of love's hers to find."

The kitchen filled with "ahhhhs" and the clapping built quickly once it became obvious the reading was over.

"It's clear what I'm saying, isn't it?" asked Honey. "Even though I haven't directly been labelled?"

"Absolutely!" said Diana, heartily applauding. "And you're not a piece of produce anyway!"

Gerty nodded. "No sensationalised slogans."

"Girl crushes are fashionable," added Dot.

Liza continued the support. "And men are such a let-down these days. The public will understand you romanticising the fairer sex. Hurrah, Meg, what a well written piece."

"Sofia, what do you think?" Honey was still frowning.

"It's lovely. It's sensitive, and it gives the reader that insight while keeping you at the safe distance a Diamond should be kept."

"Maybe I wanted to be a woman of the people."

"And join social media?" scoffed Diana, "and be called upon for even more interviews, charity patronages, discussion panels, quotes on anything even remotely related to sexuality?" She nodded. "Your song spoke the truth. This article speaks the truth. It doesn't matter who you're attracted to and you can go have your picture taken with this one for all I care." She slapped Meg on the back. "Like Dot said, it's all rather fashionable right now." She smiled. "But at least the headline won't label your love."

Svetty Sokolova, who'd been listening in a line at the breakfast bar with Liza, Heidi, Louisa and Caitlyn scrunched up her eyes. "Heff you never been driving the cars?"

Honey turned to her guest. "Delayed and somewhat random, but that's what you got from the piece?"

The Russian woman continued. "And why you not be purchasing the new sofa?"

"In my music room?" Ignoring the strange inquisition, she turned to Meg. "It's really sweet how you used that. I like the idea of people picturing me writing lyrics on my childhood sofa."

"Fleas!" continued the voice. "Rats, pigeons, now you heff fleas if you not change of the sofa!"

Liza took hold of the large lady's arm. "Honey, I'll be with you this evening. You can hold your own at the drama day today, can't you?"

"What?" said Honey with mock shock. "Where's Liza? What have you done with her? You're a different woman entirely!"

"I told you," nodded Diana. "My holistic therapist is worth every penny."

Honey frowned as the PA giggled her way from the room. "Does she charge by the hour?"

"I don't care. A happy Liza's worth its weight in gold to us all."

"True!" said Caitlyn, encouraging Honey back to the stool in the centre of the room. "We've got a breather again and it's beautiful!"

"Let's just make sure we stick to the schedule today, shall we?" added Heidi. "Tammara's coming at ten."

"It's ten," said Louisa.

Meg watched the clucking with a growing feeling of warmth. This was Honey's life and she felt privileged to bear witness. Everyone was happy. She'd done the right thing. She'd emailed a copy over to her editor and was hoping the response would be as positive. The rumour mills were still dissecting every single line of Honey's leaked song, but this article should offer answers. Yes, there had been no direct labelling, but that was the way most stars played it these days anyway. People could, and would, read between the lines.

Meg spotted the encouraging eyes of Diana and smiled at the nod of congratulations, responding with a nod of her own. The eyes she didn't notice were Sofia's, watching her with careful, cautious discretion.

****

Following Honey out of the house, Meg heard the ping of her phone. An email from her editor. She scanned quickly. It said the piece was great, exactly what *The Beacon* was famed for, with the real win being the story behind the story. She typed back quickly: The fairytale analogies? The response was instant. *Yes. Honey's world's not real. Real relationship rules don't apply.* Puzzling at the comment, Meg looked up at her host, now hurrying towards the executive car in the driveway. But that's what Honey wanted, wasn't it? A real relationship. Could it ever work? Would it ever work? Meg had to admit that so far she'd only ever seen Honey in her relaxed, day-off mode. Maybe today would open her eyes. Maybe today would show her who this woman actually was.

"Your chariot, my lady." Honey had edged in front of a perplexed looking female chauffeur, stealing her role as she pulled open the door.

Meg smiled. This woman was perfect. "Why thank you."

Honey hopped in after her. "No, thank *you*."

"What for?"

"The piece." The smile was wide. "You took a different direction to the one I was expecting, but it's beautiful. It wasn't shouty or crass, it was quietly unassuming, like you."

"Would you like the divider up?" asked the voice from the front.

"Tam, this is Meg. Meg, Tam." The face was cheeky. "And do you know what? I think yes, this time we would."

Smiling at the driver, Meg watched as the divider clicked into place, the smart glass tinting black, casting the back of the car into a soft, romantic light. That's what it felt like to her anyway. Honey was probably used to the leather seats, dreamy atmosphere and the gentle music that started to play.

"Too much?" asked Honey.

"The music?" Meg could feel her heart rate rising. She was alone, in the back of a luxury car, with Honey Diamond, amorous lighting and Maria Carey's number one hits, a better romantic fantasy than she'd ever previously created. "It's perfect," she said, ignoring the desire to pinch herself and check this was real.

"This is it now. Your work's all finished. You're here as my friend."

"And I'm relaxed. For the first time, I honestly am." Meg wasn't lying. Yes, her heart rate was going nineteen to the dozen, but the feelings she'd had of impostership, of unworthiness? They'd ebbed slowly away. Meg stared at the woman next to her, privately addressing that one lingering doubt, that deep-seated guilt about running SlebSecrets. She inhaled. It was more than just her now: Diana was involved, and her site was a sin of the past. Everyone had those, didn't they? Hidden from partners, hidden from people they were trying to impress. She stayed silent, letting herself fully accept where her train of thought had led her. She *was* trying to impress Honey. She wanted this woman to like her as much as she liked this woman herself. She wanted her. She wanted her so very much.

"I feel it too," said the voice.

Meg leaned forward, lifting her lips to Honey's.

The kiss was one of perfection.

Soft. Emotional. Honest.

CHAPTER TWENTY ONE

The loud rap on the glass divider pulled both women from their embrace. Meg was breathless, Honey was ruffled, and both parties were frantically blinking. Honey somehow managed to gather herself first. "We can't be here already?" she said, squinting out at their surroundings, wondering how an hour of kissing could pass by so quickly. Catching sight of her reflection she gasped. "My hair!"

"And your shirt," added Meg, helping to straighten it.

Honey smiled at the gesture, quickly realising that her guest was in need of some smoothing of her own. "You sort my hair, I'll sort yours."

Both women lifted their hands to the other, gently taming the wayward locks with soft fingers brushing until coming to rest on warm cheeks, the look of desire back in their eyes, their grasps growing tighter as their lips drew together once more. Honey smiled into the kiss. Meg was open, receptive; more than that, she was leading. This woman, who'd shied away from all initial contact, was now leading. She was leading and pushing for more. Honey gathered her strength and pulled back. "We need to go in."

"Can't we stay here?"

Honey looked at the intense eyes. "I had yesterday off. I can't do it again today. They're relying on me."

"What is this again?"

Honey read the eyes. This woman wasn't interested in the drama day that was planned, or the idea of a Hollywood script. This woman was interested in her. She smiled. That was all she'd ever really wanted, someone to see her, not her life or her work, just her. "It's a drama class."

"But you've acted for years."

"Yes, in the West End. I think the production company are worried I may be too jazz hands."

Meg laughed. "It's a singing *When Harry Met Sally* though, isn't it?"

"Yes." Honey paused. "Where did you hear that?"

"I'm not sure. It's getting lots of column inches, your first Hollywood role."

"Well today's just a back to basics, build your confidence, improv drama session."

"I'll enjoy watching it."

Honey shook her head. "Oh no."

"I have to wait outside?"

"Oh no."

"What do you mean?"

"You, Meg, my lovely, are living my life." She smiled as wide as she could. "I sat on your Svlasta sofa yesterday so today you're sharing my circle."

****

Meg studied the seated circle of five before lowering herself awkwardly into the chair next to Honey's. She shifted her weight on the plastic, frowning once more at their surroundings. How could a huge production company haul Honey Diamond to a run-down studio in the middle of nowhere, with grey plastic school chairs, a battered vending machine and dog-eared posters featuring the BAGA gymnastics scheme? "Are you sure this is the right place?" she whispered.

Honey nodded. "There's Bernard Remi."

"Who?" Meg followed Honey's eyes to the man sitting in the corner of the room. "Why does he get to watch?"

"He's the producer."

"Never heard of him." She flicked her eyes around the other people sitting in the circle. "And who's this crowd?"

"No idea. Bernard's renowned for his inventive methods. Actors swear by him. I'm sure we'll find out."

Straightening in her seat, Meg cringed. She'd always been crap at acting, lucky to get the role of cat or dog in the year seven drama class. She even remembered a lesson spent playing the pavement while the other more assertive girls in her group acted out an argument scene behind her. She smiled to herself. Those were the days: beginning secondary school with every subject offered up to you, no worry of real exams or assessments, just knowing you could spend an hour shuffling round as a cat or a dog, or being the best tarmac you could ever possibly be. She stopped herself. This wasn't year seven drama class and she wasn't eleven years old. This was a script from Hollywood. This was A-list celebrity meets A-list producer, refreshing A-list acting skills no doubt, but who this bunch of seated weirdos were she had no idea.

Looking around at the gathering, Meg felt even more unworthy. Not only was she there as a tag-along, but also she didn't seem to have anything captivating or memorable about herself, unlike the others. Her jeans, boots and jumper were no match for the man opposite, kitted out in grey dance leggings, Crocs and an impossibly large-knit polo-necked shrug. The woman next to him was striking as well with a large and shining pan face, highlighted by her scraped back hair and painted on eyebrows. Eager was the word that sprung to mind. Meg dropped her eyes, not wanting to connect, unsure of the protocol in such situations. No one was talking. It was as if an air of impending competition was passing between them in the stilted silence.

Of course these actors would know who Honey was, but maybe this was one of Bernard Remi's tactics, to take Honey out of her comfort zone. Or maybe these actors felt Honey, the singer, shouldn't be here. Or maybe they weren't even actors, maybe they were random members of the public plucked from the street, or the parish council in the case of the woman to Honey's left with white ruffled collar, lifted nose and precisely pinned hair. A Mrs Peacock character from Cluedo. Meg turned her attention to the man completing their circle. Wolverine. The man looked like Wolverine, with dark hair sprouting from all over his face. She couldn't resist the temptation to glance at his nails. They were long. She shuddered. Nothing worse than a man with long nails.

"Stop staring," whispered Honey.

"What are we meant to be doing?"

"We wait for instruction."

"It's been ten minutes already."

"Just relax and enjoy yourself."

Twisting her shoulder, Meg shielded them from the rest of the circle. "Enjoy what? Can't you feel the tension?"

"That's called the pre-emptive artistic atmosphere. Oh, here he comes! Here we go! Isn't this exciting?"

Looking up at the middle-aged man swishing his way into their circle, Meg felt anything but excited. The twist of his hip was complementing the twist of his handlebar moustache. The droop of his wrist, although working well with the drainpipe trousers and red beret, were taking her further away from any sense of excitement and right into the horror of unease. She shouldn't be here. She wasn't an actor or a pop star, she was a guest, and one who should be watching. Rising from her seat she kept her head low, planning a quick escape from the circle.

"Seet!" said the French accent. "Task one. Srow yourself into a bizarre stance. Make a bizarre noise. Next person reflect and invent. Commence."

Meg dropped back into her seat. If there was no escape then she certainly wasn't going to go first. She peeped up as the swish took the man back out of the circle, the twist planting him on the chair in the corner.

"*Maintenant*," came the command.

Meg tried to fold in on herself. Who would go first? She certainly wouldn't. And Honey didn't appear to be moving either. A strange trilling noise made her look up. Of course. Eager pan face was up, performing an arabesque in the centre of the circle, trilling like a sparrow. Leggings man jumped up next to her, reflecting the move, only lifting his leg slightly higher, trilling until she sat down. Meg couldn't bear it. She couldn't trill, and she certainly couldn't lift her leg like that. She watched as Leggings' pose morphed into a cherub-like statue, shooting an imaginary arrow with an accompanying whistle. But it wasn't just a regular whistle, rather it was a dynamic, multi-faceted whistle that actually sounded like an arrow in flight until it was silenced by distance. Meg gasped. She couldn't do a whistling arrow either. Old Wolverine could though, repeating the sound and action before dropping to his stomach, with arms, head and feet curved upwards, fingers together and pointing, accentuating the long nails as he clicked like a dolphin. Meg looked at Mrs Peacock; no way she'd get her spine to arch that far backwards.

Yes, and there she was, Mrs Peacock, balancing on her stomach, clicking like a dolphin. Oh good god, who were these people, and what could she do? It was Honey next and then it was her. Surely Honey would do something simple? She held her breath as Honey entered the circle, copying Mrs Peacock's frog-shaped pose with accompanying ribbit before rising up like a ballerina into a beautiful balance with a harmonious "tring" reminding Meg of a delicate music box.

Shunting forward on legs that didn't work properly she hoisted her arms up into the balance as best she could tringing in a slightly strange key, but tringing all the same. Honey stepped away. The circle was hers. All eyes were watching, staring, judging. What the hell could she do? Catching sight of the BAGA gymnastics poster, she gasped. A star jump! She jumped... slightly, legs wide, arms out, hands doing some strange jazz shake of their own. She paused. The noise! What noise could she do? Everyone was waiting. Anticipating. Meg felt her tongue drop from her mouth and couldn't help the raspberry that escaped. It was a half-hearted raspberry. A wet, half-hearted raspberry. Pan face didn't get up. No one was copying her move. She stood there a moment longer, her jazz hands waning somewhat as her eyes dropped to the floor.

"Seet!" came the shout. "Very telling. Very, very telling." The drainpipes were back up and twisting. "Exactly as Bernard expected."

Folding back into her seat, Meg stared at pan face. How did she know the game had ended? She could at least have tried to copy her move. It wasn't horrific. It might have been a slightly obvious jump into the circle and ta-dah, but still. Meg felt Honey's hand on her knee. She looked down at the fingers. Were they squeezing with encouragement or squeezing with despair? Meeting her eyes, Meg tried to signal apology. She was doing her best; she'd never claimed to be Scarlett O'Hara or Clarice Starling. She smiled. She would like to be the Thelma to Honey's Louise though. With a nod of determination, she turned back to the beret. This one she'd do better. This time she'd excel.

"Bernard wants to see what you are doing." The hands were expressive. "Mime simple activity. Group shall guess what you do."

Pan face was up, swiping what looked like a sword in front of herself.

"Filleting salmon," said Mrs Peacock.

As if she's filleting bloody salmon, thought Meg.

"I am indeed," said pan face with a bow.

Yes because everyone fillets bloody salmon with a samurai sword, don't they. And what's this now? The ruffled collar of Mrs Peacock was lifted along with the nose as the fingers strummed at chest height.

Tickling your girlfriend's tits, thought Meg.

"Playing the harp," said the man in the leggings.

Of course she was, nodded Meg, *and what are you going to do? Blowtorch a crème brulee?*

The man stood still, with thumb and forefinger on chin.

Ha, she thought! *He's stuck. He's frozen! He's fluffed it at the final hurdle.*

"You're observing art," announced Wolverine.

The bow was graceful, as was the dance back out of the circle.

Meg huffed. Oh, this was all so ridiculously pretentious. What would Wolverine do now? Open a hipster café in Shoreditch? She watched as he bent and offered out his hand with a look of sheer benevolence.

"Feeding the poor," she said, without thinking.

"That I am."

Meg cringed. She'd not meant to say it aloud, and as if anyone would actually act out feeding the poor! She stood up. Honey was watching. Remi Bernard was watching. Big old pan face was watching. She'd do something good. She'd do something better. She squatted down and lifted her hands in front of herself.

Pan face tutted. Mrs Peacock looked away. "Rather crude," sniffed Leggings.

"What?" Meg shrugged. "I'm on the Orient Express reading an Agatha Christie."

Honey patted the chair beside her.

"I was!" continued Meg.

"It's okay." The whisper was kind. "I think we're moving on now."

Meg looked towards the swish. Why did they always stop on her turn? "Let me try another?" she said.

"Non! Bernard have one final task, then maybe you seet with me."

Slumping back in her seat Meg looked around at the circle. It wasn't her fault they'd thought she was taking a shit. Fine, back to basics with this one. She listened hard. It was called "I am". The first person apparently had to announce what they were and the second person had to become something related, and the third one and so on. Oh, and here she was now, surprise surprise, pan face back up, first in the circle.

"I am a tree!" she declared, eyebrows rising even higher as she waved her arms like branches.

Leggings was straight up next to her. "I am the wind, blowing your leaves." He started to prance.

Wolverine joined the duo. "I am the sun, softening your branches."

Mrs Peacock swirled among the bodies. "And I am your scent summoned up by the sun."

Honey joined in the scene, forming a heart over her head with her arms. "I am the lover's carving, in the bark of the tree."

Meg shuffled forward, bent down and flopped onto the floor. "And I am the pavement built over your roots."

CHAPTER TWENTY TWO

The atmosphere in the back of the car was somewhat stiff to say the least. Honey hadn't taken kindly to Meg's character assassination of the people in the circle and Meg hadn't appreciated Honey's accusation that she was deliberately messing around. She wasn't. She'd been trying. Yes, after the pavement mime, which was deemed by pan face to have lowered the artistic ambition of the scene, her enthusiasm had waned, but she'd been trying, she honestly had. Staring out of the window, Meg decided to take a different tack.

"It's like the kid in the class who gets labelled as a problem," she said. "They're very often not messing around for messing around's sake. They're behaving in a manner that distracts attention from the fact they're failing, or struggling, or in my case not up to the job."

"No one was judging you, Meg."

"Mrs ruffled collar was, and so was Mr big balls in those bloody dance leggings."

"There you go again. *You've* just judged *them*."

"Oh come on, Honey, you can't seriously be that prim and proper?"

"Is that how you view me?"

Meg sighed, thankful that the glass divider was up and tinted. "No, I'm sorry." She shrugged, unsure of how open to be. "I guess I just feel inferior. No matter where I am, no matter what I do, I never feel good enough, and that's bound to get worse being around someone as perfect as you, and I mean perfect in the most genuine sense of the word. There's nothing I could possibly dislike about you. You're incredible, and I can get grumpy and sulky sometimes."

Honey reached out for the bottom lip that was protruding and gently pushed it back up. "You're writing for the nation's most established broadsheet. You're talented and successful and—"

"They liked my background at HotBuzz, that's all. They needed to step into the twenty-first century and I ticked that box."

"Don't be so hard on yourself. You just need to be nicer."

Meg straightened in her seat. "You think I'm not nice?"

"I think you judge easily and I think you're too quick to look for the negatives, for the bad in people. Geraldine said she missed you in the afternoon activities."

"Who's Geraldine?"

"The lady with the up-do."

"Cluedo piece? Mrs Peacock?"

Honey laughed. "See!"

"That's funny though, isn't it?"

"No. You shouldn't be mean about people."

"How can you *not* be? How can you spend a day in that room without rolling your eyes at their ridiculousness? Filleting the salmon? Feeding the poor? I mean come on! Who are these people?"

"They're people I have to deal with every day. The industry's renowned for its eccentricities."

"So you just turn a blind eye to all the bollocks?"

"I have to."

"Aha! You admit it's bollocks then!"

"I didn't say that." Honey laughed. "But this is my world, Meg, and I've learnt to take everything with a pinch of salt. Nothing surprises me anymore." She smiled. "I've honestly seen it all. And who am I to judge?"

"You're Honey Diamond who gets everything right!"

"So I'm right when I say you need to be nicer?"

Meg took the comment in the kind spirit it was offered. After all, they did say you should be with someone who brought out the best in you, who helped you be the best version of yourself you could ever possibly be. Honey would do that. From this one small conversation she knew that Honey would do that. Looking back out of the window, she spoke again. "I'm never going to let you meet my flatmate, Jo. She makes me look like St Sheila from Stockport."

"Was there a St Sheila from Stockport?"

"No, but I didn't want to use Mother Teresa in case you didn't approve."

"I just want you to be you."

"What if I'm not a nice person?"

"Meg, look at me. You are. You're a very nice person." Honey shifted her position on the backseat. "A very, very nice person."

Meg's eyes dropped to the lips that were smiling, encouraging. She knew she wasn't a bad person as such, but she wasn't as good as Honey deserved. She could be better. She wanted to be better. She'd try harder to be positive and always look for the good in people; it would be a challenge, but she'd try. Thinking again of her flatmate, Meg realised there'd have to be changes; she'd have to call Jo out on her sniping, even if booze was involved. Usually she'd just nod and accept it, knowing the apology would arrive the next day, but it brought her down, or worse, it sometimes encouraged her to rise up and join in.

She didn't want to be the person she became around Jo, she wanted to be the person she became around Honey. Honey thought she was someone special, and no one had ever thought that before. Her, Meg Rutherton, special. Lifting her hands, she drew Honey's mouth closer, kissing with ambition, not pulling Honey's perfection that little bit nearer the dark side, but instead drawing herself into the light.

****

Honey moaned at the contact. Meg's lips so soft, yet her tongue so searching. It was the kind of kiss that aroused you, that turned you on. She wanted more, she needed more. Pulling Meg closer, she drew their chests together, instantly feeling the heat of two bodies intensely attracted to one another. She groaned into the connection. It was as if they'd been magnets, sensing each other's presence but not fully realising the power of the invisible pull until it was too late, now locked together, not easily prised apart. She lifted her hands to Meg's neck, running her fingers through her hair until she had a hold of her head, forcing her closer, tasting her deeper.

"Wait."

Meg's words stopped her. "What?" she gasped.

Meg's eyes were glancing around the car. "We can't, not here."

"We can."

"You have?"

Honey shrugged. She might have got a bit hot and bothered in the car that one time with She-Ra, and that other time with Liza's friend Mandy, but nothing this fierce or this fiery. Maybe Meg was right. She wanted her naked. She needed her naked. The thought flushed over her in a blaze of arousal. She wanted this quirky, slightly awkward, yet totally intriguing woman, with her dark stirring eyes and nervous self-worth, all alone to herself. Yes, there had been an instant attraction on the day of the interview, opening the door and accepting that feeling, yet the draw had intensified with each further meeting. The not knowing had driven her desire to find out. Who was this woman? Why was she so distant? Impenetrable? Because she was. She had been. Meg had almost jumped out of her skin at the post-curry come on, and again at the kiss by the car. Yes, it could have been the interruption by Pia, but there'd been a definite wall. A wall that was slowly crumbling away. She liked her. Looking into her eyes, Honey knew she daringly liked her. Because it had been daring, to be so full on. To seize the moment. To try and grab this feeling and run.

Honey smiled, enjoying the emotion for what it was. It was the acceptance that for whatever reason she wanted this woman. That mysterious feeling of lust. Why them? Why had the universe thrown them together? Why had the sparks started to fly? She didn't really believe in fate or a pre-determined path, but she did believe in this feeling. This invisible bond. Two people knowing they wanted each other, and no matter the circumstance or situation it would happen, eventually. "Tonight," she said with a smile, "after *Britain Sings*, you'll come back to mine?"

The look was perplexed. "You want me to come with you?"

"Of course. This is my day."

"But you'll be on stage."

"And you'll be front row."

Honey watched with interest. On the odd occasion that she had invited people as guests in the audience they'd crowed and wailed, overcome with the idea of celebrity, the shoulders they'd rub, the stories they'd tell. But not Meg. Meg was sitting there, cogs whirring once more. "You can come to my dressing room first, help me get changed. I must try and beat Gwen tonight. She's been crowned best dressed the past two weeks."

"I'm not sure I'm the one to ask." Her eyes were down. "And I'll feel totally out of place. My job usually sees me behind the scenes, not up front and personal."

"I'll make sure you feel special."

Meg's face was back up and searching. "But why?"

"Because I like you. Is it really so hard to believe?"

The shoulders shrugged. "A bit. You're Honey Diamond. I'm just... I'm nobody."

"You're everybody to me." Honey reached out and lifted her chin, connecting with her eyes and speaking in earnest. "Who *should* I be with? Some love-themselves celebrity only intent on raising their own profile? Or some gorgeous woman who arrived on my doorstep like a gift from the gods?"

Meg laughed. "Too much. And I thought you didn't judge?"

"Something brought us together, Meg. My song? Your paper? Those awful internet trolls? Who knows? But what I do know is this happens. People come into each other's lives when they're least expecting it, and they go and turn everything on its head. Because that's what it feels like with you. I took a day off yesterday. I never take a day off." She smiled. "And then you went and played the pavement in my acting class, and it was the best pavement I've ever seen, and I knew you were special. If anything I'm the one who should be self-conscious. I've been unnaturally forward. I've dived straight in. I've probably been stalkerish to the extreme."

"You?"

Honey laughed. "Yes, me. I feel like I've been a hunter."

"You don't have time to waste. I get that."

"And you do?"

"It's that line. You're Honey Diamond."

"Stop saying that!"

"It's true. You're special, and yes I'll admit it, I dreamt of moments like these. I was a fan, a big fan. I watched you from afar, I admired you from afar. I never actually believed I'd be in your presence. Surely you can understand there are slight nerves for me?"

"We're all just people, Meg, and when we find that person who draws us in we should go with it. I want you to go with it."

"I'm in the back of a car snogging the woman of my dreams; trust me I'm going with it. But it's like: *reality check, what the hell's going on?*"

Honey smiled wickedly. "It's exciting though, isn't it?"

Meg laughed. "You're just so different to how I imagined."

Reaching out, Honey ran her fingers down the side of Meg's neck. "Tell me what you imagined."

"Oh, I imagined a lot."

The come on was sexy. "Did you?"

"I did." Meg took hold of Honey's fingers and moved them back to their owner. "I imagined I'd do the leading," she said, reaching up with her own hands.

Honey groaned, feeling herself pushed back, lips once again hard to her neck. She spoke with a smile. "Well, won't this be the battle of wills?"

CHAPTER TWENTY THREE

Following the hustle as best she could, Meg smiled, thankful for the hand that reached out to pull her into the fold. They were walking at a rapid pace down a backstage passage at the cavernous *Britain Sings* studio, scaffolding securing the seating to their right as runners rushed past on the left tasked with life or death missions if their frantic faces, buzzing headsets and flapping clipboards were anything to go by. Meg squeezed Honey's fingers as a thank you. Honey was being hurried along by a team of people, yet she'd made time to reach out and reassure her, drawing her close so their steps were in sync.

Of course Meg had been in situations like this before, but only on the other side of proceedings. She'd been responsible for the hustle, and yes she was obviously aware it would be intimidating for the person she was shaking her mic at or waving her notebook towards, but she hadn't quite accepted just how intense it could feel. If Meg was honest, the idea of dropping back and slipping away had crossed her mind twice already since leaving the car; the car that had been so cocooned, so other-worldly, their own little bubble, protecting them from this. She tried to take in what exactly *this* was because these weren't journalists, they were production people flurrying around, desperate to impart whatever essential information they felt Honey needed to know.

Meg listened to the polite but firm instructions. Justin would be at the studio at six pre-recording his set that had to appear live, so they needed the judges in position early for their reactions to be filmed, which could potentially cause continuity issues if Gwen opted for a last minute outfit change, something she was prone to do, apparently. But why Honey needed to hear this, Meg struggled to understand. "I should get going," she said, trying to speak over the voices, but not wanting to draw attention. "You've got enough going on without having to babysit me too."

"It's not usually like this. Liza deals with everything. Where is she? I knew she wasn't coming to the drama day, but I assumed she'd be here; she's always here."

"Shall I try and find her? I've got my *Beacon* press pass in my bag. I'm sure I can wangle my way around."

The voice was hushed. "I'd rather you got rid of these cling-ons."

"Right," said Meg, deciding to get a grip, step up and impress with her assertiveness. "Where's your dressing room?"

"It's down here."

"Ask for some privacy and we'll make a plan from in there."

Honey glanced around at the urgency before slowing her pace. "Excuse me," she said, addressing the crowd, "Liza will be here shortly. Could you do what you usually do and feed all this through her? I'll be in my dressing room and would rather not be disturbed."

Meg watched the faces. They weren't shocked exactly, just questioning and reluctantly complying. She had no doubt the guidance they were all trying to impart was of the utmost importance, and without Liza the next port of call was obviously Honey, but this *was* Honey Diamond after all, and she'd asked for some distance. Meg smiled as they upped their pace, forcing the pack to gradually tail off, leaving them to finish their walk down the corridor without the chattering entourage.

Honey's laugh was nervous. "I feel like a bitch."

"Don't. Tell me how I can help."

"I'm not sure. We usually arrive for the live shows at the back entrance, as we did today, but there's always a waiting runner who walks me to my dressing room where I find Heidi, Caitlyn and Louisa. Liza stays back there and obviously deals with all that."

She shook her head. "Poor Liza, no wonder she's stressed. I've always tried to make her feel appreciated, but I'm not sure I've ever quite realised the scale of what she does." She nodded at the glittering Honey Diamond placard before pushing open the dressing room door and continuing. "She must message ahead so the runner's there for the moment we arrive; she must—"

"You've arrived!" came the gasp. "I didn't message the runner!"

Meg spotted the PA first, head sticking up from some sort of portable massage table in the corner of the large dressing room, brogues tucked neatly under a nearby chair also playing hanger to a three piece suit, a shirt, slipped or thrown, down on the floor. "Hi," she said, wanting to break the awkward silence, Honey still open-mouthed at the scene. "We met at Honey's. Liza, isn't it? And Svetty?"

The Russian woman lifted her hands together and bowed. "Svetty Sokolova. I do services. Liza like me do services. Liza like me do extra services. Svetty be asked to service Liza's—"

"Enough!" The PA scrambled from the table and grabbed her clothes, squatting behind the chair as if it offered some sort of camouflage while she tried to re-dress. "I've been saying for a while you need to relax, Honey. I didn't realise your mother's holistic therapist offered off-site treatments."

"Svetty be offering the off-site treatments, the on-site treatments. On site of buttocks. On site of breasticles."

"Svetty, please!" Liza's voice was strained. "I'm sorry," she said, shirt back on, legs pulled into trousers, "I wasn't expecting you for another half hour. Tammara should have kept me informed."

Meg thought back to Honey's instruction in the car. "Just drive," she had said in the nicest possible way, neither of them wanting any interruption to the temperature that had started to rise. Tammara had possibly mentioned something about calling ahead, but the memory was hazy, as was Honey's no doubt. Both lost in the moment, in the desire to dive deeper, to explore, to feel more.

Meg quivered. Their kissing had been so intense, encompassing them in a private bubble where nothing else seemed to register apart from the moans and the contact. Tammara could have been divider-down, talking the whole time for all she could remember. And she knew Honey had been lost in exactly the same way, she'd seen it in her eyes, the trance that sucked them both in.

"You know I don't like strangers touching me, Liza," Honey's voice came from her new position on the sofa, "and there's nothing wrong with admitting Svetty's here for your purpose."

The PA turned her back on the table. "She's not here for me."

The holistic therapist looked hurt. "You be saying you like the services of Svetty. You be calling Svetty special."

"Not now, Svetty."

Meg shuffled on her feet in the centre of the room, not wanting to gawp at the lovers' tiff. Instead, she looked around at the décor. A glittering dresser table, mirror and stool against the back wall, plush sofas down the side wall and a lavish table and chairs to the right. Expensive but soulless, Svetty's make-shift massage salon in the corner the only thing out of place. Maybe it was Liza who liked everything just so, Liza the one with borderline OCD, everything having a purpose or no place at all. Other dressing rooms she'd been in had been cramped and full of the typical odds and ends, feather boas and flowers, but this one was like a waiting room.

She moved from her position and sat next to Honey. The smile came quickly. The idea that Honey didn't like strangers touching her sounded so foreign after their ride in the car and, yes, while there hadn't as yet been any intimate contact there *had* been a great contest to get closer, cheeks on cheeks, arms pulling chests together, fingers riding higher on necks, both wanting more, needing more. "You don't like strangers touching you?" she whispered.

Honey dipped her head. "You're not a stranger. And I don't mean in a diva type way, I mean in a – let me lie naked for an intimate back rub from a stranger – way."

Meg felt that chemistry once more. Shivers of lust spiking through her body as the invisible pull found its force. "I think a massage is a good idea," she whispered.

Honey whispered back, "From Svetty?"

"From me."

"What are you two giggling about?" asked Liza, fully together once more, brogues clipping at the heels, signalling she was back in the game. "And I did bring her for you." She nodded towards the massage table and the holistic therapist who was now standing obediently, hands together, head bowed, awaiting further instruction. "I have to admit she's worked absolute wonders with me. I feel like a new woman entirely, but I acknowledge I can't let this new found freedom affect my game, which it has done today." She shook her head. "I'm sorry. It won't happen again."

"You not be using the Svetty no more?" The obedience was broken.

Liza turned back around. "We've spoken about this. Please remember your place when at work."

"But you confuses the Svetty." Her eyes were upset. "You say—"

Honey cut in. "Oh Liza, don't worry about it; it's lovely to see you so happy, and we must have been early anyway."

The PA refocused her attention. "The workshop didn't run its full course?"

Meg could feel her cheeks reddening; she'd no doubt been the fly in the ointment affecting the format of the day. Trying to ignore the cringeworthy memories, she talked instead to Liza. "It certainly was an eye-opener," she said with a smile.

Liza smiled back. "I'm afraid you won't be quite as involved this evening. I'll be back in twenty minutes with the girls, please feel free to stay and watch Honey's transformation but then I'll escort you to the stands."

"Front row?" asked Honey anxiously.

Liza nodded. "Of course."

"You'll be right behind me then." Honey spoke with a smile. "And I'll come and chat in the breaks. Make sure the seat next to hers is free as well please, Liza."

"I'll do that now." Liza moved towards the door. "And Honey, please give Svetty a go."

Meg looked at the now silent woman, like an offering shared among friends.

"Sloppy seconds ain't my style," said Honey with a whisper.

Meg's smile was wide as the dressing room door clicked closed. Honey was on exactly the same wavelength. "We're racing for pinks."

"Pinks?"

Meg's excitement rose. Nothing better than a woman who could banter back and forth with great lines from great films. "Pinks you punk! Pink slips! Ownership papers."

"Oh oh ho ho ho!"

Meg laughed loudly. "Please tell me you can do the *Fresh Prince of Bel Air* rap."

"Yes," Honey nodded, "with swag."

The head was out of its bowed position. "Svetty be starting the pack up. You two not be needing the relax. You already be loose. You already want the pom pom. The bonk bonk. The sex."

Honey laughed. "Me?"

"Both. Both juicy. Juicy eyes. Juicy lips. Juicy joo-joos."

"Svetty!"

"I think she already said that," laughed Meg.

"Meg!"

"What?" Meg knew Honey's indignation was feigned. "She's on the money with the joo-joos."

"It's more fun if we tease together," said Honey, joining her with a nudge to the shoulder. She turned to Svetty. "Does Liza want the sex?"

"Ma'am not be paying me for the sex."

Honey's face straightened. "My mother?

"Ma'am be paying wages. I in-house holistic therapist at Velvet Villa."

"Yes, but surely you're here for Liza?"

"Extra cost money."

"My mother's paying you for today?"

"She says I be keeping the Liza happy, so I be keeping the Honey happy."

"But you like Liza, right?"

"Not matter what Svetty like. Everyone just be liking services. Just services."

"I think she likes you."

The plump cheeks rose into a smile. "She like the Svetty?"

"I think so."

"Liza like Svetty for Svetty? Not for beating of hand and slapping of buttocks?"

"Yes probably that too, but there's more to life than work – there's love, and love can never be bought or paid for."

"We heff confusions."

Honey nodded. "Miscommunication happens in all relationships, Svetty, regardless of translation." She smiled. "If you like someone, tell them." Her eyes turned to Meg. "If you love someone, show them."

Meg held the connection. Honey was so perfect and so kind to everyone no matter their walk of life or role in her world. She could learn from her. She could grow with her. Returning the smile she accepted the truth. Honey could teach her how to love and be loved.

The kindness continued. "Why don't you hang around? We could all go for some food after the show."

"Svetty be chiropodist tonight. Gerty got the bunions."

"Another night then? I'll arrange it."

The woman pulled her folded table towards the door. "You not be teasing the Svetty? You think Liza like her? I go find the Liza. We heff the missing communications of issues sometimes. Svetty go now, she sorting it out. But you promising you are not doing the teasing?"

Honey spoke with all seriousness. "I'd never tease the Svetty."

"Damn it," whispered Meg under her breath. She waited for the therapist to leave and the door to close before the inevitable shoulder shove came from Honey. "What?" said Meg, "it's a shame."

"It's a shame if those two don't do the Sokolova."

Meg leaned in closer. "You're quite the little matchmaker, aren't you?"

"I can spot the odd spark."

"Any fire between us?"

Honey's lips were exploring once more. "There's a whole blazing inferno," she said with a smile.

****

Taking her seat in the studio Meg marvelled at the electric atmosphere. The last hour she'd spent watching Honey transformed from her naturally beautiful state into a stylised queen, dripping in glitz and glamour, her outfit sure to blow Gwen's offering out of the water. What Meg found interesting was that there'd been no interaction between the two female judges pre-show. There was a perpetual public debate as to whether or not the two singers from opposite sides of the ocean were actually friend or foe, and so far Meg's judgement was they were neither. Liza had liaised with Gwen's team, ensuring outfits didn't clash or – worse – match, but in the build-up to the show the team had been close-knit, just Honey and her professionals. To Meg, a theme was emerging. Honey didn't have an entourage of pointless flunkies, she didn't make dressing room demands, she didn't have fame-hungry friendships or create false feuds, she was just Honey, as often as possible.

Looking at the stage, with the lights low in waiting, Meg realised Honey was playing a role: the nation's Honey, the nation's sweetheart. This was her act, all the make-up, hair, glamorous gowns and sparkling jewellery was the front that protected a very private person. Yet this person, so loved by so many, had shown her true self – to her – to Meg. Feeling the buzz of anticipation, she held her breath. Music was cued and brought up. The lights rose as the music reached a crashing crescendo, the studio doors opened with firework effects flaring from each side. Four judges were revealed, all famous in their own right, all dazzling in their own themes, but only one drawing her eyes. Honey. Her Honey.

Meg couldn't stop the smile that took over her face. She was proud. Honoured. She felt special. In this crowd of screaming people, Honey had made *her* feel special. This wonderful woman, so loudly cheered and adored, wanted her; and every bone in her body wanted Honey right back.

Meg joined the whooping audience, clapping and cheering on their feet as the four judges took their seats. She knew the live show wasn't due to start for another half hour and the judges would enter once more after Justin performed. She realised she'd have previously viewed such antics with scorn, thinking the vain judges wanted to practice their entrances. Or she'd have laughed at the famous guest singer's fear to perform live on what was ironically a live talent show, but now she viewed it as another chance to stand even taller, to clap even louder, to bask in this feeling of wonder. This secret smile. This secret bond. She turned towards the judges table. Honey, with fireworks blazing behind her, was smiling right back.

CHAPTER TWENTY FOUR

Looking down at the head resting in her lap, Meg felt the tender wash of affection course through her body once more. The evening had been a mix of emotions swinging wildly from pride to lust, back to wonder and respect. Honey had been a generous, funny and astute presence. Her judging on-point, her comments endearing, sharp but never mean, and her secret glances back to the audience had sent silent shivers of anticipation straight down Meg's spine. Honey had been sitting there, watched by millions, with a poise and purpose so far removed from her previous position, moments before, back up against the dressing room door being kissed with a passion and urgency most viewers wouldn't be able to imagine let alone comprehend. But then the show had started and the hours, although not dragging, had totted up. And it wasn't simply the live show, there was the after show as well, live from another channel, not focusing on the judges but needing their input in debates and discussions. Then came the dress down. Hair unpinned, gown given back, Liza taking quotes that were needed for headlines: Had Honey felt the right people progressed? Was she happy her outfit polled better than Gwen's? It was never ending, and now it was past two in the morning.

Honey had tried her best to stay sparkling, Meg had seen that, but once they were in the warmth and security of the car, Honey had wilted, and Meg, looking down on her, knew she should leave her in peace. The plan had been to go back to Honey's, to make the most of the day that had started an age ago with Mrs Peacock and pan face, but the idea of waking the sleeping beauty and expecting any kind of meaningful interaction was cruel, let alone unrealistic. So Meg whispered to Tammara that the first drop-off was hers. She wrote a note, leaving her number for Honey and the reasons for bailing. For the first time in her life, she genuinely wanted to do the right thing. She already felt more for this woman than she had any other, never saying no to the few and far between come-ons even if the timing had been wrong or the person not right. But this felt so different, this yearning for total connection. She wanted their moment. She needed their moment. But this wasn't it.

Carefully climbing out of the car, Meg looked back at the sleeping woman. There would be another time and another place and, yes, Honey was busy, but two people who had that pull would never be far apart, of that she was sure.

****

"But I'm in China tomorrow!" gasped Honey, holding the note up to the light. "And Thailand from there. I'm not back till next weekend's live show! Oh Tammara, why didn't you stop her?"

The driver leaned through the space the reclined divider had vacated. "I thought she was right. You look shattered. You'll see her again."

"When?!"

"Should I go back and fetch her?"

Reading the words on the note, Honey sighed; she knew both women were right. "The day just didn't finish as I planned, as I hoped. I was meant to be showing her a day in the life of Honey Diamond."

"She's seen that."

"Not all of it."

"Why, what do you usually do now?"

Honey thought honestly. "Well, I..."

"You collapse, before Liza's early morning call alerts you to flight times and journey preparations. She hasn't missed anything and if the way she was staring at you lying there asleep on her lap was anything to go by then I'd say the day ended pretty perfectly for her."

"She was watching me?"

"With wide eyes and sighs of contentment."

"She was not!"

"She was, and I like her. I like her a lot. Betty Big Boobs who?"

Honey laughed. "Do you want to know what she wrote?"

"Obviously."

Reading the neat penmanship, Honey spoke softly. "I may not be a singer, or a star in your bright world, but life is now much better with you here quietly curled. I may not be a poet, or a master writing song, but please sleep tight this evening as my heart is singing strong. We'll meet again tomorrow and every day therein, because with you I think a special bond can now begin."

"I love it!"

Honey felt the warmth rise in her chest. "So do I, but I'm not here tomorrow and I'm not here the next day or the day after that."

"You have her number."

"You know I don't have a phone."

"So get one."

"No. I hate the idea of hunching over some gadget that only ever takes you away from the real world."

"So call her from your hotels. Speak to her. Woo her the old fashioned way; not that she needs much wooing if that poem's anything to go by."

Honey smiled. "I guess a build-up could be fun." Sliding across the seat she reached for the door handle. "Don't get out, it's cold. Are you on airport duty tomorrow?"

"That I am."

"Don't tell me the time, I don't want to know."

"Let's just say your planned ending may have been somewhat rushed anyway, and no one wants to rush the important things in life, do they?"

Honey groaned. "We're talking hours, aren't we?"

"Not quite the plural."

CHAPTER TWENTY FIVE

Checking her phone for the umpteenth time that day, Meg sighed. Had she given Honey the right number? It had been late, the lighting in the car had been low, she could quite easily have scribbled what looked like a wrong digit. Or maybe it was that stupid poem? What had possessed her to write such ridiculous lyrics to arguably the nation's best lyricist she couldn't comprehend, but she had and it was stupid. Stupid enough for Honey to run a mile? Quite possibly. They hadn't exchanged numbers before. *The Beacon* and Liza prepared their first meeting, a verbal agreement to meet the next day and the day after that serving as their only method of communication so far. But Honey *could* find a way of contacting her if she so wished. It was easy. Phone *The Beacon*. Ask Liza. Google her staff profile. But Honey? How was she meant to call Honey? The public couldn't just access her any old how, and that's all she was now. A nobody. A person who'd missed their damn chance.

Rolling over in bed, Meg considered the possibility of turning up at The Alderley. Old Sal would let her through security, wouldn't she? But then what? Knock on the door like a stalker? No. If Honey hadn't messaged there was a reason for it. She counted the days once more. It was eleven p.m. Monday evening. Almost forty-eight hours since the Saturday night show. They hadn't discussed details of Honey's schedule during their time together, in fact Honey hadn't spoken much about her whirlwind lifestyle apart from the fact it was whirlwind. Albums, shows, this new film. Maybe a day or two was nothing to her? Maybe time flew in the face of all the lights, camera, action. Or maybe she just wasn't that bothered. Honey didn't have a personal phone, so she wouldn't have been glued to it like she'd been, waiting for that first initial contact. Not that Meg could make it anyway as there was no direct line to the star.

Meg huffed. She'd been expecting a text that very first evening. A few words about her departure, or even her poem, just something, anything, but no, not even a smiling emoji. Honey could have borrowed Tammara's phone, or even Sofia's. There were ways and means had she so wished. Pulling the pillow over her head, she let out a silent scream. Why had she just walked away? Why hadn't she gone back to Honey's? Why hadn't she seized the moment and woken her, kissed her, made love to her. The sound of the ringtone stopped her. She looked at the screen. International. She clicked quickly. "Honey?"

The delay was noticeable before the connection kicked in. "Meg? Hi. I'm calling from China."

Meg wiggled her toes with pent up delight under the covers. China. She was in China. "I've missed you!" The words were out of her mouth before she had time to take a breath.

"I've missed you too. I'm sorry, my flight left at seven on Sunday morning, and I arrived at gone midnight China time, and I was going to call before work but I realised it would be the early hours of the morning for you, and I was chocka-block all day and I've only now got a spare half hour before I get picked up to go to Thailand."

Meg grinned at the phone. "What time is it?"

"Six, Tuesday morning. I worked that out as eleven Monday night for you. Is it okay to call? It's not too late?"

Meg sat up, drawing her knees into her chest. "It's fine. You're sure you've got time?"

"It's hectic as always, but I'll make time for you."

Meg puzzled at the comment; for her this delay was indicative of someone not making time. Yes, phone chats may have to be scheduled in but, realistically, how long did it take to thumb a quick text message? She thought of all the methods Honey could use if she had her own phone. A WhatsApp thread. A liked heart on an Instagram post. A thumbs up on a Facebook picture. All of those gestures signalled interest. They'd keep the ball rolling until the real deal phone calls could take place. Meg stopped herself. Their worlds were markedly different. Honey didn't like social media and the apps all needed a phone, and even if she did ever get a phone the idea she'd be sitting there staring at the screen and refreshing each site every ten seconds like the normal twenty-something did while multi-tasking with the TV and at least one personal tablet was laughable. Honey had a life. She had a busy life.

"You should have dropped me a text." More words out of her mouth without thinking. Meg banged her head onto her pillow. Why was she always so needy? For an independent woman it was a chink in her armour that she just couldn't mend. Her previous, albeit on-off and somewhat lacklustre, love life, had been marred by over-thinking and second-guessing. It wasn't that she was insecure, it was that she hated the rules. If you liked someone why should you wait the three days before contact? Why was a heart on every third Instagram post acceptable, but not a heart every time you saw something you genuinely liked? Why should she comment occasionally on Facebook if she had funny comments for all that she saw? It wasn't needy, it was honest. She was honest with her feelings, yet it was this that caused her own second guessing. Had there been too many likes? Was the contact too constant? Her own *lack* of over-thinking, causing the over-thinking to happen. Like the poem. It felt right at the time. She was feeling those emotions and thinking those thoughts so she wrote it, and she left it for Honey with her number attached, the number she'd only now just chosen to call.

"I don't have a phone, sorry."

"I know, but Liza does, so does Tammara, and I saw Sofia had one at your house."

"I'm not sending you private messages on someone else's device."

"Whose phone are you on now?"

"The hotel's."

"In a booth?"

"No, in my room."

"You seriously don't have a mobile? Not one that's just tucked away for emergencies?"

"No."

"Seriously?"

Honey was laughing. "Seriously! I like proper phones."

Meg closed her eyes. This was adorable. This was old school. This would be hard. "Can you get one?"

"A mobile? I don't want one."

"We could text."

"I'd rather talk."

"But you're busy."

"I've said I'll make time."

"You're getting on a plane."

"It's only a short flight."

"How short's short?"

"Three hours twenty."

Meg laughed. "That's long! You could get to the Canaries for that." Most of her holidaying had taken place in Europe where a two-hour flight could get you almost anywhere.

"Stop with the buts. I want to hear how you've been."

Meg ignored the temptation to say she'd been glued to her phone for the past forty-eight hours hoping for any sort of contact in any sort of form. She was easy to find on every single social media platform with links available from her staff profile page, or under all of the articles she'd written. She even wore a FitBit that had a messaging facility and gave alerts when new friends came online or cheered daily progress. Its buzz earlier that day had caused a rush to the app in the hope it was something from Honey. It wasn't. It was Jan James, the fittest woman at work, requesting yet another hot step hustle. "I've been busy," she lied.

"Doing what?"

This was strange. She wasn't a social chatter. She didn't have friends she'd just dial up and call. She spoke on the phone at work, but this always involved research, questions or information retrieval. She phoned home once-monthly, reeling off the list of statements she knew her parents needed to hear: yes, she was saving her money; no, she hadn't yet found a girlfriend; yes, she was eating well. Some people thought it was harder for this new social media generation, apparently unable to communicate properly, but actually it felt easier. You'd start the relationship with accepted friendship requests. You'd like the odd post. You'd build up to the first public comment. Then, moving into the private message, you'd continue the jokes you didn't want others to see. You had time to think of your responses. You had emojis. You had gifs. You'd build up that foundation before you actually had to have conversations like this.

Meg took hold of herself. They'd spoken perfectly freely when they'd been together. In fact it had felt like they'd done it before. Old friends, slipping into that familiar territory of chat. Maybe it was just this whole phone thing. Who called anyone up these days? She paused. What did she really want to know? "Have you missed me?" she asked, before grimacing and holding her breath. Was this delay the same length as the last one, or was this delay more than just the long distance phone line? Dammit there she was again, not playing it cool then overthinking her lack of cool play.

"Is that what you've been doing? Missing me?"

"Lots," she said, smiling at her own inability to act mysterious or dangle a carrot. Jo always accused her of being a moody, chip-on-the-shoulder goth, and while she knew her blonde-haired, blue-eyed flatmate viewed anyone with dark hair and dark eyes as gothic, she struggled to understand where the brutal, if not slightly teasing, character assessment had come from. She could be quiet sometimes, but not moody. Thoughtful was possibly the word and, yes, maybe that perceived chip-on-the-shoulder could have been caused by a slight disgruntlement that her openness couldn't be met by others, or that the heart she wore on her sleeve seemed to cause more damage than good. But as Honey had said, if you liked someone you told them, if you felt something you showed them. "I've missed you lots."

Honey's voice was smiling. "And I've missed you lots too. I'll get a phone. I'll send you a message."

"Don't." Meg sat up straighter in bed. "This will be fun. Old fashioned. You can woo me. I can woo you."

"You mean that?"

"Woo hoo, I do."

"Oh, Meg, thank you."

"For what?"

"You're not trying to change me."

"I never would, and it will be nice not having to check my phone every five minutes." She meant both. People, she believed, never really changed. They might say they would, but they wouldn't, and why should they, just to fit in with someone else's idea of how a person should act or behave? Too often people lost themselves in relationships. She saw it all the time when working for HotBuzz: young girls transforming into the WAGs they thought their footballers wanted only to be replaced when a newer model became available. Vacant and airy was the fashion to begin with, then it was driven and successful, potential recruits requiring at least one clothing line or modelling contract under their belts before admittance into the world of the WAG.

Meg smiled. This whole phone thing would be a relief. She'd received a multitude of notifications from her numerous apps over the past forty-eight hours and each time the ping wasn't from Honey she'd fallen deeper into a pit of depression and desperation. Why wasn't she contacting me? Why hadn't she shown me a sign? A like. A buzz. A heart. A ping. A gif? Just anything? Ridiculous given the fact she knew she was phone-free, but the hope had been there. "As long as I know when you're going to call," she said, excited already at the novelty of this old fashioned idea, wondering what it must have been like before mobile phones. Sending a message by carrier pigeon? Throwing a rock at the one you quite liked?

"I arrive in Thailand at eleven-thirty my time now, but that's ten-thirty their time, so it will be four-thirty in the morning, your time."

Meg couldn't resist. "Honey Diamond, good at meth."

"We call it maths in this country, as you well know. But through my calculations and Liza's itinerary I should be able to call you tomorrow evening, your time at eleven."

"The same time as today?"

"Yes, I'll get up early. We have a packed schedule starting with a slot on the nation's number one breakfast show, I can't remember the name of the host, complicated sounding, which reminds me," the pause was apprehensive, "I've booked us in for a joint massage on Sunday with Svetty and her apprentice, or junior, or whatever title she goes by, another one of Mother's holistic therapists I assume."

"And she's got a complicated name?"

"Depends how you pronounce it."

"What is it?"

"Kuntse. But I think Mother calls her—"

"You're lying!" Meg laughed. "We're not having a joint massage with Svetty and Kuntse."

"We are, and I don't say that lightly. I'm very apprehensive when it comes to strangers touching me. I think it was having so many different stylists and clothing people when I was younger – pre-Heidi, Caitlyn and Louisa. I felt like a piece of meat sometimes, dressed up, dressed down, make-up on, hair pulled. It got really uncomfortable. But Liza's a different woman. She's relaxed, she's affable, she even slept on the plane, and Liza *never* sleeps on the plane."

"So what, we go for this massage and become even cooler than we already are?"

Honey laughed. "I just thought it would be nice. Relax us, before a potential evening in?"

"This Sunday?"

"Yes. I'm back for *Britain Sings* on Saturday, then I have a script meeting Sunday morning, but from six I'm free. They've said they can bring their equipment to mine so we won't have to go and see Mother, and afterwards I was thinking maybe we could get a takeaway and watch some TV?"

"You're not the type of person who strikes me as getting takeaways and watching TV."

"No?"

"You're more of a music on, book out person."

"I rarely have time for either, but I want to try. I want to try and make whatever this is we've got going on work. I can't promise plans won't change at the last minute, or that I'll always be there when you need me, but I can promise I want to be. I want to be that person you turn to. I want to be the one you spend time with and, please, I'll get you a seat for Saturday night's show again if you want?"

Meg paused. It was tempting, and it had been good, but she'd rather have Honey to herself, not share her with her fans, and anyway, watching the live show on TV meant more close-ups and not just a view of her back. "I'll see you at yours. Six on Sunday. Massage ready."

"Yes it might."

"Pardon?"

"It might."

"It might what?"

"I thought you said the massage will get us ready?"

Meg grinned. "Oh, did you now? And what might it be getting us ready for?"

"Round two?"

"As long as round two doesn't involve Svetty and Kuntse, or Liza for that matter."

"It'll involve Svetty and Kuntse if we're doing it right."

"Oh stop it!" Meg was laughing. "Are you sure she doesn't mind us borrowing her?"

"Borrowing Svetty? No, but I think we should choose treatments from the regular menu to be safe."

"Fine, and I'll offer up dessert." Meg smiled to herself. It was cringe, but she'd have typed it in a message, so why not say it down the phone?

"Oooh, you flirt."

"Embarrassing, aren't I?" This talking on the phone was easier than she'd imagined, her apprehension about the traditional communication method had been short lived. "Thank you for calling," she said.

"Get ready." The voice was smiling. "I'm calling a lot."

CHAPTER TWENTY SIX

On Tuesday afternoon, the buzz in the *Beacon* office was more charged than usual. Honey Diamond's exclusive interview was top banner front page, a story about the European Union's latest move on refugees the main headline. Any other paper would have the singer's picture splashed full-frontal for all to see, but *The Beacon* didn't approve of splashing or sensationalising, and therefore wasn't best prepared for the tsunami of interest that occurred when a story went viral. And although it had its own online edition and team of people to keep track of comments and publish updates to ever-changing stories, it wasn't on the pulse when it came to the perils of internet adaptation. Because that's what would happen, Meg knew. Stories would get quoted, misquoted, adapted, made into memes, and she was one of the few at *The Beacon* able to understand what should be tackled and what should be left to run. Her time at HotBuzz – where the aim was to always go viral – had given her a wealth of expertise in this area.

So that's where she found herself, shipped in to help the drowning online team, trying to monitor comments and react to the ever-growing interest the story had caused. People were desperate for more with numerous offers coming in from news outlets asking for a quote – "What was she really like?" – or even better, an appearance – "Come on our show and expand on the story." But that's not what they did at *The Beacon*, and Meg was grateful she was only asked to sit and advise.

Pulling herself closer to the screen, she read the latest influx of comments and smiled; over eighty percent were positive, and in the age of vicious internet trolling that was a huge accomplishment. "It's fine," she said. "Don't worry."

"But the volume!" said one of the flustered faces.

"And the calls!" said another.

"We've never had to deal with anything quite like this before!"

"I'm sure you have," said Meg, sympathetic to their bewilderment at this bizarre world where people bothered to comment more on celebrity than politics. It was the same with YouTube stars, or reality kings and queens, an older generation simply not able to grasp the concept of their huge following, asking who they were and why could they possibly matter? The new media world understood that celebrity sold, but for an institution like *The Beacon* it was all very disconcerting. Meg's Honey Diamond interview had already collected more than a hundred times the hits registered by the editor's front page European Union piece, and if early sales figures were to be believed the paper was about to experience its largest bump in circulation in over a decade.

"Just make sure you delete all the spam," she said, pointing at an html link guiding readers in the direction of miracle fat absorbing diet pills, "and watch out for anything overtly homophobic."

"Where's the line?" asked one of the flustered comrades.

"You'll know it when you see it," she said, highlighting and deleting a comment that read: *All gays shall be dragged into boiling water and suffer never-ending pain, torture and eternal damnation in the burning fires of hell. You dirty gayboy scum.* She replaced it with the banner: "This comment has been removed by the moderator."

****

"Let me borrow your glasses," said Diana, squinting at the iPad Sofia had recently rescued from the arm of Honey's sofa, the half-hourly phone calls from her tech team not enough to quench her need for insight.

Sofia passed over the half-moon frames. "Would my laptop be easier?"

"What does this one say?" she snapped, shoving the offering onto the bridge of her nose and scrunching up her face.

Sofia tried to pinch the tablet's screen and widen. Nothing happened. She peered in closer. "It says, oh hang on, glasses back, Di. Right. Let me see. It says," she coughed, "All gays shall be dragged into boiling water and suffer never-ending, oh I won't read that one."

"Read it."

"No, it's—"

Diana plucked the pass-the-parcel glasses from her friend and continued the sentence. "Never-ending pain, torture and eternal damnation in the burning fires of hell. You dirty gayboy scum." She frowned at Sofia. "Have they even read the article?!"

"Probably not, but look," Sofia tapped the screen, "it's gone. Comment removed by moderator."

"Stop tapping the screen, you're changing the size!" Diana thrust the glasses back to their owner. "I should have stayed at Velvet Villa. Benedict and his tech team have a whole incident room set up in the lounge."

"There's not been a murder."

"Hasn't there?"

"Oh Di, these comments are good, the response on the television's been good." She pointed at the broadsheet pulled apart on the coffee table and shrugged. "The story's good. And you'll always get some weirdo spouting drivel – you know this, you've seen this, that's why you have your team of people. You have to admit the reaction is overwhelmingly positive. And gayboy scum? That's just trolling. You've explained to me all about trolling. They obviously haven't the first clue who Honey is."

"Everyone knows who Honey is. That's why I can't let this get out of hand."

"It's not. She's done the right thing."

Diana dropped her head backwards onto the cushions. "And have I?"

"What do you mean?"

"You know."

"With Meg?" Sofia joined her friend, head back on the cushions. "I'm watching her. I'll report if she steps out of line."

"Isn't she as bad as that troll? And if she is, shouldn't I keep her away from my daughter?"

Sofia fixed her glasses back into position. "Of that I'm still to decide."

****

Meg replaced another comment with the moderator banner. Who were these people sitting at home spamming articles with hatred? Now *these* were the people Honey and Diana had described. Cat killers. Self-hating, porn-obsessed weirdos. Freaks with no goal in life but to hurt other people. She wasn't part of that group and she'd never left a single trolling comment in any guise on any forum. Her site had been intelligent, yes possibly not so much at the start, but it had been witty and tongue-in-cheek, and honest. The posts she'd written were honest. Drivel about burning in hell wasn't honest, or productive. At least her site made people think twice, made people question their motives. She twisted in her chair, contemplating once more the titbit she'd picked up this morning. An interview with up-and-coming artist Sandy Greer, daughter of Alexander Greer, billionaire tycoon, owner of Greer's retail empire, which included half the stores lucky to be left on the nation's high streets. Sandy had spent the majority of the somewhat pretentious interview crowing about the success of her sell-out exhibition, every single piece snatched up within the first hour of exposure. A mean feat for a relative unknown, as was last year's singing success, a drum and bass track charting in the top ten, and the year before that a party planning book categorised as Waterstones' most recommended read.

Meg knew money bought success, or at least the initial *appearance* of success, because her research had shown the single dropping out of the charts after a week and the book going on to receive dozens of horrific one-star reviews on Amazon. This time it was the pouty assistant at the gallery who let slip, post interview, that it was Sandy's father who'd purchased all the pieces with red dots displayed next to them. Meg smiled to herself, realising the slip was no mistake; she'd deliberately waited until Sandy had left the building before scurrying over to tell tales. A sympathetic smile and a further gentle question got it all tumbling out in a whisper: Sandy Greer was a horror to work with and her pieces were shit. Meg couldn't write that, just as other critics whose websites and books would undoubtedly list the Greer Fine Arts Foundation as a sponsor would know, but the whisper was there, as it often was in such circles.

What post could she write? Which daddy's girl's making it onto super-cool gallery walls because the fashionable father's buying her way in? Meg stopped herself, shocked at the thrill that had so quickly returned. It would be easy to fire up the site – she hadn't deleted it, it was simply offline. One click and it would be back, one post and people would know. Closing her eyes, she sighed. She couldn't, there was too much at stake. In fact her escape had been a lot more than just lucky. She'd been truly blessed with this fresh start, this chance to make amends. She smiled. This chance to know Honey for real.

Meg felt the familiar lurch of anticipation, the shock of sparks ricocheting around her body every time she remembered. The contact. The kisses. They'd kissed, with passion, for hours and she knew they would soon go further, much further. That wasn't luck, that was some divine intervention by some divine being giving her a glimpse of what happiness might be. She knew her life hadn't been bad as such… just a bit ordinary. Tough times, regular times, the odd memorable holiday, the odd memorable encounter, but nothing like this. Nothing so extraordinary that saw her wake with a smile, walk with a skip, sing with no cares in the world. Meg laughed to herself. She'd even sung in the shower. She never sang in the shower. Crikey, she'd gone as far as smile at her own reflection when usually she'd be faced with a grimace. She'd eaten a good breakfast and enjoyed it. She'd been gracious when faced with the customary office politics and article disputes. She'd even invited Jan James, work's fitness freak, to a FitBit daily showdown, not caring if she lost, just upbeat about getting involved. Life was good. Life was really good, and some half-hearted, short-lived desire to see Sandy Greer faced with an uncomfortable truth just wasn't worth it.

Turning to the team of anxious faces she said calmly, "This is all fine. You're doing a good job." It was strange somehow, how this had brought her into the fold, her irrational feeling that she was in some way undeserving of her new role quashed by the expertise now on display. "Keep replying to interview requests with the standard line," she continued. "Everything Honey Diamond wanted to say she's said. Everything Margaret Rutherton learnt she wrote." She got up from the desk and smiled. She would use this time to find some real questions that, when asked, would give her the real answers she'd so desperately wanted.

CHAPTER TWENTY SEVEN

Honey lazily lifted the receiver that had been buzzing for some time now. Liza's wakeup call wouldn't be coming in for a while yet, but she'd privately requested an early morning alert from her eager-to-please personal concierge. They were staying in Bangkok's Mandarin Oriental hotel, famed for its comfort, dignity and style, or so Liza had said en-route from the airport in a car that seemed to be curiously immune to the worst traffic she had ever seen. It really didn't matter to Honey where they stayed as she'd rarely get chance to walk the grounds, or use the amenities, or even see the city. Most often it was a case of settle in, order room service, go to sleep, get up, do the job and leave again and this trip was no different. A packed schedule meant her only glimpse of the slow-moving green expanse of the Chao Phraya River was from her seventeenth floor balcony. She yawned into the receiver. It had been a while since she'd requested Liza schedule in some sight-seeing stops, Venice being the last time she'd insisted they stay on. A performance in St Mark's Square had filled her with a love for the city that one day she wanted to share. She blinked, remembering why the soothing voice was waking her so early from sleep. She was calling Meg. Never before had she requested a wake-up earlier than necessary. She knew every single minute of sleep was essential for getting her through the day's schedule. Her latest album's global release called for her to promote songs throughout Asia after similarly crazy whistle-stop tours throughout Europe and the United States. Next would come the full-blown stadium tour; she had seen the draft schedule and the list had exhausted her before she'd got halfway through it. Not to mention the new album awaiting release.

Thanking the caller, she stretched with a smile. Meg. The unassuming, self-effacing mystery of intellect, complication and intrigue. Playing the pavement. Enjoying Ikea. Cute come-ons and witty remarks. She had that secret smile – something inside her, a hidden glint, a spark of excitement. A light only ignited by someone of a similar persuasion. Two strangers giving life to each other. Like a sense of adventure. A desire to take on the world. Because that's what she saw in Meg, someone yet to find their true self, and even though their lives were markedly different she felt in her a kindred spirit, a lone wolf running free. Both independent women, yet both needing that link of connection, not to stifle or suffocate, but to know someone was there, beside you, running at the same speed.

Honey rolled her eyes at herself. Why was she being so dreamy? She smiled. She knew why. She was in that romantic phase of intellectual lust. She wanted to know more, she wanted to know everything. Why was Meg the way she was? What were her hopes, her dreams, her desires? And yes of course the lust was physical too, she'd widened her eyes the very first time she'd opened the door, but for her the pull was about what the eyes couldn't see. Her life left her surrounded by models and stage stars, purportedly the world's most beautiful people, but for her beauty didn't come in flawless skin or arched eyebrows, it came in an aura, a sense of someone's being, and Meg's aura was delicate, it was fragile. She smiled. It was hidden. Her walls had been high. But they'd get there, she thought. They'd get there with phone calls like this.

Pulling open the top drawer of the bedside cabinet, she found the poem and number. The words were soft and the writing was gentle, exposing the bravery it took to put pen to paper. Meg wasn't a weak person, more likely a strong force to be reckoned with, but these lines gave a glimpse into the tender soul hiding behind those curious eyes. She lifted the receiver and started to dial, butterflies building in her stomach as they had when she was younger and asked to call her mother's glamorous friend with the instruction to confirm an invitation, or double check travel arrangements. Looking back now, Honey was sure her mother had a team of people already in charge of everything, and Diana was always on the phone to Daphne anyway, so the idea that her ten-year-old daughter would have to call and confirm plans seemed laughable now. Her mother liked to see her blush. That's what it was. A misguided idea of affection, her mother needling her afterwards and ruffling her hair.

Honey waited for the call to connect. Diana hadn't been a bad mother. She'd been there as much as she could be, and they'd made some wonderful memories during time spent abroad, but there always seemed to be others around. She never had her mother to herself, constantly sharing her with the glamorous gang and people like Daphne. The eager voice on the end of the line stopped her remembering. She waited for the excited variations on "Hello, hi, you actually called!" to stop, before speaking with real emotion.

"Was that only twenty-four-hours?" she said.

"I know! It seems like a lifetime," Meg was talking quickly, "but not in a bad way. It actually made me enjoy my day more. I wasn't checking my phone every two seconds to see if you'd called, I just had that nice knowledge you would, and it's made me smile. I've been smiling all day."

"I've been asleep, but I'm sure I was smiling."

"Really now?"

Honey laughed at the wickedness with which it was delivered. Meg was starting to flirt. Pulling herself higher in bed, she pushed a pillow behind her back. The time difference meant one was full of life from a day on the go, the other trying to chug the starter motor and get the ball rolling. She stretched her shoulders and focused, twisting the dimmer switch to softly brighten the room. "So how have you been? Busy day?"

"Busy day?!" The voice was disbelieving. "Your interview went live. Top banner, front page."

"Oh yes, Liza mentioned it. But you, how have you been?"

"Don't you want to know how it's gone?"

"Not really." The echoing silence on the line made her stop and she realised her mistake. "Except for how it affects you. Is it all okay?"

Meg's answering laugh gave her permission to breathe again.

"It's been crazy. *The Beacon* has never had a response like it. But it's been crazy good though and I really feel part of the team. Finally."

"That's great. I'm pleased for you." Pulling back the covers, Honey tucked the cordless phone into her shoulder and padded over to the tall window, peeping though the curtains at the twinkling view of the river still shrouded in night time yet alive with the lights from the boats. "I'm looking over the Chao Phraya River from the Mandarin Oriental in Bangkok."

"And I'm in a penthouse in Clapham but don't you want to know—"

"A penthouse?"

"Above a shop. Two-bed. Not enough windows. But that's irrelevant. Your location doesn't change how the story's gone. Don't you want details?"

"The world never stops turning, Meg. Life always continues." She stretched up on her tiptoes. "I was there, remember? I know what I said, I know what you wrote. Nothing either of us can do now will change how it goes down."

"It's gone down well! You're even more of a hero!"

"That's good."

"I thought you'd be frantic? I thought you'd be desperate for news?"

"The only time I was slightly anxious was when I realised there'd been a suggestion I was lying, so I dealt with it, and it's done. What will be will be."

"But it's great!"

"Good."

"Are you always like this in the mornings?"

Honey laughed. "I've always ignored the press. I've never been concerned about my public image. I sing songs. If people like them, great, if they don't, oh well."

"It's really that simple for you?"

"Yes. Isn't it for you?" She listened to the pause, imagining for a moment what it must be like to care so much about other peoples' perception. She thought of Liza, constantly getting grief for her brogues and three-piece-suits, but wearing them all the same. Did she care about the banter? If she did then she hid it well.

"If you honestly didn't mind what people said, what people wrote, then why would you choose not to read it?"

Honey pulled the curtain closed and scurried back to the bed. "Oooh, you're testing me. I like this." She tucked her legs under the plush covers and snuggled back down. "You're saying I care too much?"

"Don't you? Don't we all? Isn't it part of human nature to crave acceptance? To want to be liked?"

"You do know it's five *a.m.* here don't you? I'm all for late-night what's the purpose of life chats, but I've got hair and make-up coming in a minute." She paused. "Do *you* want to be liked?"

Meg laughed. "I've never been liked."

"Oh, I doubt that!"

"I've never been popular. I've always been there, in the groups, in the background, but I've never been the memorable one. There won't be someone sitting down right now with their partner, reminiscing over a bottle of wine about Meg Rutherton, the great fun, good for a laugh, happy go lucky girl from their past."

"Would you want to be remembered like that?"

"What else is there?"

"There's kindness, there's intellect. You're a great writer. Your name's at the bottom of some interesting pieces."

"I'm falling asleep as you speak." The laugh was kind. "You, on the other hand, are responsible for many babies, many marriages, many happy memories. Your songs bring life. They bring emotion. They bring love."

"Not to me they don't." Honey sighed and closed her eyes. Maybe Meg was right? Maybe she did care about her public perception? Maybe this image was too hard to embody, that's why she turned a blind eye?

"Tell me about your secret smile song."

Honey laughed. It was a question she'd been asked a thousand times already, but had yet to tell the full truth. She'd always say it was about inner confidence and the determination to succeed, rising up against the odds, smiling inside with spirit and daring. "It's about an affair."

"I knew it!" The pause was questioning. "You've had one?"

"No, and not in the mistress, steal-someone-from-their-partner way, just in a falling-in-love-with-someone-you-shouldn't way."

"She-Ra?"

"Yes." She'd written it that summer. The ballad that saw her catapult from successful singer to international superstar. Driven by the excitement of She-Ra. The hidden whispers. The private jokes. The secret smile that swelled inside her every time she thought of the woman, with whom she knew there was no future, but the moment was theirs and they enjoyed it covertly. "You've felt it, haven't you? That dawning realisation you're into someone and they might be into you too?"

"No."

"No?" Honey pulled herself back into her seated position. "You do know I'm into you, don't you?"

"Oh right, sorry, I thought you were talking pre-us."

"There's an us?" Honey tried to hide the smile as she spoke.

"No, sorry, I thought…"

"I *want* there to be an us."

The response from halfway around the world was quick and warm. "Thank goodness for that. I never know quite how to play it. I'll often wear my heart on my sleeve then worry I've said too much."

"You've dated a lot?" It was hard to keep from grinning. Meg was easy to tease.

"Hey! I'm the one sitting at the desk in my bedroom with a list of questions to ask you! I spent the whole day researching and rehearsing. What I wanted to ask, why I wanted to ask it, how you might respond."

"Really? Like rehearsing what you're going to say before a phone call? I used to do that."

"There are just some things I'm desperate to know. You fascinate me, Honey."

"And you fascinate me too."

"Really? I'm actually a terrible bore. My flatmate, Jo, describes me as nondescript."

Honey laughed. "And she's a good friend?"

"I don't have many. At least with her I know she'll always be honest."

"Oh Meg, you're far from nondescript. I worry I'm nondescript! Being labelled as some style and fashion icon? It's all nonsense. Come on, ask me a question. I like being probed."

"I thought you hated it?"

"By others yes, but by you..." Her tone must have encouraged as the questions came quickly.

"What's your most treasured memory?"

"When Mum came home at night."

"That's the first time you've not called her Mother."

"She was away a lot. I never slept properly. But when she came to me, and tucked me in tight, well... all was right with the world."

"So Mum's the person you had all to yourself, and Mother's the person you share?"

"Maybe, but I'm not someone who dwells. I've led a very fortunate life, Meg. I'm someone who always looks for the positives, not the negatives. I'm peaceful. I like life as simple as it can be, a difficult feat given the nature of my work, but I have a mother and sometimes she's my Mum."

"That's why you're an inspiration." The sigh was thoughtful. "I'm too hard on my parents. I resent them for being mean when I came out. It's a huge blow being told the very essence of who you are isn't what they wanted."

"Do you see them much?"

"As and when, but I will." The voice was smiling. "You've stirred me into making more effort. I definitely want to be a better person now I've met you."

Honey warmed. It was a nice compliment. "So what's your most treasured memory?"

"No! This is my list! Right, where was I? Question two. What's your most terrible memory?"

"Really? You want to know that? Right, okay. Probably when Mother would leave for a show. She toured, she travelled, she took holidays." Honey closed her eyes. It was all about Heath. Everything had always been about Heath. She'd often wondered if she reminded her mother too much of him, causing her to run, to stay guarded. "She struggled after my father died. She really did love him. Truly. Completely. That's why she acts so blasé now about love. She doesn't want it to hurt her. She doesn't want it to hurt me."

"I won't hurt you."

Honey's smile was wide as the swell of warmth built deep inside her. "How can I feel you when we're so far apart? It's like you're sitting right here next to me."

"I feel that too. Let me ask you another."

"Is that your defence mechanism? When things get too deep? Keep talking? Change the subject?"

The voice laughed. "No, I just have twenty-two more questions to get through."

Honey smiled. "Okay then, fire away, as long as you promise we can revisit all these at a later date with your responses?"

"You're on, snuggled up together, having these chats late into the night."

"With wine?"

"Always with wine. Right, number three, if a crystal ball could tell you the truth about yourself, your life, the future or anything else, what would you want to know?"

"It's still before six o'clock in the morning."

"Too much?"

Honey laughed. "What's your answer? You must have asked this for a reason. You've had time to think about it. I've only just woken up."

"Okay. I'd maybe want to know if I was a good person."

"Really?" Honey puzzled. "You don't know that already?"

"Don't we all doubt ourselves?"

"Not to that extent."

"Oh."

"Is there something you're not telling me? Some deep dark secret?"

"No. Maybe I meant more in the vein of am I on the right track? Am I making a difference?"

"That's not what you said."

"Isn't it?"

"Are you okay?"

"Yes, of course, I just—"

Honey jumped. The bang on the door was more than just forceful. "Yes?" she managed.

"Honey! It's Liza! Open the door right this instant!"

Tucking the phone into her shoulder, she rose from the bed. "You heard that, right?"

Meg questioned. "Liza?"

The shout sounded once more. "Who are you talking to? Who's in there with you?"

Pulling open the door, Honey looked at her flustered PA. "Yes?"

"Who's in there? Don't tell me it's some Thai bride." Liza bustled her way in.

"I'm on the phone."

Liza stalked around the apartment. "My call wouldn't connect. Do you realise the time?"

Honey looked at the clock. "It's two minutes past six, Liza." She pulled the handset from the crook of her neck and wiggled it at the intruder. "It's Meg. Say hello, Meg." She kept the phone outstretched.

The voice echoed. "Hello."

"Hello, but hurry it along. We've got a schedule to keep."

"Svetty's magic's worn off I see?" said Honey, slowly realising the relationship between the two forceful women may be one of extreme highs and lows. Liza almost comatose on the plane on the way over, post stroking from Svetty, only to experience a huge come down as the soothing subsided and reality hit home that the holistic therapist had chosen to stay at Velvet Villa instead of coming with them. An option okayed by Diana but rejected by Svetty. Honey had tried to talk to Liza about it on the way over here, but she'd been in the throes of relaxation, claiming the rejection wasn't of her, but now, looking at the tension in the shoulders and hearing the snap in the voice, she might have reconsidered. "You should call her, Liza."

"We're late! My call wouldn't connect!"

"To Svetty?"

"To you!"

Honey turned her back on the flapping. "I'm sorry, Meg. I'm going to have to go." She lowered her voice and smiled. "But I've loved this and I want to do it again. I want to know more about you, just everything, random things, important things, silly things, what makes you tick, what makes you cross."

"Questions seventeen and eighteen."

"What makes you smile, what makes you laugh."

"Twenty and twenty-one."

Honey laughed loudly. "Exactly, it's been fab, you're fab, this is fab. Everything's fab."

Liza looked stern. "Get off the phone, Honey."

Honey continued. "Same time tomorrow? And the day after that?"

The voice was soft and heartfelt. "And every day for the rest of our lives."

CHAPTER TWENTY EIGHT

Driving under the barrier and into The Alderley estate, Meg smiled at Old Sal, the security woman's enthusiastic wave an early indication of approval of her anticipated arrival. Honey must have called ahead, let her know she was coming. Meg smiled again. The old woman was now giving a grinning thumbs up. There'd been an exchange no doubt, Honey making the call, Old Sal asking the questions. They wanted her happy. Everyone in Honey's life wanted her happy; that had become undeniably obvious the closer she'd got to the singer, and after a week of late night phone calls she felt she knew her completely. They'd discussed childhoods, teenage years, hopes, aspirations and fears – no topic out of bounds, no topic left untouched. They'd fit perfectly into an ease of discussion, neither taking the lead or monopolising the conversation, both as keen to hear as be heard. And Honey was funny. She had a wit only seen in the observant, perceptive person, able to effortlessly amuse with anecdotes and banter.

Meg followed the short winding road, lost in her musings. It was the banter that had enamoured her the most, because it was simply so unexpected. Honey was gorgeous, talented and accomplished, all plenty to draw anyone in, yet it was the hidden personality that enticed more than anything. And yes, while Honey's stories about sell-out world tours and ridiculous celebrity parties were fascinating, it was the quick-witted one-liners that drew her further into the infatuation. Rounding the final corner before the imposing house came into view, Meg questioned herself; was infatuation the right word? Was that how you'd describe the rush of emotion when the phone started to ring? The smile constantly creeping onto your lips whenever you thought of the person? The fact you'd laugh in a totally inappropriate setting when a memory skipped into your mind? Or was it the inability to spend a single hour without that person popping into your thoughts? Every sight, smell or sound relatable in one way or another.

Saturday night had been agony, watching Honey taking her seat at the judges' table, knowing what it felt like to be seated ten metres behind, understanding the effort it took to step out looking that glam. The smell of the hairspray, the feel of the clothes, the air of excitement surrounding the show. Meg shuddered remembering the last time they'd kissed, Honey pressed against the dressing room door, both knowing the attraction was building and, yes, while she'd cursed her decision to go home and let Honey sleep in the car, it had actually served to raise anticipation levels further. The calls had become intimate, and not in a stilted phone sex way, but in a naturally progressive logical way. Of course one of their laughing innuendos would result in a sexual discussion. What turned them on? What made them want more? And Meg had been honest. It wasn't the idea of seeing a woman in sexy clothes, trying to entice with fluttering eyelashes or wiggling hips. It was the idea of that intimate connection. The invisible pull finally having its way, joining you on every level.

Jo's comment last night while watching the show of "Why haven't you shagged yet?" only made her think about it more clearly. Lesbian sex wasn't like straight sex. Straight sex: you could just lie there and it would happen. The man often the leader, the woman thinking – why not. With lesbians it was different. You both had to want it. Really want it, she reasoned. It was that slow build of growing desire that worked to make the actual act, when it finally happened, utterly explosive, utterly mind-blowing, an uncontrollable meeting of emotions culminating in an act of pure passion, pure love. Meg stopped herself. Was it love she wanted to make? Was she already that deeply involved? She nodded with vigour. Yes, yes it was. Totally, utterly, completely and without question.

Jo had quizzed her throughout last night's show, not getting their connection, not understanding what one saw in the other. Obviously she was focusing more on Honey's supposed attraction than her own, but the questions had come thick and fast and her answer of "Sometimes this just happens" didn't appease the blonde in the slightest. Jo was a cynic and didn't believe things like this *just happened*. She'd set out to snare footballer Gavin Grahams the night of the auction, and she'd worked to keep him interested ever since. She'd said the idea of some fairytale fate-like bond pulling the two women together was no more than bollocks, causing Meg, against her better judgement, to invite Jo and Gavin to the dinner she and Honey had planned later in the week. The thought process had been: show off the bond, compare it to her flatmate's non-existent one, win the argument. But now, faced with the prospect of a double date, she knew she'd probably rethink. She wasn't ready to share Honey, and she certainly wasn't ready to explain the acquired taste that was the blonde bombshell.

Stepping out onto the driveway, Meg felt a flush of anticipation. Honey had described how she was going to open the door. Slowly. Smiling. Pulling her in. They were going to hold each other's gaze. They were going to feel the energy. Drown in the arousal. They would kiss. It would get frenzied. Their bodies would get rough. They'd be desperate for more. Pulling. Pushing. Finding a wall. A table. The stairs. They'd talked about the stairs, stopping as they climbed them to kiss deeper, to feel more, before arriving at the bedroom. Meg reached for the doorbell and held her breath. She shuddered at the ring. This was it. This was their moment. She closed her eyes, feeling the rush of warmth as the door was pulled open.

"I don't know why she couldn't do my bunions at Velvet Villa," said the voice.

"And my toenail's still hanging off," said the other.

Meg stepped back in horror. Gerty and Dot were there, feet breathing freely in flip-flops, glass of sherry for medicinal purposes in hand. "H-Hi," she managed.

"Bedroom three. Top of the stairs, turn left."

Meg tried to look over their shoulders. "Is Honey here?"

"Bedroom two." Gerty was sipping her sherry. "Monopolising Svetty and Kuntse. Rushing our chiropody session. Never taken any interest whatsoever in her mother's holistic therapists."

"Yet the minute she does," continued Dot, "all the stops are pulled out."

Both women nodded in sync.

Meg tried to smile. "You can push the stops back in if you want?" The whole idea of a massage from Svetty was awkward enough without the added pressure of having someone lie next to you, someone with whom you weren't yet fully acquainted. What if she groaned? What if she pulled her sex face? Meg stopped herself. This was Honey's idea and she'd vowed to take part with commitment. "Why's Honey in bedroom two if I'm in bedroom three? I thought this was a joint massage?"

"Come in, dear, let me explain."

Meg looked at the woman with the slightly fuller face. Gerty, she reminded herself, remembering the strange family meeting on the sofas not so very long ago. "Thank you, Gerty."

"Oh, I do like you," said the face with a smile. "Right. Well." A sip was taken before the story was allowed to unfold. "We were at Velvet Villa, ready and waiting for our chiropody session. We need our chiropody sessions, don't we, Dot."

"Gerty, we do. My toenails don't know whether they're coming or going."

"Nor do my bunions." There was a pause as more therapeutic healing alcohol was consumed.

Dot continued. "Only we find out Svetty's come here. So we arrive and see her setting up some elaborate massage cavern in bedroom two."

"She's never set a cavern up for us."

"That she has not."

"So we complain about our lack of cavern."

"And our lack of chiropody session."

"So she squeezes us in."

"Svetty knows which way her bread's buttered," said Dot with authority.

"Only now she's delayed."

"So Kuntse's starting you in bedroom three."

Meg frowned. "I don't get the cavern."

"You will. She'll wheel you in."

"Who will?"

"Kuntse."

"On a stretcher?"

"Portable massage table."

Meg looked around the large expanse of hall. This wasn't at all what she'd been expecting. She'd been expecting fireworks and fumblings, not the groans and grumblings of two sozzled old women. "If she's delayed, can't she start us together?"

"Kuntse's new. Svetty's apprentice."

Dot shook her head. "She's Svetty's cousin from Laundroteria."

Meg frowned. "Where's Laundroteria?"

"The dry cleaners round the corner. The Laundroteria. She says she's the best sheet folder in town. Anyway, Svetty's trying to get her a place on Di's team."

"And she's massaging me?"

Gerty nodded. "Svetty wanted a final run through, massaging Honey so Kuntse could watch and take notes. Apparently everything's going to be synchronised."

Dot continued. "Only we messed up their schedule and Svetty's not finished."

"And our Svetty's very professional. She doesn't want to stop Honey halfway through, so Kuntse's starting you off, warming you up, giving Svetty time to finish before you get wheeled in for the real deal to begin."

"I think we should watch," mused Dot.

Gerty nodded. "It's all done to music. My bunions never get music."

Meg coughed. "So the woman from the dry cleaner is warming me up then wheeling me in?"

"Got it. Top of the stairs first on the left. She's waiting."

Meg stared at the women. "Really?"

"Yes, really. They heard the bell; they told us to get you."

Meg started towards the stairs. "And Honey didn't want to come down?"

The old women laughed in unison. "You've obviously never been therapised by Svetty."

Maybe not. And, yes, she seemed forceful, but she wouldn't be able to stop Honey from rushing down the stairs to greet the woman she'd been intimately involved with every evening this week, would she? Because that's what it felt like. Each phone call bringing them closer. But now this? A house full of people? She quickened her pace up the wide staircase. Fine. The sooner they started the sooner she'd see her. And, yes, it may only be face down on a massage table, but they'd be together. They'd feel that force. That pull. Meg smiled. They'd hold hands. That's the image she'd created. Both lying side by side, or head to head, hands finding each other.

Knocking on the bedroom door, she waited. Nothing. She tried again, this time pushing on the handle. She slipped into the room. It was huge and airy with a bed, a cabinet, some paintings – clearly not lived in, but nice all the same. In the corner, she looked to the massage table, its white sheet hanging over the sides, not quite long enough to disguise the wheels. She glanced around for the other door. Would she be lying flat while being wheeled into the cavern? Were the wheels on lock-down right now? A woman's noisy entrance stopped her, bustling in from a door she'd not noticed, hidden to the side of the wardrobe, connecting the two main bedrooms no doubt. Meg paused. No, they'd said bed two and bed three; there must be another, far grander, master bedroom hidden somewhere within the sprawling design. She smiled, hoping she and Honey might visit it later.

The voice was deep. "You are looking of the happiness. Good. I Kuntse."

Meg focused. It was Svetty, only shorter and wider. "You look like your cousin."

"Me be performing the massages like Svetty too." The face screwed up. "But Svetty not be folding of the sheets like Kuntse Krasnikova." The woman tutted at herself. "I stop the chat chat about old job. Kuntse be wanting new job." An array of oils were set on the bed before an imaginary rainbow was painted with an outstretched hand. "Velvet Villa," she said with a slight melody in her voice. The nod was forceful. "I be getting you of the ready."

Meg took hold of the outstretched paper pants. "Thank you," she said, lifting her eyes to the stationary therapist. "I think I can manage."

"I warm you up; I wheel you in."

"Yes." Meg stayed standing, smiling at the woman who was still stationary and staring just metres away. "Could I have a moment?"

"I be watching of the massages. I do you too. We be doing of the stroking in sync. Honey get twice."

"It must be good then," said Meg, still standing there clutching on to the paper pants.

"Kuntse fast learner."

"I think Kuntse needs to give me a minute to get changed."

The woman bowed and made small reversing steps out of the room. Meg glanced into the gap created as the inter-connecting door was opened once more. The other bedroom looked atmospheric, the odd twinkle of light adding a glow to the darkness. Meg inhaled. The escaping scent was definitely lavender. She quivered. This could be nice. This could work wonders. She wouldn't really describe herself as an uptight person, just a busy one who had better things to spend her money on than synchronised soothing techniques. But she'd enjoy it. She nodded. She'd try and enjoy it.

Turning towards the bed, she pulled off her top, quickly unclipped her bra and folded both onto the covers. She pulled down her jeans only to jump at the sudden dong of a bell. She clutched hold of her boobs and spun round, jeans falling around her ankles. The holistic therapist was back in the room, brandishing what looked like a small church bell.

"Svetty be using of the chimers," said the deep whisper. "Kuntse find this."

Meg looked down at herself. "You're meant to give me five minutes!"

"Kuntse be of the enterings too soon?"

"Way too soon!"

The therapist performed her reverse, accidentally bonging the bell once again. "Kuntse come back. Lady be getting under the covers."

"I'm trying," said Meg, waiting for the door to close once more. She grabbed at her jeans and pulled them off, crouching in on herself as she swapped her own knickers for the paper pants. She glanced over her shoulder at the door, hoping the bell-swinging therapist wouldn't make another appearance. She rolled her knickers and jeans into a pile and dropped them on the bed, dashing to the table and hiding herself under the covers. She breathed. She was in. Looking up at the bright lights, she squinted. Maybe Kuntse would dim them. In fact, she'd roll over. This was a back massage after all. She paused. Wasn't it? What had Honey called it? Oh dear, she thought, as the scent came again; Kuntse was back in the room.

Adjusting herself on the padding, Meg breathed. This was better. No bonging. She opened her eyes through the face hole. Yes, and the lights had been dimmed. With a slow intake of scented air, she relaxed. The week had been busy. It always was working for *The Beacon*, but this week particularly so with Honey's interview, Sandy Greer's piece and numerous other stories researched, explored and checked with no help. Being a journalist could be isolating sometimes, strange when you said it aloud, people imagining you'd race from one hustle and bustle to another, when often it was just you and your thoughts, you and your research. It was busy in that sense of the word, pieces to write, word counts to hit. But life was good, she decided. Life was starting. That's what it felt like, the beginning of something special, everything falling neatly into place.

"I not be doing of the chat chat," said the voice.

Meg smiled. Perfect. She could lose herself in her musings. She could unwind in the gentle flutters caused by the adjustment of towels. Kuntse simply pulling up the covers, gently... slowly... grazing her skin, exposing her ankles, her calfs, her knees. This was heaven, this was relaxing, this was—

"What the hellings is that?"

Meg startled from her stupor, lifting her head and looking over her shoulder.

"You got psoriasis."

"What?! No, I haven't!"

The holistic therapist had stepped back from the table, pointing at her left thigh. "There!" The face was grimaced.

Meg looked down at her own leg.

"Nasty! Red! I not be getting of the infections! I need the clean hand to fold of the sheets!"

"It's a birth mark."

The head was shaking. "That not a birth mark."

Meg nodded, feeling her cheeks flush. "It's just a birth mark. A strawberry mark."

"It be looking sore. Kuntse put light on."

Meg squinted as the room switched back to full spotlight. She waited for her eyes to adjust before looking once more at her leg. She'd had it from birth. It wasn't that big. And it certainly wasn't infected. "It's fine," she said, "it's natural."

"That not natural."

"Oh well fine, don't massage me then."

Kuntse stepped closer, daring to poke the adjacent area with a finger. "Kuntse be putting on gloves."

"You don't need gloves! It's a strawberry mark."

"It look like disease."

"It's not!" Meg glanced at the woman, her face a picture of apprehension and disgust. "Honestly, we'll stop, it's fine."

"Wait! Kuntse be wanting of the job at Velvet Villa." The forceful rainbow was painted once again. "I just be needing the care to take. Svetty tell me some story."

"About psoriasis?"

"Back that she massage. Zitty. She be squeezing up. Zit pop out. Pus hit her on forehead. She say smellings like death."

Meg tried not to heave. "I think we'll just leave it there, shall we?" Pushing up on her arms she tried to swing her legs to the floor.

"Wait! I sorry. I be turnings off of the light. I start again."

The hands were holding her in position. "Really, it's fine."

"I just be scared by some story." She dimmed the lights and spoke quietly. "Svetty be saying the one man, leave skid marks on sheet."

"Oh, for goodness sake," said Meg, "this really isn't relaxing."

"I relax you. I be using the oils. You be of the understanding though. I new to this. I not be needing to see old lady with great grey bush."

"I haven't got a great grey bush!"

"Just psoriasis. That shock me too. Svetty say one lady have prolapse. She massage too hard, see it pop out."

Meg lifted her head. "Can we stop with the chat chat?"

"I sorry. I just be doing the talkings when I scared."

"Just put a bit of oil on me and push me in. They must be ready for me by now?"

"As long as you don't do the trumpet. Svetty be saying some do the trumpet."

"You've not done anything to cause me to do the trumpet!"

The holistic therapist nodded. "Right. We begin."

Meg felt the hands on her calves, warm with oil, massaging firmly up her legs. She let her head drop down into the face hole. What if Honey couldn't handle her birth mark? She'd never questioned it before, the small fist-sized red patch on the back of her thigh. She groaned as Kuntse's fingers ran right over it, a seemingly short-lived resentment. She breathed heavily, the hands were working both legs, thumbs pushing up from calf, to thigh, to buttock. She opened one eye. Where were the fingers off to?

Kuntse's voice was knowing. "I be doing the full moon approach when massaging buttocks."

Meg's other eye flashed open. Kuntse's hands were working her glutes up and out, indeed widening her like a full moon. Don't do the trumpet, she said to herself, don't do the trumpet.

Kuntse spoke again. "You be liking the full moon."

"I'd rather you didn't."

"You need to relax."

"It's hard!"

"Howl like a wolf."

"What?"

"Howl like a wolf. It help you relax."

Meg was holding her breath, not able to loosen into the full moon's rhythm. "Maybe move onto my back."

"Not till you howl like the wolf."

Meg swallowed. "Woof." It was pitiful. Chihuahua-like. The full moon was getting fuller and the fingers were pushing wider. She tried again. "Woo-oof."

"Howl, lady, howl!"

"Haaaaw!"

The hand slapped the buttock with force. "That be my lady!"

Meg couldn't stop the trumpet escape.

"Toot toot!" shouted Kuntse, again forgetting her phobias. "I just be doing the oiling, then we go in."

Meg tried to push her burning cheeks as deeply into the face hole as they'd go. What if that happened next to Honey? What if Honey told her to go? She was about to stand and get out of this ridiculous situation when the warm oil dripped onto her back. She moaned as the fingers worked it into her shoulder, onto her neck, all over her hair. She gasped. "You're getting it in my hair!"

Kuntse lavished more oil onto her fingers before working it into the roots. "This be the full body and head massage, you need to be ready."

Meg pulled herself up. This was the final straw. She swung her legs from the table and took a moment to steady herself in the seated position.

The holistic therapist looked shocked. "Kuntse not be doing the honking of the boob!"

Meg looked down at her bare chest, covering it quickly with her hands. "I don't want the honking of the boob thank you very much and I don't want this massage!"

The hand drew the rainbow once more. "But Velvet Villa! I be needing to take you in there!"

Meg felt the table change height as it was clipped onto its wheels and shoved towards the cavern's door. "Stop it! I'm not going in looking like this!" She jumped from the travelling trolley and dashed back to the safety of the big double bed. Finding her bra, she hauled it on quickly, glancing over her shoulder at the scene at the door.

"She be doing the escape!" cried Kuntse into the other room.

Meg ignored the commotion and pulled her jeans over her pants. A hand on her shoulder stopped her. She turned. It was Honey. She couldn't meet her eyes; instead, she dropped her gaze down on herself, noticing the puff of paper pants escaping from the zip in her jeans. "Hello," she said to the floor.

Gentle fingers lifted her chin. The voice was soft. "What a disaster."

Meg looked at the eyes properly, before noticing the straw hair and oily drips. "They worked your hair too?"

"And my buttocks."

"Did you get the full moon?"

Honey was nodding. "Yep."

"The boob honk?"

"No! Did you?! Oh, that's a step too far. I'm so sorry, Meg." She looked over her shoulder at the two holistic therapists standing in the interconnecting doorway. "Go and find Gerty and Dot. They'll be more than happy to take our places." Honey rolled her shoulder. "She's been working me so hard I think I might scab."

Meg laughed while looking her host up and down. She was wrapped clumsily in a too-small towel, her hair was a mess, her face was shiny with oil, but it was the most beautiful she'd ever seen her. "I've missed you."

Honey's arms reached out quickly. "And I've missed you too."

Meg laughed as their bodies slid against one another, her eyes suddenly drawn to the two women at the door. "Do you think we could go somewhere more private?"

Honey's face was close as she whispered. "The shower's the most logical choice."

CHAPTER TWENTY NINE

Standing alone in the shower, Meg questioned what she'd been expecting. Was Honey going to ignore the fact they'd never gone any further than kissing and simply strip naked beside her, step in and soap up? Of course she wasn't and any misplaced hopes of such action only served to redden the embarrassment of the disastrous day to date. Honey had seen her half naked, hair like Worzel Gummidge, mackerel-oily skin, and paper pants protruding in an awkward fashion from her jeans zipper.

She'd been led from the inter-connecting bedrooms, along the balcony landing to a super-sized bathroom that bore a striking resemblance to the Taj Mahal. A long, rectangular bath in the centre of the room served as runway to the huge dome-shaped mirror, marble surface and sink, and pillars that had no other purpose than to frame the extravagant scene. The shower was set off to the left and was more like a room in its own right. With three marble steps up and a quick turn right, the lavishly tiled area with numerous sprinkling systems was large enough to house a whole host of people. But here she was, alone, buffeted by a blast of water from the left and an intermittent spritz from the right. Honey had explained how it all worked with motion sensitivity, each area offering a different strength of spray. She'd then said she preferred the much simpler shower in the en-suite downstairs, and Meg was beginning to understand why.

She stepped away from the sideward blast and under a circular, more traditional looking shower head. The warm water started to fall. Meg relaxed her neck, looking upwards, allowing the spray to push back her hair. This was nice. This was heaven. The water seemed scented somehow. She wiped her eyes; no, the array of shampoos, conditioners and body creams lined up on a ledge, which she'd already sampled profusely, were the reason for the sweet aroma. She reached out for another bottle: Chanel Coco Noir foaming shower cream. Honey had explained during one of their late night chats that companies would send her packages of their latest promotion – clothes, perfumes, furniture. She'd even once been given a car. Liza apparently had some system in place where offerings would be re-gifted to charities, or fans, or crowds at events. But obviously some things made their way into the house. This huge selection of goodies seemingly one of them.

Squirting some of the luxurious lotion onto her hand Meg noticed the buzz of the shower. One of the motion sensors had gone off behind her. She turned, shocked at the sight. Honey, naked and smiling. Feeling the soapy liquid seep through her fingers, she brushed her hand against the top of her thigh.

The voice was soft. "I could use some of that."

Meg looked down at the glistening soap suds. She wasn't frozen in fear, she just didn't know what she should do. Honey was standing naked... beautiful... Meg lifted her eyes, so stunningly beautiful. Her skin was pale yet peach-like and her breasts were full. She took a deep breath. She'd never been shy of her own body, she just knew she wasn't all that amazing. Her own hips didn't swell like Honey's, and her waist wasn't narrow or toned. Honey, on the other hand, was the picture of perfection: gorgeous and glistening with the water cascading over her curves. She was slim, but she still had that womanly figure, like a miniature hourglass, water droplets sliding over her like the soft sand passing through time.

Honey was reaching out, slowly, deliberately, sweeping the soap from her thigh. Meg wanted the hand to stay where it was, resting at the top of her leg, inches from the curve of her buttock, but it moved, the suds now stroked into Honey's shoulder. Meg's eyes widened. The action was slow and deliberate: Honey's fingers moving across her own collar bone, down her sternum and pausing on her slim waist.

"Do you have any more?" she asked.

Meg looked down at the bottle and held it out towards the intruder.

The smile was innocent. "Could you?" Honey turned around.

Meg could do nothing but look on as the beautifully arched back and bottom came into view. The cheeks were so pert and so sassy. Meg smiled to herself. Honey Diamond had a sassy behind. She stepped forward and mustered her resolve. *This* was their moment. *This* was their time. She reached up and drew the damp auburn hair behind Honey's ear, whispering slowly. "Why are you here?"

"For this," said Honey, finding Meg's fingers and drawing them round to the hourglass.

Meg felt herself pulled closer, her breasts grazing Honey's smooth back. Honey's moan was all it took to ignite the fire that had been sparking since the moment they met. Moving them both towards the wall, Meg replaced the cream on the shelf before locking fingers with Honey, pressing her palm up to the wall. She was behind, Honey facing away, enough of a gap between them and the tiles for her hand to slide up Honey's body towards her neck. Meg tilted Honey's head to the side, joining their eyes properly. "I want you," she said with certainty.

"Have me." The eyes were wild and pleading.

Meg realised she held the position of power. This wonderful woman with this beautiful body was hers for the taking. She kept their eyes locked. She could spin her round, please her from the front, go down on her knees as she pulled a leg over her shoulder, or she could hold their gaze and let her fingers slide slowly from the neck, past the chest, towards the taut torso. The eyes widened in anticipation as the fingers grazed lower. Honey wanted this, her quivering lips were needing this. Letting her fingers continue their downward journey, Meg paused at the top of the thigh before moving the leg to the side, widening Honey's base, water now able to find a new course. Honey moaned.

Hearing Honey's lips emit such a wanton sound was all it took for Meg to succumb. The plan had been about control: she'd take her time, she'd tease, she'd keep their eyes focused as she made Honey come. But here she was, tasting her mouth, devouring her tongue, twisting her round as she pushed their bodies hard to the wall, breasts on breasts, legs parting, thighs pressing. The gentle water continued to flow from above but there was nothing gentle about their connection. Honey, with her hand now free, had reached round to her hips drawing their bodies closer together. Meg took the hands and forced them back against the wall; she still wanted control, she still wanted to give pleasure first.

Kissing Honey deeper, she forced the legs to the side with her own, the hourglass figure now star-shaped against the tiles. Meg pulled back momentarily and waited for the eyes that opened in a haze of arousal. "You're perfect," she managed to say.

"I want you to take me." It was the same guttural tone only this time more demanding. Honey needed it. Honey wanted it now.

Meg kissed her roughly, forcing their hardened nipples together. She ran her fingers over the outstretched arms, pinning Honey to the wall, moving her mouth to her neck, soft and wet from the water. She let her tongue dart out before grinding her teeth along Honey's jawline. Honey tilted her head, offering more of her flesh. Meg grazed harder, her teeth finding an earlobe. She pulled and sucked with her lips; Honey's mouth quickly turned back into the action.

They were rampant, urgent, all-encompassing kisses. It wasn't simply a meeting of mouths, it was a meeting of wants, of desires, of desperation to get closer, to feel more. Meg moved her hands from Honey's shoulders, her thumbs stroking down to the nipples. She moaned into Honey's mouth as she felt them harden further under pressure, each pinch causing an intake of breath. Honey was one of the lucky ones, her nipples sending wave after wave to her centre. It was the same for Meg, her nipples as worthy of attention as any other intimate area. She worked them harder, knowing how close she could bring her.

Meg felt Honey's kisses become shorter, stuttering to make way for the moans and the gasps. This was her time. This was her moment. Keeping her hands in position, Meg dropped to her knees, her face exactly where it needed to be. She brought her mouth down, taking Honey completely. The wetness was different to that on her neck and her body, it was warmer, sweeter. Meg took more, widening her mouth and reaching with her tongue, flicking in time with her thumbs, working the nipples in sync with the movements. Honey was screaming, really screaming. She wasn't holding back or being self-conscious, she was riding her hips forward, forcing Meg to take more in her mouth. Meg swallowed hard, increasing pressure and suction around the lips so her tongue could work freely, darting in and out of the warmth, and up and over her pleasure.

Meg felt hands drop down to her head; Honey had hold of her face forcing more pressure, more power. Meg was the one working but Honey was the one riding, really riding. Pushing herself forward as Meg worked with her tongue. The cries got louder and the motion more frantic. Honey was coming, she was coming right in her mouth. Meg pulled the nipples as Honey's orgasm ripped right through her, legs shuddering as she held Meg firmly in place. Meg tasted the pleasure. It was so rich and intoxicating. It was Honey.

The voice was shaky. "You're amazing."

Meg looked up with wide eyes. "Only with you."

"Come here," the eyes were pleading for her to rise. "This doesn't happen by chance. This was more than just sex, Meg. This was… this was…"

Meg found the right word. "This was magic."

"Yes." The smile was knowing. "It was like starlight." Honey moved their mouths back together. "With you I get lost in the starlight," she whispered.

CHAPTER THIRTY

Feeling the weight of Meg's body on her own, Honey moaned in satisfaction. They'd been in this position many times over the past three weeks, taking it in turns to dominate, arouse and give pleasure, and as yet nothing had been too much or too far, but as Honey felt her head bashing from left to right, hitting the hard plastic either side of her with a force that was making her dizzy, she took stock and shifted away from the contact. "What the hell are you doing?" she asked, using her fingers to pull herself up to the car's glass divider. "I told you to lose them, but not at all costs."

The trail of paparazzi following the car that Honey, Meg and the infamous flatmate Jo were travelling in had grown almost three-fold since leaving The Alderley, with photographers confirming to colleagues it was indeed Honey Diamond in the back of the black saloon. How they knew was a mystery to all as both driver and passengers had played their parts in the ruse to perfection. Tammara, at the very last minute, had requested a different car to the one she was scheduled to drive, not quite as padded as Honey had just uncomfortably discovered. Jo had sat in the front, the only area of the car without black-out windows, in an attempt to fool the paps into believing she was a random Alderley resident being chauffeur-driven away, and Meg and Honey had lay prone in the footwell, enjoying their task that little bit too much. Tammara had ensured them the back windows were flash proof, meaning no clear shots could be taken even if the cameras were pressed right up to the glass, but Honey had insisted they'd better be safe than sorry and stay low.

Much giggling had ensued until it dawned on them their distraction had failed and a whole host of people were now following the car, causing Tammara's erratic driving and their refuge in the uncomfortably squashed space they simply weren't used to, the other cars being nicely carpeted with seats upholstered all the way down. Sitting properly, Honey looked out of the windows. Things with the press had escalated since the song and the interview, everyone desperate for that first shot of her woman, because that's what the rumour mills were reporting: a woman who'd stolen her heart, a woman always close by her side. Looking across at Meg, now also back in her seat, she realised they were right. There was a woman, and she'd more than stolen her heart, she'd snatched it clean away, filled it with love, life and laughter, yet they were wrong with their supposition of proximity. Meg was too far away too much of the time, both of their jobs dominating their schedules. She had suggested Meg retire and become her new personal publicist, but this was not received with humour, as it was intended. Meg had declared her independence was key, and as much as she'd love to spend every waking moment with Honey, it was simply too much too soon. Honey had confirmed she'd been joking, but had started to wonder if Meg feared true commitment.

Looking over at her now, staring anxiously out of the window, she questioned it once more. "They'll get their picture eventually," she said.

"But we're going to the back entrance, right? That's what you told Tammara?"

Honey nodded. The Muse was prepared for celebrity diners like herself, the back entrance only accessible via the underground car park manned by security personnel and fully enclosed to ensure an exit from the vehicle would be seen only by the waiting maître d'.

Jo piped up from the front of the car. "Do what you want but I'm getting dropped at the front."

Honey looked at the busty blonde. They'd met for the first time thirty minutes ago and for now she was reserving her judgement. Meg had put off their previous meetings, postponing at the last minute, always finding a reason to stay at The Alderley instead of heading back to her place where there was a chance they might meet the other woman in her life. Honey had been very careful not to sound precious, and it was true, she didn't mind where she stayed as long as she was with Meg, and more than that, she wanted to see her home, her house. Meg was constantly correcting her that it wasn't a home or a house, more of a bedsit in Clapham, but it couldn't be that bad, could it? And Jo couldn't be that horrendous, could she?

"My first time at The Muse," continued the blonde, "and I am not entering via some scutty underground tunnel. Gavin's meeting me out front anyway."

Honey smiled. There was a big difference in the celebrity world between those wanting the attention and those not needing it because they already had it. "Meg tells me he's a footballer."

"Er, like the best."

Honey watched as Meg's hand moved through the gap towards the front seat, no doubt squeezing her flatmate's arm in an attempt to control. "Who does he play for?" she continued.

"Are you serious?" The tone was disparaging.

Meg cut in. "Honey doesn't follow football."

"Everyone knows who Gavin Grahams is."

Honey put her hand up in apology. "I'm sorry, I don't."

"Well, don't tell him that, for god's sake."

Honey laughed. It was actually refreshing to have someone so snippy towards her. No one would usually dare, but Meg had warned that Jo might be a tad resentful, viewing her as the reason she no longer saw much of her flatmate. In the three weeks since their first steamy shower encounter, things had moved fast. Late night meetings, secret stop-overs and so much sex it was wild. Honey closed her eyes as she often did when remembering. Meg could arouse her, instantly. She could make her come in so many different ways, and had, in so many different places. She'd been endearingly shy about her lack of experience, so either they were a match made in heaven, or Meg was hiding some illicit past prowess, but in all honesty she didn't really care. Meg was hers now, and if only she could encourage her to take that next step and be pictured beside her. Yes, the press would go crazy, but they'd get over it, and they'd simply become the new biggest thing. Honey and Meg, Meg and Honey. They looked good together. They looked sweet. Honey opened her eyes and smiled at her girlfriend, and was met not by a returning smile, but instead by a worried gaze and anxious eyes. One step at a time, she told herself; Meg wasn't one to be rushed. "No one will see us at the back entrance," she whispered.

"But the diners in The Muse…"

"You said you've been before. They're not ones to lift their phones. Not to take pictures anyway. People know I'm seeing someone. The worst they can do is confirm with written descriptions your beautiful face and pretty outfit."

Meg looked down at herself. "You're sure I'm okay?"

"You're perfect, and if you're ever worried just make use of my girls. I did offer them today, remember; you should have come in."

Meg lifted her finger to her lips, shushing the comment as she leaned back into her seat and mouthed. "It's bad enough she's here. I had to hold her down in the car until you came out. She'd have found fault with your furniture, lifted her nose at your neighbours. No chance. I don't know why I even agreed to all this anyway."

Honey's voice was quiet. "Because she's your friend and we needed to meet eventually."

"But at The Muse? On a double date? With her boyfriend?"

"This was your idea."

"No, it was hers!" Meg shushed herself, fanning her words as they spilled from her mouth. "She said she'd only come if it was somewhere spectacular, you said we had to meet regardless, so I'm just stuck here in the middle trying to keep my head down."

"Why? Why's your head down?"

"Oh, Honey, you know this. Once we're together we're *together.*"

"I thought we were already together? You call me your girlfriend."

"Yes, but in the public eye. That suddenly escalates everything."

"And what's wrong with that?"

"It's just the pressure. I'll be judged as unworthy. I'm bound to muck up and I don't want the world watching when I do."

"You won't! Have faith in yourself. Have faith in us."

"I do have faith in us, I'm just not used to being on the brighter side of this world."

Both women paused as Jo buzzed down her window, waving like the Queen at the paparazzi all clustered round the entrance to The Muse. "I certainly don't have faith in her," said Meg, quickly upping her volume. "Close that, Jo! Now, you idiot!"

"I told you. I'm getting out."

"Not in the middle of the road you're not," said Tammara, double checking the central locking.

"I need to whet their appetites." She paused before gasping and quickly buzzing the window back up. "Oh god, what if they think I'm you?" She lifted her nose at Meg. "What if they think I'm her lesbian?" She gifted Honey with the same nose lift. "That lot behind us have been following since The Alderley. They took my picture. You said they know Honey's in the car. They're going to put two and two together and call me a lesbian." She mimed the act of being incredibly ill. "Gross. I'm definitely getting out now. Gavin and I need to make our grand entrance. I need to show them I like tail not titties."

Meg rolled her eyes. "Oh Jo, who cares what they think?"

Honey turned her attention to the woman next to her, lifting her eyebrows with a look of confirmation. "Exactly my point."

"I meant it in terms of Jo being a nobody."

Jo tutted. "You're a nobody too, Meg."

"But I'm with Honey, and Honey's a somebody."

"So's Gavin."

"Not quite on the same scale."

"Yes he is."

Tammara joined in. "I'd not heard of him."

Jo's snipes were barbed. "You lesbians don't know the first thing about sport."

Honey cut in. "Tammara's not a lesbian."

"She looks like one."

"Jo!" Meg's hand was at her mouth in shock.

"What? I'm just saying it as it is. Gavin Grahams is just as famous as Honey. He got us the reservation. He's the one who bagged the top table."

Honey bit her lip, avoiding the temptation to correct. She'd asked Liza to confirm the booking once Meg suggested it, knowing how difficult it was to get a table at such short notice and not wanting anything to hamper this meeting of friends that had taken so long to arrange. No reservation had been made so Liza had worked her magic and booked them straight in. Honey accepted it was more her name than Liza's way with words that had got them the slot, but still, her PA had done all the work, contacting Gavin Grahams' people afterwards to confirm the booking with them. He was heading straight there from a game apparently, the reason for Jo's travel arrangements. It was fine, thought Honey, smiling at the blonde in the front; it gave her a chance to get acquainted before the sit down meal began.

"So what do you like about him?" she asked with genuine warmth.

"He's got the biggest bollocks you could imagine."

"Jo!"

"What, Meg? They're big; plus he's minted as shit."

"Jo! You said it was only one glass."

"What? Don't pretend you don't swear like a trooper and don't pretend you don't drink like a fish."

"I don't!"

"You do. Unless you've changed already, which probably you have. I never see you anymore do I, so how would I know?"

"Jo, I'm busy, Honey's busy, we don't see each other that often. I'm still home a lot; you're the one who's hardly ever there."

"I'm always there."

Honey decided it was a good time to cut in. "We could go back to yours after the meal, make it into a girly evening?"

Jo grimaced. "And do what? Plait each other's leg hair?"

"What's got into you? How much have you had?" Meg was alarmed. "Can you please just behave?"

"Look at you, Miss Prissy. It's not like you to be positive and you know I like a drink when I'm getting ready. And what's changed? You'd usually be blasting all this secret entrance rigmarole and hidden appearance crap."

"I wouldn't!"

"Oh, you little liar!"

"I'm sorry about this, Honey." Meg was talking fast. "Maybe we should just call it a night?"

"And miss my grand entrance? No chance. Gavin says he'll meet me out front."

Tammara nodded to the security guard who raised the barrier and let the car into the underground entrance. "We're here now."

"Open the doors, I'm walking back out." The blonde was pulling on the handle and signalling to the central locking. "I'll meet you inside."

Tammara looked over her shoulder for guidance.

Honey shrugged. What could she do? If Jo wanted to totter back up the ramp and out into the open then so be it. She nodded to the driver who released the lock on the doors. "We'll see you inside."

"So long, suckers," came the shout as the heels clipped back through the tunnel.

The three women left in the car stared at each other in disbelief, Meg's face more embarrassed than the others. "I'm so sorry," she said, speaking first. "Now do you understand my slight trepidation?"

Honey was puzzled. "But you've been friends for so long."

"I know, right."

"Is she fun to be around? Does she stimulate you intellectually?" She watched as Meg laughed. "Does she care for you?"

"Like when I'm ill?" The laughing continued.

"So what's the pull, and I'm not being judgemental, I'm sure she's lovely."

"Don't you have friends you're just friends with? You don't question why, you just sort of slot into each other?" Meg sighed. "We've been through a lot. She's got her issues and she says having me helps. Obviously not at the time, at the time of the dramas she's yelling at me to do one, but—"

"Is it the drink?"

"Mostly."

"Some people don't want to be helped, Meg, and there comes a time where you have to lift your hands and walk away."

"Move out?"

"It's a thought."

"I couldn't do that to her. We're too similar."

"But you're nothing like her."

"Maybe I was."

"No. Stop it. You two are chalk and cheese."

"She's just an acquired taste, that's all. You'll get used to her."

"Maybe I'm an acquired taste and she won't like the taste of me?"

Meg raised her eyebrows wickedly.

"You know what I mean!"

"Jo doesn't like anyone. The meaner she is, the more she secretly loves you. And FYI," Meg lowered her voice and leaned in closer, "you taste like perfection."

Honey felt that surge of lust rise once more from deep in her stomach. It was a wash of shudders trembling through her in memory, in anticipation. "Can we go back to yours? After the meal, I mean?"

"I'm not prepared. I've not cleaned. The place is a mess."

"I want you to take me... in your bed... in your house... any which way you should please."

Meg swallowed. "Well, when you put it that way."

"Is that a yes?"

Meg glanced at the heels tottering away in the distance. "No. Actually it's a no. A definite no."

****

Entering the restaurant through the back door meant they avoided the public area below and could climb the wide staircase to the VIP balcony room from an entrance to the left. It wasn't that Honey wanted to avoid the crowds, it was just a by-product of avoiding the paps, neither of which some celebrities, including her mother, ever chose to do, loving the attention and courting the stares. Of course, the people in the VIP room stared too, but their stares were more subtle, less devouring. Maybe this time it would be different. This time she wasn't arriving alone. Reaching out, she took hold of Meg's hand.

"What are you doing?" came the gasp.

"We're nearly at the top."

"Exactly!"

Honey felt the fingers wiggle away. "We're a couple, Meg."

"But we don't want the world to know that!"

"Why not?"

"We seriously cannot have this conversation again on step twenty of this twenty-five-step mammoth staircase. It's like that one on the Titanic, only curving."

"Stop changing the subject."

"Let go of my hand and you can stay at my place."

"Deal," said Honey with a wide smile. It was going to be about the small wins with Meg, the small steps. This side of the world was new to her; of course she'd have doubts, and of course they were wise not parading themselves in front of the press in case it all went terribly wrong. Looking across at the woman walking by her side, Honey smiled to herself. This wouldn't go terribly wrong, this was all so perfectly right.

"There's Gavin Grahams." Meg was whispering as they rounded the curve, the VIP floor coming into full view.

Honey knew where they'd be seated, her eyes found him quickly. "There at the table? Wow, he's really quite suave."

"My point is he's not outside."

"Right. No." Honey found her head dropping as the gasping got louder. Diners were nudging each other, stifling their animated gossip. She kept her eyes down and followed the maître d's ankles.

"Your table, Miss Diamond."

"Honey, please." Regaining her composure, she looked up at Meg. She was like a rabbit in the headlights. Placing a hand on the small of Meg's back, she guided her towards her seat.

The man didn't stand.

"Hi, I'm Honey," she said, giving him one last chance to do the polite thing.

"And you know who I am," he said with a wink, bottom firmly in place. "Meg, nice to see you again," he continued. "Looking more sexy than usual, if I do say so myself."

Honey looked at her girlfriend, still visibly shocked from the diners' attention. "Are you okay? Shall we sit down?"

"Sorry, yes. I've just not been here for a while. It's strange seeing it from the other side."

Gavin cut in. "The side of us celebs? It's a hard life but someone's got to live it. Where's my bird?"

Honey spoke first. "Jo? She's waiting outside."

"What's she out there for, silly bint?"

Honey coughed. Was this how couples spoke to one another? "She thought you were making your entrance together."

"Too bloody cold to hang around out there." He whistled the maître d'. "Do us a favour, mate, my bird's outside, go find her for me, would you? You can't miss her, big tits." He paused. "Well, big tits, that's it really."

"Wouldn't you rather go?" asked Honey.

"And lose valuable time with you, my gorgeous, no chance."

Honey studied the man: tanned skin, dapper suit, perfectly clean cut, but a coolness behind his eyes that she knew she wouldn't warm to. "Did you win today?" she asked, despite her concerns.

"Louis fucking Laurent's fault. Over-paid toss-pot missed the penalty, didn't he."

"You know Louis? He's my neighbour; lovely family man."

Gavin exaggerated his snort. "The nanny's more his thing. I told Jo all about it first time we met. He's a right royal fucktard. I used to be careful who I told, but not no more now it's out there with that site—"

Meg interrupted. "Gavin, could you ask for the menu?"

Honey frowned. The menu? This wasn't a Harvester. Meg had said she'd been here before. "They'll bring the wine choices when everyone's arrived," she whispered quietly, "then the food menu."

"Right. Sorry."

"Are you okay? You look a bit flustered."

"She probably can't see without her glasses," said Gavin. "A right specky four eyes first time we met."

"When was that?"

"Oh, back in—"

"There's Jo!" Meg's voice was high pitched.

Looking towards the staircase, Honey grimaced. Jo looked like a drowned rat, hair slick to her shoulders, dress damp to the skin. "The rain must have started," she said, waving her hand and welcoming the latecomer to their table. "Here, have my napkin," she offered.

The snap was vicious. "You said you'd be outside, Gavin! What the bloody hell are you doing sitting up here?"

"Chatting up our Honey, aren't I my love?"

Honey ignored the come on. "Miscommunication I think."

"They wouldn't let me in," continued Jo, "said they didn't know who I was."

"Good call." Gavin was laughing. "Get your arse down and stop making a scene."

"Me? It looks like you're the one making a scene with *our* Honey*.*" She spoke with affectation.

The footballer pulled on his cuffs. "She'd be *my* Honey if I set my mind to it."

"Hello, I am here."

"No, she wouldn't," said Jo, still standing by the table. "She's a lesbian, a tit tosser."

Honey made a mental note to Google whether tit tossing was an actual thing. "I am here."

"She can toss me with her tits any day of the week."

Honey glanced around at the seated diners, all staring their way, all straining for titbits. She smiled at her own joke. Titbits. None of it really mattered anymore. She was happy. She was confident. She was in the middle of a lovers' tiff with tit talk clearly audible, but with Meg by her side nothing would phase her. The papers could write what they liked, who cared what half-truths they told? Not her, she realised as she encouraged Jo to sit down once more.

"I'm not sitting next to someone my Gavin would rather be with." The blonde had folded her arms.

"Of course I'd rather be with her. Hot Honey. Even hotter now I know she'd want her mates to join in." The footballer shook his head at Meg. "Not you though, love. No offence."

Meg spoke softly. "I think we should go."

Gavin nodded. "Yeah, you two head home and leave us celebs here."

"I'm not going anywhere," said Jo, finally taking her seat. "Where's the menu? Are we all sharing some starters? Garlic bread anyone? Do they do it with cheese?"

"I know what I want for my pudding." Gavin winked seedily at Honey.

Honey weighed up the options. Stay and let things degenerate further, or go and confirm all of Jo's suspicions. The woman clearly didn't like her. The woman clearly thought she was wrong for her friend. But what if Jo was the one wrong for her girlfriend? What if their friendship was harmful? Honey stopped herself. She couldn't be judgemental, she didn't live in the real world. Maybe this was how people spoke to each other. Maybe this was how people chose to act and behave. She'd caught a Christmas episode of *EastEnders* once and was shocked but equally drawn in to the family rifts and shouting confrontations. Maybe real people did goad each other. Maybe it was a sign of affection.

Gavin Grahams whistled. "Hey, gringo, get my big-titted bird something to swallow." He lowered his voice and turned to Jo as he sneered. "And I'm not talking about my big bollocked balls this time you thirsty bitch."

Right, that was it. Honey nodded. She'd had quite enough. "Meg, follow me, I'll show you the wine rack."

CHAPTER THIRTY ONE

Pulling Meg down the stairwell and into The Muse's underground car park, Honey questioned her actions – a claimed visit to the restaurant's wine rack her excuse for a sharp exit from their table and the horror of Gavin Grahams and his "bird", or was it "bad bitch"? Why Jo would put up with such vileness was beyond her comprehension, and even though the blonde appeared to give as good as she got, wouldn't she rather be with someone who valued her, respected her, was proud of her? Honey smiled. She'd been proud of Meg as they'd walked up that grand, curving staircase, and as much as it would have pleased her to have Meg's hand willingly in her own, she was more than happy with the runner up reward of an invitation home. If she was honest, it wasn't quite an invitation, more of a bamboozlement. She'd bulldozed Meg into having her back, with Meg immediately trying to retract once she knew they were making their grand escape.

Meg had been apologising profusely for her flatmate's behaviour, but there really was no need to say sorry. Meg wasn't Jo's keeper, it wasn't her place to hold her in check. What Jo was, however, was a litmus test indicating the level of palatability Meg could accept in a friend, and it seemed her tolerance levels were high. Wasn't it a good thing Meg wasn't judgemental? Looking over at her now, as they awaited Tammara's earlier than scheduled arrival, Honey questioned it once more, unable to shake off that old saying: surround yourself with people that reflect who you want to be and how you want to feel. The saying was right, energies are contagious. What must a night in the flat be like? Sitting, moaning, bitching? No. Meg had seemed just as aghast as she had. Jo was probably just nervous, or showing off, or maybe she'd had one too many pre-dinner aperitifs, and anyway, a text to Meg's phone had announced Jo's plans to head back to Gavin's after the meal, a reply to Meg's lie of a Honey Diamond music studio emergency. At least it meant she wouldn't be involved in any more of their evening.

"Oh no, now she's asking who's paying." Meg was shaking her head at her mobile.

"Really? Can't her big bollocked, shit-rich footballer stomach the prices?"

"Honey!"

"Sorry. All that bitching banter's rubbed off."

"It doesn't suit you."

"I can't imagine it suiting you either." Pointing towards the car, she hurried their exit. "Here's Tammara."

"I don't want to be that person anymore." Meg reached out for Honey's hand, stopping her walk.

"Were you ever that person? I was joking. I've never heard you speak like that."

The pause was thoughtful. "No. But I thought it was okay."

"It is okay. Some people might say I'm prudish."

"What, for not using your celebrity to treat others like… what did he call them? Gringos?"

"I have no clue what that even means."

"Nor do I, but my point is, I'm sorry. Maybe I should think about moving somewhere new. She takes it too far." The head was shaking. "Always too far."

Pulling on Meg's hand, Honey got them moving again. "Stop apologising. I should be the one apologising for sending us home without supper."

"It was too much for the first meeting. We should have got takeout and just chilled instead."

"Can't we do that now?"

"She's staying at Gavin's."

"I mean us, now, at yours?"

"Just don't judge me."

"On what?"

"All of this. My friends, my house, my mess."

"I wouldn't. I judge people on the way they make me feel, and you make me feel fantastic." Smiling at Tammara and the open car door, Honey signalled for Meg to get in first. Tammara would no doubt be wondering what on earth was going on, a pick-up fifteen minutes after the drop-off and the loss of a passenger, but she knew from the way the chauffeur was standing, with eyes professionally distant, that she wouldn't ask – until they were alone, maybe. "We're going to Meg's," she said with a smile.

Noticing Tammara's wink, Honey pulled herself in, pausing before she took hold of her seatbelt. "I thought you had a cleaner. Pia? The one from the hub."

"We did. She's not been for a while and even if she had the mess Jo makes when getting ready is utterly inconceivable."

"I've always loved that idea – a shared bedroom, clothes flung around, make-up scattered everywhere, music blaring as wine gets drunk."

"It's not quite like that."

"As long as your bin's not overflowing, I'll be fine."

****

Standing close to Meg's shoulder, Honey glanced back down the dark communal stairwell in Clapham. It looked like there might be one other flat on this level, but it wasn't at all as she'd imagined. Of course she knew there wouldn't be a concierge or reception desk, revolving doors or a lift, but the battered shutter next to the shop front that led up these dingy, dirty steps, to this door that Meg was now using three keys to open, wasn't quite what she'd pictured. No one had seen her make the short dash from the car through the shutters, and Alan or Andy were bound to be hidden close by, but even so, standing in this stairwell she felt vulnerable. "Are we in?" she asked quickly.

"I promise it's nicer inside," said Meg, finally pushing open the door.

Honey stepped straight into the lounge. Glancing left, she spotted two further doors, bedrooms no doubt, and then right she noticed the kitchen, and overflowing bin. "It's so small," she said without thinking.

"This is huge for the area."

"Right, sorry, yes, I've not got anything to compare it to I guess."

"Apart from your mansion." Meg was laughing. "It's fine, honestly. Of course Honey Diamond hasn't been inside a two-bed flat above a discount store in Clapham before. Oh and damn it, don't look at the bin!"

Honey felt herself turned sideways as she was ushered towards the first door. "I'd call this cluttered, not messy," she said, "and I like the feel. It's nicely unmethodical, not all rigid and stark." Standing beside Meg as the door was pushed open, she couldn't help but laugh. A bedroom, almost identical to one of the Ikea pods: tidy, rigid and stark. "I was lying! I simply can't live with a mess." Stepping into the room she smiled. "I like this. I love this. This is exactly my sort of thing. You've got a desk over there, a bookcase, a bed, some tables."

Meg was smiling, pleased that her part of the place looked okay. "It's not that impressive."

"It is! It's Ikea chic." She walked towards the bed and kicked off her shoes. "Can you climb on and we'll pretend that we're roommates?"

"I'd rather pretend we were lovers."

"Pretend?"

Meg's smiled was wicked. "I couldn't if I tried. The way you touch me…"

Honey watched as the bottom lip was sucked. Meg certainly made all the right noises, and their lovemaking did seem to be evenly matched. Neither were, apparently, that accomplished in bed, which made for more potential excitement. It wasn't like being with someone who'd been there, done that, got the t-shirt and was simply showing off their skills. It was a mutual awakening, a joint effort made better by their constant communication, not in the realms of – am I doing it right? – but in the desire to experiment and please.

"Pretend you're my new flatmate," said Honey. "I'm an out lesbian and you're bi-curious, but unsure."

"Honey Diamond wants to do role play?" Meg bent down to pull off her shoes before retreating to the door. "I have to make my entrance."

"Can I call you Petra?"

"Petra the flatmate?"

"Yes. The sparks have been flying. We know we like each other but I don't want to ruin what we've got and you don't know if you want to be with a woman."

Meg nodded. "I'm having an accent."

"Good. I'm quite a stud."

Honey watched as Meg left the room before a timid knock sounded on the door. "Ye, wassup," she said, chilling on the bed in as cool a fashion as she could muster.

Meg popped her head back in. "I wouldn't fancy someone who spoke like that."

"Petra might."

"No, she wants you girly and cute."

Honey nodded. "On it." She waited for the door to close and the knock to sound. "H-hi," the accent was American-ish.

"Hellough, can oi come in for a chat?"

Honey lifted a cushion from the bed and flung it at Meg. "You sound like the big summer blowout innkeeper in *Frozen*!"

"Fine. I'm American too. You were American, right? Role play's always better in American."

Honey relaxed back onto the bed, propping herself onto an elbow and folding one leg over the other as seductively as she could manage. The knock sounded and she performed her "H-hi".

"Hey, can I come in?"

"Sure, girl, there's always room on my bed."

"I just don't know how close I can get, girl."

"Wha-da-ya mean, girl?"

Meg was stepping closer. "There's a chemistry; can't ya feel it, girl?"

"Come closer and I'll tell ya, girl."

"How close is too close?"

"In my world you can never get close enough."

"Wha-da-ya mean, girl?"

"Sit down and I'll show ya."

Meg perched herself on the bed.

"Lie back girl, I ain't gunna bite."

"Maybe I want you to."

"Whoah, girl, you be steady now." Honey lifted herself higher on her elbow, bringing her face closer to Meg's. "How do you feel when we're a-talking?"

"I like it."

Both accents were slowly disappearing as the real chemistry charged into the atmosphere. "And when I talk closer?"

Meg's eyes were locked into Honey's. "My heartbeat gets faster."

"And when you think my lips might touch yours?" Honey was hovering millimetres away.

"I feel the sparks, the electricity. I feel the pull. I want you. All of you. On me, over me, inside me."

Honey smiled. She was going to take her time. She was going to make Meg wait. Undoing the top button on Meg's shirt she smiled. "You're Richard Gere, I'm Julia Roberts. That first scene where he's sitting in the chair and she slowly undoes him and takes him, that's what I'm going to do to you, but on the bed, you lying back."

Meg's eyes closed as her head pushed further into the pillow. "Don't tease me."

"I won't." Honey opened another button. "I'm going to hover above you, exposing your flesh, bringing my mouth close to your body, but not actually touching your skin." She opened another button and pulled the shirt apart at the chest. Meg's nipples were standing to attention under her bra. "Your nipples want me." She gently pulled down on the cups, making sure her fingers didn't make contact with the skin. "They need my mouth." The nipples were exposed, pert, erect, desperate. "They want my fingers pulling, squeezing, working." She held her palm over the breasts. "You feel me here, don't you?"

Meg opened an eye and moaned. "There's a charge coming from your hand. I feel it."

"I know you do. You feel my mouth too, don't you?" Honey brought her lips towards the nipples, opening wide and breathing freely.

The moan was wanton. "Take them. Suck them."

Honey blew gently and watched the light hairs dancing on the puckered skin. "No. I'm going to undo your shirt completely." She worked as she spoke. "I'm going to unzip your trousers. I'm going to pull them off at the ankle." Removing the socks as well, Honey's eyes widened as she devoured the beauty of the body lying in front of her. Meg, naked, all except for the lacy black pants and bra pulled under her breasts. "Sit up for a minute," she instructed, letting her hair brush over Meg's shoulder as she unclasped the bra at the back. She pulled it off gently, allowing it to rub up past the nipples as she placed it on the cabinet to the back of the bed. "Lie down. Open your legs." Honey slid from the bed and walked towards Meg's feet, standing in front of her with a smile. "Keep your eyes open. Watch me." She unzipped her dress slowly, a navy blue chiffon design with a front-fitted, over-sized gold zip the focal point. Letting the dress drop over her hips, she kicked it to the side and widened her stance as she slipped her bra straps from her shoulders. "Open your legs wider," she instructed again. "You're going to imagine me between you," she undid her bra at the back, "my nipples brushing against your stomach as I move up your body towards your mouth." Lifting her fingers to her breasts, she scissored her own nipples. "I'd trace them around your lips." She squeezed harder. "I'd force them into your mouth."

Meg groaned. "Do it."

"Imagine it." She watched as Meg unknowingly chewed on her lip. "My hand would be between your legs." She watched as the thighs twitched. "I'd slide my fingers inside your pants." She paused as she ran her own fingers down her own stomach, leaving them teetering at the top of her own underwear. "I'd part you."

Meg's moan was louder. "I want you to touch me."

"I want you to watch as I touch myself." She slid her fingers into the fabric, closing her eyes and moaning as she parted herself between her own legs.

"Oh god, Honey, I love you."

Honey stopped and spoke slowly. "You love me?"

"I love you." Meg was pulling herself up on the bed. "I love you so very much."

Honey stood motionless. "You're not acting? You're not playing Petra?"

"I'm not acting." Meg's shoulders were shrugging in acceptance. "Sorry if it's the wrong time to say it, but I do. I just know I do."

"Oh, Meg."

"What?"

Honey didn't know what to say; she was overwhelmed, moved. She felt her heart swelling inside her. "You love me?"

The smile was wide. "I love you!"

Honey sank onto the bottom of the bed, her hand clasped to her mouth. She was shaking her head. "You love me."

"Is that a bad thing?" Meg was close behind her.

"It's the best thing in the world." She dropped her eyes. "I've been feeling it too. For a while."

"Feeling what?"

Honey smiled as she returned to the gaze. "This," she said, moving her hand between them.

"This what?"

"This love."

Meg wrapped her arms around Honey's waist. "I'm never going to hurt you. I can promise you that."

"Just love me. That's all I could wish for." Feeling the lips on her neck, Honey turned into the embrace. "Make love to me, Meg. Make love to me now."

"I will." The eyes held the longing connection before flickering with mischief. "Just promise we'll play Petra again."

CHAPTER THIRTY TWO

Honey awoke to the slam of the door. She looked over at the Ikea clock gently glowing atop Meg's Ikea cabinet. It was three in the morning. She pricked up her ears. Jo. She was back and mumbling obscenities. The crack of a kitchen cabinet door, or possibly the fridge, made her open her eyes further. She glanced over at Meg, sound asleep. They'd made love for most of the evening, tender touches turning frantic, every mode of climax well and truly experienced. She smiled. She liked it best when Meg was soft, when she was delicate, when her fingers and lips showed her what true love really felt like. She smiled again. Meg had said it. Freely. The wash of joy coursed through her once more. Life was funny. Giving you everything you thought you ever wanted, then suddenly showing you none of it actually mattered at all. What mattered was love. Connection. They'd been drawn to each other and that was the start of the end. Their explosion inevitable. Because that's what it felt like. A huge burst of emotion. Attraction. Lust. Fulfilment. They brought out the best in each other. They were destined to meet from the start.

Honey stopped her musings at the sound of more cursing. Should she go out and check on the flatmate? Would her presence be welcomed? Gently pulling back the covers, she crept towards the door, straightening as she heard a slam from the bedroom beside her. Jo was in her room. She turned back towards the bed, smiling at a sleeping Meg before noticing the crisp white pad of paper sitting perfectly central on the desk, glowing somehow in the shadowy room, pulling her closer, asking for her words.

Tiptoeing towards the chair, she sat with a smile. She'd find her words. She'd write her feelings. She'd capture this moment in all its glory. Her eyes adjusted in the darkness as she scanned for a pen. Often she'd wake in the night with lyrics or harmonies rushing through her thoughts, writing equipment positioned next to every bed in every room. She smiled. She'd have to bring some here just in case. It wasn't the arrival of a toothbrush that signalled progress where a songwriter was concerned, it was the arrival of their quirks, their eccentricities, their scraps of paper and chewed pencils.

Pulling open the top drawer, Honey nodded in approval – very smooth. She'd seen one of those machines in Ikea demonstrating how many times drawers were opened and closed to ensure the furniture lasted. This was smooth, incredibly smooth. She repeated the action, pulling it wider this time. Yes, just as good. She smiled at herself. It really was the simple things in life. Bending forward she looked in the drawer. A stack of envelopes on the right, some pens on the left and a letter jumping out at her from the centre. She froze, desperate for the pens to take her attention, but she couldn't move her eyes. Her mother's crest. Her mother's signature. Her mother's lawyers.

Scanning the words, Honey reeled back in horror.

****

Reaching out from the covers, Meg silenced her phone. Her alarm hadn't been set that early, a scheduled interview with a well-known historian the main event of the day. Honey had said her load was surprisingly light too. Her morning load at any rate, a four-day jaunt to America the undertaking of the afternoon, some press-related trip announcing the actors slated to shine in next year's all-singing, all-dancing big screen blockbuster. Turning over in the bed, she reached out for Honey. She'd miss her, and yes they'd been apart for longer than this before, but the closer they grew the harder it felt. Meg opened her eyes. Where was she? Jumping out of bed, she yanked on her dressing gown. Last night she didn't mind Honey nipping to the toilet – the lighting low, her mind undoubtedly elsewhere – but in the cold light of day, their shower? Just no. Pulling on the bedroom door, she scurried across the lounge, past the kitchen, getting a whiff of the overflowing bin. Meg cringed. It had all been going so well. She stopped at the door to the bathroom and knocked gently. "Honey, are you in there? Can I get you some towels?" She paused. "If you're taking a shower be careful with the shower head; it's prone to falling off the wall and clonking you mid rinse."

Listening carefully, Meg heard the retch. "Honey? Are you okay?" Again, more heaving. "Open the door. Is it something we ate?" She thought back to her late-night scurry to the fridge, grabbing sustenance where she could find it. "I'm sure that quiche was okay."

The toilet lid slammed down and the bathroom door flew open. "You ate my fucking quiche? You ditch me with fucktard then come home and eat my fucking quiche?!"

"Jo?" Meg stepped backwards at the stench of booze. "What are you doing here?"

"I live here! And that quiche lived here too."

Meg noticed the matted hair and smudged eyeliner. "Are you still drunk?"

"He dumped me!"

"Gavin?"

"Yes Gavin. Who the fuck do you think I've been seeing for the past however long? If you were around more you'd have known!"

"Have you just got in?"

"No, he made me pay for the meal first then took me home for a fucking before flicking me away like some fucking little flea or some shit like that."

"Shhhh! Honey will hear! She doesn't like bad language."

Jo raised her voice even higher. "Well she can piss right off then! She's the reason he dumped me. Said he realised he wanted someone well known, someone his rank, someone his standard, but

I'm telling you now, she's not all that. I saw her split ends in the car and her nose has definitely got a bump in it."

Meg glanced around the flat. Where was she? This was awful, this was horrible, this was beyond a nightmare. "She's the love of my life and you need to stop it right now."

"Oooh look at you, Miss Feisty. You wouldn't know what love was if it smacked you right in that frigid little face of yours. Me though?" Jo rubbed her chipped nails on her shoulder. "All falling at my feet. Darryl last night, told me he'd missed me. Told me he could love me. In fact, I think he even mentioned marriage."

"Who?"

"Darryl! Darryl the doorman! London Town bouncer, promoted to The Muse. You seriously are so self-absorbed, Meg."

"Was Gavin there while this profession of love was being uttered? Maybe that's why he dumped you."

"What's with your hoity toity words? You're Meg, just Meg, that bitch from Sleb—"

"Jo!" Meg threw her hand to her flatmate's mouth. "What the hell's wrong with you?" she hissed.

Jo started to retch. "Move it, I'm going to be sick."

Releasing her grip, Meg dashed around the small living space, popping her head back into her bedroom and stepping into Jo's room just to be sure. She returned to the bathroom and hovered over the crouching blonde. "What have you said? Where has she gone? Did you wake her when you came in? What have you done, Jo?" She shook the shoulders. "For god's sake, what have you done?"

"Me?" The hand was clumsily wiping across the wet mouth. "You were always bound to fuck this up. Why should you get someone like her while I'm left on my own? I'm much more beautiful than you are, yet you get the job, the partner, the praise every single time you rescue me from whatever fun I've been having. That's it! That's what you are. You're the fun police, nee-naw, nee-naw, nee-naw."

"What? What are you talking about?"

Jo twisted from her knees onto her bottom, her back slumped against the toilet bowl. "You don't deserve her."

"You know what, Jo? I don't deserve this. It's been fun but... actually no, wait... it *hasn't* been fun. This is my notice. I'm moving out as soon as I can."

"No, you're not! You couldn't survive without me!"

"Watch me." Stalking back to her bedroom, Meg growled in frustration. Jo was clearly still drunk but enough was enough. Honey had shown her a better way, a brighter future. Slamming her bedroom door, she dropped hard onto the bed, her eyes catching a flash of colour on her white desk pad. She pulled herself back up and made her way to her work station. Reading the words, Meg crumpled in on herself, her stomach clenching, her arms reaching out for the chair in support. Scribbled in pressured writing were the words: DON'T EVER CONTACT ME AGAIN.

Meg threw her hand to her mouth. She was the one now feeling sick. Flying back to the bathroom, she towered over Jo, spitting her words as she tried to hold on to her stomach. "What have you done?!"

"She's no good for you, smarmy little so and so. One of those people who think they're better than anyone else." Jo pulled her matted hair behind her ears and looked up with dark eyes. "Did you see the way she was sneering at Gavin? Who the hell does she think she is?"

"What did you do?!"

"People need to know what she's really like. She's ruined it for me, and if you leave me she's ruined all that too."

"Jo!" Meg was shaking the shoulders. "What did you do?!"

The wide eyes looked up as if she was being asked the question for the first time. "I didn't do anything."

"You must have done!"

"I know what I could do though. I know what would sort all this out."

Meg felt a wash of panic rise up from the pit of her stomach. Racing back into her bedroom, she flung open the desk drawer. No! The cease and desist letter was gone.

CHAPTER THIRTY THREE

Sitting on the white lounge sofa at home in The Alderley, Honey cried into the arms of her godmother.

"She knew too," snapped Diana, from her position on the pouffe. "Why aren't you batting her arms away?"

Gerty piped up. "I didn't know."

"Nor me," added Dot.

Liza bowed her head. "I don't seem to know anything anymore."

Honey lifted her eyes and looked at the group before focusing on her mother. It was the one number she knew off by heart. A call to Diana Diamond's personal line at Velvet Villa met with the shrill panic of any call from a child to mother at three in the morning. The whole crowd had come to get her. Gerty and Dot had jumped in on the action, strutting away from their late-night boozy poker game with the yoga boys like mafiosi summoned out on a mission. Liza, upon Diana's insistence, was picked up en route, blame for this whole disaster still lying flat at her door. But with exact location instructions from Honey's security, the seek and retrieve operation wasn't, in fact, that dramatic at all.

Diana snapped at the PA. "Why weren't you there?"

Liza rubbed her eyes. "We've been over this. It was a double date. Honey can't take her PA on a double date."

"You should have taken Svetty then. Made it a sixsome."

The voice was quiet. "Svetty's not talking to me."

"Oooh, why?" queried Dot.

"Go on, why?" added Gerty.

Liza squashed further into her corner of the white sofa. "I asked for a free massage. She said I was taking liberties. She called it the taking of the joke, or was it the taking of the pissing? Anyway, it had me questioning exactly what I'd been paying for, or what Diana had been paying for, or whoever's been paying to keep me happy."

Honey interrupted the wallowing. "This is about me! Not any of you lot! I've no clue why you're all here!"

"You were alone," said Diana, "in Clapham of all places, at three in the morning. What sort of woman would leave you so vulnerable?"

"I phoned from her house phone. I wasn't out on the streets."

"But you could have been! Who does that to a Diamond?"

Gerty nodded. "Someone who spills secrets on the internet it would seem."

Honey wiped her eyes, the pain too much to bear. "Why didn't you tell me?"

"You said you liked her." Diana dared to edge off the pouffe and reach out to give Honey's thigh a reassuring squeeze. "You seemed really happy."

"Sit back down, Mother. You should have exposed her. It's not like you. You never let anyone get one up on a Diamond."

Diana shrugged. "We all make mistakes," she straightened her position and nodded, "but it's out in the open now, so let's pour some sherries and head down to the spa. What time's your flight, darling?"

Liza answered first. "It's not till this afternoon."

"I'm not going."

Yanking on her collar, Diana growled at her daughter. "Oh yes you are. The reins are back on." She clapped at the PA. "Liza, get hold of the reins. Everything worked perfectly before." She waited until Liza was in a more upright rein-holding position before giving the thumbs up to all parties. "Things will be back on track before we all know it."

"I don't want things back on track and for goodness sake, Mother, put your thumbs down."

Sofia spoke softly. "What do *you* want, dear?"

Dropping her head back into the comforting arms, Honey sniffed. "I want Meg." She lifted her eyes and looked for the answers. "Why didn't you tell me, Sofia?"

The old woman sighed. "I liked her. I liked that you liked her. The site went down. It was a sin of the past."

"Why didn't she tell me?"

"Meg? How could she?"

Diana turned on her heels. "Right. Who's for some Croft Original? I'll phone the spa, let them know we're coming."

"Mother, please."

"What?" Diana turned at the sound of the house phone. "That's probably them now. We've been here four hours already without so much as a call to the restaurant for late night snacks and they're very good here at pre-empting the wants of you residents. Word's probably filtered through that we're on the block. In fact, I'm quite interested to see if there are any plots available. I could definitely envisage myself living somewhere like this."

"Mother! Just answer the phone!"

Diana Diamond lifted the receiver and paused. "Who? No. Never. I don't care what she says. Put her on the watch list. If she returns contact the police."

Honey jumped from the sofa. "Is it Meg?"

Diana turned her back on her daughter. "Yes. Honey's right here. No, she doesn't want to see her."

"I do!" she screamed, knowing in that moment she could forgive her. The shock had been awful, as if her insides were unravelling around her, but the call to her mother and subsequent pick up by the old age posse and strangling PA only worked to soften the blow and confirm everything she'd disliked about her life to date, and everything that Meg, in her innocent normality, had washed away. Meg was flawed, obviously so, and, yes, it would take a tremendous amount of explaining to even come close to a genuine understanding of how she could do what she'd done, but she wanted to hear it. Shouting again, Honey confirmed she wanted to hear it.

Diana Diamond put down the phone and turned to her daughter. "You, my girl, need a check-up from the neck up."

"Oooh, me too," said Gerty. "Liza, could you give Svetty a ring?"

"I told you, we're not talking."

"Kuntse then. She was a bit out there in that double massage, but I think I quite liked it."

Honey waved away the chatter. "Ladies, I need you to leave." Catching sight of her reflection in the window, she used her fingers to straighten her hair and her thumbs to wipe away the smudged make-up. "I want to do this by myself."

"We'll be in the kitchen," said Diana. "We're not leaving you alone with that beast."

"But you did leave me alone, Mother! You knew what she'd done and you let me keep seeing her!"

"As if I could stop you."

"Of course you could stop me! You've always stopped me! You've stopped me from living a life."

"She's very tired," whispered Diana to the rest of room, before announcing more loudly, "Liza, ring Svetty. Honey needs something deep."

"I can recommend Kuntse's deep feet treat," said Dot.

"Go!" shouted Honey, "all of you!" She reached for her godmother's hand. "Not you, Sofia. I want you with me."

"Sofia knew too!" cried Diana once more.

Honey kept her stare chilly and waited for the troupe to shuffle out of the room, forcefully shaking her head each time one of them turned to question her demand. "That's it. Out you all go." She waited for the lounge door to close before falling back onto the sofa and questioning her choice. Meg was there, at the gates, pleading for entry. She'd obviously woken up, seen the note and sped round as soon as she could. At least she wasn't hiding. At least she wanted to confront what she'd done. Maybe it *was* Jo? The letter didn't say for sure and her mother had been very mixed with her message, first saying it was a total travesty what the site had embodied, then claiming it wasn't a big enough deal to stop the culprit from dating her daughter. Maybe Meg did the tech side of things? Surely she couldn't have written those mean words or posted those cryptic yet catty remarks, could she?

Snuggling back into Sofia's shoulder, Honey thought of all the things that hadn't made sense. The way Meg didn't want to talk to Jackie Laurent on the green the first day of their meeting, even though Jackie was wholeheartedly positive about the wonderful Miss Rutherton. Margaret Rutherton. Maybe she had a double life? A split personality? Margaret publicly writing positive things so the world would praise her, while Meg privately spilled the not so positive truth. Honey shook her head. Didn't everyone do that to some extent? Telling someone they looked lovely when actually they didn't? Praising a new haircut even though it looked worse? Honey shook her head again. Yes, people told those sorts of lies, but not all went on to sneer with friends behind backs. She shook her head again. And these people weren't even Meg's rivals. Meg had no reason to bring any of them down.

"Talk to me," said Sofia. "I see you answering your own questions in there." She kissed the top of the head and lifted her hand to Honey's chest. "But feel what your heart's singing instead." She smiled. "Because hearts do sing, Honey. They don't talk or question, they sing. And their song is the truth."

Honey sighed. "The Laurents' nanny. The one you said was flirting with Tony the handyman. Was she flirting with Louis as well?"

"Louis Laurent?" Sofia laughed. "Full on affair if the talk at the hub's anything to go by."

"And me? Was I hiding my sexuality?"

"You were never asked outright."

"So I was lying by omission?"

"No, you were... Honey, you were just very innocent."

"I was managed, and Meg was right. Her comments. The secrets on that site. They weren't lies."

"They were fishing with a very wide net, dear, but even so it still doesn't answer her motive."

Honey nodded. "So that's what I'll ask her."

"And you're sure you want me here?"

"Sofia, you're the only person I trust." Honey sighed. "And I know you have loyalties to my mother, but I've never questioned your motives." She smiled. "We have so much history together, I know I always come first."

"You do, dear." The hug was soft yet supportive. "And I'll always be right by your side."

****

On hearing the doorbell, Honey pushed her godmother off the sofa. The crowd of women were definitely still in the house as she could hear them clattering around in the kitchen, finding some early morning aperitifs or late night tipples, whichever way they chose to look at it, and if Sofia didn't get to the door quickly enough one of the others would open it first. Maybe she *should* let Meg feel the full force of her mother? Or maybe Gerty and Dot could give her a mouthful? Honey sat more upright. No, she didn't want to be mean. She wanted to understand, because at the moment none of this made any sense whatsoever. She would stay seated. She would stay calm. She would ask the questions and listen to the answers. She wouldn't let her emotions overwhelm her and she certainly wouldn't let Meg off the hook.

Lifting her eyes, she tracked the lounge door as it opened, Meg entering first with Sofia her shadow. "Oh Meg," she cried, unable to stop herself from racing towards the woman who was now standing still with a plastic carrier bag hanging from each hand. "What have you done?"

The shoulders lifted, drawing attention by consequence to the two heavy bags. "I've brought round your meatballs. The Ikea

Köttbullar ones. I went back after our visit. They've been in my freezer for ages. I've been saving them for a special occasion."

"And you think this is it?"

"You said you never wanted to see me again. I thought I'd better bring them round really quickly as you did seem to enjoy them."

Honey noticed Sofia's smile before turning back to Meg. "Is this a joke?"

"No, I just…" The voice tailed off before the bags were rested onto the carpet. "I just didn't know what to do, and then I thought of all the things I'd never be able to do," she shrugged, "cooking you these meatballs being one of them."

Honey leaned forward and peeped into a carrier. "Four packs?"

"In each bag."

"Cook from frozen?"

Meg nodded. "But I know you don't want to see me so I'd better head off."

"Don't you want to explain?"

The shoulders turned quickly. "Honey, all I've ever wanted to do was explain. I'm a fool. I'm a foolish fool. I had no clue what to do. You opened the door on the morning of the interview and I knew I was wrong. I've always known I was wrong, and now you've seen the letter so it's all over I guess."

"Why did you do it?"

"I don't know. It was just something to do. Sounds so ridiculous now, but I didn't make money, I didn't want fame. I just wanted to call people out on their behaviour."

"Why? What gives you that right?"

"I don't know. I could try and cite a nasty come-on from a famous sleazeball as the trigger, or my frustrations at seeing so many lies in the celebrity world. Models famous for body-shaming other women yet denying their latest surgical enhancement. I don't know. I just saw injustice and I felt it was okay to call it. But I know I had no right regardless of my frustrations."

"Exactly, you had no right. You didn't know these people. You didn't know me."

"But the minute I did know you, I knew I was wrong."

"Wrong for doing what?"

"Publicly discussing you. You didn't pursue the press. You didn't crave the attention. I was gossiping without reason."

"Why?"

Meg shrugged. "Sometimes we just don't have the answers for our behaviour."

"That's it?"

"I could try and justify my actions or I could just say I was wrong, and I'm sorry."

Sofia stepped between the meatballs. "Don't you want to sit down?"

"No," said both, freed somehow by this face to face standoff.

Meg spoke first. "This was me. This was all me."

"Not Jo?"

"No, me. Titbits I'd pick up through work but couldn't print."

Sofia spoke again. "The three a.m. girls do the same. But publicly. They write the gossip column in *The Mirror*. Perez too. They're freely invited to all the celebrity parties because most celebrities like the column inches. I'm sure if people knew Meg did what she did they'd invite her too."

"That's not my point," said Honey, "and whose side are you on?"

"Yours, dear. But is it really such a big deal what she did? She didn't name names, she didn't tell lies."

"She lied to me!"

Meg nodded. "And that's why I'm going. I made a mistake. I made a terrible, terrible mistake. I should have told you the minute I met you."

Sofia tutted. "You wouldn't have done that."

"She *should* have," said Honey.

"And what would you have done, dear?" continued the old woman.

"I'd have told her to go."

"Exactly, and you wouldn't have found this." Sofia lifted her hands between them. "The way you were talking to me, I knew I had to let you find your own path, and you found it. You've been happy."

"This," said Honey, turning her back on the connection, "was a lie."

Meg reached out and took hold of her shoulder. "Was it?" she asked, turning the body and forcing the eyes to connect.

Honey sniffed. "It was built on a lie."

"I wanted to tell you, so many times. At the windowsill the night of the fermented egg curry, over meatballs at the Ikea café, in your dressing room the night of the show. So many times. All the time."

"But you didn't."

"I didn't want to lose you."

"Before you had me?"

"I had one chance. One chance not to mess things up. But I did, like I always do. And deep down I knew this was coming; that's why I've shied away from the photos."

"You didn't shy away because you were unsure?"

"God no! I love you, Honey, and I want to be with you. I just knew the minute we went public I'd be putting you in an awful position having to explain why it was so short lived, because you trusted a drongo, because you fell into my trap."

Sofia cut in. "But this wasn't deliberate. You didn't set out to snare Honey?"

"As if! Look at me! Can you imagine me thinking I had any chance? Of course I fantasised and romanticised, I was a fan, a huge fan, one of your biggest, but I've always known I wasn't worthy." She sighed. "Anyway, I'm sorry. Truly I am. You deserve someone so much better than me."

Honey felt herself starting to crack. "You were doing okay."

The head was shaking. "I'm that duck who looks like they're gliding over the water, when really they're paddling like shit underneath. I've been paddling like shit since the moment I met you."

Sofia coughed. "For a top journalist you've got quite the way with words."

"She's got quite the gift with presents as well," said Honey, finally allowing herself to smile. "You brought me meatballs."

"That's not enough."

Honey nodded. "That's more than enough."

"What if they don't taste as good as the ones in the store? What if I don't taste as good now that I'm damaged?"

Honey felt her heart forgiving; she couldn't help but love this ridiculous woman with all her insecurities and high walls. So what if she ran some stupid site? So what if she spilled silly secrets? It had stopped, and the idea of not holding her again, not touching her again, well that was far more painful than any betrayal she'd felt when reading the letter. She paused, one final point she wanted addressed. "So my mother sends you that letter and you pull the site. Why? Fear of exposure? Fear of a law suit?"

"It was meeting you, and I know this sounds too hard to believe but that letter meant nothing. It was a threat. My site wasn't illegal. I didn't name names. I didn't tell lies—"

"Only to me."

Sofia chastised her goddaughter. "Honey."

"Sorry." Honey shook her head. "I'm letting it go."

Meg reached out for Honey's hands. "I don't need you to let it go. I fully deserve to be punished. I was wrong. I should have told you. But whether I'd received that letter or not, the site was coming down. I knew the minute I met you that I couldn't live with what I'd done... what I'd said. You're a private person, Honey, and I should have respected that, knowing you or not."

Honey felt the warmth and honesty in the words and pulled her girlfriend in close. "I'm sorry for walking away." She lifted her shoulders with a smile. "But I've realised I don't want to be private. I *want* all the secret sites screaming about us. I want the pictures. I want the gossip. I want to show you off and parade you around. I'm in love with you, Meg, and I think you're in love with me too."

"I am. I love you so very, very much. You've changed me. You've made me want to be a better person." She smiled. "I *am* a better person when I'm with you."

The cough sounded first, then the rustle of plastic. "I'll go and pop these in the freezer, dear," said Sofia, lifting the bags.

"Get some of them cooking," instructed Honey. "I want us to party."

"PARTY?!" came the scream. "PARTY?!" Diana Diamond crashed into the lounge with her mobile phone outstretched and collar at an all-time high, her entourage of OAPs following in quick succession. "GET OUT OF MY HOUSE!"

Honey stood protectively in front of Meg. "This is my house, Mother."

"LOOK! LOOK WHAT SHE'S DONE!" The phone was waggling. "She's posted again! Benedict just pinged me! You shagged She-Ra, Honey?! SHE-RA?! SHE-RA?! I can clear up some messes but this shit'll stick!"

Honey grabbed the phone and read quickly. The purple site and shushing finger filled the screen. Which ginger singer shagged She-Ra? She's a lesbian and she glitters like a crap bit of glass. "Meg?" she cried, throwing her hand to her mouth as she stepped back in horror.

"GET OUT OF THIS HOUSE!" cried Diana.

"Yes, shoo," said Gerty.

"Piss off," added Dot.

"Meg?!" Honey felt the horror turn into tears. "How could you?"

"What?" The eyes were wide.

"I walk out and you start up again?"

"Start what?" Meg was trying to edge a look at the phone. "What does it say?"

"WHAT DOES IT SAY?" screamed Diana. "It says law suits and emergency PR stunts and boyfriends. You need a big burly boyfriend, Honey, that's what we'll do, but you might not come back from this one; she'll sue us! She'll sue you. It's She-Ra! She won't want any of this out there!"

"What's out there?" asked Meg, her face still a picture of confusion.

"WHY'S SHE STILL HERE?!" Diana pointed at the door. "Ladies, remove her!"

"Meg, how could you?" cried Honey.

Diana sneered. "This one could do anything! Has she told you I bribed her into changing your story?"

"My what?"

"Your interview." Diana nodded. "My interview. Her interview. We colluded. No lesbian labels, no need to reveal her true self."

Honey cried out. "No!"

Meg was gasping. "No, it wasn't like that!"

Diana offered her arms to welcome her daughter back into the fold. "It was, my darling. Now come back to me where it's safe."

"No to all of you!" screamed Honey, racing out of the room.

CHAPTER THIRTY FOUR

Two months later:

Sitting at the make-up table in the arena's dressing room, Honey looked at the scene reflected in the mirror. Her mother, Sofia, Gerty and Dot were all squashed up on the sofa, quaffing drinks from the never-ending supply they had on request from the eager-to-please runners. Caitlyn, Heidi and Louisa were busying around, making her perfect, talking politely and getting involved, but still not playing a true part in her life outside of work. Looking in the top of the mirror, she caught a glimpse of step-siblings Nick and Nadia Diamond as they flashed onto the flat screen TV, Liza quickly trying to change channel. Another exclusive interview no doubt, giving their spin on the She-Ra rumours that simply refused to die down. The fact the singer had left her husband added more fuel to the fire. Had she left for Honey? Had the affair been going on for the whole of her marriage? The bisexual community bore the brunt of the drama, the age-old once a lesbian always a lesbian rhetoric a nasty undercurrent in all the main papers. The fact that She-Ra had indeed contacted her to reminisce about good times and praise her for being true to herself didn't need to be known. She-Ra wasn't angry about the rumours; yes her PR machine was now in full flow, but she wasn't personally angry. She'd called it a memorable time in her life and one she wouldn't mind revisiting. Honey smiled to herself. It was no more tempting now than it had been two months ago when originally offered. All she'd been able to think about was Meg, all she *continued* to think about was Meg.

Remembering the scene, Honey sighed. Meg, dragged kicking and screaming from the house by the Golden Girls, professing her innocence, saying she had proof it was Jo. And, yes, even though it transpired the gossip was indeed posted as Meg was standing in her living room next to two bags of meatballs, the fact remained that she'd told her. Meg had told Jo her secret about She-Ra, and it hurt. Had she gone home and gossiped about their meeting? Laughed at her lesbian lust? Had she sneered? Judged? And this wasn't even mentioning the details with her mother, not telling her she'd changed the interview to save her own skin. Plotting. Scheming. Honey shook her head. Once more, Meg had professed her innocence, claiming that's the way she'd written the article to begin with, claiming she'd wanted to explain all that too.

But that was the crux of it. Meg *trying* to tell her about the site. Meg *wanting* to tell her about her mother. Meg *needing* to be honest, but never quite getting to that point. Meg was clearly a person who couldn't face up to the truth. The one who'd turn the blame on to you for not giving them the opportunity to be open. "I'd have told you if I didn't think you'd react." Or: "You've not made it easy for me to be truthful." No. There would always be a reason, an excuse, or a passed blame. Meg was just too far into that grey area, and yes the site had gone down within hours of the She-Ra post and was as yet to reappear, but the damage had been done. She didn't need someone like that in her life.

It wasn't simply a case of saying sorry and moving on. The rumour had been copied, there were screenshots, discussions, interviews. Honey tutted as the channel flicked past Nick and Nadia Diamond once more, milking every moment of what could potentially be the fall of her mother's ridiculous Diamond dynasty. That was the reason for everyone's presence in the dressing room, supporting her in this one-off make or break concert. That's what her mother had called it anyway, her grand idea to assess damage to the brand. A night in the O2 arena. The fact the tickets had sold out within three minutes still not enough to appease the irrational anxieties of her mother.

Honey had stood firm when declaring her song list, her new one appearing in the middle of the mix. It wasn't called the sexuality song, but that's the way everyone referred to it. She had in fact given it the title of *Honest Love*. She'd slowed it down and turned it into a more typical ballad, but she'd been advised that singing it live onstage for the first time in front of such a big audience would be too much too soon. Even so, this was the route she wanted to take, singing songs that meant more than just words, and if she was honest the past two months had seen her writing some of her best, most heartfelt and meaningful lyrics to date.

Hearing the knock on the door, Honey watched her PA's reflection. Liza was back to her usual self: overbearing, dictatorial, moody and cross. Cross at her, cross at the girls, cross at Tammara, but mostly the PA was cross with herself. Svetty had tried to make up on many occasions but Liza's stubborn streak had got in the way, and now Svetty was holed up at Velvet Villa, no longer performing any treatments off-site. Honey watched as Liza's face burst into smiles. "What is it?" she asked quickly.

Liza's mouth stayed turned at the corners. "The runner's just announced the arrival of your holistic therapist."

"Oh Mother," said Honey, spinning around in her seat. "I don't want Svetty Sokolova channelling my chakra before I'm on stage."

"She can channel my chakra any day of the week," said Dot.

"I prefer Kuntse," said Gerty. "Her suction cup's deeper than Svetty's."

Diana lifted her collar. "Svetty resigned. Kuntse's in charge." She nodded. "And here she is now. Set up in the corner would you please?"

The holistic therapist giggled. "I be sorry. I be needing Svetty. I not be good with the making of portable table." The voice giggled again. "I not be good at driving big wagon either. You got big wagon, Madame Diamond. Madame Diamond's wagon be huge."

"Svetty's here?" gasped Liza, the disappearing smile now back on her lips.

"Outside in big wagon. I get her. She be driving better than Kuntse and she be setting portable table better than Kuntse," the therapist wagged her finger, "but Kuntse be folding the sheet with more neatness than Svetty."

"She's resigned?"

The therapist nodded. "For you. You be thinking she dip her feet deep only if you pay her. But now she show you she dip her feet deep all by herself."

"Because she wants to? For me?"

"Svetty wanting to go deep in here," Kuntse waved her hand in the general area of Liza's womb, "and in here," she slammed her fist against Liza's heart.

Liza's brogues started to riverdance. "Go and get her! Quickly! Go and get her."

Diana snapped. "Stop acting like a schoolgirl."

"I won't stop, and you, Diana Diamond, need to find love, doesn't she girls?"

The three stylists kept their heads low and ignored the question but Sofia, Gerty and Dot all seemed to shrug in agreement.

"It frees you," continued Liza, "it lightens you. You'll be a different person entirely."

"Oh will I?" Diana sniffed. "It seems when people do fall in love they always end up wallowing in tears. Look at the pair of you." She nodded in Honey's vague direction. "Miserable for months."

Preaching to the room, Liza's brogues continued to tap. "Sometimes you just need to forget about the doubts, the arguments, the miscommunications and questions and just feel what you feel. Svetty taught me that."

"When she was foot deep in womb?" Diana finished her drink. "I think we've all heard quite enough about what Svetty's feeling. Ladies, let's escape to the bar. I've heard there's a VIP section."

Dot pulled herself up. "Oh goody. It's been a while since we were spotted in *Tatler*."

"Speak for yourself," added Gerty. "I made the who's who column in *Vogue*."

"Mother, I'll be singing my song."

Diana Diamond turned on her way out of the room. "As long as you don't make any dedications then it should be bearable."

"Oh, Mother, you know I've been right about everything. No one cares who I love. My sales are higher than ever, my..." Her mother had gone, Sofia was the only one still sitting.

"Sing your song, dear; sing it loud from the centre of your soul."

"Sofia, thank you, I will." She smiled at her godmother before signalling her to go after the others. "Go on, have fun." She'd been the one by her side through it all: the sleepless nights, the midnight feasts, the quiet lulls in the house. Listening, comforting, but never advising. It must have been the same when she'd found out about Meg, not wanting to judge Diana's decision, not wanting to influence anyone in any way. She was good like that, but it was also incredibly frustrating. She'd have loved her godmother to have tried to convince her that Meg was the one, that the onslaught of various Ikea items left at the front gate on a weekly basis was a sign of her sorrow, a sign of atonement. But she hadn't, so they'd both carried on mourning something that never quite was.

"All this reminds me," Liza said, clicking through her PDA. "Give us a minute would you please, girls."

"We're not even half way through her hair," said Heidi.

"A minute."

Honey watched as the stylists sulked out of the room after Sofia, leaving her and her PA standing alone. "It's something private?"

Liza passed over her handheld. "It's from the editor of *The Beacon*. He's awaiting my response."

"What is it?"

"Read it. It's a piece by Meg."

"About what?"

"She's like Svetty, given her notice, but I guess she wants to go out with a bang."

"It's about us? Our affair?" Honey gasped. "How could she?"

Liza's head was shaking. "SlebSecrets. She's fessed up."

"What?"

"Just read it."

Honey scanned the draft copy. Meg was outing herself as the site owner, claiming she created it because of resentment at the false world she observed and was resigning from her job due to the guilt she now felt. There were professions of malpractice, culpability and disgrace, and an awareness of the hurt and upset she had caused. There was no attempt to sway favour or even really justify her reasons for sharing the secrets, just an admission of error, her hands held up high as she confessed to her readers the poor judgement of her past. The tagline at the bottom simply saying: Meg Rutherton, formerly Margaret Rutherton of *The Beacon*, lives alone in East Dulwich.

Honey gasped. "She left her flatmate? She quit her job?"

"It looks that way."

"Oh no! She's done that for me! Jo needs her! I advised her badly. It's admirable the way she puts up with her. She was clearly drunk when she did what she did. Maybe Meg's put her in rehab? She can't leave her alone. I was the one being judgemental. Everyone needs someone like Meg. I need someone like Meg. *The Beacon* needs someone like Meg." The voice was panicked. "They can't print this!"

"That's why they sent it over, because you're mentioned several times. She's truly sorry, Honey. Obviously it looks bad for *The Beacon*, their lead correspondent bringing their paper into disrepute, but apparently she's said she'll send it somewhere else if they don't print it. She wants to make the grand gesture, the big public apology."

"They can't print it. No one can print it. I love her. Oh Liza, I want her. She'd do this for me? She'd really do this for me?" Honey was scanning the passages, feeling the sorrow in the words.

"I want us to be together, side by side. People can't know she's the one who said what she said. I want people to love her, to see her, to see her like I did. Like I do. She's wonderful, she's sexy, and yes, she's a little bit strange sometimes but I love that. I love her. Oh Liza, you have to go find her."

"I can't go and find her. You're going on stage in an hour."

"For me? Please, Liza, I don't ask for much."

"I can't! I'll ring the paper and make sure they cancel the story then you can call Meg after the show, make her see sense, show her she doesn't need a public flogging because you've forgiven her."

"I have forgiven her! Genuinely, right now, standing here, my heart feels full again. She's given up her job, she's changed her life... for me." Honey spoke quickly. "Will they take her back? Call them, find out. She needs that job, she needs her independence. Even through all the moaning, I know she loves what she does."

Liza took back her handheld, using it to call the number attached to the piece. "The signal in here's just dreadful," she said, speaking as firmly as she could manage. "Hello, it's Liza Munroe. Yes, I know you've been calling. The piece, we want you to bin it. No, I can assure you it won't appear elsewhere. Her job though, is that out of the question? What? She's left? Where? Yes, you said, but... Right, I didn't realise. And when's she going? Okay, not to worry, thanks for your help."

"What? What is it?" Honey was frantically pacing.

"Meg's leaving the country. She's making a fresh start some place abroad."

"No! Liza, she can't! That's so ridiculous and clichéd."

"People run." Both turned at the sound of the door. "But I'm not running! Svetty!" she cried. "You're here!"

The Russian woman bowed. "I heff no more confusions. I be loving of you."

The brogues clipped. "You love me?"

"I be loving of you." The nod was firm. "Our story heff ended."

Liza raced over with wide arms. "You mean our story's complete."

Holding on to the chair Honey gasped. "Isn't the happy ending meant to be mine?"

CHAPTER THIRTY FIVE

Despite the odds, the true professional in Honey had kicked in and she'd made it to the mid-point in her concert without so much as a tear. She hadn't wanted to go on stage knowing Meg could be boarding a plane at any moment, all attempts to call her mobile met with an offline tone, her social media sites sending an awaiting delivery note back to Liza's PDA. They'd even used Heidi's FitBit to try and make contact, but as yet nothing had got through. The signal in the arena was notoriously bad and they couldn't work out if it was a fault at their end or hers, and Honey, as much as she loved the idea of a mid-concert dash to the airport, was a realist. If it was going to happen it would happen when the timings were right. Maybe Meg did need this space. She'd contact her and let her know she was sorry, because she honestly was. She should have just sat down and talked without the entourage, without the flared tempers, just her and Meg, talking, and listening, and kissing... she smiled at the crowd, she'd missed the kissing the most.

"Are you ready?" she said to her fans, speaking softly into the microphone, her lips right up to the mesh, making each person in the starlit arena feel as if she was talking directly to them. "I have a new song. You might have heard it was coming."

The crowd erupted into a frenzy of cheers.

"I want to dedicate it to someone special."

The crowd cheered even louder.

Honey looked up and over her shoulder at the huge screen now displaying the sweeping faces in the audience. "I want to dedicate it to you," she pointed her finger at a woman overcome with emotion and laughed at her wide-eyed wailing response, "and you," she said to the young man now shown on the screen. It was a bit like a kiss-cam, cruising the crowd, picking out people, giving them something to remember for the rest of their lives. "It's for all of you," she continued. "This world's a tough place, so be kind. Show support." She smiled. "Support your friends, your family, those who are struggling, those who need love." She lifted her arms as if drawing the crowd into her heart. "Because your support means everything to me." The roaring response was emotional. "Just go out there and love who you love. Because I love you." The camera started to sweep once more. "Yes, you." She started pointing again. "And you." She nodded with enthusiasm at the disbelieving faces. "Yes I do." She smiled. "And this song is for you. And for…" Honey stopped. "GO BACK!" she screamed. "Quickly, go back!" She was waving at the sweeping camera. The image on the big screen jolted forward and backwards, the crowd going crazy as the cheering people came in and out of view. Honey turned her back on the audience and looked right at the screen. "STOP!" she shouted, waving and pointing with the biggest action she could muster. "This song… this song is for YOU!"

Focusing in, the camera momentarily picked up a woman before her face ducked away in the crowd.

"Get her!" cried Honey, swept along with the whooping. "Her! Yes, her! Bring her down here!" She watched with excitement as the woman was finally found and lifted high in the crowd. "I love you!" she shouted. Spinning away from the screen, she spotted the scene in reality about ten rows back. "Everybody, this is my girlfriend! This is the love of my life!"

The arena erupted into a wailing, stamping roar of support as Honey watched the lift turn into a seated crowd surf. Meg, her Meg, being swept to the front. "This is Meg! She's the love of my life!" Taking the microphone off the stand, Honey raced towards the edge of the stage, reaching out her hand. "Take my hand. Hold it forever."

The crowd melted into a sea of adoring whimpers.

Meg was bustled to the front but instead of climbing onto the stage she slid down, in among the people who were inches away from Honey's feet. She looked up, eyes wide at the microphone.

Honey laid it on the stage and dropped to her knees.

Meg's voice was quiet. "I'm just a fan. I've only ever been a fan. And I don't even deserve that acclaim."

Honey left the microphone where it was, speaking to the one person in the whole arena who mattered the most. "You, Meg Rutherton, are the reason I sing."

"So sing."

"To you, up here, in front of the world." She reached out and caressed Meg's face, as high behind her the gesture was captured and repeated on the giant screens.

Meg's eyes turned to look at the huge audience and then up at the expectant faces and raised glow sticks relayed all around the arena in real time. "You want me up there?"

"I want you up here, by my side." Honey smiled. "For the rest of our lives I want us singing together."

"What if I pull you off-key?"

"You're my harmony, Meg, my accompanying tune." Reaching down, she found Meg's hands. "Let's rise together. Let's show the world our true strength because nothing can break us now, Meg. We've been through all this and look where we are." Feeling the fingers tighten around her own and watching the bravery build in the eyes, Honey let go momentarily and lifted the microphone. "Who wants to meet her?" she shouted. "The love of my life."

The cheers were deafening as the glow from raised phones lit the arena, everyone desperate to capture this moment. "Let's do this, Meg," she said, reaching out once more.

Meg nodded and lifted herself into the light. "Let's change the world, Honey."

"I understand now, that's all you wanted to do." The smile was wide. "But you have to admit, this way will work better."

Meg laughed and lifted her hand, waving shyly at the cheering audience. "Hello," she whispered.

Honey threw her arms around Meg's shoulders and kissed her lips with true love. "Be you, Meg, just always be you." Stepping back slightly, she raised the microphone and signalled the start of the music, speaking her words for the world to embrace. "Love," she said with true meaning, "is the worst thing to hate." She smiled at the woman standing beside her and held her hand as the song started to play. "This one, my love, is for you."

THE END

About the author:

Kiki Archer is a UK-based lesbian fiction novelist and winner of the Ultimate Planet's Independent Author of the Year Award in 2013. She also received an honourable mention in the 2014 Author of the Year category.

Kiki won Best Independent Author and Best Book with **Too Late... I Love You** at the 2015 Lesbian Oscars.

Her debut novel, the best-selling **But She is My Student**, won the UK's 2012 SoSoGay Best Book Award.

Its sequel, **Instigations**, took just 12 hours from its release to reach the top of the UK lesbian fiction chart.

Kiki topped the lesbian fiction charts in 2013 with her best-selling third novel, **Binding Devotion**, which was a 2013 Rainbow Awards finalist.

One Foot Onto The Ice broke into the American contemporary fiction top 100 as well as achieving the US and UK lesbian fiction number one.

The sequel **When You Know** went straight to number one on the Amazon UK, Amazon America, and Amazon Australia lesbian fiction charts, as well as number one on the iTunes, Smashwords, and Lulu Gay and Lesbian chart.

Her latest novel **Too Late... I Love You** has been her most successful to date winning the National Indie Excellence Award for best LGBTQ book, The Gold Global eBook Award for best LGBT Fiction and making that transition into the mainstream contemporary romance charts. It was also a Rainbow Awards finalist and received an honourable mention.

Novels by Kiki Archer:

BUT SHE IS MY STUDENT - March 2012

INSTIGATIONS - August 2012

BINDING DEVOTION - February 2013

ONE FOOT ONTO THE ICE - September 2013

WHEN YOU KNOW - April 2014

TOO LATE... I LOVE YOU - June 2015

LOST IN THE STARLIGHT - September 2016

Connect with Kiki:

www.kikiarcher.com
Twitter: @kikiarcherbooks
Instagram: kikiarcherbooks
www.facebook.com/kiki.archer
www.youtube.com/kikiarcherbooks

Printed in Great Britain
by Amazon